OLD SINS, LONG SHADOWS

OLD SINS, LONG SHADOWS

by
JUDY JACKMAN

Copyright © 2025 by Judy Jackman
All rights reserved.

The right of Judy Jackman to be identified as the author of this work has been asserted in accordance with sections 77 and 78 of the Copyright, Designs and Patents Act, 1988.

No part of this book may be reproduced or transmitted in any form or by any means without prior permission in writing from the publisher.

The story, all names, characters, and incidents portrayed in this production are fictitious. No identification with actual persons (living or deceased), places, buildings and products is intended or should be inferred.

MALTHORP HOUSE 1909
VALENTINE

Valentine Taylor was only seven years old when he learnt the meaning of true hatred. At the same time, he also made a discovery which, although he did not know it, would have disturbing repercussions on many lives.

The discovery he made was this; that the hatred he was experiencing was, by far, a more powerful, pleasurable and potent emotion than that of love.

It all started with Baba and the day he discovers that she has left him forever. No one will say where she has gone or why she has left without even saying goodbye.

"But I *want* her," he declares tearfully. "She always reads me my story at bedtime. We're almost halfway through *Treasure Island* and Jim Hawkins is hiding from the pirates. Baba *wouldn't* go away without finishing the chapter."

His mother, Beatrice, sighs as she sits by his bedside gently stroking the dark, damp hair back from his forehead. She knows from past experience that his distress is a sure precursor to an uncontrollable tantrum and such an outcome could in turn lead to a punishment that will be utterly beyond her control.

"Oh, Valentine, my dearest boy, I beg you, please don't make a fuss. Your father has decided, quite rightly, that you are becoming too old to remain in the nursery with a nanny. He is engaging a young man to tutor you, and you will begin proper lessons with him very soon. It will be good for you to learn more and I am sure that the person he chooses will be kind and patient and help you to learn so much. It will be very beneficial to you."

"But, Mama, I don't want a tutor. I want Baba. I do! I do!"

His voice has risen, and he begins to tremble now with rage and frustration. He throws the bedclothes back and kicks out at her ineffectually with his wasted legs. She looks on helplessly as he begins to scream hysterically, his face turning red with fury.

"I hate being a cripple! I hate not having Baba! I hate *you*!"

"What is this noise? The whole household is being disturbed!"

It is his stepfather who has violently flung open the door. Beatrice looks round fearfully, her mouth trembling as she puts out a restraining hand to her angry son.

"Richard, my dear, Valentine has become a little distraught. I have had to break the news that Nanny Bartlett has left us and I am afraid it has very much upset him. Perhaps, if you had allowed her to say goodbye…" Her voice falters as she sees her husband's face darken. "But, of course, you are probably right that it was for the best. I am quite sure that given time Valentine will accept that it is necessary."

"I *won't*! I want her back. I want Baba, not some silly old tutor!" The boy speaks through clenched teeth as he glares at his stepfather.

"That is quite enough, Valentine!" His stepfather regards the distraught boy coldly as he takes a menacing step forward, speaking slowly and deliberately. "As your mother has probably explained, you are far too old for a nanny. The very fact that you still refer to her by that childish name tells me that it is time you had the discipline of a male tutor. Miss Bartlett has left us, and I have today interviewed a very satisfactory replacement for her. Mr George Hopkins is to commence his duties on Monday. Hopefully he will be able to instil into you some semblance of good manners and behaviour as well as improving your general knowledge of literature and arithmetic which, by the way, is appallingly backward for a child of your age."

His contemptuous glance flickers again over the boy's withered legs and hunched back. "If The Almighty had not seen fit to afflict you with these abnormalities you would, of course, have been going to boarding school. As it is, I am willing, for your mother's sake, to go to the expense of giving you a decent education. The least you can do is to accept it with good grace. Come, my dear, it is time to leave and allow the boy to settle down."

He grips his distraught wife firmly by the arm; she winces in pain but meekly allows him to guide her to her feet, placing her other hand on her swollen stomach as she rises. She looks with a pitying glance at her small son who still glares defiantly at them.

"What must you say to your father, Valentine?"

The child's mouth trembles; he is very near to tears, but his face is still flushed with anger and defiance as he replies.

"*He's* not my father, Mama. *My* father is dead and would never have treated me so!"

"Why – you insolent young…"

Richard Cartwright releases Beatrice's arm and lurches towards the bed. Beatrice gave a cry of fear as he raises his arm to her cowering son, believing that this time he will surely strike Valentine. But at the last moment he turns, to sweep to the floor the contents of the night stand near the bed, smashing the water-glass and the music box which stand upon it. He also sent Valentine's wire spectacles skittering across the floor where they come to rest against the wall. Valentine lets out a cry of pure anguish at the destruction of his precious toy but Cartwright ignores his distress and, raising his hand again, makes his intention clear; to this time strike his stepson. His swarthy face is suffused with the utmost fury but Beatrice catches his arm before the blow can fall, her voice breaking with tearful appeal.

"No, please Richard! Valentine is overwrought. He doesn't know what he is saying. Let us just leave him – I am sure he will come to see it is all for the best." She throws her son a mute plea for his compliance as he gazes at her husband with both terror and a deep loathing.

Cartwright lowers his arm, his face still dark with rage, but then his eyes fall to the soft swell of his wife's belly and his expression softens a little.

"Very well, my dear, if that is your wish. You should be resting in any case. Such anxiety is not good for you in your condition." He looks thoughtfully at the cowering boy. "However, I cannot allow such insolence to go unpunished, so tomorrow, Valentine, you shall remain in your room for the day, with only bread and cheese for your luncheon and I will set you six short verses from the Bible to learn by heart. If you are unable to repeat them perfectly to me by three o'clock in the afternoon you will receive a beating. Do not venture to suppose that your disabilities will prevent me from carrying out my threat." He thrust his face close to the boy. "Do you understand me?"

Valentine's face is no longer flushed but chalk-white as he glares from under lowered brows, but his mother's distress and the sight of her pale and anxious face by his stepfather's shoulder prevent him from retaliating further. He nods slowly, knowing she will only suffer for it if he shows more defiance.

"Good. Then that is settled. Now I suggest you say your prayers before sleeping. Ask God to forgive you for your transgressions, and to help you to accept with gratitude the blessings bestowed upon you, despite your weakness and infirmity."

His mother bends towards Valentine awkwardly as though to embrace him, but is abruptly pulled back and away as Richard ushers her out of the door. He bestowed one final sneering look upon his stepson as the door slams shut firmly behind them.

Valentine turns slowly and painfully on his side, clutching a handful of his pillow as he regards the precious, ruined music box that had been Baba's last gift to him. He wants to cry, oh so badly, but the tears that moments before threatened to spill from his eyes, do not come. Instead, deep inside his soul flares a white-hot flame of passionate anger, so great that he feels instead a thrill of pure pleasure.

"I hate him!" he whispers fiercely into his damp pillow. "I *hate* him!"

CHAPTER 1

The train was nearly twenty minutes late as it drew into Winchester station. The doors opened and spewed forth the usual Monday-morning quota of anxious-faced, world-weary commuters, most of whom were cursing British Rail under their breath for yet another late start at work.

Adam Ellis stood back on the platform, allowing the initial rush to clear. He looked at his watch; it was lucky he had allowed an extra couple of hours for his journey. His interview wasn't until ten forty-five, so he had plenty of time to look round the town and maybe have a coffee before his appointment at the hospital. He made his way out of the station and strolled down towards the top of the high street.

It was a beautiful day, and Adam felt his spirits rising. He had always liked Winchester. As a child his parents had brought him and his brothers here several times, and they had explored the city thoroughly – the Great Hall with the Round Table, said to be the very one used by King Arthur and his Knights; the magnificent Cathedral with its surrounding ancient buildings, usually finishing up with a walk past the walled Bishop's Palace and round to the weir to watch the swans with their cygnets negotiate the fierce current. He always remembered being fascinated by the huge statue of King Alfred which dominated the skyline at the bottom of the town. He strolled on slowly, savouring the atmosphere.

The town was quite busy, its pedestrianised pavements already thronged with shoppers, and he enjoyed looking at the various small shops with their air of old-fashioned solidity. He was not at all nervous about this, his second interview. He felt quite confident; his qualifications were more than sufficient, and he knew his composed manner and smart appearance never failed to impress people. At twenty-eight, and with four years' experience as a junior doctor in a famous paediatric hospital in London where he had worked with some of the best-known consultants in the country, he felt he was more than ready to tackle the challenge of becoming a senior registrar in the children's ward at the city hospital here in Winchester.

Adam had been born in Bracknell, Berkshire; the third of four brothers. His parents were affluent and lived in a large, modern, mock-Tudor style house in a desirable residential area. Adam's father, John, was a successful stockbroker in the City; his mother Audrey had been a secretary in a firm of solicitors before they married. Within six months of the wedding, she became pregnant with her first son; three others, including Adam, followed at two-yearly intervals. The boys were raised well and lacked for nothing money could provide. They all went to private school and, when they reached the age of eleven, the eldest two, David and Neil, were sent to a prestigious public school as boarders. Adam, and his younger brother, Simon, would have followed suit, but Audrey began to suffer bouts of severe depression and was referred to a psychiatrist. After numerous sessions it was pronounced that it was the thought of losing her two younger sons that was causing her distress, so it was decided to keep the boys at home. Adam was quite happy with this arrangement; he was settled at his excellent school and meant to stay there until the sixth form – he had already decided on his career as a doctor and intended to go on to university to obtain a degree in medicine. Simon, however, resented being kept at home; he was not academically inclined, but he thought that boarding-school sounded a lot of fun. David and Neil had regaled the family with many stories of their escapades and he had been looking forward to joining them. As his sense of resentment grew, especially against his mother, his achievements at school and his behaviour at home worsened. His parents despaired of him; luckily, they had no such worries with their other sons. David left university with a degree in engineering and now worked in the Far East, earning very good money. Neil also did well; as a talented musician, he won a prestigious award and was eventually offered a place in the Royal Philharmonic Orchestra, with whom he spent much of his time touring to various parts of the globe. Adam's career, too, had followed its course as planned. Only Simon continued to cause his parents heartache, drifting from one dead-end job to another, but lately he had seemed more settled and was managing to hold down a position as a junior reporter working for a local newspaper. Neil had married, but it had not worked out, so he and Jo had split up after three years; later they had agreed to an amicable divorce.

"I suppose we'll be grandparents *one* day," commented Audrey at the time; she secretly longed for a granddaughter after her four boys. "Though I hope Simon won't think about marrying too soon; he can hardly look after himself."

"I don't think that's very likely, my dear," replied John. "He's too fond of playing the field to commit himself to one girl."

Audrey nodded sadly.

"I've tried to read the cards to work out what might happen," she said. "But it's unclear at the present time."

John sighed inwardly. Audrey had, since her depressive illness eighteen years before, been dabbling in the occult, ranging from séances to Tarot cards, and was becoming ever more obsessed as she tended to do these days. John thought it was a lot of nonsense, and often looked back wistfully to the sweet-natured, level-headed girl he had married. However, he humoured her and tried to show an interest when she brought the subject into their conversation.

"Never mind, my dear," he said now. "I'm sure everything will turn out for the best."

Adam headed for a little café halfway up the High Street, near the ancient Butter Cross. He remembered from a previous visit that they did delicious coffee. It was nearly ten o'clock and they were already quite busy; all the tables were occupied, but near the window was one occupied by a young woman. She had a half-empty cup before her and seemed totally absorbed in her book. He moved over to the table and coughed politely.

"Excuse me asking, but is anyone else sitting here?" he asked.

She looked up and smiled. "No, and I've nearly finished. Please feel free."

Adam caught his breath. She was undoubtedly one of the most beautiful girls he had ever seen. Her skin was like thick cream; she had long, wavy, chestnut hair that cascaded halfway down her back and her eyes were the most incredible blue flecked with green. For a moment he stood there mesmerised. She smiled again, her eyes crinkling at the corners.

"Don't you want to sit down?"

"Um... yes, of course," said Adam, recovering himself. It wasn't often that he was lost for words. The waitress came over and he ordered coffee and, as he was now feeling rather hungry, a scone.

The girl continued to read her book. Adam noticed the title: *Art and the Renaissance*. He presumed she was a student; she looked about eighteen. His coffee and scone arrived, and he started eating, desperately trying to think of a way to start a conversation. She finished her coffee and slid her book into a large shoulder-bag which was slung over the side of her chair. Adam knew it was his last chance. He opened his mouth to speak, but as she stood up she knocked the table and most of his coffee slopped out onto the saucer and over the table. She gasped.

"Oh no! I'm so sorry – how careless of me."

"Don't worry about it," Adam would have forgiven her anything. "It really doesn't matter."

"But you'd hardly touched it! Please, let me get you another one."

"No, really," he said. Then he smiled. "Well... not unless you join me, that is."

"I... I don't know."

"Please," said Adam, giving her an appealing look.

She laughed. "Okay then, I will, seeing as I spilt your coffee."

She called the waitress over, who cleaned up the mess and took their order for two more coffees. There was an awkward silence until the waitress returned. Adam thought desperately of something to say and, as they started to sip their drinks, he took a deep breath and took the plunge.

"I couldn't help noticing the book you were reading. Are you an art student?"

"Not now," she replied. "I was until quite recently but, as a matter of fact, I'm starting a new job today."

"Really? Me too, at least I'm being interviewed, but I think it's in the bag. Where are you going to be working?"

"In a local art gallery. I'm not starting until half-past-ten because the owner had to go to Southampton to pick up some paintings. What about you?"

"The County Hospital. I'm hoping to become a senior registrar in the Children's Department. Actually," he continued, glancing briefly at his watch, "I'd better get a move on." He swallowed the rest of his coffee in haste.

"Me too," said the girl. She went to pick up the bill, but Adam was too quick for her.

"Let me get this," he said, ignoring her protests.

"Which way are you walking?" he asked when they stepped outside.

"The top of the High Street," she replied. They started walking up the hill along the busy street. Conversation was difficult and Adam began to feel quite desperate again. He felt unaccountably drawn to the girl, but after today he might never see her again. They reached the top of the hill, and the girl indicated a road to the right.

"There's the gallery down there," she said. "Thanks for the coffee, and sorry again for being so clumsy."

"Not at all," said poor Adam, feeling tongue-tied again. In another moment she'd be gone. "Look," he said, and found himself blushing, something that hadn't happened to him since he was sixteen. "You'll probably think this is an awful nerve, and you can say no if you don't want to, but I don't know a soul in Winchester and I'd really like to see you again. Have you a phone number I could reach you on? If I get this job, I'll be starting in about two weeks. Maybe we could meet for dinner or something."

She hesitated and his heart sank. Then she gave him her beautiful smile and suddenly it all felt right.

"I'd like that," she said. "We could compare notes on our new jobs. I could phone you."

"Great!" He delved into his pocket and found an old receipt. He scribbled his mobile number on it. "I'll be there until the twenty-third," he told her.

"I'll ring before that," she promised, as he looked at his watch again.

"God, I am going to be late if I don't go now! I'd better get moving. Look forward to hearing from you." He started to walk away then realised that he'd forgotten to ask her something quite important. "What's your name, by the way?"

"Beth," she replied, "Beth Morgan."

"I'm Adam, Adam Ellis. See you soon I hope, and good luck with the job!"

"You too, and all the best with your interview."

Beth stood for a moment watching Adam as he hurried away. She wasn't in the habit of conversing with strange young men, but he'd seemed nice enough, good looking too, with his fair, floppy hair and square, dependable kind of face. She looked down at the phone number in her hand. She wasn't yet sure whether she would give him a ring; but it would be nice to be taken out for dinner as also she knew few people in the city. She smiled to herself and walked down the road to the art gallery. Mr Desmond, her new boss, had just arrived back from Southampton and was unloading his latest acquisitions from the back of his car.

"Ah, Beth," he exclaimed. "Glad to see you m'dear. Give us a hand with these, will you?"

She helped him into the little gallery with the paintings.

"Picked up some good bargains," he said, lighting a cigarette. "We'll sort them out in a moment. First things first though, let's pop the kettle on. I'm gasping for a cuppa."

Philip Desmond didn't fit the usual mould of an art expert. He was a large, untidy man of about sixty, with a balding head and nicotine-stained fingers. But his eyes behind the steel-framed spectacles were shrewd, and he could spot a forged Old Master a mile off. He had been in Winchester for thirty years and his little gallery was surprisingly successful. Beth considered herself privileged to be working for him.

She had been recommended to him by her last boss, Joe Campbell. She had worked for Joe, in Southampton, since getting her art degree at the university. He had owned a small gallery in the city but it had been struggling for a while; he'd finally decided to cut his losses and sell up. Philip was an old friend and Joe knew he had been looking for a reliable assistant he could train to run the gallery when he was away on one of his buying trips. Philip had come down to the shop to interview Beth, they'd hit it off straight away and he had offered her the job on the spot.

After a cup of tea, they unpacked the paintings and Beth helped Philip to catalogue them. Once again, he was impressed by her knowledge.

"I can tell you're going to be an asset, m'dear!" he said, lighting his ninth cigarette of the day. "Beauty and brains are such a rare combination these days." He patted her hand. "Will you be able to cope if I nip out for a while? I have to run a few errands."

"I'll be fine," Beth replied.

It was a quiet morning and only a few people came in to browse around. In between customers Beth wondered how Adam had got on with his interview. He had seemed very confident and she had liked him very much. She found herself looking forward to seeing him again. She had been out with only a few young men before him. Years ago she had suffered a terrible experience and it had affected her so deeply that she found it difficult to form any long-term relationships. She was fine as long as a boy only wanted to hold her hand, or even put an arm around her, but she could bear no further intimacies. She knew she needed help to overcome this, but still found it impossible to confide in anyone, even a doctor, about her experience.

She had spent many of her teenage years in a children's home and for a long time had been so traumatised that she became withdrawn and barely spoke. Eventually, with the little help she would accept, she began to come out of her deep depression, made a few friends and started to settle in. Although she suffered terrible nightmares they lessened in time, but she still found it difficult to talk about her past to anyone, even rejecting the chance to have counselling. Her education continued at the local secondary school, where she did well in her exams, gaining high grades. When she was sixteen, she was told by the governors that, although she was considered too old to stay at the home, they had decided to offer her a place as a helper and allow her to remain living in and attend college part-time. She was relieved and agreed to the arrangement; she had been very worried about what would happen to her if she had been forced to leave. She stayed there for a further two years, managing to get three A Levels in English, Art and History and was accepted at Southampton University. She found a part-time waitressing job to pay for her digs and finally obtained a First Class Arts Degree. Then, through one of her tutors, she met Joe and had been offered the job working in his shop.

"Though you're worth much more," he told her. "You've got a huge talent there, Beth. You ought to be using it." But she had felt safe with Joe. Now she had this job with Philip and fairly comfortable lodgings in Winchester. She had taken one leap of faith, though – she'd sent a few of her sketches off to a publisher of children's stories. Perhaps something would come of it, but if not she had lost nothing. She looked at the piece of paper with Adam's number on it again and made a decision.

She would ring him in a week.

Adam received her call when he was chatting to his father in the lounge. He hurried out into the hall.

"Hi!" he said, immediately recognising her voice. "Great to hear from you. How is your job going? Sold many paintings?"

She laughed. "Not many. How did the interview go? Did you get it?"

"I did. I start on Monday."

"Oh, well done! I thought you would. What area did you say you're hoping to specialise in?"

"Paediatrics." He paused, "Listen, do you still want to meet up?"

"I'd love to. Where and when?"

Adam thought rapidly. "I passed a nice little Italian restaurant just past the street where your gallery is. How about there on, say, Wednesday evening about seven-thirty?"

"I know the one you mean. I'll see you there, then. I'll have to go – some customers have just come into the shop. See you on Wednesday."

"Look forward to it," said Adam. He ended the call and punched the air. "Yes!" he proclaimed ecstatically. John, who was just coming out of the living room smiled tolerantly at his son.

"Hope she's worth all the excitement," he said mildly.

"Oh yes, Dad, she definitely is," replied Adam. "This one is special."

When he got to the restaurant on Wednesday, there was no sign of Beth. Adam's heart sank. Surely she hadn't changed her mind? Then, after a few moments, he saw her hurrying towards him.

"Sorry I'm a bit late," she said breathlessly. "Philip needed help with some important clients at the gallery and I didn't get home until nearly quarter to seven. I'm afraid I didn't have much time to get ready."

"You look lovely," said Adam sincerely. The evening was warm and she was dressed in a blue sleeveless, slightly flared dress with a slashed neckline. Round her shoulders she wore a light, cream-coloured, fringed shawl. Her long chestnut hair gleamed in the evening sunlight.

The restaurant was very quiet and they had no trouble getting a table. They studied the menu, and Beth confessed that she had rarely eaten Italian food, so had no idea what to order.

"The lasagne's probably the best bet," said Adam, touched by her frankness "Minced beef with herbs and tomatoes layered with sheets of pasta. I'm sure you'll like it."

They settled for the lasagne and a bottle of Chianti. As they ate Beth asked Adam about his new post at the hospital, and he told her that he was enjoying it, even though the consultant he was working under was rather a terrifying figure.

"He's known universally as 'God'," he said gloomily. "I can't imagine anyone ever daring to disagree with his opinion."

"Maybe you'll be like that when you're at the top of the tree," she said. "Perhaps it happens to all consultants."

"I hope not," he replied. "I'd like to think I'd remember what it was like to be one of the lower branches."

The evening flew by as they chatted. This time there was no awkwardness and Adam couldn't remember ever feeling so at ease with a girl before. Beth was intelligent, but she also had a good sense of humour, and they seemed to talk about anything and everything. He told her about his childhood, about his parents and his brothers, and as he was doing so noticed a look of sadness in her eyes.

"You've been lucky," she said.

"What about you?" he asked. "I've noticed you have a slight accent, but I can't quite pin it down. Where were you brought up?"

She looked at her watch.

"Is that really the time?" she said. "I ought to be getting back. I've an early start tomorrow."

Outside they stood in silence for a moment.

"Can I walk you home?" said Adam. He felt dismayed at her sudden withdrawal.

"No, really, it's not far." She smiled at him. "Thank you for a lovely evening, Adam."

"Look, I'm sorry if I upset you in there," he said. "I didn't mean to put my foot in it."

"No, it's not you," she replied. "I… I just find the past a bit difficult to talk about, that's all. One of these days I'll tell you about it."

"Does that mean I can see you again?" She laughed at his hopeful expression.

"Of course, I'd really like to go out with you again. How about lunch down by the river one day soon? Pop into the gallery and we'll arrange it."

"I'll do that," said Adam happily. He bent to kiss her cheek and felt her recoil slightly. "Sorry," he said again, rather surprised. He wasn't used to having such a negative effect on girls, especially when they'd had such a pleasant evening.

"Don't be, please. It's not you." She leant forward and gave him a quick hug. "See you soon."

She hurried off, leaving Adam staring after her, somewhat bewildered. She was a lovely girl and he had thoroughly enjoyed being with her, but something was not quite right. Perhaps when they knew each other better she would feel able to confide in him. Meanwhile, he decided, he would avoid asking her too many personal questions. For the time being they could enjoy being just good friends.

CHAPTER 2

Six months later Adam took Beth home to meet his parents. They had been meeting once or twice a week and their relationship had changed and deepened over the weeks. As her trust in him grew, Beth had been able to tell him a certain amount about her unhappy past, although she still did not feel ready to disclose the whole story. She knew he would like to make love to her and, although she too had felt for the first time, stirrings of desire, she still could not relax enough to allow him to stray beyond the boundaries of the preliminaries to lovemaking.

Then one evening, back at Adam's flat, after they had shared a bottle of wine and were warm, sleepy and contented, his kisses grew urgent and more demanding, and slowly he began to undress her. He kissed her breasts, and his fingers slid gently down between her legs. He undid his jeans and placed her hand on his stiffening penis.

Beth cried out in terror. She snatched her hand away and pushed him off her. She sat up and wrapped her arms around her shivering body. Hunching up her shoulders she began to cry.

"Beth!" exclaimed Adam, horrified. "What is it, darling? I'm so sorry – did I hurt you?"

She shook her head, sobbing softly. Adam picked up her cardigan and put it gently around her shoulders.

"I'll make us some coffee," he said. He took some time out in the little kitchen, clattering round with the cups and saucers, giving her time to compose herself. He took the tray in and poured the coffee.

"Adam, I… I'm so sorry," said Beth. She looked like a bewildered child, with her red eyes and her hair pushed back over her ears. "I… I just can't bear anyone to touch me like that. Please forgive me."

He handed her a cup of coffee.

"There's nothing to forgive," he said. "But I do think you need to talk about it to someone, Beth. If not to me, there are people who are trained to help you."

"Psychiatrists, you mean," Beth said. She gave a tearful laugh. "Sex therapists."

"Not necessarily," said Adam. "There are many types of specially trained counsellors." He paused, "But nobody can help you if you keep it all bottled up inside. You've got to want to talk about it."

Beth looked at him. Over the past months she had become more than fond of him. She didn't know whether she was in love with him yet; she only knew that she liked him tremendously and trusted him far more than any man she had ever known. And she knew suddenly that if she could tell anyone, it would be Adam. She took a deep shuddering breath.

"When… when I was thirteen," she said, so softly he had to bend his head to hear her, "I was raped by my uncle." Haltingly, she told him the whole story.

She had been born in Wales and she and her parents lived on a remote farm near the Welsh mountains. Her father worked as a shepherd but, when she was eight, her mother had left her father, Owen, for another man and Beth had never seen her again. Eventually she had been sent to live with her father's sister, Auntie Glenys and her husband, Kevin Webster, in Liverpool. Owen, distraught and embittered by his wife's desertion, had not felt able to cope alone and had decided to leave Wales and make a new start without her. He had promised Beth faithfully that their parting was only temporary and that he would send for her eventually when he had settled. However, as the years went by she heard nothing, and had come to feel a deep sense of hurt and betrayal. She had been very unhappy at first in her cramped and shabby surroundings which were in such contrast to her former life in the green hills of Wales, but had eventually accepted the situation. Auntie Glenys had been kind, if not overly affectionate, and one of her three cousins, Trevor, had looked out for the lonely little girl and stopped other children bullying her at school. Kevin was a different matter; she had disliked and feared him from the start; he drank heavily and was often out of work, forcing Glenys to be working all hours taking on menial jobs to make ends meet. When he was drunk, which was most of the time, Kevin often struck his wife and sometimes his own children, though he never laid a hand on Beth. When she reached puberty, he had started to corner her and make crude comments about her looks and figure which made Beth feel very frightened and uncomfortable. She had desperately wanted to confide in her aunt but felt unable to do so as she wasn't sure that Glenys would believe her. Then, one evening when everyone was out and Beth had gone to bed, Kevin had come unannounced into her room. He had pinned her to the bed and although she had done her best to fight him off, he had easily overpowered and then raped her violently. Terrified and traumatised, she had run away after he threatened to do it again, telling her that nobody would believe her and that he would say she had led him on if she told anyone.

She was found by the police and eventually was persuaded to confide in a sympathetic police officer. Kevin was arrested and Beth had to go to court, aged only thirteen, to face the trauma of the courtroom. Kevin, of course, had denied everything and the defending counsel had taken the line that Beth had flirted and encouraged him to have sex with her. Fortunately, the sympathetic judge and jury believed Beth and the evidence presented by the doctors of forced intercourse. Kevin was found guilty and sentenced to fifteen years imprisonment. One of the worst things for Beth was that her aunt had refused to believe her and had stood by her husband throughout. The police had tried to trace Beth's father but without success so she had been sent to live in the children's home.

Adam listened to her story with growing anger and incredulity. He was racked with pity for her. When she had finished her story, they sat in silence for a few moments. Then he held his arms out to her and she went into them.

"Beth," he said softly, "Beth, what happened to you is terrible. But none of it was your fault, and until you can accept that you won't be able to come to terms with it."

"But I couldn't *stop* him," she said tearfully. "I was powerless and that is what has always haunted me. That and the fact that my aunt thought I was a liar and my parents deserted me when I needed them most."

"You were a child," he reminded her, "and the people who should have been there to protect you let you down. In a sense you were almost raped again in that witness box, having to re-live the whole experience. Then you had nobody to help you come to terms with it. There was no way you could have stopped him from doing what he did, but you need to learn to put it behind you. You're a beautiful young woman with an enormous talent and you can't let this thing blight your life. You've taken the first step towards overcoming this tonight by talking about it to me. I'll help you as much as I can – but if you say the word I'll find you other people you can talk to. We'll beat it together – that's if you want me to help you."

She took his hand and looked into his compassionate blue eyes.

"I want you to," she said simply.

Their relationship had changed to something much deeper from that day, and Beth had been able to talk many of her darkest fears through with Adam and the excellent counsellor he found for her. Adam knew he was falling deeply in love with her and eventually persuaded her to come to his home for the weekend. She was very nervous about meeting his parents even though Adam tried to reassure her.

"They'll love you," he said. "Especially my mother. She's always wanted a daughter, and she's been dying for me to settle down with one girl."

"Is that a proposal?" asked Beth, laughing at him. He grinned back, but his eyes were serious as he said lightly,

"Do you know I think it might just be that."

They went down by train and got a taxi from the station. Audrey and John were on the doorstep to greet them as they drew up outside their large, red brick house. Beth felt more nervous than ever as they got out of the taxi, but their greeting was warm and she soon felt her tension lessening. She especially liked Adam's father, a tall, handsome distinguished-looking man with thick greying hair. Adam looked very like him.

"It's wonderful to meet you, my dear," he said sincerely. "Adam's been very remiss not bringing you down before, although he's done nothing but talk about you on his visits to us. Now we've finally met you, I can quite see why he's so smitten."

"Oh, be quiet, John, you'll embarrass the poor girl," said Audrey sharply. "Come in, Beth, and we'll have a drink before lunch." She led the way into the large, airy living-room. "By the way, Adam, Simon's here, and Neil said he might drop in and join us later."

"Sorry, Beth," whispered Adam as the drinks were being poured. "I didn't realise you were going to be subjected to a family inspection!"

"Don't worry," she whispered back, "I think I'm beginning to enjoy myself."

She hoped that she could grow to like Adam's mother as much as she did John, though she sensed a certain amount of restraint in Audrey's attitude towards her. Perhaps she felt that no girl would be quite good enough for her son, Beth thought, watching Audrey, with her fine-boned, elegant features and her immaculately coiffured hair, holding forth upon the vagaries of the National Health Service, whilst Adam listened with amused, but patient resignation.

"And that's why I prefer to go private, my dear," she was saying as a tall, dark, well-built and very handsome man entered the room. "Ah, Simon, there you are! Come and meet Beth."

"So, you're the famous girlfriend." He took her hand and bent over it with exaggerated courtesy. As he straightened up, he swept his startlingly blue eyes across her. "Hmm... now I understand perfectly why my big brother's been keeping you under wraps."

Beth smiled, but she felt a little uncomfortable. Simon appeared charming, but her first instinct was that she wouldn't trust him an inch. If anything, this feeling grew stronger as lunch progressed, even though Simon put himself out to be attentive to her and talked very amusingly throughout the meal. Adam's other brother, Neil, also joined them; shorter and stockier than either of his siblings, he was much more reserved than Simon, but of the two Beth liked him better. After lunch, she and Adam went for a walk.

"Sorry about Simon," he said, "he's a bit of a black sheep as far as Ma and Dad are concerned, and he always tries to take over the conversation."

"I liked Neil," said Beth. "He's quiet, but he strikes me as the dependable sort."

"Oh, Neil's solid gold. He's like Dad – you could set your watch by him, but you can always turn to him in a crisis. Simon, though, he'd run the other way. I don't know how long he'll stay in this reporter's job – he doesn't stick at anything for long. I think my parents are quite relieved that he's moved out at last; Dad thought that they were going to be stuck with him at home forever."

The rest of the day passed pleasantly enough, but that night, Beth excused herself and went to bed early, leaving Adam talking to his parents, downstairs. She fell asleep almost immediately, but woke about two. She lay there for a while, tossing and turning, but she couldn't get back to sleep. She felt wide awake now and very restless. She found herself thinking about Adam, lying asleep just down the passageway. Somehow, the thought of his nearness brought her a warm glow of satisfaction, and she realised that she felt something more than that. For the first time, deep within her, there was a desire to be with him.

She got up and quietly opened the door. The moonlight was flooding in through the big window at the top of the stairs. Did she dare? She crept silently past John and Audrey's room, praying the floorboards wouldn't creak, and made her way down to the end of the passage to where she knew Adam's bedroom was. She paused for a moment outside the door then quietly turned the handle.

Adam wasn't asleep. He, too, had been lying awake, thinking about Beth. He could scarcely believe it when the door opened and she slid silently into the room. He half sat up. She moved closer and put a finger to her lips. He smiled, hardly able to take in the fact that she had come to him.

"Aren't you going to let me in there?" she whispered.

He opened the covers. In one swift movement, she let her nightdress drop to the floor and stood there for a moment letting the moonlight flood over her slender, exquisite body. Then she slid in beside him.

"Are you sure you…" he started to say, but she put her lips lightly against his mouth. "Love me, Adam," she said simply. His mouth covered hers with fierce possessiveness and to his joy he felt her return the kiss with equal passion. This time, as he explored her body, he felt her respond; her nipples beneath his eager mouth stiffened, and as he ran his tongue down to the shadowy secret cleft between her legs he felt her wetness, and groaned. He took time to give her pleasure, taking her to heights she had not known existed; she cried out softly in ecstasy as he made her come again and again, then finally he could wait no longer and slid deep into her with a gasp of elation. They moved rhythmically, as one, until he could not hold back any more, and allowed his own climax to explode within her with almost agonising pleasure.

They lay for a while, neither able to speak. Then Adam cupped his hands around her face and kissed her gently.

"Beth, I love you," he said. She looked at him, her face tender and serious.

"I know," she said. "I think you've chased away a few ghosts tonight."

"Beth," he said. "I mean it. I love you and I want to marry you."

She looked away. "I don't know, Adam. I don't know if I'm capable of love. What just happened between us was wonderful. I didn't know anyone could make me feel like you've just done – but I don't know if that's love."

"Love will grow, Beth," he said. "This is just a start. Give it a chance, and I know it will work out. Say at least you're prepared to give us that chance."

She smiled at him suddenly, "I'll try."

He smiled back and hugged her to him. He would make it work between them; he wanted her so desperately that he knew in that moment that nothing would stop him. He would dedicate his life to making her happy and fulfilled and do his utmost to wipe away her unhappy memories forever.

He could only hope that, along the way, she would find herself falling as much in love with him as he was with her.

CHAPTER 3
TEN YEARS LATER

Beth drew her brush carefully and delicately over the final line of the elaborate watercolour. She leaned back in her chair, stretched her aching limbs and surveyed the finished painting with deep satisfaction. It had taken her weeks to complete this commission, but she felt strongly that it was amongst the finest work she had ever done. When Guy Turner of the publishers, Crombie and Turner, had first approached her about doing the illustrations for the new publication of Desmond Franklin's *The Wizard of the White Mountain* series, she had been very flattered but rather apprehensive. Franklin had been hailed as the new Tolkien of the twenty-first century; his books sold like the proverbial hot cakes and this undertaking had been one of the most important moves of her career. She, too, had read the books and was as hooked as the rest of the population, making her nervous about meeting the great man. Despite her reservations, her initial sketches had been well received by the small, surprisingly modest, bespectacled author and she'd been hard at work ever since.

She looked at her watch. Three o'clock. She had better get moving; it would be time to meet the boys from school soon. Danny wouldn't thank her if she was late – he had football practice at five-thirty and the traffic would probably be bad today on the main A31 to Jamie's school as there were roadworks yet again. She sighed and switched off the lights. This attic room was far from ideal for her work; she must talk to Adam again tonight about the possibility of moving. So far, he had been less than enthusiastic as they had lived in Winchester for the nine years they had been married; he loved the city and it was convenient for the hospital. But Beth had felt restless for some time and still felt a yearning for a house in the country, somewhere with a big garden and plenty of space for the boys to run wild. She would be paid a hefty sum for this commission and Adam was earning good money as a senior consultant. He had been taking on some private work lately, too, so they might even be able to consider somewhere much bigger, away from these city suburbs which were becoming increasingly congested. She clattered down the wooden stairs and into the spacious lounge. Grabbing the telephone, she quickly dialled a number.

"Guy Turner, please," she said as it was answered, "Beth Ellis." She tapped her foot impatiently as there was a short delay before she was put through.

"Beth?" Guy sounded anxious as usual. "How's it going? I've had John on to me again today. We're really going to need the first illustrations by next Monday. I told him these things can't be hurried, but you know what he's like and..."

"Relax, Guy," interrupted Beth, laughing down the phone at him. "They're all done. That's what I'm ringing to tell you."

"Really! Oh, that's marvellous. I knew you'd do it. I said as much to that daft old bugger, but he's panicking like mad as usual. When can you get them to us?"

"I'll be up tomorrow with them, straight after I've dropped the boys off. Be with you about eleven hopefully."

"Wonderful. I'll take you out to lunch to celebrate. See you then."

Beth rang off, grabbed her handbag and left the house, slamming the front door after her. She jumped into the Range Rover and drove down the busy roads to the outskirts of the city and Danny's school. She was a few minutes early and managed for once to find a parking space without too much trouble. She glanced at the newsagents across the road from the school. She had time to pop over and pick up a *Property Weekly*. She had been doing this regularly for the past few months, and had even been to view a few properties without Adam's knowledge, but so far had seen nothing suitable for their needs. She wasn't even sure that she knew what *was* suitable, but she had the feeling she would know straight away when she saw it.

She scanned through the usual crop of detached, semi and terraced houses in the first few pages and pulled a wry face. Nothing of any note caught her eye. Then she turned a page and gasped.

There it was... *the* house – her house. A square built, large solid mansion, set in a tangle of neglected gardens. She started to read the blurb.

> **NEWLY OFFERED!** A fascinating Edwardian property (built circa 1907), set in four acres of secluded gardens, in a much sought-after rural location. There is great potential in this six-bedroomed property which retains many aspects of its past. Four spacious living-rooms on the ground-floor, plus a large garden room. A spacious kitchen, with scullery and pantries off. The second-floor consists of six large bedrooms, three with dressing-rooms off and a large family bathroom. Upstairs to a third floor containing attic rooms.
>
> The property has been vacant for some time and is in need of some renovation, repair and updating; hence offers in the region of £950,000 would be considered. Contact Telfer and Giddings, 21 High Street, Upper Melcombe. Tel: 04856 876543.

Upper Melcombe. That was about two miles away from Jamie's school. Perfect. Beth stared again at the grainy photograph. She jumped as there was a sharp tap at the Land Rover's window. Danny was staring in at her. She reached over and unlocked the passenger door.

"You were miles away, Mum. What are you reading?"

"Only the boring old property guide." She grinned at him, "Have you had a good day?"

"Not bad. No maths today, so not bad at all." He scrambled into the front seat and fastened the seatbelt. "Got anything to eat, Mum? I'm absolutely starving."

"You always are." She reached into the glove compartment and fished out a Twix. "Here, this do until we get home?"

"Magic!" He tore off the wrapper and took a huge bite, chewing blissfully. Beth looked at him fondly. His sandy hair was untidy as usual and his school blazer and trousers looked as though they could do with a good brush, but he was a cheerful child. At eleven, still young enough to need her, but mature enough to hold a sensible conversation if required.

"I finished the commission, Dan," she told him.

"Brilliant! Can I see it when we get home? Everyone at school's dead jealous that you've met Desmond Franklin. I told them that we'd probably get the first copy of the new book when it comes out so I hope we do."

Beth laughed at his enthusiasm and swung the Land Rover out into the traffic. Danny pulled his DS out of his backpack and lost himself in his latest game.

Danny was adopted. Beth and Adam had intended to start a family straight away, but it just hadn't happened and after they had been for innumerable tests and IVF had been tried and failed, they had begun to lose all hope of having a child of their own. So, they decided, after much heart-searching, to begin the long process of adoption. It seemed the only way forward. Beth had been convinced that the rape had been to blame, although there was no medical evidence for this, but they both desperately wanted a child. The adoption process had been painfully hard; ten months of gruelling interviews and stringent checks on their suitability. Considering their circumstances – Adam a successful paediatric consultant and herself a well-established illustrator – Beth had often wondered what it must be like for people in a less advantageous situation. However, finally, approval had been given and Danny, a lively and robust five-year-old had come into their lives. His parents had split up when he was three and his young mother had moved in with a new boyfriend. Neither had truly wanted the responsibility of a child and, after several incidents, neighbours reported to Social Services that the little boy was being grossly neglected, often left alone at night while his mother and her new partner were out partying. Danny was taken into care and spent the next eighteen months with a foster family. His foster parents had been kind and caring people who had treated the bewildered little boy well, and Beth and Adam were concerned at first about his reaction to yet another upheaval in his young life. But, although there were a few problems initially, Danny had settled down well and the rewards had been enormous. They had always been honest with him about the facts of his first few years of life and he had seemed to accept the fact that he was adopted, never expressing any wish to contact his 'real' mother. Beth and Adam had planned to adopt a sister for him if all went well, but a year later, just as they were beginning the process all over again, Beth had discovered she was pregnant.

At first neither of them could believe it. Even throughout the nine months, as her stomach swelled to enormous proportions and the baby kicked inside her, Beth would sometimes feel a strong sense of unreality, as if the whole thing was happening to someone else. Not until the December morning when she pushed their new son out into the world in the maternity unit near Winchester hospital, did she finally believe that she and Adam were really parents again. The sense of ecstatic wonder stayed with her for weeks; even though Audrey, Adam's mother, couldn't disguise her obvious disappointment at another grandson, not the longed-for granddaughter.

Looking back, those first months at home with Adam, Danny and Jamie had been amongst the happiest in her life. At first, Jamie had seemed to be the perfect baby. True, he had not wanted to breastfeed, but after the initial disappointment she accepted it and put him on the bottle, on which he had thrived. He slept well and rarely cried. He was an exceptionally beautiful child, with downy dark hair and big blue eyes, which often seemed to be thoughtfully gazing into the far distance. People who saw him in the street being wheeled in his pram would stop and admire him, remarking how handsome he was and how lucky Beth was to have such a placid baby.

It wasn't until Jamie was nine months old that Beth began to be seriously concerned about her son. It was on the day she had taken him for his check-up to the local clinic. It was a hot day, the clinic was stuffy, and it was full of harassed mothers with crying, wriggling infants. She had Jamie on her knee, with Danny sitting beside her. Jamie was gazing into the distance as usual in his serene, unfocused way, showing no interest in anything around him. Next to her sat a young girl with a baby girl about the same age as Jamie who was laughing and gurgling at an older lady, obviously the child's proud grandmother, who was playing peek-a-boo with her. It occurred to her suddenly that she had never seen Jamie react in this way; he rarely smiled or showed any pleasure in anything. In fact, none of the other babies around her had that air of impassive detachment; they were all making their presence felt in one way or another. When she was called in for Jamie's check-up, her fears were exacerbated by his failure to respond to the usual tests. The health visitor remarked that he seemed a little slow in his reactions.

"But I'm sure it's nothing to worry about, Mrs Ellis," she said cheerfully. "Babies often differ at this age. We'll test him again in another three months, and I'm sure he'll have caught up by then."

But Beth didn't want to wait three months. She talked it over with Adam when he came home.

"I've been a bit worried too," he admitted. "I'll arrange for a proper assessment at the hospital."

Jamie had been assessed by his colleague, Laura Simmonds, who agreed that he did seem to have a slight developmental problem, but she felt he was still too young to make any definitive diagnosis. They would have to monitor the situation as he grew. As time went on, it became obvious to everyone that Jamie was not developing normally. Physically he was a lovely child; very much like Beth in looks, though his hair was dark like that of his maternal grandfather, but he retained his air of other-worldliness and showed little response to his parents or brother. He would shy away from any physical contact, detaching himself firmly from any attempts to cuddle or kiss him, avoiding any eye contact. As he grew older his behaviour became more unpredictable and he started to have temper-tantrums during which he would throw himself on the floor, uttering a high-pitched wailing which could go on for hours on end. His sleep patterns became erratic; some nights he would sleep well, but often he would be awake all night, disrupting the rest of the family. His speech, too, did not develop and was mainly unintelligible apart from the odd word, although he was fascinated by the television and would sometimes pick up a phrase from it which he would repeat over and over again. At four he was finally diagnosed as severely autistic.

Beth and Adam were devastated and, although they had been partly prepared for the diagnosis, it took many months for them to come to terms with it. Adam had seen quite a few cases of autism in his career and knew that the condition was unlikely to improve dramatically and always put a tremendous strain on the families affected.

"I'm worried about Beth," he confided to Laura, "she's had so much to cope with in her life. She gets so tired dealing with Jamie and trying to look after Danny as well. I don't know if she's going to be able to handle this. I don't even know if *I* can."

"It's awful for you both," said Laura sympathetically. She had become a close friend of theirs as well as a colleague. "Look, I don't know if you and Beth want to think about this at the moment but there's a marvellous school just opened up not far from here. An American guy runs it – he's had a lot of success in the States using new methods to help children like Jamie. He prefers them to board, but they can go as day pupils if the families would rather." She opened a drawer in her desk. "The booklet's in here somewhere – ah, this is it. Yes, his name's Tom Mitchell and the place is called Hopelands." She handed him the book. "At least talk it over with Beth."

At first Beth had refused even to consider it. Jamie was too young; he was too vulnerable; she wanted to be the one to help him. He wasn't going to a 'special school' with all its obvious connotations, to be shut away from the world as if he was some sort of freak.

"It wouldn't be like that," said Adam patiently. "At least let's go and have a look, Beth, and talk to this Tom Mitchell. We might be pleasantly surprised."

"I'll go," she said, "but don't expect me to jump at it."

However, in spite of her misgivings, she had been impressed. Tom Mitchell was older than she had expected, a stocky, balding, bearded man in his late fifties and she immediately liked him. He explained to them that he had been studying autistic children for thirty years and had grown to deplore some of the methods that were used to 'help' them. Because of this, he, along with other enlightened child psychiatrists, had been working on other ways to break through the barriers of autism.

"Our methods are based on something called Applied Behaviour Analysis, or ABA. It was developed during the sixties and seventies by a psychology professor called Ole Ivar Lovaas. He believed in treating autism through strict routine and by rewarding the children using praise and encouragement. We also involve the parents at every stage of the treatment. Autism cannot be cured, but our methods have helped many of the children to integrate into society and to develop more awareness of others around them. We have also had remarkable success with developing language skills."

He took them round the school and showed them the various bright and airy classrooms, and introduced them to some of the dedicated teachers who worked with the children, using gentle but persistent and repetitive methods to help in the development of their basic skills.

In one of the classes the children were playing with water, pouring it from a jug through a series of pipes leading down to various cogs and wheels which turned as the water hit them. He indicated a little boy of about five, who was clapping excitedly as the cogs turned.

"That's Michael. When he first came here a year ago, he basically sat in a corner and stared at the wall, rocking backwards and forwards. That's when he wasn't having the mother and father of all tantrums. Now, he's joining in and even enjoying himself. He's also starting to respond to his parents and his two sisters. A big part of what we try to do here is to teach the child's family how to carry on the therapy outside school; that's particularly important for our day pupils. When we see a child like Michael reacting to play situations with such obvious pleasure, that's what makes this job so rewarding."

Back in his office he poured them coffee.

"I'm sure you must have a heap of questions. But I suggest you go home first and talk about it. Think over what you've seen and decide whether you feel that it's right for Jamie. You'd be welcome to bring him for a few visits if you like. I don't believe in putting pressure on people to make up their minds too quickly, I'd rather let the reputation of the school speak for itself. You know your own child and your own situation best when all's said and done."

Beth nodded.

"I think we're both impressed by what we've seen. It's certainly different from what I expected."

Jamie had started at Hopelands the following autumn, although Beth refused to let him board. It meant a thirty-mile round trip, but she wanted him at home every night. She knew only too well what it was like to be sent away from your family. In the last two years he had come on by leaps and bounds and, despite a few setbacks, he was a much calmer, happier child these days, and that was what counted.

She drew in at the wide gates of the school, admiring as always the elegant façade of the white Georgian building. It was a quarter to four and the teachers were already bringing children out onto the gravel drive. She left Danny in the car and joined the other mothers at the front of the school.

Jamie was holding his teacher's hand, but as soon as he saw her he detached himself and ran over. This was a recent development, and one which warmed Beth's heart each time it happened. He grabbed her hand and gazed up at her for a moment, his blue eyes wide.

"Hello, sweetheart," she said softly, bending to kiss him. He looked away and she felt the usual keen sense of disappointment. One day, she thought, one day he might even get to kiss me back…

In the car Danny turned to ruffle Jamie's hair as Beth strapped him in his car seat.

"Hi there, Spud! How about this then? I scored top points on Super Mario. I'm the champion!"

"I'm champion," repeated Jamie wide-eyed. "I'm champion… champion… champion!"

Beth laughed.

"You certainly are, Jamie. What time do you need to get to football practice, Dan?"

"About a quarter-past-five. Why?"

"I just want to take a slight detour, that's all. It won't take long."

CHAPTER 4

"Where are we going, Mum?" asked Danny as they swung off the main road down a narrow country lane.

"You'll see in a moment," she replied, negotiating the Land Rover skilfully around the sharp twists and turns in the road. After about ten minutes they reached a sign saying UPPER MELCOMBE and in smaller letters: Please Drive Carefully Through Our Village. She drove on past picturesque, half-timbered houses, a large church with a Norman spire and a well-kept village green and duck pond. There was an old whitewashed pub called The Blacksmith's Arms, a small row of shops which included a newsagent with a post office, a small convenience store, a pharmacy and a little gift-shop called Norah's Knick-Knacks. Right at the end of them was a small glass-fronted building with a sign over the door: *Telfer and Giddings, Estate Agents and Valuers*. Beth swung the four-by-four into the pull-in by the shops.

"I won't be a moment," she told the boys, as she got out and approached the door. She glanced quickly in the window, but surprisingly the house was not displayed on any of the boards. She opened the door and went in, finding herself in a small room with a large desk in one corner behind which sat a distinguished-looking elderly gentleman with silver hair and a pair of half-glasses on the end of his nose. He peered at her over these and gave a brief smile.

"Good afternoon, Madam. How can I be of service?"

Beth smiled back. "You have a house advertised in the *Property Weekly*." She showed him the paper. "I wondered if you could give me any further details."

He peered at the article. "Ah, yes." He frowned and cleared his throat. "Hrmm... that is Malthorp House... quite so. Built in 1907 and an unusual property if I might say so, but individual – yes – highly individual." He opened a drawer in the desk and rummaged around whilst Beth looked on, rather amused at his eccentric manner. "Ah, here we are," he said, producing a sheet of paper which he handed to her with a flourish. "Can I interest you in any other properties, Madam? We have one or two very nice modern detached houses in the area?"

"No thank you," she replied. "I'm really looking for something a bit different; that's why this one caught my eye. I want to show my husband tonight and if we decide we're interested, perhaps we can get back to you soon and come down to view the house."

"Yes, yes, by all means." He coughed again, and said, "Of course, you must realise that the house hasn't been lived in for a considerable time."

"Yes, so it says in the paper," replied Beth. "How long, exactly?"

He seemed strangely reluctant to give her an answer.

"Hrmm…. Well, I think about… yes, well it must be all of… let me see now… twelve years, I suppose."

"Twelve *years*!" Beth stared at him in disbelief. "Hasn't it been on the market before this?"

The estate agent looked uncomfortable. "Well, no, I don't believe so – though I'm really not quite, well, *clear*, on the precise reasons for that. I think some legal requirement stated that it couldn't be sold until it was inherited by the present owner, although the previous one died some years ago. It was all rather complicated I believe. The house has rather fallen into disrepair. I think it may need a *considerable* amount of work done on it. I don't want to put you off, but…" He seemed loathe to complete his sentence.

"Well, as I've already said, I'll be talking to my husband about it," said Beth, who was beginning to feel rather strongly that he was indeed trying to put her off. Most unusual, she thought, for an estate agent. "If we do want to view, I'll give you a ring Mr?"

"Giddings," he replied putting out a large, well-manicured hand. "Joshua Giddings at your service, dear lady. Let me give you one of our cards."

"Thank you. I'm Beth Ellis," she replied, shaking his hand. "Goodbye, Mr Giddings."

"Goodbye Mrs… er… Ellis."

She left the estate agents feeling amused and more than a little puzzled by Mr Giddings' manner. She got back in the car and Danny leant forward curiously to look at the piece of paper in her hand.

"What's that, Mum? We're not moving, are we?"

"I'm not sure, Danny. I'm just looking around at the moment." She showed him the picture of Malthorp House. "What do you think?"

"Wow!" he exclaimed. "That's a mansion. We're not going to buy that, are we?"

"I do rather like the look of it. I need somewhere where I can set up a proper studio. There would certainly be heaps of room in a place like this. But I've got to see what Dad thinks first; I haven't even told him I've been looking yet."

"Can I have a snooker table in the attic? In fact, can I have the attic as a games room? That'd be really wicked."

"Wicket!" echoed Jamie, gazing dreamily out of the window. "Wicket… wicket… *wicket*!"

Beth had been home about half-an-hour and the boys were sitting at the table with their tea, when the phone rang. She sighed inwardly as she heard her mother-in-law's strident tones.

"Oh, hello Audrey, how lovely to hear from you." She tried hard to sound enthusiastic. "How are you? Is John feeling better?" There had been a bit of a scare with Adam's father a few weeks back when he had suffered what the doctors feared could be a mild stroke. After extensive tests he'd been diagnosed as suffering from a heart condition probably brought on by a combination of exhaustion and stress. Beth was not in the least surprised; over the years since she and Adam had been married, she had often wondered how John coped with his wife and her strange moods – one moment

Audrey could be charming and warm, the next she could sink into a dark depression, during which her only comfort seemed to be her obsession with Tarot cards and the Ouija board. She had gathered together a like-minded circle of friends, and many evenings at their home would be spent on what Audrey liked to call their 'spiritual and occult sessions', during which John's main function seemed to be chief coffee-and-sandwich-maker. He had often remarked to Adam privately that, for followers of the ethereal world of the spirits, their consumption of these earthly pleasures seemed boundless. His only escape was the office and he had been spending as much time there as he could; this in turn had led to his present problem. He was slowly recovering, much to the family's relief, and had recently talked of retiring. Audrey was the only one who seemed totally unconcerned about her husband – she was far too wrapped up in her own world.

"Oh, Beth, dear, thank goodness you're there," she said now, blithely ignoring Beth's query about John. "I simply had to telephone you straight away. I've had Faith Bulmer here with us this afternoon and the cards have been *so* informative. But it was our séance that I'm really ringing you about. Now, Beth, I know you and Adam don't really believe in our little sessions, but Broken Arrow came through so strongly and then there was this extraordinary message for you. You won't credit this but…"

"Audrey," interrupted Beth, half amused, half annoyed, "I'm sure it's very interesting and I'd love to hear all about it another time, but to be honest this isn't the best moment. I'm not being unkind but I haven't a clue who this Faith Bulmer is, let alone Broken Arrow, and as you say I don't really believe in any of this nons… um… séance stuff. I'd love to stop and talk, but Danny has football practice in half an hour, so I'm rather pushed for time."

There was a short but frosty silence at the other end of the phone. Oh dear, thought Beth, I've done it now. Then Audrey spoke.

"Well, of course Beth, if you feel Daniel's sport is more important than spending five minutes listening to something that may be extremely relevant to your and Adam's life, then I suppose there's no more to be said."

Beth took a deep breath and willed herself to be patient. She knew John would be the one to suffer if she upset Audrey, and she was very fond of her father-in-law.

"Of course it's not more important, Audrey. It's just been rather a busy day and…"

"I knew you'd want to know, my dear, and I won't keep you long I promise." Audrey's tone resumed its enthusiastic stridency. "Faith Bulmer is one of the top mediums in the country. She's had astonishing success with her predictions. Her guide is Broken Arrow, a Red Indian chief who lived in the last century. Anyway, we'd had our usual session and he had come through for several of the followers when, all of a sudden, Faith seemed to go into an even deeper trance than normal. Then this woman's voice said something in Welsh."

"Welsh?" Beth's heart missed a beat. "Go on, Audrey."

"Well, it was just a few words. I can't repeat them, obviously, because I don't speak it, but Maisie Gould was there and her husband comes from Wales, so she wrote it down. After the session she rang him and you will never guess what he said it meant?"

For some reason Beth suddenly felt cold. Audrey's tone was gratified as she continued, sensing she now had Beth's full attention.

"Apparently this spirit said: 'Tell Beth, Beth Morgan that she and the children must not go. Look again elsewhere or it will begin again'." She waited for a reaction. "Beth? Beth, are you still there? Your name was Morgan before you married Adam, wasn't it? Have you any idea what the message could mean?"

Beth mentally shook herself. "No, I have no idea whatsoever, Audrey. Look, I really have to go now. Speak to you soon." She hung up and stood staring at the phone for several minutes, until Danny's voice broke in on her thoughts.

"Mum? Mum, I'm going to be late if we don't go soon. What did Grandma want?"

Beth came back to earth and smiled at her son.

"Oh, nothing Dan, she was just telling me about one of her gatherings."

"Her drivel and slush sessions as Granddad always calls them," grinned Danny. Beth laughed at the mischievous expression on his face.

"Something like that." She pushed Audrey's conversation to the back of her mind and called to Jamie who was still sitting at the table pushing the last of his chips round with his fork.

"Come on, sweetheart, it's time to take Danny to football practice. Daddy will be home soon."

Jamie climbed down from the kitchen table. He was clutching something in his hand and Beth saw it was the sheet of paper with the details of Malthorp House.

"Oh, give that to me, Jamie," she said. "I want to show it to Daddy later."

He shook his head and sat down on the floor beside her. With extreme care he spread the paper out flat in front of him and studied the picture with seemingly intense concentration. Beth smiled and hunkered down on the floor beside him.

"Do you like the look of that house, Jamie?" she asked softly. "Would you like to live there?"

He raised his head and looked at her, and for a split second she thought she saw understanding and a deep wisdom in his eyes. Then he turned away, and she felt that familiar sense of disappointment. She got up and went to fetch her car keys.

Left alone, Jamie fixed his gaze once again at the grainy photograph of Malthorp House and gave one of his rare smiles.

"*Valentine*," he said softly.

CHAPTER 5

Adam saw the door shut after his last consultation of the day with a sigh of relief. It had been a particularly busy day and a traumatic one in which he had suffered the loss of a patient. The death of a child was one of the things he had always found difficult to come to terms with, in spite of the fact that he saw a lot of it in his line of work. He'd fought so hard to save little Kirsty Reed, but in the end the battle had proved too much for her tiny body and the cancer had won. It had been hard as always to maintain an air of professional detachment in the face of her parent's grief and bewilderment; even harder when Chris Reed had grasped his hand and whispered brokenly, "We know you did your best for her, Mr Ellis." He rubbed his forehead where he could feel the beginnings of a headache. Sometimes he wished he had chosen an easier field than paediatrics.

There was a knock and his colleague Laura Simmonds put her head round the door.

"Hi," she said cheerfully, "thought you'd probably finished." She frowned at the expression on his face and came into the room. "God, Adam, you look terrible. Bad day?"

"We lost the little Reed girl."

"Oh." She shook her head sadly. "We never bloody well get used to it, do we?" She pursed her lips. "Tell you what, let's pop into the White Horse on the way home and I'll treat you to a pint. Geoff's not finishing until seven tonight and I could use some company."

He smiled at her. Laura was an attractive blonde in her late thirties; she had worked with him now for the past eight years and had become a close family friend, often coming over for an evening meal with them and staying the odd weekend. The children both adored her and she them; she had given Beth and Adam invaluable support with Jamie and had endless patience with him. Adam had often thought what a marvellous mother she would make, but she'd remained firmly unattached over the years until quite recently, when she had met and fallen deeply in love with Geoff Dunbar, a lab technician who had transferred from Edinburgh to the south for work. Adam and Beth had been delighted for her; Geoff was a big, warm bear of a man who obviously worshipped Laura and the four of them had spent several highly enjoyable evenings together. A few weeks ago, they had announced that they intended to get married in the not-too-distant future and they had all spent a memorable weekend celebrating.

"I would love a pint," Adam said now. "But I can't, unfortunately. Beth's arranged for us to view this house at six-thirty so I've got to shoot off and pick up Debbie, who's babysitting for us."

"You decided not to take the boys with you after all?"

"No, I think it'll be easier without them, and Debs is very good with Jamie. Beth trusts her, and we won't be that long, hopefully."

Laura looked at him quizzically.

"You're still not too keen on the idea of moving, are you?" she said. "Or is it just that you don't want all the hassle?"

"I don't know," he said honestly. "I know it's what Beth wants, but I'm not sure that a move is the best thing for us at the moment, and this place she has found is so big. It's going to need a hell of a lot of work done to it by all accounts and most of the arrangements for that are going to fall on Beth's shoulders. On the other hand, she does need more room for her work, and it is a lot nearer to Jamie's school."

"But further away from Danny's," pointed out Laura.

"Well, there's a pretty good school bus service or we can drop him off first. I'm trying to seem enthusiastic for Beth's sake – she's really keen as you know, so I think I'll have a job to dissuade her if she falls in love with it. I must admit it would be nice to have a lot of ground for the boys to run around in. Danny's already throwing out hints about having a dog if we move to the country." He looked at his watch. "I'd better get going. See you later, Laura."

He picked up Debbie in good time and was home by just after five. Beth was on the phone when he got in, and he could see by her face that something was wrong.

"Yes, Mr Giddings," she was saying, "I appreciate what you're saying, but I think it's only fair to let us view it first. After all, we may decide it's worth paying more than they're offering. Yes… I realise that… yes… well, we'll still be there at six-thirty as arranged. No, not at all… Right… Goodbye, Mr Giddings."

She banged the phone down. "Honestly, that bloody man! If I have to listen to one more 'Aaahrm… well' I shall go stark staring mad!" Adam laughed and put his arms round her. Debbie, an attractive blonde, gave a grin and went in the lounge to see the boys.

"What's up? Is there a problem with viewing the house?"

Beth kissed him. "Apparently he's had a lot of interest from an American client who owns a chain of 'gracious country manors' that he leases as conference centres. He wanted to know if we thought we'd really be interested in Malthorp House as his client is preparing to make a direct offer to the vendor and with the house needing such a lot of work, blah… blah… blah… He's done nothing but try to put me off ever since I asked about the place."

Adam grinned. "Well, he hasn't succeeded, so he obviously doesn't know you very well. Come on, love, relax. We're still going to look, aren't we?"

"Too true. I'm more determined than ever now. Go and see the boys. There's a cup of tea and I've made you a sandwich – I thought we'd stop at the local pub on the way home and have a meal; I noticed they did food the other day."

"Fine," he called as he went into the lounge. Danny was sprawled on the settee watching *Tom and Jerry*. Jamie was sitting on the floor with Debbie lining up his toy cars, something he would spend endless hours doing.

"Hi, Dad," Danny bounced up into a sitting position. "Guess what? We made the semi-finals; we thrashed 'em – four-nil!"

"That's brilliant, Dan. Who's the play-off against?"

"Redmond. We'll beat them *easy*."

Adam shook his head in mock despair. "Such confidence for one so young." He hunkered down beside Jamie. "Hello, Tiger, and how was your day?"

Jamie nodded and picked up a yellow MG, placing it carefully behind a blue Lancia. His expression as always was serious and reserved, his blue eyes showing little emotion. Adam sighed inwardly. He would have given anything to see his little boy smile or laugh; if anything, his love for him grew more every day and with it the sadness that his son would probably never be able to experience a full and normal life. Beside him, Debbie gave Jamie a gentle nudge.

"Come on Jamie. Show your Daddy what you learnt today."

Jamie gave Adam a sideways look. Adam gave him an encouraging smile.

"What did you learn, Tiger?"

In a clear voice Jamie said,

"My name is Jamie and I'm six years old."

Adam grinned delightedly. "That's wonderful, Jamie. Have you heard this, Beth?"

"I have," she said coming into the room with his tea and sandwich. "Tom's really pleased with his progress. I spoke with him today and he said that Jamie was actually starting to come forward voluntarily to play, and he sat on Mrs Foster's knee this morning and listened to a whole story without getting down."

"We'll have him playing football soon, won't we Spud?" said Danny, jumping off the settee and sitting on the floor next to his brother. He picked up another car and handed it to Jamie, who solemnly took it and lined it up.

"My name is Jamie and I'm six years old," he said with quiet dignity.

Beth laughed. "Come on, sweetheart, time for your bath," she said. "Debbie's going to take you up tonight because Daddy and I have to go out." She held out her hand, but Jamie ignored her, seemingly intent on his cars.

"Jamie?" Beth said again.

"N...n...No-o-o-o!" screeched Jamie suddenly. He threw himself on the floor and began the high-pitched screaming that heralded one of his hysterical attacks. Beth bit her lip. From past experience she knew that this could go on for hours.

"Don't worry, Mrs Ellis!" shouted Debbie above the noise. "I'll see to him, you go on. He'll be okay."

"I can't leave you with this," said Beth. "Adam, you'd better ring Mr Giddings and cancel. We'll go another time."

Suddenly Jamie stopped yelling. He bottom-shuffled over to Danny and buried his head in his brother's lap, snuffling and hiccupping softly.

"He's okay now, Mum," said Danny. "I 'spect he's tired. We'll play for a bit longer and then Debs and me will put him to bed. You go."

"Well..." said Beth.

"Come on, love," urged Adam. "He'll be fine. We'll be late if we don't leave now."

She followed him out of the room. Adam grabbed his sandwich to eat in the car on the way and then they picked up their coats and hurried out.

"It's been ages since he had one of those attacks," said Beth miserably as they headed towards the A31. "I spoke too soon about the improvement."

"Oh, come on Beth, he's ten times better than he used to be. It didn't last long, did it? Danny's right, he's just a bit tired. Now let's just concentrate on Malthorp House. Is Giddings meeting us there?"

"He should be. Through the village, past the church and the turning's on the left."

"This looks nice," said Adam, as they passed through the little village. "I like the look of the pub. How much further to the house?"

Beth consulted the sheet. "There's a little road in about a quarter-of-a-mile on the left. About five hundred yards down there and the gates to the house are on the right."

The little road proved very narrow. After about two hundred yards a crumbling, high brick wall appeared on the right hand side. A little further on they saw two big rusty wrought-iron gates between tall stone pillars which were topped by a pair of lichen-covered, rather sinister-looking stone lions. There was an ancient black Rover parked beside the gates. As they drew up, the car door opened and Mr Giddings emerged, beaming at them benevolently.

"Ah, Mrs Ellis, how nice to see you again! And this must be… hrmm… *Mr* Ellis? Delighted to make your acquaintance my dear sir! I trust I find you in good health?"

"Fine, thanks," replied Adam, amused by the man's rather old-fashioned bonhomie. "Sorry we're a bit late."

"Not at all… not at all. As a matter of fact, a slight… hrmm… *problem* has occurred."

"We're not going to be able to view the house," said Beth flatly.

Mr Giddings looked shocked.

"No… No… Not at all, dear lady. I should have telephoned you had that been the case. No, unfortunately I have been summoned to Winchester for an important meeting and I won't be able to show you around the property. However, if you don't mind… hrmm… showing *yourselves* around, as it were, and then dropping the keys back to my office."

"That will be fine," said Adam, taking the bunch of keys from the estate agent's hand. "Please don't worry about it, Mr Giddings. We'll make sure we bring the keys back."

"Oh, thank you. I really can't apologise enough. If you just push the keys through the… hrmm… you know… the *letterbox* that would be too kind. See you soon, I hope."

He climbed back into his ancient car, which coughed and spluttered rather like its owner as he started it up and roared off up the road, scattering leaves in his wake. Adam and Beth heaved sighs of relief.

"Thank God for that!" said Beth. "I wasn't looking forward to him showing us round." She gazed up at the stone lions. "Spooky, as Danny would say. Let's leave the car here, shall we, and walk up to the house?"

CHAPTER 6

Overgrown rhododendron and azalea bushes lined the winding driveway, and the only sound was the faint crunch of their feet on the weed-choked gravel. Adam found the silence rather oppressive as in the town there was always some noise to be heard – a car door slamming, a raised voice – but here even the birdsong seemed to be faintly subdued. He shivered a little in the chill evening air and glanced at Beth.

Her face was bright with anticipation and, as they rounded the final curve of the drive, she gasped. Adam, too, felt a sense of detachment from reality as he gazed on the house before them.

The evening sun shone warmly on the red brick, reflecting off the bay windows and ornamental stonework. The two tall, patterned-brick chimneys were set in a warm terracotta roof and the whole building had an air of surrealness as if it had been frozen in time. As they approached, they saw that the ornamental porch was surmounted by another stone creature – an eagle this time, with outstretched wings and a curved, cruel-looking beak. Adam whistled.

"This place isn't true, Beth. It looks like something out of a bad horror movie. When did Giddings say it was built?"

"1907," said Beth dreamily. "Adam, it's wonderful."

"I don't know about that," he said looking up doubtfully at the brickwork. "Look at those cracks and some of that stonework on the upper balustrades doesn't look too safe either. If it's not been occupied for twelve years then I've a nasty feeling that there's going to be a lot that needs doing to this place, Beth."

"Oh, don't be such an old pessimist. Let's at least look inside and see what it's like before we dismiss it out of hand. Look at all this ground, the boys could go wild here."

Adam thought the garden would need quite a lot of work too, but he smiled at her enthusiasm as they mounted the worn stone steps to the front door. "This is good and solid anyway," he said as he inserted the key into the big brass lock. It grated slightly as he turned it and the door swung open with a creak.

"Velcome to Dracula's humble abode!" he intoned in a sepulchral voice as they entered.

"Idiot," said Beth. "Wow, this is some entrance hall!"

The hall was enormous and covered with a dusty red carpet. The walls were lined with some sort of thick flock paper which showed pale squares where once pictures had hung. In front of them was a wide staircase. Several doors led off the hallway.

"Look, Adam," said Beth. "Even the old gas brackets have been left on the walls. We could make a feature of those."

They began exploring, opening the doors that led off the hallway and exclaiming afresh each time at the size of the rooms beyond. Each one had a fireplace, and one had obviously been used as a library judging by the bookshelves lining the walls. In one they discovered a sheet-shrouded object which proved to be an old piano.

"Hey," said Adam as he examined it, "Neil would love this. It must be pretty old and I think it's a Bentwood. I wonder if it would work if it was cleaned up?"

"Probably. Come on, I want to see what the kitchen arrangements are like. Did you notice the green baize door down the passage at the end of the hallway? They used to put those in so that the smell of the cooking wouldn't permeate through the house."

They went through the door which closed with a soft whispering sound behind them. A short flight of stairs led downwards and through another door into the kitchen itself.

"I see what they meant by 'Upstairs, Downstairs'," said Adam. He surveyed the gloomy, cavernous kitchen and shook his head. "I can see this needing a lot of work."

A huge, rusty old kitchen range stood against one wall, with a dilapidated oak dresser next to it. Pushed back against the other wall was a massive pine table. A door to the side of it led into a small room lined with shelves with a high, mesh-covered window, that had obviously been used as a larder. Another door opposite them led down two more steps into a large scullery that housed an old boiling copper and a cracked Butler sink. A passageway led along from this to a set of wooden stairs. Everywhere was thick with dust and cobwebs.

"These must be the back stairs used by the servants," said Beth. "Shall we use them or shall we sweep up the main staircase in style?"

"The main staircase, of course," replied Adam. "We are the prospective Master and Mistress of this desirable property after all."

They made their way back to the hall, noticing on their way the set of bells used to summon the servants in days gone by, which still hung above the kitchen door.

"Can't have been much fun in those days," remarked Adam. "I bet they had to work pretty long hours for very little pay. Imagine having to run up and down all those stairs every day, their legs must have been worn out!"

The staircase rose up steeply from the hall and split two ways. They turned left first and examined the three large bedrooms on that side. They all smelt musty and had peeling wallpaper and creaking floorboards. There was also a large walk-in linen cupboard, lined with slatted shelves. They retraced their steps and took the right-hand branch of the split. This side of the house contained another three rooms, one of which had obviously been used as a nursery, judging by the bars at the windows. There was also a large bathroom with an old claw-footed bath in it.

"Nice," said Adam. "You pay a fortune for these, you know."

"Mmm…" said Beth. "Did you notice that some of the bedrooms had dressing rooms? They could easily be converted into en-suites."

He looked at her quizzically. "Don't get too carried away, love. There's an awful lot to think about before deciding whether to take this place on or not."

"You don't need to tell me, but…" she smiled at him, "…I don't know what it is about this place, Adam, I just fell in love with it the first moment I saw it in the paper. Now I've seen inside I'm more convinced than ever that it's right for us. Before you say anything…" she raised her hand as he opened his mouth to speak "…I realise it's going to be an awful lot of work and that it will cost quite a bit of money, but with my fee from *Wizard of the White Mountain* and this other commission that's in the bag, I'm sure we can manage it."

"Okay, okay," he raised his own hands in mock surrender, "you've nearly convinced me. What's down this little passageway at the end?" he said leading the way.

"Aha, the other end of the servant's staircase. And this stairway going up here must lead into the attics."

They mounted the steep, narrow stairs and he pushed open the door at the top. They found themselves in a large room with shutters across the window and a cupboard at one end.

"This might have been used as a schoolroom or another nursery," remarked Beth as she crossed to the window and struggled with the shutters. Adam came to help her, and the evening light flooded in as they folded them back. There were heavy iron bars at this window too. They looked down on the tangle of blackberry bushes below. "Look, over there are some old outbuildings. I wonder how big the grounds are."

"It will be getting dark soon – the light's already beginning to fade," he replied. "Do you realise it's a quarter-past-seven? We'd better be making a move soon if we're going to have a meal at the pub."

"Look, Adam, there's a fireplace in here, just like all the other rooms. I wonder what's through here," said Beth, indicating a door on the other side of the room. They went through and found it led to four small poky rooms, each one dusty and full of cobwebs. "Servants quarters," she said. "They didn't have much in the way of home comforts, did they?"

He shook his head.

"They certainly didn't. I'm just going down to take another look at that piano. If it is a Bentwood, then it will be worth restoring."

He clattered off down the steps, leaving Beth looking round the attic. She crossed to the big cupboard and opened the door. It was lined with shelves, but totally empty. She closed the door and crossed to the window once more. The sun had nearly set now and the shadows were growing long and dark across the sky. Behind her she heard a long, whispering sigh.

She spun round. There was nothing there, but in the corner by the cupboard there was one shadow that seemed deeper than the rest. She took a step towards it. Suddenly the room seemed very cold. She frowned. The shadow almost looked like a small person. She shivered, feeling increasingly uneasy.

The shadow seemed to shift. It was as if it were stretching out a small arm towards her…

"Beth!" Adam's voice echoed cheerfully up the stairs and she started towards it in relief. He appeared in the doorway.

"What on earth are you doing mooching round up there in the dark? That piano *is* a Bentwood. I must tell Neil about it. I'd better put those shutters back and then we'll make for the pub. I could murder a pint."

<hr>

They dropped the keys off at Telfer and Giddings then, over shepherd's pie at the Blacksmith's Arms in the village, they discussed the advantages and pitfalls of buying Malthorp House. At least it was Adam who pointed out the pitfalls while Beth enthused over the advantages. By the end of the evening, Adam knew he was beaten. He decided to indulge in another half of the Blacksmith's finest brew as consolation, whilst Beth popped outside to ring Debbie on her mobile to ensure all was well at home. He leant against the bar and lifted the foaming glass gratefully to his lips.

"Haven't seen you in here before, sir," said the landlord. He was a short, rotund man with a shock of bright ginger hair. "Just passing through, or did someone recommend the food?"

"No," he replied. "Though I must say it was excellent and this is a lovely pint. Actually, we're thinking of buying a house near here."

"Oh, yes?" He took a glass from another customer who had just come up to the bar. "Same again, Bill? Where might that be, then?"

"A place called Malthorp House. It's just down the road there, to the left."

"Oh, I know where it is, sir." He gave Adam a strange look. "Everyone knows Malthorp. And you're thinking of buying it, you say?"

"Yes," he replied. "That's if we can manage to get all the work done on it that needs doing. Can you recommend any good builders around this area should we decide to go ahead?"

"Well…" began the landlord, but he was interrupted by the man to whom he had just served a pint.

"You won't get nobody round here to work at Malthorp."

"Now then, Bill," said the landlord.

"Come on, Ted, you know it's true. No one will touch it with a barge-pole. Too much has gone on there."

"But I thought it had been empty for years," said Adam, somewhat bemused. Mr Giddings told us it hadn't been lived in for at least twelve years."

Bill sniffed.

"Joshua Giddings! What do he know? It's not the living I'm talking about."

"I beg your pardon?" said Adam, even more bewildered. "What do you mean, not the living?"

Bill took a long swig of his pint and wiped his mouth with the back of his hand.

"Haunted, isn't it? Has been since living memory. My old gran used to work there as a girl, an' she had many a tale she could tell about the goings-on up at Malthorp. Something bad happened there, something nobody wanted talked about. That's why the family won't live there. The Martins, scared to death of it they are. Ask anyone."

"Shut up, Bill!" said Ted. "Don't you take no notice of him, sir. Spins many a tale he does. Likes to make himself heard." He leant forward as Bill, still muttering, took himself over to a table near the door to join his cronies. "His old gran was a bit touched in the head, poor old soul. I've never seen anything wrong with Malthorp; the family only lived there on and off it's true, after old Mr Cartwright, who built the place I believe, died sometime back in the twenties. I heard there was some complication over a will or something. Young Mr Robert Martin owns it now, his great-great-grandson, but maybe he feels it's too big for him."

"Quite," said Adam, feeling a little bewildered by all this information. He smiled as Beth joined him at the bar. "It is a big place. This is my wife, Beth, by the way. I'm Adam Ellis."

"Ted Chambers. I hope we'll be seeing a lot more of you if you do buy the house. We do a good Sunday roast if you want to bring your family in. I expect you've got children?"

"Two boys," replied Beth with a smile. "That's one of the reasons we like the house – there's plenty of room for them to run around in."

"Talking of the boys we better be getting back," said Adam. "Goodbye for now, Mr Chambers. See you again soon, I hope."

"Call me Ted, please. Good luck with the house."

On the way out they passed Bill, who shook his head and muttered, "Don't say I didn't warn you!" before subsiding once more into his pint. In the car Beth said,

"What was all that about?"

"Oh, just one of the local yokels trying to scare me to death by telling me some tale about Malthorp being haunted. I can see how it got that reputation, though. It is rather creepy in some ways."

"It won't be once we've finished with it," said Beth. "I do hope things will work out for us, Adam."

"So do I," he replied. "So do I."

<hr>

At Malthorp House the sun had deserted the darkening sky, a few stars were beginning to show and a thin sickle moon had appeared, to chase the long shadows away.

But one, deeper than the rest, remained.

CHAPTER 7

Negotiations to buy Malthorp House proved long and complicated; at times Beth and Adam despaired of ever completing the transaction. Firstly, the conglomerate that had wished to purchase the property with a view to turning it into an upmarket conference centre, increased their offer to Robert Martin, the vendor, so they were forced to match it. Then, after the initial survey, there was so much dry rot and damp discovered that there was talk of the whole building being declared unsafe. Beth and Adam also had problems with their own purchasers, who nearly pulled out once because of financial problems; eventually they managed to resolve them and got back on track once again. But then once again the conglomerate that had been interested renewed their offer. At that point they had been close to giving up the whole idea. But, in the end, Martin agreed to sell them the house after Adam had bypassed Telfer and Giddings and rang him personally one evening. Adam had been surprised how young he sounded.

"I hope you don't mind me ringing," said Adam, "but we're really keen on the place. I know it needs a lot of work, but my wife and I feel it would be criminal to turn it into something as soulless as a conference centre. It seems to us that it must always have been a family home and we'd love to have the chance to restore it into just that again."

"Really?" said the voice on the other end of the phone. "I've always felt it was a bit of a monstrosity, but I'm glad you feel that way about it. I don't know if you've been told, but it has actually been in my family for nearly a hundred years. It was built by my – let me see – yes, my great-great-grandfather in about 1907 or thereabouts. Personally, I could never stand the place, but my great-grandfather, Robert Cartwright, left it to me in his will when I was about ten. That's why it's been empty for so long. There was a clause in the will which stated that it had to stay in the family until I was twenty-one, then I was free to do whatever I chose with it. My grandmother, his daughter, never wanted to live there after my grandfather died, and I think the old boy hoped that I would, but frankly I could do with the money, so I'll be glad to be shot of it." He paused. "When you went to view the house did you go up into the attics?"

"Yes. If we get the place, we want to turn the big room into a playroom for our two boys."

There was a short silence.

"I see. Did you..." he cleared his throat "...did you feel anything... well... strange when you were up there?"

"No. It was very cold, but apart from that, nothing out of the ordinary," replied Adam, puzzled. "Why do you ask?"

"Oh, no reason really," said Robert. "Look, I'm glad you rang me and I think you sound ideal for the house, so I would like you to have it as you're so keen. I'm going to ring Joshua Giddings now and tell him that I have accepted your offer."

"Really!" exclaimed Adam delightedly. "That's wonderful. My wife will be over the moon – she fell in love with Malthorp from the first time she saw it. Thank you so much, Mr Martin."

"I just hope you realise what you're taking on," the younger man replied enigmatically, but rang off before Adam could ask him what he meant.

Robert Martin put the phone down thoughtfully and went into the kitchen where his Italian wife, Maria, was preparing their evening meal. A delicious aroma of tomatoes and herbs rose from a steaming pot on the stove. Maria looked flushed and beautiful as she chopped mushrooms and peppers. She looked up enquiringly,

"Who was that on the phone, Robert?"

"The prospective vendors for Malthorp."

"Conference International?"

"No, a chap called Adam Ellis. He and his wife are crazy about the old place so I've agreed to let him have it." He picked up a piece of pepper and chewed on it gloomily.

"Well, that's good news, isn't it?" She added the mushrooms and peppers to the pot on the stove. "So why don't you look happy about it?"

"I just wonder…"

"What?" She turned to him. "What is it about that house, Robert? Why wouldn't you let me go and see it? With the baby on the way, we might have even wanted to do it up ourselves and live there."

"*No!*" He bit his lip. "Sorry, Maria, I don't mean to snap. It's just that I hated that house when I went to visit as a kid; to me it never seemed the right place for a family. That's why I'm wondering if I've done the right thing by letting the Ellises have it."

He walked away from her into the living room, poured himself a large shot of Scotch and sat down. A shiver ran down his spine as he made himself remember back…

Back to when he was ten years old.

THEN

The tall, thin, dark-haired man standing on the gravelled drive hunched up his shoulders against the steady drizzle. He found himself shivering even though his waterproof jacket was lined and warm, remembering suddenly the way this house had always made him feel – cold inside and out. He sighed and strode resolutely towards the front door, trying not to look at the menacing stone eagle above the porch. It had always spooked him whenever he had visited this place. Reaching into his pocket he pulled out a brass key which he inserted into the large keyhole. As the panelled wooden door swung open, he paused and looked round.

"Rob!" he called. "Sarah! Where are you?" There was no response. He called again, more loudly. "Robert!"

His two children, ten-year-old Robert and five-year-old Sarah, appeared from round the side of the house. They were giggling rather guiltily and their mouths were stained red with juice. The man smiled in relief.

"There you are! What have you two little devils been up to?"

His daughter giggled again.

"We found some blackenberries, Daddy. Round there by the wall."

"*Blackberries*," corrected her brother. He saw his father frown. "Sorry, Dad – we were just exploring."

Harry Martin sighed. He hadn't wanted to bring the children with him today, but Lorna had been called into the office at the last moment and there was nobody else to look after them at such short notice. He had promised his mother-in-law faithfully that he would carry out her grandfather's last wishes, and as he was due to go away on business, today was his last opportunity. He hadn't been looking forward to it; he had never liked the house and had always felt uncomfortable on his rare visits there. In a way, he reflected, as he pushed the door further open it was good to have Robert and Sarah's company. He entered the house, the children following closely behind him.

They were in a large hallway, lined with thick, faded flock wallpaper which had once been a rich red but had now faded to pale pink. At the far end rose a wide imposing stairway with an ornately carved banister. On the walls, between the old gas brackets, hung some dark and gloomy oil-paintings, mainly of rural scenes. Several doors led off the hall; to the left of the stairway was a smaller door covered in green baize. By his side his son shivered.

"Spooky, Dad!" he said, and jumped as his voice echoed. Little Sarah's lip trembled.

"I don't like it here!" she wailed suddenly. "Want to go home!"

Harry stooped and picked her up.

"Don't be silly," he said gently. "This won't take me long. I just have to check round and make sure everything is alright. I promised Grandma. Then the house can be locked up safely and we can go. Okay?"

They both nodded and, still carrying Sarah, he began opening doors and checking all the rooms.

"Why does it have to be locked up, Dad?" asked Robert. "Don't Grandma and Gramps want to live here?" He opened one of the doors and peered into the shadowy room beyond. "These rooms are really big – they'd have lots more space here. Gramps would have loads of room for his trains." His grandfather was a model railway fanatic, and was banished to the loft of his grandparent's modest three-bedroomed house.

His father laughed.

"I don't think Grandma would appreciate having to clean this big place just so that Gramps would be able to play with his trains, son. Besides, it was your great-grandad Cartwright's wish that the house should not be lived in for now."

"Who was he?"

"He was Grandma's father."

"Why doesn't he want anyone to live here?" persisted Robert.

"You ask too many questions," said Harry. "Come on, it'll be getting dark soon. We'd better be getting on."

He opened the green baize door and walked down the long passageway beyond, followed closely by Sarah. The door shut behind them with a whispering sound. Robert decided not to follow them and opened another door discovering a smaller room beyond. There was a large rectangular object in it covered by a yellowing sheet. Curious, he crossed the dusty floor and lifted one corner of the sheet. Beneath was a shiny piano.

"Wow!" he exclaimed pulling off the rest of the cover. He lifted the lid and pressed one of the keys. It let out a mournful *dong* and he jumped slightly even though he had been expecting it.

"*Robert!*"

He jumped as he heard a voice behind him and turned, but there was no one there. It had sounded like Sarah, but he'd thought she was with Dad. He covered up the piano and crossed to the door.

"*Ro…obert!*"

Now the voice sounded as if it was coming from upstairs. It was a funny voice, thin and tinny, a bit like the voice on his robot toy that Grandma had bought him for Christmas a few years ago. Maybe Sarah was playing a trick on him. He started cautiously up the stairs and heard a faint sound, a sort of hollow tapping that echoed off the walls as he reached the landing where the stairs split two ways. Robert took a turn to the right.

"Sarah!" he called softly. "Sarah! Is that you?"

There was a muffled giggle. He found himself in a corridor with yet more doors going off it. He opened two or three of them but beyond were only big, dusty, empty rooms. Then at the end of the corridor, which narrowed into a small passage, he found a set of narrow, wooden stairs leading downwards; to the right was another set of stairs leading up to another door.

Robert heard the sound of another stifled laugh and the *tap, tap, tapping* noise he had heard before. It definitely was coming from upstairs.

"Sarah!" he shouted "Are you up there? You'll be in big trouble from Dad if you don't come down!"

"*Robert!*" called the tinny voice enticingly, "*Come up here...*"

He hated to admit it but he felt a little scared.

"I don't want to," he called, his voice trembling a little. He shook himself mentally. It was only his little sister up there after all, he told himself firmly. "You come down here."

"*Ple...ease, Robert!*"

Reluctantly he mounted the stairs. When he reached the top the door was partially open. He pushed it slowly and stepped inside, half expecting to see his sister grinning at him, but the big oblong room beyond was empty. There were two square windows facing him both with iron bars and wooden shutters. A big cupboard stood at one end of the room and a faded rug lay on the dusty floorboards. He crossed to one of the windows and looked down over the deserted garden. From here he could see the wall against which grew the tangle of blackberry bushes, the same ones he and Sarah had feasted on earlier, and beyond, a few old brick outbuildings.

There was a faint sound, a sort of whispering sigh, behind him. He turned sharply expecting to see his sister, but there was nobody there. She was hiding from him, he thought, playing a silly trick. He strode over to the cupboard, took a deep breath and pulled the door wide open.

It was empty.

His eyes swivelled sideways. He could sense something behind him. Something bad.

Something he didn't want to see.

"*Ro...o...bert! Help me...e!*"

The voice was now a menacing faint echo and the room seemed to darken as he turned. In the corner of the room was a darker shadow, almost human in shape. He couldn't seem to move and as he stared at the shape it appeared to be lifting a small arm towards him, an arm holding some sort of stick...

Then the door of the room slammed. He gave a cry and ran to it twisting the handle frantically, panicking as it slipped and turned in his grasp but refused to open. He tried to shout but his voice stuck in his throat and nothing came out but a hoarse yell. The tapping he had heard before started again, but this time louder and more rhythmically.

Tap… Tap… TAP… TAP… TAP…

He covered his ears with his hands and slid to the floor, sobbing with terror.

TAP… TAP…

The door opened and he gave a terrified scream – then he heard his father's anxious voice above his head.

"Robert! Rob – what happened? Did you get shut in?"

He threw his arms round his father's legs, almost hysterical with relief.

"Dad! Oh, Dad! I heard… I thought I saw… I heard…"

"What?"

Robert gulped.

"I – I don't really know. N… nothing – I'm not sure…" He stood up and wiped his eyes.

"Come on, old son. Let's get you out of this." His father put a comforting arm around his shoulders. "Look, Sarah's downstairs – why don't you go and find her? I've finished now, anyway. I'll just put the shutters across these windows and then we'll lock up and go home."

Robert sniffed and nodded.

"Okay." He watched from the doorway as the heavy shutters were pulled across the windows. "Dad?"

"Yes, son?"

"Do you believe in ghosts?"

His father frowned and shook his head.

"Not really, Rob. You don't think you saw one did you? Is that why you were so frightened? Old houses have a lot of strange noises in them, you know. And sometimes our imagination can play funny tricks on us."

The boy nodded thoughtfully.

"I don't ever want to come here again," he said. "I won't have to, will I?"

"Well…" he paused. "I suppose you're old enough to be told, although your mum thought we ought to wait. Your great-granddad's left you this house in his will, Rob. It's yours to do with as you like when you're twenty-one. You can live in it then if you want, or you can sell it. It will be up to you."

The boy stared at him, wide-eyed.

"I'll *never* want to live in it," he said firmly as they went downstairs.

He watches as they drive away. His anger and frustration burning deep within – that boy should have been the one to release him from this purgatory in which he is forced to exist.

He is of the same blood of the one he hates and fears beyond all others. He needs a child such as him, a vulnerable and receptive child, whom he can use to sustain his own strength and then perhaps he will soon be strong enough to take his revenge upon those who betrayed him – especially that dark soul he cannot reach. The final words that the boy had spoken echo in his tortured, twisted soul.

"I'll never want to live in it."

In his private hell he screams with fury and anguish. He had wanted desperately to enter the boy, to overpower his spirit and use him to the ends he desired – and now his chance had gone.

But one day fate will give him another opportunity, of that he is sure. He can wait.

He will wait.

One day soon his time will come.

CHAPTER 8

A month later, at the end of December, just after Jamie's seventh birthday, when the contracts were on the point of being exchanged, they took the boys to see the house. It was a cold and wet day, so they drove up the winding drive. Jamie sat in the back humming tunelessly, but Danny's mouth dropped open as the house came into view.

"It's wicked!" was his only stunned comment.

Inside, while Beth and Adam measured windows and discussed colour schemes and all the things that had to be done, the boys ran around the house, exploring each room in turn, Jamie following Danny like a little shadow. They discovered the piano and Danny clunked out a very off-key version of *Three Blind Mice* while Jamie watched him solemnly. They tore down the passage into the kitchen and whooped loudly as they discovered the dusty pantry and damp scullery. Then Danny found the wooden staircase and they clattered up it. At the top, Danny paused.

"Those must be the attics up there. We'll look at them in a minute. The bedrooms are this way. Come on, Jamie!"

He darted in and out of the bedrooms, but Jamie didn't follow. Instead, he walked to the bottom of the attic stairs and concentrated his gaze up them, cocking his head on one side as if listening. Then he opened his mouth and his blue eyes lit up.

"Valentine?" he said softly as he put his foot on the first tread.

"Hey, Jamie!" Danny's voice echoed behind him. "Come and see the bathroom. It's got this really weird bath in it…" He broke off as he saw his brother's rapt expression. "You want to go up there first? Okay, no problem. We'll look at the rest afterwards. This is going to be our games room up here. Dad's promised us a snooker table and he's going to set up his old Scalextric set for us as well."

He followed his brother up the narrow stairs. "Wow!" he exclaimed as they entered the room. "This is so cool – it could be really something."

He pressed the light switch but nothing happened. "Oh, I suppose there's no power," he said. He crossed to the window and, after a struggle, managed to pull back the heavy shutters. The dull light flooded into the room. He looked down into the garden and through the rain-spattered window saw a dark figure gazing up at him.

"Hey!" he said. "Who's that woman down there?"

He peered more intently. The woman was dressed in a long, white dress and wore a strange old-fashioned hat, with a veil that covered her face. As Danny watched, she lifted the veil and raised her head so that he could see her sad, pale face gazing up at him. Then she walked towards the front of the house and disappeared from view. He frowned.

"I wonder if Dad knows she's in the garden," he said. "Stay here, Jamie. I'll go and ask him."

He ran back down the stairs. Left alone, Jamie sat down on the dusty floorboards and took a small, red toy car out of his pocket. Slowly, in front of him the door of the cupboard at the end of the room swung open. Jamie gave a half-smile.

"Valentine," he said again very softly, and pushed the car towards the cupboard. It skittered across the floor and stopped about a foot in front of the door. There was a sigh like a breath of air.

Slowly, and to Jamie's great delight, the car rolled back to him.

Downstairs Adam and Beth were in the kitchen having a deep discussion on whether to keep the old fuel-burning Aga, or whether to replace it with a modern gas-fired version. They looked up in surprise as Danny burst in on them through the scullery door.

"Mum, Dad, there's a lady in the garden! I saw her through the attic window. I think she's gone round to the front door."

Adam frowned. "I don't know who that can be," he said, "as far as

I know we're the only ones here."

"Perhaps it's one of the neighbours checking up on us," remarked Beth. "Though I think our nearest one is quite a way down the road."

"I'd better go and see," said Adam. "You can come with me, Danny."

"Where's Jamie?" asked Beth.

"I left him up in the attic," Danny called as he and Adam went up the passage to the green baize door. "He's fine, Mum."

Outside, the rain had stopped but there was no sign of the woman he had seen.

"Where exactly did you see her?" asked Adam.

"Round here." Danny led the way round to the side of the house where there was a wall with a tangle of blackberry bushes against it. "She had really funny clothes on, Dad, sort of old-fashioned looking, and she was just staring up at me."

"Well, there's no sign of her now." Adam peered at his son closely. "You're not winding me up, are you Danny?"

"No, I did see her, honest Dad. She was dressed all in white. Bit scary really."

"It was probably like Mum said, just one of the neighbours being a bit nosy. Come on, let's get back inside."

Beth met them at the door looking worried.

"No sign of anyone," began Adam cheerfully, but Beth shook her head.

"Never mind that now, I can't find Jamie."

Danny frowned. "He was up in the attic. I told him to stay there."

"Well, he's not there now. I can't find him anywhere. I've looked in all the rooms."

"I'll go and look," said Adam, hurrying off.

"I'll check the kitchen again," said Beth. She ran down the passage, Danny at her side.

"Don't worry, Mum," he said, "he won't have gone far. He's probably curled up and gone to sleep somewhere."

There was no sign of Jamie in the kitchen and after a few minutes

Adam joined them.

"I've looked everywhere," he said. "He's nowhere in the house. He must have wandered outside, but I don't suppose he's gone far."

"He never usually wanders off," said Beth her voice full of concern. "You check round the other side of the house, Adam. Make sure he's not in any of the outbuildings. I'll go round the other way. Danny, you run down the drive and make sure he's not gone back down to the gates."

"Right, Mum." Danny paused, biting his lip. "I'm really sorry... I should never have left him on his own."

Adam ruffled his son's hair affectionately. "Don't be daft, Dan. As Mum says he doesn't usually wander off like this. We'll soon find him, don't you worry."

He set off round to one side of the house, whilst Beth went to the other, past the wall with the tangle of blackberry bushes where Danny had thought he'd seen the strange woman. The sun was just beginning to break through the clouds but the wind felt cold and she shivered. Just past the wall was a brick-built outbuilding, obviously once used as a garage. She tried the door but it was firmly locked, so she peered through the dusty windows. There were a couple of wooden ladders leaning up against the walls, some old sacking and an ancient galvanized bucket on the floor, but apart from that it was empty. She walked round to the back of the building, but there was no sign of Jamie. Further on round, at the back of the house there were two old wooden sheds; they, too, were empty, and there was nowhere else that a small boy could hide. Adam appeared from the other side of the house.

"Nothing!" he called as he saw her. "We'd better check the rest of the garden."

Beth felt her anxiety rise as they began to systematically search the rest of the overgrown grounds. Danny joined them, having checked the driveway and found no sign of Jamie. They called him again and again, but there was no reply and Beth began to feel a real sense of panic. Where could he be? She reached the old wall which surrounded what had once been the kitchen-garden. You could still make out the trenches where potatoes and other vegetables had once been grown. She turned to the others.

"He's not here. Perhaps we'd better check the house again."

"Sshh!" Adam lifted his hand. "I thought I heard something."

They all fell silent, listening.

"I can hear it now, Dad!" exclaimed Danny. "Someone's singing. Over there."

He ran over to the right, towards a tangle of undergrowth. Beth and Adam followed. The singing grew louder and now they could make out the words.

> *In the sky so clear above me*
> *The moon doth brightly shine,*
> *Give me your heart, then I will be*
> *Forever your Valentine.*

There was a grassy clearing in the middle of the undergrowth and Jamie was sitting cross-legged on the damp ground in the middle of it, clutching a small red car. He was staring at a patch of ground in front of him, rocking backwards and forwards gently as he sang the words over and over again.

"There you are, Jamie," said Danny thankfully. "You had us pretty worried."

"Hello, sweetheart," said Beth, squatting down beside the little boy. She smoothed his silky dark hair back from his forehead. "We wondered where you'd got to."

Jamie turned his head to look at her; in his deep blue eyes there were unfathomable depths. For a moment Beth felt a sharp frisson of fear. It was as though she were drowning in those depths. Then she came back down to earth and pulled herself together. This was Jamie; her baby, her vulnerable, dependent baby. He looked away again, focusing his gaze once more upon the ground.

> *In the sky so clear above me*
> *The moon doth brightly shine,*
> *Give me your heart, then I will be*
> *Forever your Valentine.*

"I've never heard him sing that one before," said Adam. "In fact, I don't think I've ever heard him sing a song all the way through. It sounds sort of old-fashioned." He frowned suddenly and crossed to the piece of ground just in front of Jamie. "Hello, there's something here, sunk into the grass." He hunkered down for a closer look. "Hmm... looks like an old wooden cover. There must be a hole under there, maybe an old well or something." He pulled at the iron handle but it wouldn't budge.

"Well, it seems secure enough," he said. "I wonder where he heard that song – I certainly don't recognise it? I suppose he must have learned it at school." He straightened up. "Come on, I think it's time we made our way home. We can't do too much more here now, we'll get back and have some lunch and go to the shops this afternoon." He bent down and picked Jamie up, swinging him up onto his shoulders. "Come on, let's go and lock the place up."

From his high perch, Jamie wriggled. "Take Valentine!" he said. "Daddy! Take *Valentine*."

"Who's Valentine?" Adam asked Beth. "One of the kids at school?"

Beth looked puzzled. "Not one that I know," she replied. "I think I'd remember that name, it's a bit unusual." She shivered suddenly. "I'm getting cold. Come on, let's get a move on. I'll get the kids in the car while you lock up."

In the car, Danny gazed thoughtfully out of the window at the house while they waited for Adam. "I wonder who that lady was," he said, "we never did find her."

"As I said, just one of the nosy neighbours," Beth replied. "Did you like the house then, Danny?"

"Yup." He paused and then gave her a mischievous look. "I think something's missing though."

Beth raised her eyebrows. "Oh, yes? What's that then?"

He grinned. "I'll give you a clue, Mum. It's got four legs, a waggy tail and, um… it's furry."

She grinned back. "I haven't a clue. You'll have to see if your father can guess that one."

"I will." He leaned back in his seat as Adam ran down the steps and towards the car. "What do you think, Spud?" he whispered. "A dog would be great, wouldn't it?"

Jamie nodded and twisted in his seat to look out of the back window. Slowly, as the car began to pull away from the house, he raised his hand and waved. Then, very quietly, he began to sing once again.

Please say you'll always love me
With a promise oh so true,
If you say that this will be so
My heart will belong to you.

CHAPTER 9

The next four months passed in a whirl of activity, involving solicitors, estate agents, builders, electricians, plumbers, carpenters and surveyors. It was discovered that, despite the dry rot, structurally Malthorp House was fairly sound although the roof needed some repairs and there was crumbling masonry that needed urgent attention. Also, the plumbing was out of date, most of the pipes needed replacing and the whole house also needed rewiring. To Beth's great regret the ancient Aga was pronounced beyond repair and a more up-to-date version was purchased ready to be installed.

Despite Bill's gloomy prediction, Adam had no difficulty in locating an excellent builder. Jon Faber had recently taken over the running of his father's long-established business in the nearby village of Darley and proved to be both reliable and industrious. Jon found all the workmen they needed and it was a great relief to Beth and Adam to be able to leave everything in his capable hands. By the end of January, the sale of their own house had finally gone through and they decided to rent a property until Malthorp was habitable. However, on a flying visit to Adam's parents, without the boys who had been left for the day with Laura and Geoff, this idea was dismissed out of hand by Audrey. She insisted that they came and stayed in Bracknell until such time as the house was ready.

"I don't think that would be such a good idea," Beth whispered to Adam, when Audrey and John had gone out to make coffee. "Surely it will be a strain on your father? You know how tense and agitated your mother gets – I can't imagine her being able to cope with two lively boys around the place. Plus, it would mean you having a long train journey each day. And what about school?"

But, as she served the coffee, Audrey brushed these last two difficulties aside.

"There is a perfectly wonderful school near us that Danny can go to for just this short time," she said airily. "I know Roger Thompson, the headmaster personally, and I'm quite sure he would be willing to help. Then, when you move in, he can return to Rackham. And, as for Jamie..." she paused.

"Jamie can't change," said Beth firmly. She hated being organised. "It could be disastrous if he was disrupted at this stage in his development."

"I wasn't going to suggest it, my dear. But surely you told me that Hopelands takes weekly boarders? He could stay there during the week and come home at weekends."

"No!" said Beth adamantly. "I wouldn't consider it for a moment. He's far too young for one thing, and he's never been parted from us for even a single night. Sorry, Audrey, we'll just have to think of another solution. Perhaps it would be more sensible to rent after all."

"Quite right," said John, who had been sitting in his armchair ostensibly reading *The Times*. "You can't just pack Jamie off like that, he'd wonder what on earth was happening."

"Nonsense," retorted Audrey, "it would only be for a few weeks. What do you think, Adam? It wouldn't do him any harm, would it?"

To Beth's fury, Adam sided with his mother.

"He does love it at Hopelands and Tom Mitchell would look after him. It would certainly be an answer, Beth. We could always give it a try. If he hated it, then we could think again."

"That's right," said Audrey firmly. "Jamie won't know the difference. Let's face it he is, after all, in a world of his own, poor child – what is the term they use, special needs? Perhaps it would even do him good to be permanently among his own type."

Beth felt her anger bubble up and boil over, and for the first time in her married life she shouted at her mother-in-law.

"How dare you! How dare you speak about my son being among his *type* as though he was some sort of interesting animal. He's a human being with feelings and needs, the same as any other child, and he is not going to be packed off like some sort of parcel because he doesn't fit in with your plans!"

Audrey subsided on to the sofa, looking very hurt.

"I didn't mean..." she began, but Beth was in full flow now and the resentments of the last few years began to surface.

"You've never cared for Jamie, have you? Just because he wasn't the precious granddaughter you've always wanted. Even Danny's noticed how you practically ignore him every time we see you. Well, you won't have to be bothered with him, because we won't be staying here, now or ever!"

"Beth..." Adam started to say, but she shook his hand off furiously and stormed out. Audrey burst into tears. John bit his lip, and shook his head as Adam went towards his mother.

"You go after Beth," he said quietly. "I'll see to your mother."

Adam found Beth in the garden, gazing unseeingly at John's prize roses. He went to put his arm around her, but she shrugged him off and turned away.

"Come on, love," he said gently. "She didn't mean it the way it came out."

"Didn't she?" She turned and looked at him, and he saw she was very white. "How could you have sided with her, Adam? You know what I said was true. She's never taken to Jamie, has never been a real, loving grandmother to either of the boys. Oh, I'm sure she would love to send him away, so she wouldn't have to look at him, to be reminded that not only is he not the granddaughter that she always wanted but he's also not 'normal'. She blames me for that, did you know? I heard her one day talking on the phone to one of her friends." She did a passable imitation of Audrey's strident tones. 'Of course, there's nothing like that on our side of the family. But Beth... well, my dear, you know what they say about the Welsh. And, another thing, we know nothing about the family she comes from; she keeps very quiet about that. Frankly, I had my doubts about the wisdom of the marriage at all, but dear Adam was so determined...'

"How do you think that made me feel?" Her eyes suddenly filled with tears. "Danny and Jamie are our children, Adam. If they're not welcome here, then how can you even consider us staying?"

He put his arms around her, and this time she didn't push him away.

"I'm sorry, sweetheart," he said contritely. "I had no idea that Ma had said that and you're right, I should have supported you. Of course I don't want to send Jamie away – you know how much I love our boys. I suppose I'm used to placating my mother – ever since we were kids, she's been difficult and we've all let her get away with murder. Listen, we'll do what we were going to in the first place and rent somewhere. I'll go back in and speak to Dad – I know he agrees with you and he'll back us up."

"No, I'll come with you, I ought to apologise." Beth pushed her hair back from her face. "I know I was rude, and I really don't want to fall out with Audrey otherwise John will suffer. But we'll have to stand firm on this and tell her that we're not going to stay."

They went back in to where Audrey was lying back on the sofa, John sitting by her with a glass of water. He smiled at them but Audrey looked away.

"Audrey," said Beth. "I'm very sorry I spoke to you like that. I know you were only trying to help and we do appreciate your offer, but it would be difficult with the boys, so we've talked about it and decided we will look around for somewhere to rent."

"I see," Audrey's voice was very stiff. "Is that how you feel too, Adam?" He nodded. "Well, there's no more to be said and you must do whatever you think best. I'm very tired, so I think perhaps you'd better go now."

"Goodbye, Ma. We'll see you soon," said Adam, and bent to kiss her cheek.

"Goodbye, my dear," she replied faintly, turning her head away on the cushion.

"She'll come round," whispered John as he saw them to the door.

"If it's any consolation, I think you're doing exactly the right thing. It would never have worked out."

"I am sorry…" began Beth, but John shook his head.

"Don't worry about it, my dear. It does her good to hear the truth occasionally. We're all guilty of pussyfooting around where her feelings are concerned; believe me, I'm the worst. Now don't leave here feeling guilty, it will all blow over."

Beth gave him a hug, which was returned warmly, and they got into the car.

"Give those two little rascals my love!" he called as they pulled away. He waved until they were out of sight and then returned to the lounge. To his relief, Audrey seemed to be asleep. He picked up his paper and crept quietly out of the room to his study to finish the crossword in peace. Audrey opened her eyes and her lips thinned as she heard the study door close.

"How dare she!" she muttered to herself. "How dare she speak to me like that. And *he's* on her side as usual. Well, she's forced poor Adam into this move and I know it isn't right for him – I feel it strongly." She rose from the sofa and went to the bureau in the corner of the lounge. Opening a drawer, she took out a pack of Tarot cards and, crossing to the table, sat down and began to lay them out face-down in a particular sequence. She began to turn them over and gazed down at the exposed faces of the cards, pursing her lips in satisfaction.

"Just as I thought," she murmured with satisfaction. "The Wheel of Fortune is reversed and adjacent to the Ten of Swords. That means bad fortune and destruction." She frowned as she turned over the next card, and her hand went to her throat as she gazed down upon the picture of two people falling from a high Tower.

"A harbinger of terrible change, or even death!" she whispered, closing her eyes.

Beth and Adam spoke very little on their way home after their disastrous visit. Both were busy with their own thoughts – Beth going over the argument with Audrey in her mind, and bitterly regretting her outburst; Adam wondering whether this move had been the right thing to do. Already they seemed fated to encounter nothing but difficulties. Malthorp had cost them a packet already and now there would be the added expense of finding a suitable property to rent; their buyers wanted to move in at the end of the following week, so they wouldn't have a lot of time to find somewhere.

When they arrived at Laura and Geoff's house they found the boys in the front room with Geoff, playing happily with a large train set. Danny was lying on his stomach switching the points as the two trains whizzed around the tracks, whilst Geoff sat on the floor with Jamie on his knee, encouraging him to blow a large silver whistle every time the trains passed. From the look on his face, he was enjoying himself as much as the boys.

"Hi!" said Danny. "This is really cool. Do you know, Dad, Uncle Geoff had this when he was a *boy*?"

Geoff looked wistful. "Many, many moons ago," he uttered in a sepulchral voice. Danny chuckled. On his knee, Jamie wriggled.

"More whistle!" he exclaimed. "More whistle, Uncle Deff!"

In the kitchen, Laura was busy at the stove, stirring the contents of a large saucepan.

"Mmm," said Adam, "something smells good."

"Lamb stew and dumplings. I've done plenty, so you will stay, won't you?"

"Try and stop us," said Beth.

"Help yourselves to wine, or if you want a beer, Adam, there are plenty in the fridge."

"Cheers," said Adam. He opened the fridge door and took out two bottles of Becks. "From the look of him, Geoff could do with one of these."

"Nonsense," called Laura as he disappeared back into the front room. "He's just a big kid himself – he's been dying for an excuse to get that train set out."

"He's marvellous with the boys," said Beth, pouring herself and Laura a large glass of red wine. "I shouldn't be having this really; I expect Adam will want a few beers and I'll have to drive home."

"You can always stay the night," Laura said. They had recently bought the property that they had previously been renting in Twyford, near Winchester. The owners had decided to move abroad permanently and the chance had been too good to miss. All the furniture, curtains and carpets had been included, and they had purchased the four-bedroomed house for a good price.

"That's true." Beth hitched herself up onto one of the stools at the breakfast bar and took a long sip of her wine. "God, I needed that."

"Mother-in-law a bit of a trial?" asked Laura. She had only met Audrey once, but Beth's description of her as rather neurotic had seemed to her to be an understatement. It had struck Laura that the woman was on the edge of paranoia.

"A bit more than that," said Beth gloomily. She told Laura what had happened. "Trouble is, I feel rather guilty now. I know I shouldn't have shouted at her like that, after all she was only trying to help us."

"Rubbish!" exclaimed Laura stoutly as she drained the vegetables. "I would have reacted in exactly the same way if she'd spoken about my child like that. And besides…"

"What?"

"Well, let's face it, Beth, she strikes me as the kind of woman who's very likely always resented you taking her little boy away from her. She probably couldn't wait to have Adam home so she could fuss over him and have him dancing attention on her again. The fact that you and the boys come along as part of the package was the downside to the situation, but with Danny at school and Jamie packed off to board at Hopelands she could make the best of a bad situation."

"You could be right," said Beth thoughtfully. "I've always known that she resents me," and went on to tell Laura about the conversation she had overheard.

"There you are then," said Laura. "Now, let's set the table, I thought we'd eat out here. Then we'll call them in for dinner, if we can drag them away from their train set, that is!"

The meal was delicious, accompanied by plenty of red wine. Adam and Beth decided to take up Laura's offer of a bed for the night as they were both well over the limit for driving. One of the bedrooms had bunk beds and they tucked the boys up about nine o'clock. Danny wanted to read so Beth left the overhead light on.

"I'll be up to turn it off later," she told him. She bent down to the lower bunk where Jamie lay snuggled up under the duvet. "Are you okay, sweetheart?"

He looked up at her, his eyes already filled with sleep. Then, suddenly and totally unexpectedly, he put his arms up and round her neck. She hugged him back, scarcely able to believe that her withdrawn little boy was showing her his first spontaneous display of affection. As he withdrew his arms, she saw that he had something clutched in his hand. It was Geoff's train whistle.

"Valentine play with it too," he murmured as his eyes closed. Beth frowned. He hadn't mentioned that name since the day they had found him sitting in the grounds of Malthorp. She must remember to ask his teacher if he had made a special friend of this Valentine.

Downstairs, Geoff was pouring whiskies. Beth went over and gave him a kiss.

"Hey," he said in surprise, "what was that for? Mind you, it was very nice. Are you thinking of leaving the old guy and running away with me?"

"I just wanted to say thank you for giving our sons such a happy time," and went on to tell them about Jamie's spontaneous hug.

"That's terrific," said Laura. She patted the sofa. "Sit down you two. Listen, Geoff and I have talked it over and, if you want to, we'd like you all to come and stay with us while you're waiting for

Malthorp to be finished." Adam and Beth looked at each other.

"Are you sure?" said Adam. "That's a very generous offer, but it's going to be at least another twelve weeks. That's an awfully long time to put up with house guests."

"Well, it would be with most. But you two are like family, and you know how much we adore the boys. It's not too far from both their schools either. We thought you could have the back bedroom, and if the boys are happy to share, we can turn the little spare room into a temporary studio for you, Beth, so you can get on with your commission. What do you say?"

"We'd love to," they both said in unison, "but only on condition we pay our whack with all the bills," added Adam.

"Of course," said Geoff, winking at Beth. "Thank goodness that's been settled so easily. Let's drink to it," and he replenished their glasses. "To friendship," he said, raising his.

"To friendship," they echoed.

CHAPTER 10

It was March, the birds had begun nesting and the spring flowers were starting to appear by the time the Ellis family were finally ready to move into their new home. Fortunately, it coincided with the beginning of the Easter holidays for both Danny and Jamie, so there was no problem with the school runs. Their furniture and household goods had been put into storage for the duration of their stay with Laura and Geoff and so they only had their clothes, the boys' toys and Beth's drawing equipment to worry about. The evening before the move they took Laura and Geoff out to a family restaurant nearby, where the food was excellent, to thank them for their hospitality.

"And for putting up with us for so long," said Danny as he tucked into an enormous plateful of gammon and chips. "I know Jamie and I were no trouble, but Mum and Dad!" He rolled his eyes in mock horror and grinned at Geoff.

"Watch it, you," growled Adam, cuffing him lightly on the side of the head. "Seriously, though, you two have been saints to cope with us all, especially as it's taken so much longer than we had hoped."

"We've loved having you," said Laura sincerely. "In fact we're going to miss you terribly; the place will seem very empty without you all, especially these two."

"Yes, who am I going to play football in the park with now, Dan? Who's going to beat me at chess? And worst of all, who's going to help me play with my trains when Jamie's gone?" Geoff sighed heavily and pulled a funny face at Jamie, who responded instantly with a giggle, a development that had recently come about. He loved Geoff, and had become very responsive with him over the past weeks. Beth only hoped that the move would not prove too traumatic for him and that he would not miss Geoff and Laura too much.

"When are you taking your illustrations up to London, Beth?" asked Adam. "Not this week, I hope."

"No, Guy wanted me to but I told him there was no way I could come up sooner than next Monday. He offered to collect them, but I need to go to the British Museum anyway to check up on those Japanese illustrations. The deadline is the fourteenth of April so I'm in plenty of time, but you know what an old woman Guy is."

"They're certainly wonderful drawings," said Laura. "If anything, they are even better than the first series."

"I am pleased with them. Apparently, so is Desmond. He told Guy that the scenes inside the Black Magician's stronghold were exactly as he had envisioned them, even down to the troll's toenails!"

"If we can get off the fascinating subject of toenails, we'd better order dessert," said Adam. "We've an early start in the morning. The removal people have promised to be at the house by eight. What are you going to have, boys?"

"Chocolate mountain sundae," said Danny. "It looks massive! Do you know, if you can eat another dessert afterwards, they give you the second one free? I bet I can manage that *easy*!"

"Oh no you don't," said Adam. "Mum and I aren't sitting up with you all night while you throw up. What about you, Jamie?"

Jamie's dark eyes regarded them solemnly.

"Jamie have that one," he said, pointing to a Knickerbocker Glory. "Bigger than Dan's."

They all laughed and as she watched Jamie join in, Beth felt a surge of optimism. Things were going to be good for them in their new home, she just knew it. Lovely though it had been staying with Laura and Geoff, she had missed her own space and she knew that Adam felt the same. Over the past months Malthorp had been transformed into a delightful family home and when their furniture and belongings had been installed, they were all going to be very happy and settled, she was sure of it. She turned to Adam and squeezed his hand.

"I love you," she whispered. He smiled at her.

"Looking forward to tomorrow?" She nodded. "Me too," he said. "I can't wait to spend our first night in our own bed."

"Come on, you two, none of that," said Geoff, overhearing the last part of their conversation. "Not in front of the children."

"Idiot," said Laura. "Come on, finish your desserts everyone and let's get home. Geoff's dying to have one more game of chess with Danny – he might actually beat him for once."

As they rose, Danny shook his head in mock resignation.

"I'm afraid, Mr Dunbar," he said in a tone of great regret, "that the result is a foregone conclusion."

That night Beth dreamt of her early childhood for the first time in many years. She saw herself running in the flower-studded meadow that lay in the shadow of the mountain. Lady and Bryn, the sheepdogs, were there, pink tongues lolling as they rounded up the sheep on the far side. She could see the distant figure of her father and hear his piercing whistle as he controlled the dogs. She grew tired of running and threw herself down on the grass to make a daisy chain. Beneath her fingers the grass felt warm and soft and she lifted her face to the sun, feeling happy and secure. A voice called, sweet and clear in the crystal air.

"Beth! Beth! Where are you, my darling?"

She turned and there, coming through the gate, was her Mam, Gwen. She was dressed in her favourite blue dress, the one Beth loved, and her luxuriant auburn hair lifted gently in the soft breeze.

"Mam!" called Beth and rose to run down the field to her. Then she saw that Gwen was not alone, by the hand she led a small, dark-haired boy who Beth, child though she was in her dream, recognised instantly. "Jamie!" she cried out joyfully. She did not question for an instant how he came to be in her Mam's company; somehow it all seemed so natural. But as she started towards them, a cloud blocked the sun and it became suddenly cold, grey and misty. The mountain and the surrounding meadow darkened and became unclear. She could still see Gwen and Jamie, but they, too, had become hazy and distant. Then she saw another figure walking on the other side of her son. She screwed up her eyes, trying to see it more clearly. It was a little taller than Jamie, but a child still, and under each arm it held what looked like a wooden pole. As they came a little nearer, she saw the boy's lurching, uneven gait and realised that the poles were crutches. She could still see no details of his face, but suddenly she knew that Jamie was in terrible danger. She opened her mouth to call out but her voice would not function. She tried to run to him but her legs felt like lead and would not move. Suddenly, the figure that was her mother called out again, this time her voice sharp with fear.

"Help him, Beth; you must help him!"

"I can't reach him," she cried, finding her voice at last. "You must."

"No, I am not allowed." The reply was distant but clear. "Only you can do it."

To Beth's horror and despair, she saw the unknown boy raise his crutches and felt, emanating from him, a terrible sense of malevolence. Suddenly, her mother gave a piercing cry and fell to the ground. As the boy turned towards Jamie, Beth found the strength at last and ran towards them. But a huge pit suddenly yawned open before her feet, and to her unutterable despair she felt herself pitch forward and fall into the unyielding blackness…

Beth woke with a start, trembling, her body soaked in sweat. The first light of dawn was just beginning to filter through the closed curtains of their room. She lay for a few moments waiting for the feeling of terror and despair that the dream had engendered to subside. It had been so vivid that the reality of her awakening seemed almost to be a dream too. By her side Adam stirred and snuggled up to her hot body.

"Mmm…" he murmured sleepily. "You feel warm this morning. What time is it?"

"Half past six," she whispered. "Adam, I had the most awful dream."

"Too much wine, followed by whisky last night," he replied. "We'll have to get up about seven."

"I know." She snuggled closer to him. "Hold me."

"Hey, you're shaking a bit. Was it as bad as all that?"

"Worse." She kissed him.

"Want to tell me about it?" She shook her head.

"No." She frowned as the memory of the fear returned. "No," she said more firmly. Her hand reached down and caressed him and he smiled sleepily as his body responded. "Make love to me."

"Now, how can I refuse an offer like that? But I thought we were going to christen our new bed later."

"That's hours away. I want you now."

She was eagerly responsive to his passion, as he kissed her deeply on the mouth and let his lips travel down to her firm breasts, flat belly and the warm wetness between her thighs. She rolled on top of him and they made love with a fierce intensity until he came with a muffled cry of delight. Her own orgasm shook her a moment later and she subsided down upon him, breathless and satiated. He let out a long breath.

"Phew!" He smiled up into her face. "I hope you have a bad dream rather more often."

"I can't even remember what it was all about now," she said. That was true, the dream was fading now, leaving behind only a confused memory of despair and terror. She rolled off him and threw back the bedclothes, "Come on, Ellis, we've a busy day ahead. You go in the shower first and I'll go down and make the tea."

"Make it strong," he said, "I've a feeling we're going to need it."

CHAPTER 11

Simon Ellis stepped through the wide glass doors of the *Daily Issues* offices near Kensington High Street, and breathed a sigh of relief. After two hours of fast-talking and flattery, he had finally managed to get the features editor, Sarah Lincoln, to accept his article on down-and-outs in London. Not a new subject, it must be said, but Simon had brought in what he thought was an entirely new and original dimension to the whole problem, and finally the attractive forty-ish something woman had accepted his article. He'd had to invite her to dinner the next day, but that would be no hardship; although she was hardly his type, with her brusque and business-like manner, but he felt sure she would relax after an evening in his company and a few glasses of wine. He took out his mobile phone and rang up a small, exclusive and quite expensive restaurant in Piccadilly that he had tried a few weeks before with his current girlfriend, Fiona. Luckily, they had a table available at nine. Perfect, he thought as he rang off; he was picking Sarah up at eight, so they would have time to go for a drink before the meal. And, afterwards, if she was willing, they would go back to his place for a nightcap and whatever else might follow. Fortunately, Fiona was away on a five-day course, so there would be no danger of her finding out.

At thirty-six, Simon had lost none of his good looks; in fact, maturity had only sharpened the appeal of his clean-cut features. He'd never married, but had never lacked a series of young, mainly stunning, girlfriends. His relationships didn't usually last long, primarily because he was completely amoral and found it impossible to be faithful to one woman. Much to his family's surprise he had stuck with his career in journalism, though for some years now he had worked freelance, earning himself a reasonable reputation and enough money to afford a flat in Finsbury and an expensive car. Lately, though, he had become increasingly discontented;

life was a constant struggle as young, ambitious kids, many fresh from university, entered the fray. More and more frequently, as had happened today, he was finding he had to fight for recognition and that kind of effort was not something he enjoyed.

As he walked along Kensington Road, heading up towards Knightsbridge, he reflected moodily on his lifestyle compared to that of his three brothers. David was still a successful engineer working in Kuwait, Neil was working with the London Philharmonic Orchestra and was also becoming very well known for his compositions of popular film and television themes. He had married again and he and his wife Kate lived in an exclusive complex in Kingston-upon-Thames. That left Adam… Simon gritted his teeth as he thought of him, so smug and self-satisfied, living his life of luxury with all the things Simon most wanted, a successful career, a big new house and Beth. Yes, most of all, Beth.

Simon had wanted her from the first time he'd seen her sitting there in his parents' lounge, so shy and vulnerable with her incredible eyes and that mane of thick chestnut hair. He had made a play for her then, but she'd only had eyes for Adam and it was still that way, even after all these years. He didn't see much of her these days, but still found her incredibly sexy and often secretly fantasised about her when he was making love to other women. She was the one woman he had lusted after who'd been totally indifferent to his charm, and that still rankled.

He jumped on a bus and alighted at Knightsbridge, strolling down towards Harrods. Perhaps he would kill some time in there; he could do with a new shirt for tomorrow night, something to impress Sarah. Then, as he approached the front of the famous store, he stopped dead and stared in disbelief. Surely that woman was Beth? For a split second he thought his fevered imagination had created an illusion, but then he saw that it was indeed her. She was standing near the entrance, leaning back against a window and seemed to be staring down the road as if transfixed whilst people jostled and pushed past her. He reached her side.

"Beth!" he exclaimed. "I thought it was you. What are you doing here?"

She turned to look at him, but her eyes were glazed and unseeing and her face ashen.

"Beth?" he repeated uncertainly. "Are you okay?"

For an answer she gave a little sigh and slumped sideways into his arms.

Half an hour later they were sitting in a little bistro off Oxford Street. Simon had wanted to take her to the hospital for a check-up, but she had refused. She'd recovered quickly from the faint and he insisted on taking her somewhere for a drink. He'd tried to persuade her to have a brandy but she had insisted on a strong coffee instead.

"I really feel I ought to call Adam," he said, noting with relief that a little colour had come back into her cheeks as she sipped the hot coffee.

"No, honestly, I'm feeling fine now," she told him. "It was so stupid. I set off early from home this morning and I didn't make time for a proper breakfast."

"What are you doing in London, anyway?" he asked. "I thought you'd be busy with the new house. You only moved in last week, didn't you?"

She nodded. "Yes, actually we're still in a bit of a muddle, but I had to come up and see Guy Turner. I've just completed the illustrations for the new book and needed to discuss them with him." She stiffened as the door of the bistro opened, then visibly relaxed as an elderly couple, laden with shopping bags entered. Simon frowned.

"Look, Beth," he said gently. "I know it's none of my business, but has something else happened? You looked terrified out of your wits when I saw you outside Harrods, and even now, you seem pretty jumpy. It might help to talk about it."

Tears came into her eyes. She had never particularly liked or trusted Simon, but he was being so kind now, and she needed to tell someone.

"You'll probably think I'm going nuts," she said shakily.

"Try me," he said.

―⁂―

The day had started fairly well for Beth. She'd arranged for the boys to spend the day with Debbie as it was the Easter holidays, and had arrived at the station in plenty of time to catch the 8.05 to Waterloo. The train was packed as it always was at that time in the morning, but she had reserved a first-class seat and so was able to relax on the hour-long journey. She'd had to wait ten minutes for a taxi outside the station, but was in Guy Turner's office by nine-forty, with the precious folder containing her illustrations intact. He was delighted with them.

"Desmond is going to love these," he said warmly. "You're a genius, Beth. How are things going at the new place?"

"Oh, it's wonderful," she told him. "So much space. The boys absolutely adore it. I've hardly seen them since we moved in. They've either been up in their playroom in the attic, or else running wild in the grounds. We're looking round for a dog for them at the moment."

"So, Danny finally talked you into it, huh?" he said, grinning. She laughed.

"Yes, but I've told him, definitely not a puppy. I've enough to do without clearing up puddles of pee on my new carpets."

"Quite right," said Guy. "Tell you what, you ought to look in Battersea Dogs Home. A friend of mine found a lovely mutt in there."

"I hadn't thought of that. I'll talk it over with Adam. Anyway, Guy, you'll have to come and see us. Stay for a few days and get away from the London smog. The house looks wonderful now, the builders and decorators have done us proud."

"I will," he promised. "When I can manage it. We're snowed

under at the moment. I'd love to take you out for lunch later, but I'm afraid it will be a quick sandwich at my desk today."

"That's fine," she told him. "I've got to check out something at the British Museum anyway, and then I'm going to do some shopping. I thought I'd go to Knightsbridge first and then on to Oxford Street. I haven't got to rush back, so I'll make the most of this opportunity."

As she left the publisher's she glanced at her watch. It was just past ten. Perfect. She'd get a taxi to the BM, then on to Harrods, and treat herself to some lunch in their restaurant before heading to Oxford Street for some serious clothes shopping.

After the peace of the BM. Harrods seemed a bit frantic, crowded with shoppers and sightseers. Many of them were foreign tourists – Japanese rubbing shoulders with Germans, French and Americans. In the furniture department where she had gone in search of a new dining table and chairs, it was a little quieter and she managed to find a set she really liked, plus a matching dresser. It was rather more expensive than she had planned, but just what she had visualised for their new dining room. She paid for it and arranged a delivery date. Then she went to the china department and spent a happy hour browsing around the dinner services and cutlery. She spent some more money and arranged for the new dinner service to be delivered too. It was nearly one o'clock and she'd had enough of Harrods so she decided to get a taxi to Oxford Street and eat there.

Outside it was busier than before. She scanned the road anxiously, looking for a taxi. Usually, there were quite a few waiting outside, but today there wasn't one in sight. Never mind, she would take the short walk to the tube station. Just then, a taxi did draw up and she hurried towards it thankfully, dying to take the weight off her aching feet. She climbed in and closed the door.

"Oxford Street, please," she said. There was no response.

"Oxford Street," Beth said again, thinking perhaps he hadn't heard her.

The driver turned slowly and Beth gave a gasp of horrified disbelief.

It was Kevin.

His thick blubbery lips parted in a hideous grin, showing yellowing, crooked teeth, his bloodshot eyes glistening.

"I'll take you wherever you want to go, sweetheart," he rasped. "Remember – I know what you like…"

His tongue came out and slowly licked the cracked lips.

Beth couldn't breathe. She couldn't speak. She couldn't move. Then, somehow, she found the strength to wrench open the door of the taxi and half-fell out onto the pavement. The taxi revved up and roared away, ignoring the half a dozen other people who were now waiting by the rank. Beth moved back towards the doors in a daze and, ignoring the jostling crowds, leant back against the window. Her heart was beating rapidly and she felt faint. Suddenly, a voice said,

"Beth?"

She looked round petrified he had found her again. Then she saw who it was, and for a few moments everything went black.

Simon hadn't taken his eyes off Beth's face while she recounted her terrifying experience to him. She didn't go into the details of what Kevin had put her through as a child, but she told him enough for him to realise that he had inflicted some sort of sexual assault upon her that had left her utterly traumatised. He leant back in his chair and lit a cigarette.

"Are you absolutely certain that it was this Kevin?" he asked after a few moments' silence. "After all, it's been what – twenty-odd years – since you last saw him? You could have been mistaken, maybe it was someone who just looked remarkably like him."

"I wasn't mistaken," Beth's voice was firm. "I'd know him anywhere. He looked exactly the same."

"That's the whole point," Simon said. He leant forward and stubbed out his half-smoked cigarette. "Surely, he'd have changed a lot, gone grey or bald or something? After all he'd be, what, in his late sixties by now?"

"It was him," repeated Beth shakily, even though she knew what he was saying was true. She rubbed her eyes and Simon saw she was very close to tears again. An unusual feeling of protectiveness towards her came over him, and he put his warm hand over hers.

"I believe you," he said. "Listen, what I'll do is dig into some records and see if I can find out when he was released from prison. This happened when you were thirteen, right?" She nodded. "Well, it shouldn't be too difficult to find out whether he served the whole of his sentence or not. I might even be able to find out if he's living around the London area. I've got some contacts that should be able to help me. If I dig anything up, I'll let you know. Now, would you like another drink, or shall I see you to the station? You won't want to get in a taxi on your own, will you?"

Beth accepted his offer gratefully and, although she protested, he insisted on coming onto the platform and seeing her onto her train. He gave her what he hoped was a brotherly peck on the cheek as he helped her up into the carriage.

"Thank you, Simon," she said. "Look…" she hesitated "…I probably won't mention this to Adam. He's had enough on his mind lately, what with the house and everything. So, if you do ring me, make it during the day."

"Will do," he reassured her, enjoying the feeling of conspiracy her words engendered. "And don't worry. If anyone's threatening you, I'll sort it out."

After leaving Beth, he hesitated about heading for home. Then he made a sudden decision. He bought a ticket and made his way down the escalator to the tube station, where he boarded a tube and finally disembarked at St Pancras. Coming out of the entrance, he crossed over the road and walked to the Newspaper Library, which housed the British Library's collection of thousands of newspapers many on microfiche to enable journalists and others to do research. Entering the building, he showed his pass and filled in a form with details of what he wanted.

A couple of hours later he emerged, gratified with his afternoon's work. In a folder he carried photocopies of the *Liverpool Echo*. He had read the accounts of Kevin Webster's arrest and subsequent trial, and scanned copies of later papers in the hope of finding out when he had been released. Unfortunately, he had been unable to find out this particular piece of information but among his acquaintances was a police officer who, for a couple of bottles of whisky, would scan the police computer for him. Simon smiled to himself, and decided to treat himself to a large scotch in the nearest pub. With any luck Beth would be very grateful to him, he reflected with a warm glow of satisfaction, especially as he had promised to keep it just between the two of them.

He was determined to make the most of her gratitude.

CHAPTER 12

Adam had finished early at the hospital for once, so he decided to have a quick sandwich in the canteen and pick the boys up from Debbie's. As he made his way across to an empty table he saw his junior colleague, Tim Shaw, on a nearby table. Tim waved him across, and Adam sighed inwardly. Tim was a nice enough chap, but very serious and extremely dedicated to his job. Adam knew that once he started discussing a case there would be little hope of an early getaway. Sure enough, Tim began to tell him about one of their more difficult cases and they were soon in a deep discussion about it. After about half an hour, Adam looked pointedly at his watch.

"Goodness, is that the time? I'd better be getting along. I'm due to pick the boys up soon."

Tim looked crestfallen.

"Oh, I was hoping to talk to you about little Ryan Forbes. He's developed complications after that routine tonsillectomy. It's rather unusual actually…"

"Sorry, Tim, I really do have to go," said Adam, getting up hastily. "Perhaps we can discuss it tomorrow. I've promised the boys that we'll look in the local paper to see if there are any dogs advertised. We've been promising them for weeks that they can have one."

Tim raised his eyebrows.

"That's a coincidence," he said, "I might be able to help you there. My sister is trying to find a home for her mutt at the moment. They're off abroad for a couple of years because of her husband's job, and they don't wish to take him with them as they'll be travelling around. She's been asking everyone she can think of, but no luck so far. She's getting quite desperate, and was even thinking of sending him to the animal shelter if she can't find someone soon."

"That would be a shame. What sort of dog is he?"

"A golden retriever, three years old. He's a lovely dog, very friendly, and she's done a lot of training with him, so he's quite obedient. I'd love to have him myself, but Sue's not keen on dogs."

"He sounds ideal," Adam said. "Could you give me your sister's phone number and I'll arrange to go and see him."

"I'll ring her now if you like," said Tim. "I'm pretty sure she'll be in this afternoon."

Adam rang Debbie to say he'd be a bit late to pick up the boys and fifteen minutes later, was on his way to Bishop's Waltham, where Tim's sister, Eileen, lived. Just before he reached her house, he rang Beth's mobile, but the answerphone was on, so he left her a message for her to ring him. Hopefully, if she wasn't too late back from London, and the dog was what they wanted, they could all go and have a look at him together that evening.

Eileen Perkins lived in a pretty cottage near the centre of the village. She was a plump, attractive, outgoing woman, not a bit like her serious younger brother and she ushered him through her untidy lounge where boxes and bin liners were stacked against the walls.

"Excuse the mess," she said. "As Tim probably told you, we're off in about three weeks, and I'm in utter chaos trying to sort everything out. Come through to the kitchen and meet Finn."

She opened a door at the far end of the lounge and the beautiful, deep golden dog rose from his bed and trotted over as they entered, his feathery tail swishing from side to side in greeting.

"This is Phineas Finn," said Eileen, stroking the top of his head. "Named after one of my husband's favourite fictional characters. Mind, we never call him Phineas, he's always just been Finn; so much easier when you're calling him."

"He's lovely," said Adam, running his hand along the soft furry body. Finn responded immediately, pushing his warm silky muzzle into Adam's other hand. "Is he good with children?"

"Gentle as a lamb. In fact, I don't think he knows how to be anything but good-natured." Her eyes filled unexpectedly with tears. "We're going to miss him," she said unsteadily. "That's why we'd like to know that he's gone to a good home, with people that will really care for him. When Tim rang up and told me about you and your family, it sounded ideal."

Adam left a few minutes later, promising Eileen that he would ring her later with a decision. He had already fallen in love with Finn, but he had to make sure that Beth would approve of his choice. He looked at his watch. Three-thirty. He would make his way to Debbie's and ring Beth again there. Just as he was getting into the car, his phone went, Beth had beaten him to it.

"Adam? I'm on the train, and I'll be at the station in about forty minutes. Any chance you can pick me up?"

"Sure. Did you get my message?"

"Yes. How did you get on?"

"Fine. You'll love him, Beth. He's just what I would have chosen for the boys. He's three years old, house-trained, and as soft as they come. I thought if you like we can take the boys over to meet him this evening and, if Mrs Perkins is agreeable, pick him up at the weekend."

"Yes, that sounds good." He felt her voice sounded a little strained and Adam frowned.

"Everything okay, love? You sound tired. Did your meeting go well?"

"Yes, fine. And I did some furniture shopping for our dining-room table and things."

"You usually sound a lot happier when you've been spending money."

She laughed. "I'm a bit tired, that's all. See you about half past four. 'Bye for now."

Adam frowned again as he started the car. She had definitely sounded very strained. Maybe the stress of the past months was catching up on her – they had been waiting so long to move and the house still needed a lot of sorting out. Perhaps he would take them all out for a meal down at the pub tonight after he had taken them to meet Finn. He would pick the boys up now and take them with him to meet the train and they could discuss it together. He smiled as he drove back towards Winchester. He had a good feeling that Finn was going to be a great addition to their family.

Danny and Beth also fell in love with Finn as soon as they saw him. Jamie seemed a little wary at first, but after going out into the garden with Danny, and throwing a ball for the big dog to run and fetch, he began to relax a little round him. He even managed a rare laugh when Finn sat and offered him a large paw in return for a treat. Eileen's husband, Mike, arrived home in the middle of all the excitement and seemed as pleased as his wife that the Ellis family was so taken with the dog.

"Eileen's been worried sick," he confided to Adam as they watched Danny racing after Finn. "To tell you the truth, I think she might have stayed here with him if you hadn't turned up. I'm sure he's going to be fine with you; he seems to have taken a shine to your boys at any rate."

"Beth's hoping that having a dog will be good for Jamie; perhaps bring him out of himself a bit more," said Adam. "What we hoped is that we could collect Finn this weekend; the boys are on holiday for another week after that, and I can be there for the first couple of days while he's settling in."

"That will be fine," said Mike. "Hopefully we'll be pretty busy this weekend, seeing friends and family, so that will help take Eileen's mind off him going."

They called the boys and said their farewells to the Perkins. Finn whimpered a little as they left and Danny knelt down and put his arms around the furry golden neck.

"Don't you worry, Finn," he whispered, as he hugged him. "We'll be back in a few days, then you'll be with us for *ever!*"

Finn swiped the boy's face with his big wet tongue and they all laughed. On the drive back to Malthorp, Danny chattered excitedly about Finn, asking endless questions about him; most of them Adam answered as Beth seemed far away in her own thoughts. He glanced at her once or twice as they drove along and noticed that her face was set and very pale. He interrupted Danny's flow of questions. "How would you two like to go with us to the village pub for a meal tonight, to celebrate getting our dog?" he asked them.

"That would be great, Dad," replied Danny.

"Jamie, too. Jamie wants to go."

"Of course," said Adam. "How about it, Beth?"

Beth smiled, trying to inject some warmth and enthusiasm into her voice, as she agreed. Adam said nothing, but when they arrived back at the house, he pulled her to one side as the boys clattered up the stairs.

"Come on, love, what's going on? You've been like a wet weekend since you got back. Look, if you're not happy about Finn, I wish you'd say. I don't wish to push you into having him if you don't really want to."

Beth put her arms around him hugging him tightly.

"Of course, I'm happy about him. I think he's absolutely gorgeous, just what we wanted. Sorry, sweetheart, I didn't mean to come over as unenthusiastic. I guess I'm just tired and a bit crotchety after a long day." She snuggled further into him, biting down on her bottom lip as she savoured the safe feeling of his warm arms around her. However, try as she might, she couldn't forget the shocking sight of Kevin's coarse, blotchy face and bloodshot eyes. It had been there, in her subconscious, all the way back on the train. She knew she would be frightened to go to sleep tonight and see him again in her dreams. Making a huge effort she raised her head, smiling warmly up into her husband's anxious face. "By the way, you'll never guess who I saw in Knightsbridge today."

"Uh, let me see… Johnny Depp? Hugh Jackman?"

"No, silly, your brother Simon."

Adam pursed his lips. He hadn't had a lot of contact with Simon these past few years; they had very little in common and he knew Simon still resented him and envied his successful lifestyle. He said lightly, "And how was my little brother? Conning the public as usual?"

"Actually, he was good company today. He'd just sold an article to *Daily Issues* and was full of amusing anecdotes about the trouble he'd had getting it accepted. I've a feeling from the way he was talking that he'll have to wine, dine, and probably sleep with the features editor as a pay off."

"As long as it's a female, that shouldn't be a problem," said Adam. He kissed her upturned nose and turned her towards the stairs. "Now, tell me about this dining table you bought while we're getting changed."

Upstairs, Danny and Jamie were in the attic playroom. It had been redecorated and made much lighter and brighter. The walls were painted cream and a bright blue carpet with oblongs of orange, yellow and mauve covered the old wooden floorboards. The cupboard at the end of the room had been retained, re-shelved inside now to hold toys and games. Two big pine bookcases stood against one wall, and a large television set with a DVD player beneath, against the other. A CD player stood on top of a small square pine table next to the television. Scattered around the room were three or four brightly coloured beanbags. Altogether it looked a far different room from the gloomy old nursery it had once been. The tiny rooms leading off it had been knocked into one large one, and Danny had been tentatively promised his own snooker table for his birthday, which was coming up in a few weeks. He was sprawled now across one of the beanbags half-watching a Disney DVD. He glanced across at Jamie, who had climbed up onto the wide windowsill and was staring down into the garden. The bars at the window had been retained, although they were now painted cream.

"When we have Finn, we'll have to walk him every day," he said.

"Mmm…" murmured Jamie.

"And we'll have to take it in turns to feed him."

"Mmm…"

"And brush him."

This time there was no answering murmur. Jamie was gazing intently downwards. Danny frowned.

"Who are you looking for, Spud?" he asked curiously.

Jamie looked at him.

"Want Valentine," he said. "Want Valentine to come an' play. Why won't he come, Danny?"

"Who is this Valentine?" asked Danny, stretching. "Is he one of the kids from school? I expect Mum will ask him round if you tell her."

"No!" Jamie wriggled impatiently on his window seat. "Valentine lives *here* with Jamie. But he gone away now an' he won't come to play with me anymore."

Danny yawned, his eyes still on the television. Jamie hadn't mentioned this Valentine for ages, but Dad reckoned it was probably an imaginary friend like the 'Mr Stan' Danny himself had insisted lived under his bed when he had been about Jamie's age. Mr Stan had come everywhere with them for about two years until Danny had grown out of him.

"Never mind, Spud," he said cheerfully. "He'll be along soon enough. He's probably gone on his holidays or something. Hang on, was that Mum calling?"

He switched off the TV and ran off down the stairs. Left alone, Jamie continued to stare wistfully out of the window for a few moments. Then he cocked his head to one side and listened intently. A half smile lit his face as he turned towards the old cupboard. Slowly, of its own accord, the door swung open. As he watched, a pack of cards lying on one of the shelves rose slowly into the air, bent backwards, and then released into a fluttering arc onto the floor.

Jamie broke into a broad grin; his eyes sparkled with excitement as they followed an unseen entity as it crossed the room to the nearest bookcase. A book, one of Danny's, was pulled out slowly by an unseen hand, opened and the pages ripped out, one by one. Jamie gave a gurgle of delight.

"Valentine!" He jumped down from the window and crossed to the bookcase. He seemed to listen again then, from the shelf, he took another book and began to tear out the pages, carefully and deliberately. "Jamie missed you," he said. "Where was you? Was you on your holidays?" He finished the destruction of the book, and reached for another. Danny appeared in the doorway.

"Come on, Jamie, Mum says it's time to get ready to go out…" His voice tailed off as he took in the scene of destruction before him.

"*Jamie!*" He crossed the room and knelt down next to his brother, staring in disbelief at the torn books. "What… what the… *hell* do you think you're doing! That's my Harry Potter book – my Christmas present from Debs. And the other one – ah no – it's my special edition of the *Wizard of the White Mountain*, the one Mum signed for me!" He grabbed Jamie's shoulders and shook him. Jamie's head snapped backwards and forwards like a rag doll, but he didn't utter a sound. For the first time in his life, Danny swore at him. "You… you fucking little *shit*!"

"Danny!" Beth's shocked voice came from the doorway. "Don't you dare swear at your brother like that? Let go of him. What on earth's going on?"

"Ask him!" yelled Danny, jumping to his feet, his face scarlet with anger. He raced out of the room, slamming the door hard behind him. Beth looked down at Jamie and saw the ruined books.

"Ah, Jamie, no," she said. She hunkered down beside him. He turned away from her rocking slowly backwards and forwards. She took his cold, unresponsive hand in hers. "What made you do that, Jamie?" she asked gently. He turned his head and she saw that far from the distress she had expected to see, his face was expressionless, and that his wide blue eyes looked into hers with calm indifference. "Jamie!" Beth said, more sharply this time. "You know that it was very wrong, don't you, to destroy Danny's books?"

For a moment he continued to stare at her dispassionately. Then he gave her an angelic smile.

"Valentine told Jamie to do it. He's been waiting Mummy, he's been waiting for me. He wants to come back to play."

CHAPTER 13

Audrey Ellis sat back on her heels, trowel in hand, and surveyed her neat garden with great satisfaction. At one time she would never have considered spending her time doing such a menial task; John had always dealt with most of the gardening, but with his worsening heart condition she had started to do much of the weeding and tidying-up herself. A man came in once a week to cut the grass and do any heavy jobs, but to her surprise she found being out here rather pleasant as she pottered gently round. Also, it was another means of escape from her husband, whom she found increasingly irritating these days. Before his enforced retirement, he had been able to go out on his days off, playing golf, but now his ill health forced him to be at home most of the time and she found he was increasingly under her feet. To her dismay, he had even discovered a latent interest in cooking, and was often to be found in her kitchen concocting the latest dish he had seen on some cookery programme or in his newspaper.

Even her spiritual interests seemed to have waned these days; she had not held any meetings for some time and had not even glanced at her Tarot cards of late.

Frankly, Audrey was bored. Life seemed to have taken on a dreary, monotonous routine and sometimes she longed for a bit of excitement and sparkle. Even her children seemed to have deserted her. She saw her eldest sons very rarely; David was abroad, so obviously he could not make it home very often, Neil travelled all over the place with the orchestra so his visits were very fleeting. As for the two youngest, Simon, whom she had longed to be rid of at one time, scarcely ever bothered with her now he had moved to London. Then there was Adam…

Her lips tightened as she thought of her favourite son. Since her falling out with Beth, before the family had moved, she had only seen them twice and relations had been rather strained. She missed him. Of all her boys, Adam had been the one with whom she could always talk, and his success, above all the others, had made her extremely proud. But her feelings for her daughter-in-law had always been ambiguous. When Adam had first told them about her, she had been dismayed at his choice. As far as Audrey was concerned, Beth was a nobody; a rootless Welsh girl, product of a broken home and, although she disguised her feelings well, she had secretly hoped that his infatuation for the girl would wear itself out. However, when he had announced his decision to marry her, she'd accepted it with good grace, frightened of alienating Adam by showing her true feelings. As time went by and they failed to have a child, she couldn't help feeling a sense of satisfaction that her fears had been justified and that her son had indeed made the wrong choice. For, above all things, Audrey was obsessed with the longing for a granddaughter. Her desire for a girl had been paramount during her last three pregnancies and, when her last-born had turned out to be yet another boy, she had been devastated. Indeed, that was the main reason that she had never bonded with Simon, and often felt that his rebellious behaviour as a child was rooted in the fact that he could sense that she had never forgiven him for not being the longed-for daughter.

With no sign of her other sons having children, all her hopes had become centred on Adam and Beth. When they had decided to adopt Danny she gave up hope; and although she treated him with kindness, as far as her self-centred nature permitted, she never truly looked on him as her grandson. Then, when Beth became pregnant, Audrey's feelings for her became transformed. Although Beth and Adam had opted not to have a scan to determine the baby's sex, she was sure in her heart that the child would be the longed-for girl, and for the first time she began to treat Beth more as a daughter. She took her shopping, buying minute vests and stretch suits. She insisted on purchasing the very best Silver Cross pram and also a brand new cot. So certain was she of the baby's sex that she even went secretly up to town and bought, from Harrods and Selfridges baby departments, pretty frilly dresses, lacy tights and an expensive pink and white snowsuit.

Consequently, when Jamie was born, she was shocked and disappointed beyond all reason. She could scarcely even bring herself to visit Beth in hospital, though John, who alone knew something of her feelings though not the true depth of them, insisted that she made the effort. She had tried to put on a good show, but scarcely even glanced at the baby; and when Adam offered Jamie over for her to hold, she'd muttered some excuse about an impending cold to avoid doing so.

From that day forward all her old feelings of resentment and dislike for Beth resurfaced, and if it hadn't been for her love for her son, and John's insistence on her maintaining contact, she would have had little to do with her or the two boys. When Jamie's developmental problems became apparent, and his autism had been finally diagnosed, she felt that her darkest fears were finally vindicated. Such a condition could not possibly stem from either her side of the family or John's; it must originate somewhere in Beth's uncertain, unstable Welsh background. As for the child, she could hardly bear to look at him; as far as she was concerned, he should be sent away to a mental institution, as others of his ilk had been in days gone by.

The sound of the phone ringing in the house brought her out of her reverie. Mrs Mason, her cleaning lady, who came three times a week to do the housework, appeared at the French doors.

"It's Simon on the phone, Mrs Ellis. Wants to know if he can come down for lunch today."

Audrey rose stiffly to her feet.

"Tell him I'm just coming, Mrs Mason. Isn't Mr Ellis there?"

"No, he said to tell you he's just popped down the shops for some tarragon."

Audrey removed her shoes at the French doors and picked up the telephone.

"Simon? What a surprise. We don't usually hear from you during the week. Is anything wrong?"

"Of course not, Ma. Just thought I hadn't seen you and Dad for a while. I've got a free afternoon, so I thought I'd get down to you for about one. Any chance of some lunch?"

"I'm sure that can be arranged, dear. In fact, I think your father's planning something with tarragon – Jamie Oliver's latest creation no doubt. We'd love to see you."

"Wonderful! Be with you as soon as poss. Cheers."

As Audrey replaced the receiver John came back, brandishing a carrier bag.

"Salmon *en croute* with tarragon sauce for lunch," he said cheerfully. "Who was that on the phone?"

"Simon," said Audrey. "He's coming down to see us. He'll be here for lunch."

John frowned.

"That's rather unusual. We haven't had the pleasure of his company for ages. Now, let me guess. Either he's been thrown out of his flat and needs somewhere to stay, or else he wants to borrow some money. Which do you think, my dear?"

"Oh, don't be so cynical, John," replied Audrey. "Hasn't it occurred to you that he might simply be seeking the pleasure of *our* company?"

"If he is, my dear," said her husband as he made his way towards the kitchen, "then it will be the first time ever in his life. No, mark my words, if I know Simon, he's after something."

Simon arrived about the time he had arranged, much to Audrey's astonishment, with a large bouquet of flowers for her and a bottle of Grants for his father.

"To make up for not seeing you for so long," he explained as he handed her the flowers. "It's been very remiss of me but I can only blame the pressures of work, you know, the trials of a freelancer and all that. Still, I'm here now, and looking forward to all the latest gossip."

"There's not a great deal of that!" remarked Audrey wryly. "Unless you count Mrs Pemberton trying to persuade me to join the Women's Institute, and Mrs Mason's youngest son running off with a married woman twice his age as gossip."

"Hmm… you sound a bit fed-up, Ma," remarked Simon. "How's Dad been?"

John was in the kitchen seeing to the vegetables while they sat in the lounge enjoying a pre-lunch gin and tonic.

"Oh, much the same," sighed Audrey. "Doing his crosswords, going to the shops and cooking his meals. Doctor Shaw says the last attack was the most serious warning yet, so he still has to take things very easy. No stress, that sort of thing." She sighed again, "Sometimes I feel I shall go mad if something more exciting doesn't happen than going to Laura Smythe-Patterson's for coffee!"

"You need a break, Ma," said Simon. He stood up and stretched, then took his drink over to the window. He stared out for a few moments and then turned to face her. "Tell you what – how about going to Adam and Beth's new place next weekend and staying for a few days? They've not long moved in and I bet Beth would appreciate some help with getting things sorted out."

Audrey stared at him as if he had gone completely insane.

"I doubt Beth would want me there," she replied frostily. "I'm quite sure she has plenty of friends who can help her if she needs it."

"Nonsense," said Simon briskly. "Who better than her mother-in-law? I bet she'd love to have you there and so would Adam," he added slyly.

"So would Adam what?" enquired John, appearing in the doorway, a small glass of whisky and soda in his hand and stripy apron tied around his waist. "Lunch in five minutes. Jolly nice of you to bring this whisky, Simon, even though I'm not supposed to indulge too often."

Simon raised his glass in acknowledgement.

"I was just saying I think Ma could do with a break, Dad," he said. "I suggested she might go and stay with Adam and Beth for a few days."

"I think that's a jolly good idea," agreed John. "You have been looking a little off-colour, my dear. It would do you the world of good to go and see them all. Have a break from boring old me and enjoy our grandchildren."

Audrey suppressed a shudder of distaste at the thought of the boys.

"But how would you cope? And perhaps Beth and Adam wouldn't want a visitor so soon. And if you're not coming, I'll have to get the train, and I hate train journeys these days." Audrey was desperately trying to think up excuses, but John and Simon brushed them aside.

"Of course I can cope. I'll have Mrs Mason popping in most days, and you know me, I'll be quite happy mooching around. I'll probably invite Gerald Carney down for a meal and a drink. It's been ages since we got together. Anyway, let's have some lunch and we'll give Beth a ring. See how she's fixed."

"And there's no need to worry about getting the train," added Simon. "I can easily arrange to take you down and pick you up – I'd like to see this wonderful new house in any case, and I shall enjoy a day out as well."

As his parents led the way into the dining room Simon suppressed a satisfied smile. He had felt sure his father would be on his side in persuading Audrey to go down to Beth's, and it had given him the perfect excuse for turning up as well. He would prefer to tell Beth what he had discovered about Kevin Webster face-to-face, and it would be far easier to snatch a moment alone with her if Audrey were there to distract Adam. A warm glow spread through him at the thought of seeing Beth alone, and of their clandestine conspiracy; not least was the gratifying thought that he would be deceiving his brother about his real motive for being there.

All in all, it was turning out to be a very satisfactory day.

CHAPTER 14

Beth sighed as she unpacked yet another box in the living-room and thought about the phone call she had received yesterday. She had not been able to think of a ready excuse when Audrey had rung up to ask if she could come down to see them the following weekend and stay until the Friday. She had pretended to be delighted at the thought, but in reality her heart had sunk. She'd spoken only briefly to Simon about their time of arrival, but he had hinted broadly that he had some news for her about Kevin; obviously he couldn't give too much away over the phone, and had said that he would speak to her when he came down. She dreaded Audrey's visit because they had never really been completely reconciled after their disagreement so felt Audrey might create a difficult atmosphere. Besides which, she didn't want any visitors yet; for the time being she wanted Malthorp to herself, to savour and enjoy.

The house was looking much more like a home now and she loved it. Jon Faber had proved an excellent workman; the fabric of the house had been rendered structurally stable again; the decorators he had found for the inside had done their job efficiently and, as both she and Adam had wished, the house had been restored as far as possible in the style of the period. The garden room had been transformed into a spacious and sunny studio for her to work in; the living room and dining room had been refurbished and another smaller room converted into Adam's study. A downstairs cloakroom had been installed and, in the kitchen, a gleaming new Aga stood resplendent in place of the old rusty one; the old walls had been re-plastered and painted cream, and a completely new kitchen fitted in pine. A new dresser stood against one wall, and the old table had been sanded and varnished and chairs found to go with it. The former larder contained, side by side, a huge American-style fridge and freezer. The old scullery, too, had been cleaned up, although the old butler sink had been retained for character, and it now housed the washing machine and tumble dryer. Upstairs, the largest bedroom, which was Beth and Adam's, boasted an en-suite bathroom, and the two boys also had bright and cheerful bedrooms. Adam had decided to turn one of the other three bedrooms into another bathroom; the other two were to be guest rooms. The big bathroom was now fully tiled and a shower had been fitted in one corner, although they had retained the old-fashioned claw-footed bath, which they both loved.

All in all, Beth was more than happy with it all, but she could have well done without Audrey and her snide remarks and unspoken criticisms. Besides everything else, they were due to collect Finn on Friday, and she didn't know how her mother-in-law would react to a big furry dog galloping around the place. It would have been nice to have a family weekend while they all got used to each other. Still, she reflected, at least Simon would have some news for her, even though in a way she dreaded to hear it.

There was another reason, too, why she was uneasy.

Things had not been right between Danny and Jamie since the incident with the books. It wasn't that Danny hadn't forgiven his brother; although naturally he had been very upset over the whole thing for a day or two. Luckily, Danny, with his sunny and cheerful personality, could not be down in the doldrums for long and he was soon back to being his usual patient self with Jamie.

No, it was Jamie who had subtly changed towards Danny. Normally, especially when they were on holiday, he followed Danny everywhere like a little shadow. Danny never minded; he adored the little boy, and made a point of trying to include him in his games. But now it was noticeable that Jamie was pointedly ignoring Danny. These last few days, instead of trotting after his big brother in his usual fashion, he would go off on his own, either to play outside in the garden or in the attic or, if Danny was up there, in his bedroom. Often, Beth would hear him talking out loud but when she went in, thinking he was with Danny, but she would find him alone, dedicatedly lining up his toy cars or scribbling in a drawing book. At these times, he would look up at her, eyes shining and lips parted, as if he was in the midst of enjoying some tremendous joke with an unseen companion. If she tried quizzing him about who he was talking to, or what the joke was, he would close his lips together gently but firmly, simply shake his head or turn away. He had always been detached from her because of his autism, but she had felt lately that they had been making some sort of progress. Now he seemed further away from her than ever. She was worried.

On an impulse she picked up the phone and dialled Tom Mitchell's number. All the parents had been given his number to call out of school hours if they were concerned about their child's behaviour. Up until today, Beth had never felt the need to use it, but now she felt she needed some of Tom's impartial advice. Marie, Tom's wife answered the phone.

"Oh, hello Beth, how are you?" she exclaimed. "I was only saying to Tom yesterday we must give you a ring and see how all is going with the new house."

"Everything's fine with the house; we're starting to get straight at last, thank God. I wondered, Marie, could I have a word with Tom?"

"I'm sorry, Beth, you just missed him. He's gone to Reading today for a conference. Can I help at all? Is it a problem with Jamie?"

"Yes… No… To tell you the truth, Marie, I'm really not sure what's going on."

"Tell me from the beginning."

"Well, it all started when we brought the boys on their first visit here."

She told Marie all about it. There was a short silence on the end of the phone. Then Marie said,

"Well, I don't think it sounds too much to worry about, Beth. I think that maybe what is at the root of it all is probably quite simple. Autistic children generally don't like change and Jamie has had to cope with a lot of changes right now. The move, of course, a new bedroom; getting a dog etcetera – it's a lot for him to take in. So, I think he may have created this Valentine as a sort of safety blanket. He can talk to Valentine, tell him anything he likes, and he knows Valentine will only give him the answers he wants. As for destroying Danny's books, perhaps that was the only way he could get rid of his anger and confusion at that particular time. But, of course, he would blame 'Valentine' for it, because in his mind, he knows it was wrong, so 'Valentine' can take the blame. A lot of children resort to an imaginary friend, though it is a little unusual for a child with Jamie's problem to do so. Does what I've said make any sense?"

"Yes," said Beth. "Yes, I see what you're saying, Marie. But I don't know, sometimes, there seems to be something more than just imagination. There's something almost knowing in the way Jamie looks, as if he's laughing at us all. I've never seen him look like that before. I can't really describe it."

"Look, if you're still worried, I'll get Tom to give you a call when he gets back. It may not be until tomorrow now, because this conference may go on quite late. Can I get him to do that?"

Beth thanked her and rang off. For a moment she sat and thought about what Marie had said. It did make a lot of sense but somehow she wasn't convinced. She looked at her watch. She'd better go and get some work done, in a couple of hours the boys would want their tea. She walked through from the living-room into the hall and went into the garden room which was now her studio. It felt quite hot with the sun streaming through the French doors. She crossed the room and unlocked them, opening them both wide. She stood for a moment breathing in the fresh air, admiring the tangled beauty of the garden and listening to the birdsong.

Suddenly, she became aware of another sound. Somewhere, quite near, she could distinctly hear the sound of a woman crying bitterly. She swung round. Where could it be coming from? Had she left the radio or television on? She checked the television first but it was turned off at the plug. The radio, which was in the kitchen, was also unplugged. The sobbing became louder and she began to walk through to the hall to check the other rooms.

Abruptly, the sobbing stopped. Beth frowned, even more puzzled, and returned to the studio. The wind had got up and one of the doors was swinging, banging back against the wall. She went across to close it.

Suddenly, from somewhere beyond the trees, there came a blood-curdling scream.

CHAPTER 15

Out in the garden, which Beth and Adam had not yet had time to tame and was still quite overgrown and wild, Danny was building a den. He had chosen a spot just beyond the old vegetable garden, at the beginning of a small wooded area where there was a tangle of rhododendron and azalea bushes. He had hacked a way through them with a rusty old scythe he found in one of the outhouses, and had discovered that, in the very middle, was a sizeable space ideal for planning secret missions and launching counter attacks on unseen enemies. He had spent the best part of two days out there and he'd even furnished his hideaway with an ancient tatty rug, originally from the attic, an old mattress and a small worm-eaten cupboard, all of which he had rescued from the workmen's skip. In this last, he intended to store provisions and had already acquired, out of the larder, two tins of baked beans, a packet of chocolate biscuits and half a dozen apples. All in all, he was extremely pleased with his handiwork.

He dragged the last of the branches he had gathered from the wooded part at the bottom of the garden, and arranged them over the front of the den. There, he thought, surveying it with proprietary satisfaction, it was a brilliant den. Only one thing remained to be done. He had prepared a notice on an old piece of plywood and intended to place it on one of the oak trees leading to the place where his den was concealed, but he needed to find a hammer and some nails. He didn't want to ask Mum, for the same reason he hadn't told her about using the scythe; she would fuss and insist on making him wait for his father to do it and Danny didn't want to wait.

"*Danny!*"

He jumped and glanced round, hearing the sudden whisper behind him. There was no one there. He frowned a little and turned away.

"*Daanny...y... y..!*"

He spun round at the sound of the thin, tinny whisper, so quiet, yet it seemed to resonate through the woods with a menacing echo.

"Who's there?" he said loudly. "Who is it?" There was no answer, but he could sense someone was watching him. "If you're trying to scare me," he continued, with commendable bravado, though his voice was trembling a little, "then it's not working. Come out here and show yourself."

There was a rustling in the bushes to the side of him, and a small dark head appeared.

"Jamie!" exclaimed Danny with relief. "What are you up to? You scared me half to death!"

Jamie's face broke into a rare smile and he clambered out from the bushes.

"What Danny doing?" he asked.

Danny grinned back, glad that his little brother seemed to want to be with him again.

"I've built a cool den," he said. "Come and see." He pushed the concealing branches aside, and proudly showed Jamie his handiwork.

"What d'you reckon then, Spud?" he asked. "Cool or what!"

"Cool!" echoed Jamie. "What you doing now?"

It was rare for his brother to ask direct questions and Danny was pleased.

"I'm going to find a hammer and nails to put up this notice." He held the board up for Jamie to see. On it was written in large red letters: 'DANGER! THIS AREA IS OUT OF BOWNDS. KEEP OUT!! Jamie's eyes widened and he gave a nod of approval as Danny read the notice out to him.

"Come on, then, let's go and find a hammer. I can't wait for Finn to get here on Friday; he's going to love our den. I'm gonna be Captain, but you can be my second-in-command, and Finn can be the private…"

His voice faded away as they headed towards the garage in search of a hammer.

Left in the clearing, he listens to the fading sound of the boys' voice. Things are progressing, but the One he has chosen has not quite yet fallen under his spell. He is too close to the other boy. Something will have to be done. Nothing can be allowed to stand in the way of his design. He needs the One to help him reach through the mists of time, to resist those who will try and stop him reaching his objective. This child is ideal, he has little will to resist, and so all other distractions must be set aside.

Must be eliminated if necessary.

That should be easy.

Danny had found a claw hammer and some rusty nails in an old wooden box in the garage and he and Jamie bore them triumphantly back to the clearing.

"Now, you'll have to hold the board while I bang them in," he said. "Can you do that?" Jamie looked serious.

"Valentine can help too," he said.

"Oh, you're not still on about that Valentine," scoffed Danny. "Come on, Spud. That'll only get you into loads of trouble. Forget about him."

"No!" shouted Jamie. "Valentine my *friend*, Danny!" His lower lip trembled.

"Okay, okay, keep your hair on," said Danny. "Well, do you think that maybe you *and* Valentine can hold this board straight?"

Jamie nodded fiercely and proceeded to hold the board as straight as he could while Danny tried to bang the nails into the tree. It wasn't as easy as he had thought, but after a lot of effort he managed to get two in. He put the hammer down on the ground and stood back to take a look at his handiwork.

"Hmm… Think we need the other two in, Jamie," he said. "What do you think?"

"Hmm…" echoed Jamie. He had picked up the abandoned

hammer and was standing back a few yards from his brother. He began swinging the hammer backwards and forwards as he looked.

"Careful with that, Jamie," said Danny. "You don't want to drop it on your foot."

Jamie swung it more vigorously.

"Come on, Spud, that's enough!" said Danny, a little more emphatically. "Mum's gonna kill me if you have an accident."

But Jamie ignored him and began to swing it even more violently, backwards and forwards, so that for a moment Danny watched fascinated as the hammer gained momentum in Jamie's small hand. Danny tried to walk forward to attempt to grab the lethal implement out of his brother's hand but he couldn't move. His legs seemed rooted to the ground, like the big old oak tree beside him. There was some sort of mist before his eyes and he screwed them up, trying to see his brother more clearly. The hammer was making a whooshing sound now as Jamie swung it above his head like the shot putters Danny had once seen in the Olympics on TV. Danny tried to cry out but his voice stuck in his throat.

Then, for a split second, he thought he saw another small, shadowy figure standing next to the small, hammer-wielding boy, a figure leaning on what looked like two sticks; a boy not much older than Jamie himself.

Danny found his voice.

"*JAMIE!*" he yelled at the top of his voice.

Jamie looked at him with an evil grin...

Then he released the hammer.

Danny tried to throw himself to the side, but the hammer hit him on the temple, just above his left eye, and he dropped like a stone.

For a moment there was silence. Then Jamie began to scream.

CHAPTER 16

Adam was at the end of an extremely complicated and delicate operation when the message came through for him. As he came out of theatre, tired after five hours of non-stop surgery, Laura was waiting for him.

"What's wrong?" he asked, seeing the expression on her face.

"It's Danny. He's had an accident at home. He's down in A & E. Now don't panic, Adam," she added as he began to tear off his mask and gown. "I've had a look at him and he's going to be fine. He was knocked unconscious for a short time, but his reflexes are good and, although he's got a bit of a headache, I think everything is okay. I've arranged for an immediate CT scan just in case."

"What happened?" he asked as they hurried along the corridor and down the stairs to Casualty. "How about Jamie – is he okay?"

"He's fine. I'll let Beth explain. Ah, here she is," she added as they rounded the corner into the emergency department. "I'll leave you together while I check on the patient."

"Beth, love." He took one look at her face and folded her into his arms. She began to cry quietly into his shoulder. He gave her a moment, then said gently: "How did it happen?"

"I... I don't know exactly." She swallowed her tears and gave a shuddering sigh. "I had just finished unpacking some boxes and I was in the studio when I heard this awful screaming. For a moment I didn't know what it was. To tell you the truth it didn't sound human. Then I thought it must be Jamie, that Jamie was hurt, and I rushed out into the garden." Her tears broke through again and Adam drew her over to a nearby seat.

"Go on," he said as they sat down. Beth screwed the handkerchief she was holding into a tight ball.

"It was awful. I couldn't see them at first and then there was another scream. I ran past the old wall of the vegetable garden and down towards the little wooded area. Danny..." she swallowed again, "...Danny was lying on the ground by the big oak. He wasn't moving and there was blood running into his eye. There was a hammer lying next to him and Jamie just kept on screaming and screaming. In the end I... I had to slap him to get him to stop." She turned her tear-filled eyes to him, "Oh, Adam, then he hunched up into a little ball and wouldn't even look at me. Danny started coming round, but he was so dazed and confused. Luckily, I had my mobile in the pocket of my jacket, so I was able to phone for an ambulance without having to leave him."

"Laura seems to think he'll be alright. I'll go in and take a look at him in a moment. Has he said what happened?"

"No. He still seems very confused. I didn't like to question him too much."

"We'll talk to him again when he's feeling better. Where's Jamie now?"

"I called Debbie. Bless her, her car's off the road at the moment but she got a taxi and came straight over. She's so good with him, said she'd give him something to eat and try and get him to sleep. I must give her a ring in a minute."

"Do that now and I'll pop in and take a look at Danny."

Beth nodded.

"I just can't believe it's happened. What on earth was Danny thinking of, playing with a hammer when Jamie was around? It's not like him to be so irresponsible."

"He probably didn't give it a thought. Go on, now, and ring Debbie and put your mind at rest at least about Jamie."

When Adam pushed the curtain aside and went into the little cubicle, Danny was lying, white-faced and silent, on the narrow trolley he'd been brought in on. Above his left eye was a nasty gash, still oozing blood and the eye itself looked bloodshot and swollen. A nurse was by his side gently holding a cooling pad to his face. She smiled at Adam.

"I'm afraid he looks a bit of a mess, Mr. Ellis."

She left the cubicle and Adam went over to his son.

"Well, you've certainly been in the wars, old son. You're not supposed to try and knock yourself about with hammers, you know. How are you feeling?"

"My head hurts, Dad, and I still feel a bit dizzy."

Adam took out his little torch and examined his eyes.

"Look up... hmm, that all seems pretty good. Can't see many brains in there though. Maybe they'll have more luck with your CT scan."

"What's that, Dad?"

"They put you through a machine that takes a sort of X-ray of your brain, just to make sure there's no permanent damage. Nothing to worry about." He bent and gave Danny a hug. The boy's arms went up and round his father's neck.

"I'm sorry, Dad," he whispered. "I shouldn't have been playing with the hammer without asking you. Will I be able to go home after the scan?"

"No, I think you'll have to stay in overnight," said Adam. "We have to be sure that you aren't concussed. That's a nasty gash on your head. Can you remember how it happened, Dan?"

Danny's face clouded at his question and he looked away.

"It's... it's a bit hazy at the moment, Dad. Can we talk about it tomorrow?"

"Sure." Adam gave him a quick kiss. "Mum's going to come and sit with you for a while. She's just gone to ring Debbie to see if Jamie's all right." "What's the matter, Dan?"

"N... nothing, Dad. Can I close my eyes now for a bit? My head's throbbing."

Adam turned to look at him as he left. Danny looked very small and vulnerable lying there. Outside, Laura was waiting to speak to him.

"He'll be going up for the scan in about ten minutes. What did you think of him?"

"Everything seems okay. He's just rather quiet, which is definitely unlike our Danny. He's going to have a nasty bruise there."

"Yes, I don't think it will need stitching because the hammer just broke the skin, although it bled quite a bit, as wounds on the temple always tend to, but it will spoil his good looks for a couple of weeks. Did he say how exactly it happened?"

"No," said Adam thoughtfully. "He didn't seem sure at all."

The next morning when Adam and Beth arrived at the hospital they found Danny in a side ward, resplendent in a hospital gown several sizes too big for him, tucking into a large bowl of cereal and watching cartoons on the small television at the end of his bed.

"Well," said Adam, "There doesn't seem to be too much wrong with you, if your appetite's anything to go by."

"No, my TC scan was fine," said Danny. "Laura says I can go home today."

"What's this TC scan then, Laura?" asked Adam in mock severity as she came up to join them. "As a leading consultant I'm supposed to be kept informed of all the new developments in medical technology!"

"I think it means that Danny is Top Cat again," said Laura as Danny chuckled. "Or is it Terrifically Cheerful, Dan?"

Danny stuffed his mouth full and nodded enthusiastically. He went back to watching his cartoons.

"No, honestly, he's absolutely fine," she went on. "No sign of any lasting damage. He can definitely go home today. How are you, Beth?"

Beth gave a wan smile.

"Not too bad. I didn't get much sleep last night. Jamie was a bit restless and I was worrying about Danny."

"How does Jamie seem?" asked Laura.

"He's a bit quiet," said Beth, glancing at Danny, who was seemingly absorbed in his programme. "But then, he often is. I am not sure whether he can remember what happened, but strangely he's not asked for Danny."

She didn't mention what she had heard Jamie saying during the night. She hadn't even been able to tell Adam. About one o'clock in the morning, unable to sleep herself, she had heard Jamie tossing and turning and muttering to himself, so she had gone in to check on him. He was lying with his back towards her and the bedclothes were rumpled down to his waist. She had crossed the room to cover him up. The bars on his bedroom window reflected off the moon shining in through the half-open curtains, tiger-striping the pale duvet which lay half off the bed. He was still muttering as she pulled the covers over him. She bent her head to hear, but could not make it out. Then suddenly, quite clearly, he said, "I didn't want you to throw it, Valentine. Why did you hurt Danny?"

Beth had frozen in shock and disbelief. One part of her wanted to believe he was just having a bad dream – but she knew that deep in her heart had been the fear that Jamie had deliberately tried to hurt his brother.

Now, looking at her elder son finishing his breakfast, and seeing that he was going to be fine, she decided that she had to know the truth.

"What exactly happened yesterday, Danny?" she asked quietly.

He looked away and his bright expression faded.

"I… I can't really remember," he said unhappily.

"Come on, Dan," Adam said. "We need to know."

"Was it anything to do with Jamie?" Beth asked gently. Danny's eyes filled with tears.

"I don't think he meant to, Mum. I was putting my notice up on the tree, and Jamie was playing with the hammer, you know, sort of swinging it. I tried to get it off him – honest – but everything went really weird and I couldn't seem to move, and then Jamie let go of the hammer and it hit me. That's all I really remember."

"What do you mean, everything went weird?" asked Adam.

"I can't really describe it. It was, like, sort of misty, and my legs wouldn't work properly. Then I… I thought I saw…" He paused.

"What?" urged Beth. Danny took a long breath.

"It looked like there was someone standing next to Jamie. It looked like another little boy. He was leaning on something, but I couldn't make out what it was. It was only for a split second and then I think the hammer hit me and everything went black."

There was a short silence.

"There couldn't really have been anyone there, could there? I probably imagined it didn't I, Mum?" Danny said beseechingly.

Beth closed her eyes for a second, then looked at him and tried to smile.

"I'm sure you did, Danny," she said feebly. "I'm sure you did."

CHAPTER 17

In the car, on the way back from the hospital, Adam glanced at Beth's white, set face and said quietly,

"I'll ring Ma this evening and tell her what's happened. I'm sure she'll understand that we couldn't possibly have her to stay now."

Beth turned and glanced at Danny on the back seat, who was engrossed in reading one of the comics they had taken to the hospital.

"No, Adam, let them come down. Danny will be fine by Friday, and I know Audrey wants to see the house. Besides, I'm sure your father is looking forward to the break."

"All the same," said Adam. "You know what Ma's like and Simon will be his usual extrovert self, taking over the conversation as he always does."

"The boys think the world of him, especially Danny," interrupted Beth. "And we'll have Finn to distract us all anyway."

"Yes, let's hope Ma will be okay with him – she's never been that keen on dogs; we were never allowed pets when we were kids. Too much noise, mess and so on."

"Grandma won't be able to help loving Finn when she sees him," put in Danny, who had put down his comic and was leaning forward in his seat. "He's the nicest and best-looking dog in the whole wide world."

"Certainly better looking than you at the moment, Dan!" laughed Adam. "You look as if you've gone ten rounds in the boxing ring. I don't know what Grandma and Uncle Simon are going to say when they see you."

Beth laughed.

"We'd better warn them. I might phone Simon this evening and tell him so they know what to expect."

"I'll do that," said Adam. "I want to ask him to bring down some of that red wine he recommended. Geoff and Laura really liked it and I can't seem to find it locally."

Beth nodded, feeling disappointed. She'd hoped to have a quiet word with her brother-in-law over the phone. At the back of her mind had been the thought that, if he could tell her what he had found out, she might be able to say she had changed her mind and put Audrey off coming down. Despite her earlier words to Adam, she really didn't feel like coping with the idiosyncrasies of her mother-in-law; the only reason she had wanted her to still come was so that she could talk to Simon. She turned to look at Danny again.

"Jamie's really looking forward to you coming home, Danny. He's drawing you a lovely picture."

Danny nodded, but his face clouded at the mention of his brother's name. He turned away and stared out of the window. Beth sighed. Since the accident, Danny had turned quiet whenever Jamie's name had been mentioned. She hoped fervently that once they were back together, they would resume their old easy relationship.

Debbie, Jamie and Finn were waiting by the front door as they arrived. They had collected the big dog early that morning so he would be there to greet Danny and he ran down the steps, tail wagging furiously, barking enthusiastically. Danny laughed as he knelt down to greet him and Finn swept a wet tongue over his face. Then Jamie did something quite unprecedented for him; he also ran down the steps and threw his arms round Danny. He looked up into his brother's battered face and his lip quivered.

"Valentine drew you a picture, Danny. He's *really* sorry."

Danny frowned for a moment, then smiled at his brother and ruffled his hair. Debbie laughed as Beth glanced at Adam and bit her lip.

"No, *you* drew the picture, Jamie," she smiled. "He's been up in his room for ages doing it, Danny, but he won't show it to me. My goodness, but you have got some war wounds, haven't you? Never mind, they'll soon fade. Come on, I've just made some hot chocolate for you boys, and there's a fresh pot of coffee on as well."

Chatting away, she led the way indoors. To Beth's relief, Danny took Jamie's hand and followed her. Beth and Adam exchanged glances.

"Valentine again," whispered Beth. "If this goes on, Adam, I think we ought to talk to someone about it. After all, Danny did think he saw someone with Jamie. Maybe this Valentine is some local boy who's getting into the grounds without us knowing. Jamie seems to have this obsession with him – I don't like it at all."

"I think you're worrying about nothing," said Adam. "As Marie said, Valentine is just someone that Jamie's made up; Danny only thought he saw this boy with Jamie and you have to remember he was in shock at the time."

"But he saw him *before* the hammer hit him. I think we should..."

"I think we should forget it," said Adam firmly. "No," he said as Beth opened her mouth to speak. "I think you're making too much of it, Beth. A lot of kids have imaginary friends and, although it's a bit unusual in a child with Jamie's problems, I'm sure that's all this Valentine is. Now let's go and have our coffee before it gets cold."

He marched off indoors, leaving Beth open-mouthed. She couldn't believe he was being so casual about it. She had almost decided to tell him later today about her experience in London and that Simon had been finding out about Kevin's whereabouts. But now she made up her mind to say nothing. If he could be so dismissive of Jamie's problem, then he would certainly be less than sympathetic towards her.

She would wait and see what Simon had come up with. Hopefully there would be some sort of rational explanation for her frightening encounter.

After lunch, which he tucked into enthusiastically, Beth insisted Danny went to lie down for an hour.

"But I feel fine, Mum," he protested. I want to go out in the garden and play with Finn. How's he ever going to get to know me if I don't even play with him?"

"There's plenty of time for that, Dan," said Adam firmly. "Your Mum's right. You've had a nasty blow to the head and you should take things easy today. Remember, Grandma and Uncle Simon are coming Friday, so we'll have a busy day. You'll be able to play with Finn tomorrow and on Friday you two can keep him out of Grandma's way as she's not too keen on dogs."

"How could anyone not like *Finn*?" grumbled Danny. "Okay, okay, I'm going," he added as he saw his father's face. "But I won't be able to sleep!"

Jamie was still in the kitchen with Debbie finishing his lunch so he headed upstairs, Finn trailing in his wake. Once he was in his bedroom, he grabbed a book off the shelf and threw himself on the bed. He read for a while, but soon his eyes drooped and he drifted off to sleep.

In his dream he was back in the woods. But this time Jamie was with him and they were running together, hand in hand. Finn was ahead of them, his golden plumed tail leading the way as they ran faster and faster, dodging round trees and bushes, brambles scratching their legs. Danny felt his legs tiring; he couldn't keep up with Jamie.

"Slow down, Jamie!" he called, but his brother didn't seem to hear him.

Suddenly, they reached a clearing in the woods and Jamie let go of Danny's hand. A woman was standing on the other side of the clearing. She was the woman he had seen before in the garden; tall and slender, wearing a long white dress and Danny saw that she was weeping.

"What's wrong?" he asked.

At first she didn't answer him, she just kept sobbing quietly into a lacy handkerchief. Then she looked across at him, her face swollen with grief.

"It's my Valentine," she said softly. "Have you seen him? I have looked everywhere but I cannot find him. His father will be so angry."

Danny turned to look at Jamie, but his brother was no longer there. Instead, a small, wizened boy leaning on two wooden crutches was standing next to him. He had dark hair, a thin, lined face and behind his round wire spectacles his dark eyes glared at Danny with malice and hatred. Danny cried out in terror.

"Valentine!" cried the woman. "Valentine!"

The boy turned his terrible gaze on her.

"You didn't save me," he said in a strange thin, tinny voice. "You let me die."

"No!" she reached out towards him. "No, Valentine, I would never have let you come to harm, never!"

For an answer the boy raised his arm and pointed at her with the crutch. The woman fell to her knees, writhing as if in pain. "Please, Valentine, *no*..." she cried out, her face a mask of agony. Danny yelled at the boy to stop, but he just laughed softly, menacingly, and Danny knew he could do nothing. He started forward to try and help the woman and...

He woke up and lay there, dazed and shivering.

The dream had been so real that for a moment he didn't know where he was. Then he saw Finn's anxious brown eyes gazing at him from the end of the bed. The dog gave a soft whine.

"It's okay, boy," said Danny. He sat up slowly, feeling weak and cold, the dream vivid in his mind. Suddenly, Finn gave a low growl, deep in his throat and his hackles rose as the door slowly opened. Jamie appeared, clutching a crumpled piece of paper and the big dog jumped down from the bed and ran from the room. Danny gave a shaky laugh.

"Oh, it's only you. I had this weirdest dream, Jamie. What's that you've got there?"

"Valentine drew this picture for you," said Jamie softly. He handed Danny the paper.

Danny looked, and took a sharp intake of breath as he saw what was on the piece of paper...

It had three crudely-drawn people on it. Two stick figures, one taller than the other, both dressed in shorts and tee shirts were standing in front of a tree. But it was the other, smaller figure that stood just in front of them that Danny was staring at in horrified fascination.

The figure was also small, dressed in longer trousers and wore round spectacles on his face. Under his arms were two sticks.

Jamie smiled dreamily and pointed to the figure.

"Valentine," he said. "See, Danny – that's Valentine!"

CHAPTER 18

Audrey and Simon were due to arrive about midday on Friday. Adam had taken the day off, as he knew that Beth was not really looking forward to his mother's visit and thought it better that he should be on hand. Although Beth was pleased that he would be there she wondered how she would be able to have a quiet word with Simon, who was only staying until that evening.

Tom Mitchell had rung her as promised and had been very reassuring about Jamie's strange behaviour. He had promised to keep a very strict eye on him and report to her immediately if he had any concerns. But to Beth's relief, Jamie had seemed much calmer these last couple of days and had not mentioned Valentine once. On the other hand, Danny had not appeared to be himself at all which Beth put down to shock following the accident, though, she had to admit, today he seemed more cheerful.

The weather had turned unseasonably warm for early April and Adam had unearthed the sun-loungers from the depths of the garage. He and Beth were sprawled comfortably on them, enjoying the sunshine, whilst the boys played ball with Finn on the lawn.

"Thank goodness Danny seems more like his normal self today," Beth remarked, watching them laugh as Finn raced after the ball for the umpteenth time. "I was getting a bit concerned because he seemed so quiet yesterday – not like himself at all."

"Sometimes the shock of something like that can set in afterwards," said Adam. "Danny was just having a bit of a delayed reaction, that's all. I've seen it lots of times with kids. He'll be fine."

Beth nodded. "I suppose so. He and Jamie are okay now so that's one thing to be grateful for." She stretched and yawned. "God, this weather's gorgeous! I'm glad I decided to do a cold lunch, though I'm sure your mother will expect something a little more special."

"Now, Beth, I'm sure she'll be more than happy. You make the best Chicken Caesar Salad ever. Anyway, by the time she's had a few glasses of Chardonnay she'll be past caring!"

Beth threw a cushion at him and he caught it, laughing, just as they heard the crunch of car tyres on the gravel at the side of the house, indicating that their guests had arrived.

Despite her misgivings, lunch passed off well. They had decided to eat out on the terrace at the back of the house and Adam had put up a gazebo to give them some shade. Although Beth had expected her mother-in-law to find at least one thing to criticise about the house, she had obviously decided to be as charming as possible and praised the lunch and the house with equal enthusiasm.

"Though I shall expect a proper guided tour after lunch," she said. "But the downstairs is wonderful – so spacious, and I adore your kitchen. Your father would be in his element in it, Adam."

"I'm sure the boys would love to show you the upstairs," said Beth. "We've turned the attic into a lovely play room for them. It's great, isn't it, Danny?"

Danny nodded enthusiastically.

"Yep," he replied, through a mouthful of chicken. "We'll show you all round, Grandma. The bathroom is really cool – it's got the biggest bath you've ever seen!"

Audrey smiled a little frostily.

"Thank you, Daniel dear. I would like to see that. But perhaps you should wait to speak until you have no food in your mouth. Manners cost nothing, as I was always telling your father and Uncle Simon when they were your age."

Simon laughed out loud, unable to contain himself.

"Indeed, you did, Ma. Pity that it worked on Adam but not on me." He winked at Danny. "Tell you what, Dan; I still talk with my mouth full. Ask Fiona – she's always telling me off for it."

Danny grinned back. He thought his Uncle Simon was really cool. Pity he wasn't the one who was staying instead of Grandma. She was so boring with all her rules. He glanced at Jamie, who was eating his salad in silence. Jamie didn't like Grandma very much. Although he couldn't express himself to other people, Danny generally knew what he was feeling. He could sense that Grandma didn't really cotton on to him or Jamie. She never acted like the grandmas that his friends had; rarely showing them any affection or buying them sweets or comics. He sighed. Well, they would just have to make the best of it. Maybe this time would be different.

Beth glanced at Danny. She knew what he was thinking. Well, tomorrow they would go out somewhere nice; maybe to Marwell Zoo or to the New Forest and show Audrey some of the beautiful countryside that surrounded them. If this weather held maybe they could even take a picnic. She caught Simon's eye and smiled ruefully. He raised his glass in a mock salute.

"Wonderful lunch, Beth. And the wine's good too; I'll have another glass please, Adam."

"I think you've had enough, Simon," said Audrey firmly. "After all, you have to drive home this evening."

"Oh, don't worry about me, Ma. I'll go on the back roads and avoid the cops. Anyway," he said teasingly, "You're not doing badly yourself. Is that your third or fourth glass?"

"*Simon!*"

"I'll get dessert," said Beth hastily, trying not to laugh.

"Come on, Si," said Adam as Beth went into the house, "I think Ma's right. You probably have had enough."

"So speaks the successful older brother," said Simon, draining his glass. "Tell me, Adam, how does it feel to have it all – top job, big house in the country, two kids, gorgeous wife? Everything's so bloody perfect for you, isn't it?"

Adam shook his head, choosing to ignore the bitter undertone in his brother's voice. He was used to Simon's occasional spiteful outbursts and understood the reasons for them.

"Ah, but I don't have the advantages of your bachelor lifestyle," he replied lightly, as Beth appeared carrying a huge cream trifle. "The lovely Fiona, pad in London, going out clubbing till all hours – those days are long gone for me, Si – not that I'd want that now, of course," he added hastily, seeing his mother frown.

There was a moment's awkward silence, then his mobile rang.

"Damn!" he said as he picked it up. "It's work. I'll have to get this, folks. Sorry."

Beth followed him as he went into the house. He finished the call and turned to her with a rueful expression.

"Sorry, love, I'll have to go in. There's been a crash on the motorway and a little girl has been seriously injured. They need me to assess her – Tim's not sure whether we can operate or not. Will you be okay coping with Ma and Simon?"

"Of course. Oh, Adam, I hope the little girl's alright." Beth tried to suppress the unworthy thought that this might give her the opportunity she needed to talk to Simon.

Audrey was less than happy that Adam had to leave them. "Oh, darling do you *have* to go – and before dessert?" but cheered up visibly after another large glass of Chardonnay. She even laughed when Danny, after his third helping of trifle, took her hand and said,

"Grandma, I think you'd better come and see upstairs before you have any more wine."

They went off into the house, Danny leading the way and chattering nineteen to the dozen; Jamie, as usual, trailing behind. Finn barked and turned pleading eyes on Beth, but she said,

"No, Finn, you stay here." He sighed deeply and flopped down at her feet. Simon looked ruefully at Beth.

"Sorry about earlier. Ma's really been winding me up about things on the way down here and I rather took it out on poor old Adam."

"Don't worry, Adam knows very well what Audrey can be like," Beth said. "He's used to dealing with awkward parents all the time in his job. It's a shame that he's been called in today though. He's been working so hard and really needed this break."

Simon leant forward.

"I'm sorry too, but at least it gives me a chance to talk to you. I've been in touch with my policeman friend and he's come up trumps. He's tracked down Kevin Webster and found out what happened to him."

Beth bit her lip and her heart began to race.

"Well?" she said. "Please tell me, Simon."

Simon looked at her solemnly. She was looking particularly beautiful today, he thought, with her skin tanned faintly by the sun, and her lips parted as she waited to hear his news. She was dressed in cream cropped trousers, which showed off her long, slim legs, and a bright pink figure-hugging top. He took a deep breath.

"Beth, I know this is going to come as a bit of a shock to you, but my friend checked it twice to be sure. Kevin Webster was stabbed by another inmate in prison seven years ago. The ambulance got there straight away and they rushed him to hospital but…" He paused and took her hand. "Beth, he died in the ambulance before they could get there. So, you see, it can't have been him that day can it?"

Audrey staggered slightly as Danny led her up the stairs. Her head felt more than a little muzzy; she wasn't used to drinking so much at lunchtime, but the wine *had* been delicious. Danny threw open the door of the first bedroom they came to.

"This is my room, Grandma, and Jamie's is next door. We've both got our own bathrooms."

"Very nice," murmured Audrey. "Though I think you need to hang up some of your clothes, Daniel. I would never have allowed your father to leave them strewn all over the floor like this."

Danny sighed inwardly. He could tell it wouldn't be easy to impress his grandmother. He gave a rueful grin.

"I know, Grandma, I've got to have a tidy up. Come and look at Jamie's room. Come on, Jamie, you show her how big it is."

Jamie pushed open the door of the next room, but Audrey merely glanced in and tutted as she saw the lines of cars stretched across the carpet.

"Such a mess! Why doesn't your mother make you clear away all those toys on the floor?"

Jamie stared at Audrey in silence with his big blue eyes.

"Well, James. Aren't you going to answer me?" Audrey stared back at her grandson. Really, the child was definitely backward. It was as she had said all along; he should be in a home.

"Well?" she said again. Jamie's bottom lip trembled.

"They Jamie's cars… not put away…"

"Really! Can't you speak clearly, James? I think your mother needs to be stricter with you boys altogether. You both get away with far too much as far as I'm concerned."

Danny was beginning to dislike his grandmother more than ever. He wanted to defend Jamie but knew it would do no good so he took a deep breath and said lightly,

"Grandma, I don't think Jamie really understands. Look, come upstairs and see our playroom. We tidied it all up specially."

"Oh, very well. Where is it?"

"Just through this passage here and up these stairs." Danny ran ahead up the stairs. Audrey put her foot on the first stair and then hesitated as she felt first a strange sensation of unease, then an inexplicable feeling of fear that sent a shiver down her spine. She turned and looked down at Jamie, who met her gaze blandly, but this time was sure she saw an icy, almost menacing look in those deep blue eyes. She turned away hastily and hurried up the stairs.

Her first impression of the room was that of light and space. The cream walls and bright carpet made it look inviting and Audrey breathed a sigh of relief as the feeling of unease subsided.

"This is nice!" she exclaimed, with genuine warmth in her tone that had been lacking until then. You are very lucky to have such a lovely playroom."

"There's another room through here," said Danny. "It used to be four little rooms but now it's one big one and Dad's promised to get us a snooker table!"

"Well, I think…" Audrey jumped as the door crashed open and Finn appeared. The big golden dog bounded joyfully across the room, nearly knocking Audrey over and jumped up at Danny, who nearly fell over too.

"Well, really!" exclaimed Audrey. "That dog's a menace. Surely, he shouldn't be allowed in the house?"

Danny grabbed Finn's collar. "Sorry, Grandma. He's not really supposed to be up here. Mum and Dad are going to train him to stay downstairs but he doesn't really understand yet. I'll take him down."

He marched the dog away. Jamie stood by the door for a moment, watching Audrey as she walked round the room looking at the books and games that were stacked on the shelves. For a moment he cocked his head to one side as if listening to something or someone. Then a smile crossed his features before he turned and went out of the room, shutting the door softly behind him.

Audrey turned, frowning slightly as silence descended and she began to experience the same feeling of unease she had felt on the stairs. She half-laughed at herself. She really shouldn't have had that last glass of wine. It had definitely affected her, making her imagine all sorts of things…

What was that?

From the end of the room, where there was a large cupboard, she was sure she had heard a soft whispering. She walked towards it and stopped abruptly.

There it was again. She took another step.

She heard a muffled giggle…

"Who's there!" she called sharply.

Silence…

Then the whispering again. It sounded almost menacing…

"James? Is that you?"

Audrey reached the cupboard. She lifted her hand to the handle but paused, feeling an icy shiver run down her spine as she heard the long, drawn-out sigh that seemed to come from within the cupboard…

She frowned as she heard a soft but unmistakeable *tap… tap… tap* echo from behind the door.

Driven by an impulse she could not control her hand came out and grasped the handle and slowly she began to turn it…

CHAPTER 19

Beth stared at Simon in utter disbelief.

"No – that can't be right, Simon! It was definitely Kevin. I know it was him – I could never mistake someone else for him. Those bloodshot eyes and those horrible thick lips of his. And what he said to me… Your friend must have got it wrong; he needs to check again."

"No, Beth," Simon said gently. "I thought the same and so I got him to double check. It's on the police computer, and just to be sure I asked him to look at the death records for that year. There's no mistake – Kevin Webster died on…" He reached in his pocket and took out a slip of paper, "…on the thirteenth of November, seven years ago. He was cremated in Liverpool; see, there was a report on it in the local paper." He handed her a photocopy. She unfolded it slowly and saw a grainy picture of a man. She shuddered as she recognised Kevin's coarse, blubbery features. Underneath was written:

LOCAL MAN CREMATED ON HOME GROUND

Kevin John Webster, aged 60, a local man imprisoned for fifteen years for the rape of his 13-year-old niece, was today cremated at Stonehurst Crematorium. He was apparently stabbed to death by another inmate, Gary Maxwell, 24, whilst serving his sentence. He was due to be released pending parole in six months' time. Maxwell will appear in court next week accused of his murder.

Amongst the mourners at Webster's funeral were his widow, Mrs Glenys Webster, and two of her children, Mrs Leah Stockwell and Mr Brian Webster. Her other son, Trevor Webster, did not attend as he is currently out of the country. A family friend said:

"Although Kevin was accused of this terrible crime, Glenys has always stood by him, believing he was innocent and the

> girl led him on, then lied in court. I know he was looking forward to his release and making a new life for himself and Glenys. This was an awful thing to happen and we are all shocked."
>
> Mrs Webster and her children refused to comment, but we understand she will be moving away from the area shortly.

Beth's lip trembled and, as she handed the piece of paper back to Simon, he saw there were tears in her eyes.

"So, Auntie Glenys still believed I was lying. How could she, knowing what he was like. Well, I'm glad he's gone, but I just don't understand what I saw that day. I must be going mad or something."

Simon leant forward and took her hand again.

"Beth," he said gently. "Think about it. You've been under an awful lot of pressure lately, what with the move and the amount of work you've had to do. Maybe this guy looked a bit like Kevin and you just…"

"Imagined the rest," she finished bitterly, pulling her hand away. Then she slumped back in the chair. "I'm sorry, Simon. I shouldn't be getting annoyed with you. Only it's been such a strain the last few days, thinking about it all the time, knowing I can't say anything to Adam because I don't want to worry him. And then the incident with Danny. Maybe you're right; perhaps I did just have a flashback or something. But it seemed so real at the time."

Simon smiled and got up.

"Don't worry about it anymore, Beth. Just try and put it all behind you. Hey, where's that mutt of yours got to?"

"He's probably gone into the house to find the boys." She stood up and smiled. "Thanks for everything, Simon; I know you did your best and I'm very grateful." She put her arms round him and gave him a hug. His arms tightened round her and he pulled her closer.

"You know I'd do anything for you, Beth," he murmured against her hair.

She pulled away, suddenly feeling embarrassed by his intimacy.

"Let's go and see if your mother's finished her guided tour."

She led the way into the house and saw that Danny was just coming down the stairs holding a sheepish Finn by the collar.

"He sneaked up to the playroom, Mum. I don't think Grandma likes him very much."

"Is Jamie still up there with Grandma?" Beth asked.

"I think so. She was looking at our books and things. Shall I…?" He stopped as a muffled thumping and yelling came from above. Beth and Simon ran up the stairs. As they reached the top Jamie appeared out of his bedroom clutching one of his cars. He smiled angelically at them.

"Grandma in playroom," he said solemnly. "Valentine locked her in."

The thumping grew louder. Simon raced up the stairs followed closely by Beth. The door was wide open and the thumping was coming from the cupboard. Simon strode across the room and pulled open the door. A white-faced Audrey fell into his arms.

"Thank God!" she whimpered. "Simon… the cupboard… there was whispering and tapping in the cupboard! It made me… it *forced* me… I looked inside and something was in there. Someone pushed me in and I tried to get out but the door was locked." She paused and gulped, then raised an accusing, trembling finger at Jamie, who was peering at her from behind Beth. "*He* pushed me and then locked me in there with *it*!"

Simon shook his head.

"No, Ma, the door wasn't locked and Jamie was downstairs. Look, there isn't a key. Perhaps it just jammed." He went into the cupboard. "What did you think you heard in here?" He smiled reassuringly. "Look, see for yourself, there's nothing in here – just shelves and toys."

Audrey shuddered.

"I tell you, there was something – or someone – in there. It whispered to me. It pulled me in. And there was this tapping, like a stick. Beth, what is it... what's going on?"

Beth put her arm round her mother-in-law. She felt she must reassure her, even though she felt a deep sense of unease.

"I think you must have imagined it, Audrey, and then when the door jammed, you panicked. Look, it's really hot up here. Come back downstairs and have a cool drink."

"I did *not* imagine it. For God's sake why won't you believe me?" Audrey's lips trembled and she shrugged Beth's arm off. "I... I think I would like to go to my room and lie down if you don't mind. Perhaps you could bring me up a cup of tea?"

"Of course." Beth escorted Audrey down to her room and saw her settled. Simon grinned as she came out, closing the door behind her.

"Poor old Ma! If you ask me, she had one Chardonnay too many."

Beth frowned.

"I'm not so sure," she said thoughtfully. "There *have* been one or two unexplained incidents since we've been here. And Jamie is always mentioning this Valentine. I'm beginning to wonder if this house has a ghost."

Simon snorted with laughter.

"I don't believe you're saying that, Beth. What would Adam say if he heard such nonsense – or does he think so too?"

"No, of course not." Beth was beginning to feel annoyed with Simon. "Look, hadn't you better be getting back? It will be getting busy on the roads and you don't want to hit the rush-hour traffic."

"Okay, I can take a hint," said Simon. "I'll leave you with Ma and the ghosts. But remember, Beth, I'm always around if you need me." He gave her a light peck on the cheek and went to say goodbye to the boys.

Beth waved him off and made tea. She took a cup up to Audrey, but she seemed to be fast asleep, so Beth placed the tea on her bedside table, closed the door and left her. She went downstairs to check on the boys and found them watching cartoons on the big television in the lounge. She knelt down by Jamie who was watching with his thumb plugged firmly in his mouth.

"Jamie," she said gently. "Did you play a trick on Grandma up there in the playroom? Did you hold the cupboard door so she couldn't get out?"

Jamie didn't answer. His eyes were fixed on the bright, gaudy images on the screen.

"Jamie, tell me," Beth persisted. "I won't be cross. I just want to know what happened."

There was still no response from her son. On the screen the images flashed and the strident music blared.

"Jamie!" Beth's voice was sharper now and she picked up the remote, snapping off the television.

"Hey!" exclaimed Danny. "We were watching that…" His voice trailed off as he saw the expression on his mother's face.

Jamie at last turned to look at Beth. His eyes held hers for a long moment. When he spoke, it was without his usual hesitancy.

"Valentine was angry so he locked the door. He doesn't like Grandma. He says she's mean, like *him*."

"What do you mean Jamie? Who is this Valentine you keep talking about?"

Jamie smiled; a secretive, enigmatic smile. He took the remote control from her hand and switched the television back on. As the raucous sound of the cartoon echoed round the room, she had to bend her head to hear his next words,

"Valentine lives here with us, Mummy. He's always lived here and he's my friend. My *best* friend."

CHAPTER 20

Beth slept badly that night. Adam hadn't arrived home until late and he looked tired and drawn. Despite all their efforts to save the child injured in the motorway accident, she had died on the operating table and, as always, it had affected him deeply. Both Audrey and the boys were in bed and Beth hadn't the heart to tell him about Audrey's traumatic experience in the playroom or about Jamie's strange behaviour afterwards. All Adam wanted to do was have a hot drink and go to bed. He made love to her before they went to sleep with a fierce intensity, and held her tightly afterwards.

"Christ knows what I'd do if we ever lost one of our boys," he whispered against her hair. "I can't imagine what that poor kid's parents are going through at the moment."

"You'll never lose any of us, my darling," she whispered back, but he was already falling asleep. Eventually she dropped off, but woke at about six. She crept out of bed quietly so as not to disturb Adam, and went to check on the boys. Danny was lying on his back, gently snoring. Jamie was curled up in a ball, covers halfway down the bed. She stroked his hair gently; his forehead felt damp with sweat. She pulled the covers up round him and he stirred and opened his eyes for a brief moment.

"Go back to sleep, sweetheart, it's early yet," she whispered. He smiled sleepily and closed his eyes obediently. She felt a sudden rush of love for both her boys. These strange things that had been happening, there must be a rational explanation for it all. They were happy, they were living in this wonderful house and they were together as a family. Everything was going to be fine, wasn't it?

An hour later she'd had a quick shower and was in the kitchen drinking her second cup of tea, Finn curled up by her feet. The sun was beginning to break through the early clouds – it was promising to be another beautiful day. Later she planned to pack a picnic;

they had decided to take Audrey and the boys to Beaulieu Motor Museum in the New Forest. They had all been a couple of years ago and Jamie had loved seeing the old cars – in fact they'd had to cope with a major tantrum when it was time to go home. She hoped that now he was a bit older the same thing would not happen again, especially with her mother-in-law there to witness it. Adam had planned to come with them, but she was not at all sure he would be feeling up to it after his traumatic afternoon. She sighed as she put her cup in the dishwasher.

"Never mind, Finn," she said, as the dog stood and stretched lazily. "I'll just have to cope, won't I? Come on," she added as he cast a longing glance at the back door. "I'd better take you for a nice long walk, in case you're going to be left on your own all day."

Just then, a very tousled and sleepy-looking Danny appeared in the doorway.

"Morning, Mum," he said, yawning widely. "What's for breakfast?"

"It's all laid out on the table," said Beth. "Orange juice, cereal and milk and there's some bread cut ready to go in the toaster. I'm just going to take Finn for a walk. Is Jamie still asleep?"

"He's in talking to Dad. I think they're on their way down."

"What about Grandma?"

"She's still asleep, I think."

"Okay. Well, tell them I'll be about an hour. I want to give him a really good walk this morning. See you later."

※

Audrey was not asleep. She'd been awake about two hours, had heard Beth go into the boys' rooms, had heard the shower running and then Beth heading downstairs. Her sleep had been restless, punctuated by strange dreams, in which she was being pursued down endless corridors by something unknown and terrifying. Then, just before she woke, she had dreamed that she was standing in a dark forest. In front of her was a deep, black hole surrounded by a low brick wall.

She sensed there was a presence in the murky darkness, something evil and threatening and, although she did not want to know what it was, she felt inexorably drawn towards it. As she approached the gaping mouth of the hole, she felt a soft touch on her arm. Turning, she saw a woman standing there. She was dressed in a long white dress and gazed at Audrey with intense blue eyes that shimmered with unshed tears.

"*Help him,*" she said softly.

"What do you mean?" Audrey asked, but the woman shook her head, wringing her hands as a fierce wind began to blow. Her long brown hair streamed out behind her and, as the sound of the wind increased, howling and moaning through the shadowy trees, she began to move away as if pulled by an inescapable force.

"*Please help him….*" her voice faded, and then Audrey felt a flicker of fear as a faint tapping began deep within the hole.

"No!" she cried, and woke abruptly, shaking with fear. The dream was so vivid that for a few moments she could not think where she was. She got up and put her dressing gown on, shivering a little in the early morning chill of the room. She went to sit in the armchair by the window until it was light enough to draw the curtains. She could not get the woman's pleading voice out of her mind.

"Who does she want me to help?" she muttered to herself. "There *is* something wrong in this house." She glanced at her bedside clock. "Seven-fifteen. I wonder if it's too early to ring…" She sat for a moment biting her lip. Then she made a decision. She opened her bag and took out her mobile phone, screwing her eyes up as she scrolled through her contacts. "Ah, here it is…"

With shaking fingers, she pressed the call key.

Beth walked Finn across the fields behind the house. She felt confident enough now to let him off the lead and the big golden dog ran ahead, his feathery, plumed tail wagging joyfully. They walked for about half an hour without seeing a soul, apart from a few early-morning rabbits who dived for cover before Finn had a chance to catch them. Beth decided to do a circuit and head back towards the village. She needed some milk and was pretty sure the little convenience store would be open by now. If not, she thought the newsagents probably sold it.

To her surprise, Upper Melcombe was quite busy for an early Saturday morning. Several people passed her and said good morning; most heading for the newsagents. The little shop was open so Beth tied Finn up outside next to the big bowl of water that was always left there for the dogs to drink. She was pleased to find they had a nice selection of cakes and fresh bread. She picked up some crusty rolls and doughnuts for their picnic as well as the milk and went to pay.

The woman behind the counter looked to be in her fifties, large and untidy with frizzy dark hair pulled back in a rough ponytail. She looked at Beth through small, shrewd, brown eyes.

"Settling in well up at Malthorp, are you?" she asked as Beth paid for her items and packed them into the canvas bag she'd brought with her.

"Yes… yes, we are, thank you," Beth replied, somewhat surprised that the woman knew who she was. She laughed, showing uneven, yellowish teeth.

"Oh, you'll have to get used to everyone knowing your business here," she said. "You can't keep anything secret here. Everyone knows everyone in a village. I'm Maureen Tidy, by the way."

"Beth Ellis," she replied, thinking what an inappropriate name Tidy was for the woman. "I haven't really had the chance to meet anyone much yet. We've been so busy with the house."

"Oh, well, I daresay you'll get to meet folk now. We've got plenty going on around here. Coffee mornings, jumble sales and things in the village hall; bingo and quiz evenings and such like. Depends how much you want to join in."

"Of course," murmured Beth, not knowing quite what to say.

There was a moment's awkward silence, then, from behind the woman, a short, balding man with a big beer belly appeared, wiping his forehead with a large hanky. He looked vaguely familiar, but Beth couldn't remember where she had seen him before.

"I'll tell you, Maureen; those sacks of spuds get heavier! Morning…" He nodded at Beth.

"This is Mrs Ellis who's moved into Malthorp House," said Maureen. "This is my husband, Bill."

Beth suddenly remembered where she had seen the man before.

"I think we've met," she said. "In the pub – the Blacksmith's Arms? My husband Adam and I were in there the evening we came up to view the house." She gave a short laugh. "I seem to remember you warned him against buying it."

Bill looked a little uncomfortable and Maureen shot him a swift disparaging glance.

"Probably half-cut, he was. 'E's always on about that house. Just 'cos his old Gran used to tell tall stories about the place."

"They wasn't tall stories, Maur, you know they wasn't. She worked there as a girl. Why, even your Mum used to say she wouldn't dare go near the place after dark. There's something amiss with it, always has been."

"Oh, go on with you, you old fool. You'll be putting the fear of God into poor Mrs Ellis. She'll be thinking we're a lot of superstitious country bumpkins."

"Not at all," interrupted Beth, hastily. "What sort of stories did your Gran tell you, Mr Tidy?"

"Never you mind that now, Bill," said Maureen as he opened his mouth. "Hurry up and get the rest of that milk up. I need to get it out before we get our morning rush. We haven't got time for all this chit-chat."

The look she gave Beth was distinctly frosty and she decided not to push her luck. There was no point in getting on bad terms with Maureen Tidy on her first proper visit to the village. But she was determined to try and get Bill Tidy on his own one day and find out more about Malthorp House's reputation. Perhaps something had happened there long ago that had left some sort of mark on the place. She knew Adam would be annoyed if he knew her concerns; he, like his father, believed that everything had a rational explanation, but Beth was beginning to wonder.

She untied Finn and made her way back along the road. She had noticed when driving back through the village that there was a path that led along the wall at the side of the church, which she was pretty sure was a short-cut to Malthorp. She decided to give it a try. As she walked along it, she noticed a small gate set into the wall; just beyond it a silver-haired man in a checked shirt and tatty jeans was vigorously pulling up weeds between the rows of ancient lichened gravestones. He straightened up and put his hands to his back with a groan. He caught her eye and smiled ruefully.

"I often wonder why the Good Lord saw fit to make these grow so much stronger and more prolific each year!" He came towards her and she saw he was younger than she had first thought and rather nice-looking. Finn jumped up and laid his paws on the gate, wagging his tail. "My, you're a fine chap, aren't you?" He stroked the dog's head. Finn's eyes sparkled as his pink tongue lolled out in what looked like a cheeky grin. The man smiled at Beth. "I'm Peter Bowers, by the way, the vicar of St Andrew's."

"Beth Ellis," she smiled back, "and this is Finn. It's nice to meet you. I've been meaning to come and look round the church. We've just recently moved into Malthorp House."

Peter Bowers looked a bit sheepish.

"I knew that there were new people in there. I'm so sorry I haven't called in yet – it's on my to-do list, but that just seems to grow longer every day. Please forgive me." He looked so crestfallen that Beth laughed.

"Don't worry, we've been busy too. The church is beautiful."

"It is rather splendid. Do you want to come and look inside it now? We have a very fine hammer-beam roof and a rather interesting rood-screen. Fifteenth century you know."

"I'd love to, but I do have to get back. We're taking our sons to Beaulieu today and I have to prepare a picnic."

His eyes lit up.

"The Motor Museum? How splendid! One of my favourite places. How old are your sons?"

"Danny's coming up to twelve and Jamie's seven. They've been before, but they really loved it." She hesitated. "Can you tell me if this path cuts through to Malthorp?"

"Yes, it does. Look, I don't know if you are churchgoers, but do come to the service tomorrow if you'd like to. We are a very friendly community here and we have a special children's service during our main one; the children have stories and colour in pictures; your youngest might enjoy it."

"Thank you," said Beth. "I'll mention it to my husband; I'm sure we'd all love to come." She hadn't been to church since she was a child and still had strong doubts about the existence of God but maybe it was time to give it a try. After all, it was an integral part of the village community and it might be good for the boys to have the experience, though she had slight reservations about how Jamie would cope. She found herself liking the vicar immensely; he was so friendly and enthusiastic.

She said goodbye and set off home, hoping that Adam would be coming with them to Beaulieu and that he would like the idea of going to church the next day. The path came out just near Malthorp on the opposite side of the road and, as she reached the entrance gates to the house, she glanced up at the stone lions. Even in daylight they looked sinister, streaked with green lichen, as though both were glaring balefully at her. I must speak to Adam about getting them cleaned, she thought as she walked past them and along the winding drive. About halfway down, Finn suddenly stopped and growled. Beth tugged on the lead.

"Come on, boy! What is it?"

Finn continued to growl; he stared into the thick rhododendron bushes and his hackles rose. Beth frowned.

"Finn! Come on, stop that! What have you seen? Is it a rabbit or something in there?" She tried to peer through the thick, glossy leaves, but could see nothing. Then she heard a stifled giggle. "Danny? Jamie? Is that you two, playing tricks?"

Suddenly, Finn gave a frightened yelp. He pulled hard on the lead and it flew out of Beth's hand. He took off down the drive towards the house.

"Finn!" Beth shouted but he had gone. She frowned. What on earth could have spooked him and made him act that way? A cloud blocked out the sun and she shivered suddenly, feeling uncomfortably as if someone was watching her. She snapped herself out of it. It was her imagination, that's all it was. Bill Tidy had obviously spooked her with his talk of Malthorp's mysterious past. Finn was fine; he'd probably just been scared by a fox or something in the undergrowth.

"I'd better get back and start this picnic," she said out loud as she started walking. The sun broke through the clouds again as she came to the end of the drive and her unease vanished as she gazed at Malthorp, serene and lovely, before her. We are so lucky to have this, she thought happily – sod Bill Tidy and his stupid insinuations!

Adam was at the front door with the boys, fussing Finn, who seemed to have quite recovered from whatever had frightened him. He smiled as she approached and Beth was relieved to see him looking relaxed and happy.

"The boys and I have had our breakfast and are raring to go," he said. "I think Ma is getting ready – she didn't want anything to eat – says she had a really bad night, but she still wants to come. Do you want some help with the picnic?"

"Yes please. I'm so glad you feel up to coming and I do hope Audrey's going to be okay. It will be a fairly lively day with these two."

"I'm sure she'll be fine. Danny, take Jamie upstairs and make sure he cleans his teeth and goes to the toilet, please. And don't forget *your* teeth either," he shouted as the boys ran into the house. Beth laughed.

"I'm really looking forward to today," she said as she sliced open the rolls and began buttering them. "By the way, I met the local vicar; he seems very nice. He wants us to go to the church service tomorrow. I thought it might be a good thing to do – get our faces known and meet some of the villagers."

Adam pulled a wry face as he opened the fridge door and took out some ham.

"Mm… I'm not so sure. Church isn't particularly my thing these days and I don't see Jamie sitting quietly through a church service. Come to that, I don't know that Danny would either."

Beth felt a stab of disappointment. For some reason that she couldn't fathom, she felt that going to the church tomorrow was important.

"Peter Bowers, the vicar, said they had a special service for the younger children. Why don't we at least give it a try, Adam. We can always take Jamie out if it doesn't work out."

"I think going to church would be a very good idea."

Audrey had come to the door behind Adam. She stared at Finn distastefully as he wagged his tail at her. She was dressed immaculately as usual in a cream linen two-piece suit, hair and make-up flawless. But Beth could see that behind the mask her face looked strained and drawn.

"Are you feeling better, Audrey?" she inquired politely.

"I'm fine, my dear. Just a touch too much sun yesterday. I think. As I was saying, I think church is an excellent idea. You haven't been for far too long, Adam. When you were a child you all went regularly."

"Yes, but in fairness we didn't really have a choice, and we had to listen to old Duggan droning on for hours. His sermons had to have been the most boring in the world. All I remember is coughing to try and cover up the fact that my tummy was rumbling – I couldn't wait to get home for Sunday roast."

"Really, Adam!" Audrey exclaimed. "That's just the sort of remark I would expect from Simon. You know you used to tell me how much you enjoyed going."

Adam cast his eyes up in mock exasperation. "Okay, okay, we'll go. Now come on, we'd better get this picnic done or we'll have rebellion from Danny. He's already put his order in."

"Just one thing…" Audrey looked a little embarrassed. "I… I hope you don't mind, Beth, but I've asked an old friend of mine down tomorrow. She lives in Winchester and I haven't seen her for a while. Will it be any problem if she comes for lunch?"

Beth and Adam exchanged glances. They knew what Audrey's friends could be like.

"Well – er – no, that should be fine," said Adam. "Beth?"

Beth saw to her surprise that her mother-in-law looked rather nervous and uncomfortable, which was very unlike her. She made herself smile warmly.

"Of course, it's alright!" she said. "I'll put the roast in before we go to church, so we'll eat about two. What time's she arriving?"

"At about one. Her name's Gloria – Gloria Nash. I'm sure you'll like her; she's a very interesting woman." Audrey's voice had resumed its normal confidence, but Beth was sure she detected a note of relief as well.

Oh well, she thought, as she started to fill the rolls with ham and cheese, let's hope Gloria Nash will keep Audrey happy for the day.

CHAPTER 21

The little church was surprisingly full as Beth, Adam, Audrey and the boys entered it the following day. Jamie clutched Beth's hand, staring wide-eyed around him in wonder at the narrow wooden pews with their carved angel's heads, the stained-glass windows filled with brightly-coloured figures and the stone pulpit surmounted by a lectern in the shape of a brass eagle.

"Magnificent roof," whispered Adam, and Audrey nodded in agreement.

"Very impressive," she murmured. "Though I think our church at home is a little more in proportion."

Their day at Beaulieu had been an overall success, although Audrey had not been at all interested in the wonderful display of cars. However, she was very happy to go with Beth and look around the Palace House and gardens, which were resplendent with spring flowers. Whilst they did that, Adam took the boys on the monorail and the open-top bus. After their picnic there was just time for the two of them to have a ride on the go-karts before they left, tired but happy. Much to Adam and Beth's relief, Jamie had shown no signs of having a temper tantrum this time round.

Beth saw Peter Bowers by the choir stalls, talking animatedly to a plump woman in a burgundy chorister's robe. He raised a hand in cheery acknowledgment and Beth smiled and nodded. A few people smiled and nodded a greeting as they took their seats towards the back of the church. Danny nudged Adam and whispered loudly.

"Dad, do I *have* to sing the hymns? Only, I don't think I'll know them. We have to sing some in assembly at school, but they're always the same ones."

Adam smiled reassuringly.

"Don't worry, Dan. I won't know them either so we can sing out of tune together."

"Look Jamie," whispered Beth. "There's the little room where you go to hear stories and do colouring with the other children. Would you like to do that?"

Jamie didn't respond. His expressionless gaze was fixed on the altar which was adorned by two silver candlesticks. Just then the woman who'd been talking to the vicar approached them. She had a pleasant, open face and her brown eyes twinkled behind her gold-rimmed spectacles as she said,

"Hello, you must be the Ellis family. I'm Janet Bowers, Peter's wife. He told me you might be coming this morning. So glad you could make it!"

"Thank you," said Beth. "I'm Beth and this is my husband, Adam. These are our two boys, Danny and Jamie. And this is Audrey, Adam's mother."

Janet beamed benevolently.

"So lovely to meet you all. And I do hope that Jamie and Danny will come to our children's service. We call the children out just before the sermon and hold the service in that room there. We have a story and then the children generally colour in a picture or two. We've been making a collage all about the history of St Andrew's."

"I'm sure they would love to come and join in," Beth replied, ignoring Danny's look of anguish. "Won't that be lovely, Jamie?"

Jamie looked up at Janet with his solemn blue eyes and nodded. "Jamie likes colouring."

"Good," she said, smiling warmly at him. "Well, I'll see you then." She hurried off.

"*Mum!*" began Danny indignantly.

"Now, Danny, you know Jamie won't go without you. Please don't make a fuss. Just go with him this once, please."

"Okay," he sighed. "As long as nobody at school gets to hear that I went to a kid's service, did colouring and listened to a *story!*"

Audrey frowned and regarded him frostily but Beth and Adam exchanged amused glances. A couple hurried past them and took their seats near the front of the church and Beth recognised Maureen and Bill Tidy from the village shop. She was about to point them out to Adam when the church organ began to play, heralding the beginning of the service.

All went well at first. Despite his fears, the first hymn was one that Danny knew, and he sang at the top of his voice, eliciting amused glances from the surrounding worshippers. Audrey was not so impressed as her rather disapproving expression showed, but Danny was too busy enjoying himself to notice. Peter Bowers spoke well; his voice resonated around the church clearly as he welcomed everyone to the service and Jamie sat quietly listening, with his eyes fixed on the vicar as if fascinated. Beth felt very proud of both of them.

Just before the sermon, all the children in the church got up and began to quietly file out into the little room at the back. Janet Bowers smiled at the boys in passing and Danny sighed resignedly but got up and held out his hand to Jamie.

"Come on, Spud," he whispered. "Let's go."

Jamie shook his head firmly. "No, Jamie stay *here*."

Beth bit her lip. She had been worried that this might happen.

"Come on, sweetheart," she whispered encouragingly. "Go with Danny and listen to the stories and colour in some pictures for Mummy. You can come back in a minute."

Jamie's lip trembled. "No, don't want to. Jamie stay."

Adam leant forward, frowning a little.

"Hey, Tiger! Do as you're told and go with Danny."

"Leave him, Adam," whispered Beth. "It really doesn't matter if he doesn't want to."

Audrey glared at Beth. Really, she did let that child get away with murder. Well, she was on Adam's side in this. She leant forward, frowning fiercely at Jamie.

"Come along, James," she hissed. "Do as you are told. You are being a very naughty boy!"

Jamie shook his head and glared at her; his mouth set in an obstinate line.

"Audrey…" Beth began, but before she could say anything else, Audrey took matters into her own hands. She rose and, pushing past Adam, grabbed hold of Jamie's arm to pull him to his feet. Jamie let out a piercing scream like a train whistle, but Audrey ignored him and continued to try and tug him to his feet. She succeeded and he half-fell, only Adam's legs preventing him from falling to his knees. He straightened up and turned towards her; she recoiled, shocked as she saw the malice in his eyes.

"*Leave us alone, you stupid, ugly old bitch! Curse you to hell!*"

The congregation turned to stare in disbelief as his words reverberated around the church. Adam and Beth froze, hardly able to comprehend that this was their small son speaking; his eyes blazed with hatred and the timbre of his voice was completely different as he spat more vitriolic profanities at Audrey who stood, white-faced with shock. Then, without warning, Jamie wrenched his arm from Audrey's grasp, pushed by Adam and Danny, passed by where Janet Bowers stood, transfixed, and ran headlong out of the door.

⸎

Beth, Adam and Danny dashed through the stone porch and out of the door after Jamie, but there was no sign of him. "Jamie!" Beth screamed.

"I'll go this way," said Adam, his voice tight. Beth could see that he was close to tears and felt her own throat tighten. She shook herself mentally. This was no time to break down. Jamie could have run off anywhere; they had to find him before he came to any harm. Danny tugged at her arm.

"Where do you want me to go, Mum? I can run back home and see if he's there."

Adam nodded. "That's a good idea, Dan, but let's see if he's anywhere about here first."

He set off round to the left side of the church. Beth and Danny went to the right, along the little gravel path. Gravestones stretched from the path right to the boundary wall. There were yew trees dotted here and there, monstrously large, casting deep shadows over the graveyard. Beth shivered.

"Jamie!" she shouted. "Where are you? Come out, darling, you're not in any trouble. Don't be frightened."

There was no answer. It was suddenly eerily quiet as a cloud passed across the sun, making the shadows appear deeper and darker. Even the birds seemed to have fallen silent.

"Jamie!" cried Beth again, but there was still no response and she felt sick with despair. Then, out of the corner of her eye, she caught a flash of blue in the far corner of the churchyard. Her heart leapt. Jamie had been wearing a bright blue sweatshirt.

"Adam!" she yelled. She and Danny raced over the uneven grass between the gravestones. Beth caught her foot on a tussock and nearly went flying, but recovered her footing. She reached the corner. Jamie was huddled in a tight ball on the rough grass and she knelt down and gathered him in her arms. Adam reached her a few seconds later.

"Thank God," he said shakily. "Is he okay?"

Beth looked up through tear-filled eyes "I… I think so. Jamie… Jamie, sweetheart?"

Her son lifted his head, his face streaked with dirt and tears. He took a deep, shuddering breath.

"I – I'm sorry, Mummy. I didn't mean to do it."

Beth hugged him tighter and Adam rested his hand gently on the boy's dark, shiny hair, shocked and bewildered. What was happening? He had never heard Jamie apologise for anything before. In fact, one of the things that Tom Mitchell had told them was that severely autistic children like Jamie very rarely understood the concept of feeling sorry for their behaviour. The other thing that astounded him was that Jamie had used 'I' instead of referring to himself by name as he had always done. He wondered if Beth had noticed as, still holding Jamie, she stood up slowly. The little boy wrapped his arms and legs around her tightly and buried his face in her neck as Janet Bowers came hurrying up to them.

"Oh, you've found him, thank the Lord. Is he alright?"

"Yes, just a little distressed," said Adam. "Mrs Bowers, I can't tell you how sorry we are… we should have told you that Jamie's autistic. We didn't realise that he would get so upset. It's so out of character for him to use that sort of language."

"Please, don't worry," she replied briskly. "It certainly livened up a dull Sunday." She smiled ruefully. "I think, though, that it may be a bit of a talking-point amongst some of our parishioners for a while. Please don't get upset." She hesitated, "Mind you, I think your mother is still in shock. I left her sitting in the vestry. One of our ladies made her a cup of tea, but I think she could do with a strong brandy!"

"I'd better go and face the music and see how she is," said Adam ruefully. "Come on, Dan."

"Are you alright, Mrs Ellis?" asked Janet. "You look very white. Do you want me to stay here with you?"

"No, it's okay, I'm fine," said Beth. "You go on. I'll just stay here with Jamie for a few more minutes, until he's calmed down. Then we'll walk home."

"Very well. I'll come back up with you, Mr Ellis, and we'll see if your mother is feeling fit enough to walk back to Malthorp. Otherwise, I can always run her back in the car."

"That's very kind of you. Sure you'll be okay, Beth?"

She nodded as he reached down and squeezed her hand. He ruffled Jamie's hair gently. "See you later, old chap."

Beth watched them walk off up the path and gave a long sigh. Jamie was still clinging desperately to her and she put him down gently.

"Are you okay now, darling? Shall we walk home slowly?"

He nodded, his head still down. Beth took his hand and led him past the short row of gravestones that jutted out from the corner. As they drew level with the last of them, she noticed that his shoelace was undone and bent down to tie it. As she stood up, she saw that she was standing in front of a large gravestone topped by a weeping stone angel. She gave an involuntary shudder. She had always hated stone angels, ever since she had been small and had been running through the local graveyard with a friend. They had rounded a corner and were confronted by a large stone angel on top of a monument, hand uplifted, gazing sightlessly at the sky. To her childish eyes it had seemed massive and threatening, and she had suffered from nightmares for weeks afterwards in which the angel had come to life and pursued her down endless paths. This angel, however, was quite a lot smaller and covered in lichen. Its face had been partly worn away by the weather and it seemed to Beth to be smirking at her in an almost obscene way. Her gaze involuntarily dropped downwards to read the words etched deeply into the gravestone's surface:

> **Here lies**
> **VALENTINE EDWARD TAYLOR**
> **Beloved Son of Beatrice and Edward Taylor**
> **Born: 16th April 1902**
> **Cruelly taken: 18th May 1911**
> **Sleep today, Oh Early Fallen,**
> **in thy Green and Narrow bed.**
> **Dirges, from the Yew and Cypress,**
> **mingle with the Tears we shed.**

Beth felt a chill in her very bones as she stared at the words.

Valentine Edward Taylor. Early fallen. A young boy, 'cruelly taken'.

Valentine. The same name as Jamie's 'friend'. She looked down at her small son and saw that he, too, was staring at the stone. Coincidence? It had to be because Valentine didn't exist. He was a figment of Jamie's imagination, wasn't he? The same as her encounter with Kevin had been. She took Jamie's hand firmly in hers once more and led him away, towards the path home.

She didn't see the small figure in the darkest corner of the churchyard who watched them as they walked away.

Nor hear him as he whispered quietly:

"Come back soon and play with me, Jamie."

But Jamie heard.

CHAPTER 22

When Beth and Jamie arrived home, there was a delicious aroma of roasting meat and Adam and Danny were in the kitchen preparing the vegetables for lunch. Audrey was upstairs in her room. Beth and Adam exchanged concerned glances.

"She says she'll be down for lunch," said Adam. "I think she's been trying to ring Gloria Nash to put her off coming but it may be too late. Hello, Jamie, old son, you okay now?" He ruffled his son's dark hair fondly. Danny opened his mouth to say something but Beth shot him a warning glance and shook her head. Jamie was best left to forget what had happened.

"Oh Lord, I'd forgotten all about Gloria!" she exclaimed. "Well, we'll just have to make the best of it and try and have a normal family lunch." She smiled down at her son, who was yawning and rubbing his eyes. We're having your favourite, Jamie, roast pork and crackling!"

Jamie yawned and rubbed his eyes again.

"Jamie not hungry. Want to go to sleep, Mummy."

Beth and Adam exchanged glances. Maybe it *would* be better to keep Jamie out of Audrey's way for a while and he did look very pale and tired.

"I'll take him up to bed," said Beth. "Are you two okay to carry on with lunch?

"Course, Mum," Danny said, his mouth full of carrot. "You know how I love cooking."

"You mean you love eating half of it before it's cooked!" said Adam, and laughed at Danny's hurt expression. "Have a good sleep, Jamie."

Almost as soon as Beth laid Jamie down, he fell asleep, thumb plugged firmly in his mouth. She felt a rush of protective love for him. He looked so beautiful lying there and she found it hard to remember the transformation that had taken place earlier in the church. She frowned as she thought of the child's grave they had seen in the churchyard. Surely it had to be a coincidence? Was there some way she could find out who this Valentine was and why he had died so young? Tomorrow, she decided, she would have a word with Peter Bowers. He was probably the best person to ask and if he didn't know he might be able to help her find out.

As she made her way downstairs the front doorbell rang. Lord, she thought, that will be Gloria Nash. Opening the door she was confronted with a well-built woman of about fifty, dressed in a bright pink top and a black, ankle-length skirt. She had faded blonde hair, piled up high on her head, fastened with a black shiny comb. She gazed at Beth through large pink-rimmed glasses and gave a beaming smile.

"Hello! I'm Gloria, Audrey's friend. You are expecting me I hope?"

"Of course, we are. It's nice to meet you. I'm Beth, Audrey's daughter-in-law. Do come in."

In the hallway there was a small, awkward pause.

"I'm sorry," said Beth. "I – I think Audrey's upstairs having a rest. We had a bit of an upset earlier; I'm sure she'll be down shortly. Would you like to come into the living room? I'll get you a drink."

"What a wonderful house," said Gloria staring around. "An upset you say?" She frowned slightly and closed her eyes. "You know there is a strong sense of happiness and contentment since you and your family have moved in here. But beneath that… underlying, there is also a powerful feeling of anger and deep grief." She blinked and smiled at Beth who was looking somewhat bemused. "I'm so sorry, my dear, I don't know if Audrey's told you but I am sensitive to these things. You see, I'm a natural psychic medium. Now what were you asking me?"

Before Beth could answer she heard Audrey's voice from the bottom of the stairs.

"Gloria! Oh, my dear how wonderful to see you. I'm so glad you could come. I see you've already met my daughter-in-law. We'll have drinks in the living room if that's alright with you, Beth, and please do send Adam in to meet Gloria. Come on through, Gloria."

She ushered her friend through the living-room door and closed it firmly in Beth's face. Beth shook her head wryly. She didn't know whether to laugh or be annoyed at Audrey's overbearing attitude, but she certainly seemed to have recovered from the shock of earlier. She made her way back to the kitchen and told Adam, though she left out what Gloria had said about the house.

"Honestly, your mother made me feel like a paid servant. She's definitely feeling better. You'd better go and meet the wonderful Gloria who, by the way, is one of her strange psychic cronies, and pour them a drink. You, too, Danny. I'll sort the rest of the lunch out."

"Oh, Mum do I have to? I'll meet her at lunchtime. Okay," he sighed as he saw Beth's expression. "I'm going, but you'd better give me the best bit of crackling to make up for it!"

Lunch turned out, on the whole, to be a far easier affair than Beth had expected. Gloria and Audrey chatted away about various spiritualist meetings they had attended and, apart from an occasional comment, Beth and Adam half-listened to the conversation, exchanging an occasional wry glance. Nothing was mentioned about the incident in the church, much to Beth and Adam's relief. Adam had opened a couple of bottles of wine, but Gloria would drink only water.

"I don't touch alcohol, dear," she murmured "I find it interferes with the force of the spirits."

Danny, chewing blissfully on a piece of crackling, stared at her curiously.

"Is it a bit like Star Wars?" he asked innocently. Gloria frowned.

"Sorry, dear, I don't quite follow."

"Well, you know, are you a bit like Obi-Wan-Kenobi?" He

swallowed the crackling and deepened his voice. "May the force be with you!"

"Well, really!" Audrey glared at her grandson. "This is a very serious subject, Daniel, and if you are going to make facetious remarks like that then perhaps you had better go and finish your lunch in the kitchen."

"Sorry Grandma," said Danny, not quite sure what facetious meant, but biting his lip and trying not to grin. Gloria caught his eye and laughed.

"Don't worry Danny," she said. "I suppose it *is* a bit like Star Wars. It's all about feelings and intuition, like a sixth sense, you see."

Danny didn't, but he nodded politely anyway. Beth found herself suddenly warming to Gloria and smiled at her.

"I'll get dessert," she said. "Hope you like lemon cheesecake, Gloria?"

"Love it, dear, thank you. That was a wonderful meal."

Audrey glared again at Danny. Honestly, that child got away with far too much. She held out her empty glass to Adam, who half filled it with a wry glance.

"I think Gloria and I will go out for a look round the garden after lunch," she said rather icily. "Then we can have a good chat without any interruptions."

"Good idea," Adam said, trying not to smile. "I'll just pop out and see if Beth needs a hand." He picked up the other bottle of wine as he went out and joined Beth in the kitchen. She was sliding the cheesecake on to a serving plate.

"Oh, get the cream out of the fridge, would you, Adam," she said. She took a serving knife out of the drawer. "What do you think of our Gloria?"

"I think she's quite nice. Though, as you know, I get a bit fed up with all this spiritualist nonsense. I had enough of it when I was growing up, to be honest. Ma's well away with the wine, so I thought I'd better bring the other bottle out – she doesn't seem to know when to stop these days."

"We'd better get back and rescue Danny," said Beth. "I think your mother's getting a bit fraught with him and you never know what he's going to come out with next."

"Don't worry," replied Adam, grinning. "He'll be too interested in the cheesecake to say much more. Anyway, I think Gloria's taken a bit of a shine to our Danny."

Up in his bedroom, Jamie awoke suddenly. His curtains were drawn and for a moment he thought it was night-time. Then he realised there was a chink of sunlight coming through the gap where they didn't quite meet and remembered that Beth had put him to bed before lunch. He was aware that firstly, he was very hungry and secondly that he needed the toilet really badly so he threw back the covers and padded over to his bathroom. He was peeing blissfully into the toilet, when he became aware that he was not alone. Finishing, he zipped up his trousers and turned around. Valentine stood there, eyes shining through his wire spectacles.

"*Come with me, Jamie,*" he said, in his funny voice. "*Time to play!*"

CHAPTER 23

Audrey and Gloria wandered round the garden for a while in silence; earlier Audrey had told her friend everything that had happened, including Jamie's strange outburst in the church. Gloria had listened without interruption and now appeared to be deep in thought.

"Well?" Audrey demanded. "What do you think? Are there malevolent spirits here? Is the child possessed?"

"I think 'malevolent' might be a bit strong," said Gloria. "Certainly, I can sense great unhappiness in the house and, yes, there is definitely something here that is not at peace. Perhaps I need to talk to Jamie to see if I can get any sense of something that might be communicating through him."

"I tell you, Gloria, the boy is evil," said Audrey quietly. "I knew it right from the moment he was born; knew there was something wrong with him. Those *eyes*, they look right through you. And after what happened today in the church… if you could have seen and heard him! I tell you, Gloria, I firmly believe that children like him should be locked away at the very least. Years ago, he would have been burned at the stake!"

"Now, Audrey, that's a bit strong," Gloria said. "I believe you told me he's autistic? These children need special help; they are often savants and have very special talents. Because of their condition they can be far more receptive to the spirit world than others."

"I suppose you may be right," sighed Audrey. "But if you had been there today…" They had reached the outskirts of the woods where Danny had built his den. Under a massive oak tree some previous owner had installed a narrow wooden bench. Audrey sank down onto it. "I feel so very weary, my dear. It has been a very trying few days. I think I may go home tomorrow."

"That might be wise," said Gloria. "I do feel very strongly that there is a certain amount of hostility and resentment towards you."

"I know. I have always felt from the start that Beth resents my closeness to my son. I've always made excuses for her and put it down to her unstable upbringing, but lately I have noticed that she has become positively disagreeable towards me. I do hope she isn't trying to turn Adam against me."

"I didn't mean Beth, my dear. It's here in this house; there is definitely some sort of negative aura surrounding it. I believe something very tragic has happened here in the past and if I could communicate with whatever unhappy souls are still here, I think…" She paused. "What was that?"

"I didn't hear anything."

"Something… in those bushes… maybe a bird or an animal… Oh!"

The bushes parted and a small dark head popped out.

"James!" Audrey leant forward, her lips tightening disapprovingly. "What on earth do you think you are doing? How dare you hide in those bushes listening to a private conversation! You should still be shut away in your room after the way you behaved earlier."

Gloria walked towards the bushes. "Now, now, Audrey, I'm sure he meant no harm. Come out, Jamie. I'd like to talk to you."

Jamie looked at them impassively. He crawled out from the bushes, stood up and stared at them blankly for a moment, then he turned to Gloria and smiled angelically. His gaze held hers and, despite herself, she felt a frisson of fear. His eyes left hers and travelled upwards into the fresh green leaves of the oak tree under which Audrey sat. His gaze was so intense that Gloria felt compelled to follow his eyes.

"What is it, dear? What are you looking at?"

Jamie raised his small hand and pointed.

"Valentine," he said and gave her a sudden dazzling smile. She followed his finger and saw… and saw…

There was a sudden sharp crack followed by a terrible tearing, creaking sound and a massive branch broke off and fell from the old tree straight onto the bench where Audrey sat. For a moment

Gloria stood, frozen with shock, then she dashed forward.

"Audrey! Oh, my God ... *Audrey!*" She scrabbled frantically, sobbing as she tried to part the mass of dense green leaves and twigs, scratching her face so that the blood ran down her cheek, but she couldn't reach her. She pulled back and turned to where Jamie had been standing just a few moments before.

"Quickly, go and get help!"

But neither he, nor the other one she had seen, were anywhere to be seen. Once more she tried in vain to find Audrey but it was no use and, abandoning her efforts, she turned and ran stumbling and sobbing back to the house.

CHAPTER 24

Audrey's funeral took place in the middle of May. An inquest had been opened and adjourned, but it was established that she had almost certainly died instantly. The oak tree had been thoroughly examined by an expert and declared sound, so it was a mystery as to why the branch had suddenly fallen.

Beth and Adam had decided to leave the boys with Geoff and Laura when they travelled to Bracknell for the funeral, feeling it would be better if they did not attend. Debbie had agreed to look after Finn and they were going to stay with John overnight, partly as they wanted to give him all the support they could and partly because the funeral was not until one, and it would mean travelling back late in the day. The sun was shining in a cloudless blue sky as they reached the lovely parish church in Easthampstead. Adam felt tears well up as Audrey's coffin was lifted out of the waiting hearse. He stood, head bowed, with his father and three brothers as it was carried past them, while Beth stood a little behind them with Kate, Neil's wife. She still felt a sense of disbelief that Audrey had gone. She felt terrible guilt, too; for when Gloria Nash had come bursting into the kitchen to tell them that there had been an accident involving Audrey, her initial reaction had been one of annoyance and impatience. Before realising the true horror of the situation, she had believed only that her mother-in-law was spoiling yet more of the day. Gloria, her face scratched and bloody, was hysterical and had been jabbering incoherently about two boys, and it wasn't until after the police and paramedics had come that she had thought to check on Jamie. She found him peacefully asleep still and felt a rush of relief that he had not been near to see the awful event. He had woken as she was bending over him and smiled sleepily. She tried not to think about the fact that, as she was straightening his bed up that night, she had found what she was certain was a young oak leaf under his pillow. Coincidence, she was sure of it, but still a little niggling doubt had remained. She had tried to talk to Gloria on the phone a few days later to ask her what she had meant by 'the boys', but the woman had cut her off abruptly, saying she did not feel able to discuss it. Before ending the conversation, she had told Beth that she would be unable to attend the funeral as, after the inquest, she would be going away for a few weeks.

The church service was very moving and afterwards they travelled the two short miles to the crematorium. After the brief service there, Beth and Kate left the family who were speaking to the many friends and relatives who had attended and made their way back to the house to make sure that the caterers had everything prepared for the gathering. After a while people began arriving and were greeted with a glass of sherry. At first the atmosphere was subdued but then people began to chat and the mood lightened a little. Meanwhile, Beth and Kate were kept busy offering sandwiches and sausage rolls whilst Adam and the others mingled. It was very hot in the house and she noticed that quite a few people had drifted outside so, after checking that Kate was alright to carry on, she stepped out into the garden to get a breath of air. She found John sitting in his favourite deckchair in the shade of the lilac tree and sat down on the grass next to him. She reached up and put her hand on his arm.

"I know it's a stupid question, John, but are you okay?"

He smiled fondly at her.

"It's silly, I know, but I was just thinking how Audrey would have been in her element today. She loved social gatherings, even funerals. Seems rather unfair that she can't be here."

Beth reached up and squeezed his hand.

"I'm so sorry, John. We still feel responsible somehow; if she hadn't been with us…"

"Nonsense, my dear, it was a tragic accident, that was all. And they said it was very quick; she'd have known nothing about it. Please, you really must not think like that."

"Have you decided what you are going to do now, John? I don't like the thought of you being here on your own." She paused. "I know you may not want to, in view of what's happened, but you do know that you would be more than welcome to come and stay with us for as long as you want?"

"Bless you for that, and it wouldn't be a problem for me to do so, but I think I will just stay here at present. I've got you and Adam staying tonight; David's back off abroad in a few days so he'll also be here until he goes. Neil and Kate have already offered to have me stay with them and even Simon said he would keep me company, but I'd just as soon be on my own for the next couple of weeks at least. When I'm feeling up to it, I will come and see you and spend time with my lovely grandsons but not just now." He stood up and smiled. "If you'll excuse me, my dear, I'd better go in and talk to people."

As Beth got up, he gave her a brief hug and walked briskly across the lawn and through the French doors. Beth knew she should go back in and be with Adam but she felt she couldn't bear to be indoors for the moment, so she walked over and stared down at the flowerbeds that Audrey had so lovingly tendered.

"Hello Beth."

She looked up to see Simon standing there. He lit a cigarette.

"I thought you'd given up smoking?"

"I had, until this. Poor old Ma…" He shook his head, exhaling a cloud of smoke. "Hell of a thing; I still can't really take it in. How are you, Beth?"

"I'm okay, but Adam's taken it very hard. We both feel so terrible that it happened when she was staying with us. Your father's been marvellous though. I just hope he'll be able to cope on his own."

"Oh, Dad's pretty resilient, you know." He paused. "This may not be the time to ask but I wondered if I could come down and see you sometime soon, Beth."

"Of course. I'll have to let you know when Adam's got a weekend free. He's pretty tied up for the next couple of weeks."

"Actually, it was you I wanted to see. I thought of coming down during the week, if that's okay. I've been doing a bit more research into the Websters and, Beth, I think I may have found something out about your father."

"My *dad?*" Beth stared at him. "But how did you know – I mean I don't think I've ever mentioned anything about my dad to you."

"Oh, I think Ma told me something about it all, a long time ago," said Simon casually. "Anyway, I'm going to do a bit more digging and then I'll let you know. Say, end of next week?"

"Yes, please, Simon. I can't take it in. I think I've just put all that out of my mind, but I suppose it would be good to at least find out what happened to him and why he never contacted me. I must tell Adam when today is over with."

"Oh, I should keep it under your hat for the moment," Simon said easily. "I would really hate to get your hopes up for nothing. I'll ring you."

He sauntered off. Beth stared after him. Could it be that he had really found out what had happened to her dad after all these years? As a child she had hoped and prayed that he would come for her, but as time had gone by, she had given up any hopes that she would ever find out why he had deserted her.

She couldn't wait to find out what Simon had discovered.

CHAPTER 25

Beth dropped Jamie off at Hopelands with a feeling of relief. They'd had a very bad weekend with him following Audrey's funeral. Although he had been fine with Geoff and Laura, as soon as he saw Beth and Adam he had thrown one almighty temper tantrum. They had eventually managed to calm him down but that night he was very restless, constantly getting out of bed and calling for Beth. In the end she had resorted to sleeping with him but she hardly slept at all and consequently felt completely shattered. The following day he withdrew into his own world, spending most of it endlessly lining up his toy cars and refusing to eat. That morning he had eaten some breakfast but still seemed very listless and Beth voiced her doubts about sending him to school. Adam thought he should go, especially as Beth was so tired and it was Debbie's day off, so it was with strong reservations that she had been persuaded to take him. She had been prepared for hysterics when she left him with his teacher, but Jamie had gone into his classroom without any trouble, though he was very quiet and subdued. She explained the situation to Marie and Tom and they promised to watch him carefully over the next few days and to ring her straight away if there were any problems.

As she drove back through the village, she decided on an impulse to call at the village shop and see if she could speak to Bill Tidy. She pulled into a parking space opposite the shop. She knew that Monday was usually the day that Maureen went to visit her daughter, so with any luck she wouldn't be there. She was intrigued to find out more about Malthorp House's past history and she felt sure that Bill would be more open to talk if his wife wasn't around.

Sure enough, Bill was on his own. There were no customers to be seen and he was leaning on the counter, deeply engrossed in reading the *Daily Mirror*. He looked up guiltily as the shop bell rang then smiled as he saw her.

"Mrs Ellis! How are you and what can I get for you this fine morning?" He hesitated. "Sorry to hear about your loss, by the way."

"Thank you," said Beth. "I'd like some bacon, please. About a pound."

"Smoked or green?"

"Smoked, please." She watched as he weighed it. "Mr Tidy..."

"Bill, please – nobody calls me Mister round here. There, that do for you?"

"Lovely." He started to wrap it. "Bill – when we first met, in the pub, you told Adam that Malthorp was haunted. You said that your Gran had worked there as a girl and that she had told you some stories about what went on. Can you tell me about that?"

Bill looked a little uncomfortable as he finished wrapping the bacon and put it on the counter.

"That'll be two pounds eighty-nine, please. I don't know as I ought to say anything about that, Mrs Ellis. Maureen wouldn't be happy if she knew I'd talked to you about it. She always says the past is just that – the past – and it should be left dead and buried like the folks as lived then."

"Please, Bill," said Beth as she handed him a five-pound note. She leant forward and smiled persuasively. "I wouldn't say a word to Maureen. It's just that..." she hesitated a moment. "It's just that one or two odd things have happened."

He frowned as he handed over her change.

"You mean besides what happened to poor Mrs Ellis?"

"That was a tragic accident," said Beth, sharply. "No, there have just been one or two unexplained incidences."

"Hmm..." Bill looked unconvinced. He sat back on his stool and folded his arms. "Well, if you really want to know, I'll tell you then. My old Gran, Florrie Baker as she was then, was a kitchen maid up there, back before the First World War and she was always telling us stories about the family. It was the Cartwrights as lived there then; well-to-do they were, at least *she* was – the wife, Beatrice. Her father lived up in the Cotswolds or some such and he'd made his money up north in the cotton mills.

Well, Beatrice married this Richard Cartwright and they had Malthorp built, mostly with her father's money. Her second marriage it was; her first husband died young and she had the one boy by him, about five I believe he was when she married Cartwright." He paused. "My Gran said it was a shame about the little lad. You see, he'd been born not quite right, with a twisted back and withered legs, so he could never walk properly. Went everywhere on crutches or in a wheelchair and Gran said it was pitiful to see him drag himself around. She was good friends with the nursery maid they had there at the time and this girl, Jenny her name was, told Gran that Richard Cartwright hated the boy and treated him horrible, especially after his own boy was born. Kept the lad shut away in the attic, couldn't bear to look at him. He wouldn't even let his mother near him half the time."

"How terrible…" Beth frowned. "What happened to the little boy?"

"He was drowned," said Bill with relish. "Fell down the well near the kitchen garden one day when all the servants were out. Gran said there was a terrible to-do when they came back and the boy was missing. They searched the grounds for hours before they found him. Reckoned he'd leaned over to look down, see, and toppled in. His mother never got over it – she went into what they called a decline and died about a year later. Gran left soon after; said she couldn't bear to stay there a minute longer. She said…" he leaned forward conspiratorially, "…she said that she, and some of the others, *heard* things."

"What sort of things?" asked Beth, shivering despite herself.

"Well, sobbing for one. Reckoned it was Beatrice crying for her son. Not only that, though. She said the cook often heard the sound of the little lad's crutches tapping along the passageway leading to the attic."

"What was his name?" asked Beth, although she was pretty sure she knew the answer. "The boy, I mean."

"It was a funny name… Victor or summit like that, no… Valentine, that were it," said Bill. "Valentine Taylor. I believe he's buried in the churchyard, right near his mother's grave."

The shop bell jangled sharply and Bill jumped guiltily as Maureen bustled through the door.

"Morning, Mrs Ellis. Bill, I told you to put the potatoes out the front and you still haven't done it. Don't tell me you've been that busy?"

"Sorry, Maur, I forgot. I'll do it now. How's Janice?"

"She had to go to the dentist. That's why I haven't been long." She turned to Beth, "How's Mr Ellis? Bearing up, I hope after his sad loss?" She put her head on one side and said, with a hint of relish in her voice, "Had some real bad luck lately haven't you, what with that and your oldest boy's accident?"

Beth suddenly found herself disliking Maureen Tidy very much indeed, but she murmured her thanks and made her exit as quickly as possible. Bill was at the front putting the potatoes in the tray and she smiled reassuringly at him as she passed.

As she walked back towards the car, she thought about what Bill had told her. She remembered the day of Danny's accident, when she had thought she heard the sound of a woman sobbing. Then there had been Audrey's hysterical outburst when she became trapped in the cupboard in the boys' attic playroom. She had said that she had heard a tapping, like a stick. Or could it have been crutches? And, on the day they had brought the boys here for the first time Danny had seen a woman in the garden, a woman dressed in old-fashioned clothes. Jamie had been lost and they had found him in the garden, sitting near what could have been an old well…

Beth stopped by the car and her hands flew up to her mouth as she closed her eyes. An old well. Could it be the very one where Valentine…? She felt faint as nausea rose up into her throat. Jamie had sung that song – that song that she had never heard before…

"Mrs Ellis … Beth? Are you alright?"

She opened her eyes to see the concerned face of Peter Bowers looking at her.

"Mr Bowers, I'm sorry, I just felt a little unwell for a moment."

"Do call me Peter, please. You've gone very pale. Look, come across to the vicarage for a moment. Janet's gone to a Mother's Union meeting but she'll be back soon. I'll make you a cup of tea."

"It's very kind of you, Peter, but I ought to be getting back. I'll be alright in a minute."

"I won't take no for an answer," said Peter firmly. "I don't think you should be driving if you're feeling unwell, and the tea will make you feel a lot better. Come on."

He took her arm and steered her firmly towards the vicarage.

"*Yoo-hoo…* Mrs Ellis!" The strident voice behind them stopped them in their tracks. It was Maureen Tidy, bustling across the road towards them, clutching a brown paper bag.

"You forgot your bacon," she said breathlessly. She peered closely at Beth as she thrust the bag into her hand. "What's up? Not feeling so good, then?"

"Mrs Ellis is feeling a little faint, Maureen, so I'm taking her into the vicarage for a cup of tea," said Peter.

"Oh, is Janet back from her meeting then?" Maureen raised her eyebrows.

"No, but she will be shortly. Please excuse us, Maureen; I think Mrs Ellis needs to sit down."

He turned away and left her standing there staring after them. As they went through the front door, he laughed tersely.

"Dear, oh dear, that woman! You do realise, Beth, it will be all round the village in a matter of hours that you came into the vicarage with me when my wife wasn't here. Before too long we'll be having a full-blown affair! Ah, well, it gives them something to talk about I suppose."

Beth gave a weak smile as he ushered her into the large, untidy kitchen. He cleared a pile of papers off a chair.

"Sit down there and I'll pop the kettle on."

He made the tea and sat down with her. After a couple of sips, the colour started to come back into her face and he nodded approvingly.

"That's better. Now, if you don't mind me saying you seem a little distraught. Can I help at all? I'm a very good listener if you do want to talk about anything?"

She opened her mouth to deny it, but instead found herself pouring out her story. He listened in silence until she had finished.

"So, you feel the house may be haunted by the ghosts of this poor boy and his mother?"

"Yes… no… I really don't know. It's just that so many odd things have happened. There was an incident when I was in London a few weeks ago as well. I thought I saw somebody from my past, someone who I've found out since has been dead for years. It… it was frightening. And then, poor Audrey…" Her eyes filled with tears.

Peter took a large white handkerchief out of his pocket and handed it to her.

"It is clean," he said. "Beth, I know things are very difficult for you at the moment. If you really feel there is a problem with the house, I'd be more than happy to come over and see if I can do anything."

She stared at him.

"An exorcism, you mean?"

He smiled. "No, I'm not qualified to do that, but I could certainly say a few prayers. If there are any poor souls who are not at rest, then it may help."

"Do you believe in ghosts then?" she asked.

"I believe there could be some souls that have not passed over fully into Our Lord's care," he answered quietly. "And I am a great believer in the power of prayer. I'd be more than willing to come over and help you and Adam find peace within the house."

"Adam mustn't know," she said quickly. "He doesn't believe in any of it. He would say that it's all nonsense."

Peter frowned.

"I don't think we can keep it from him, Beth. I wouldn't feel right about that. Look, let's leave it for a few days; see if things settle down."

"Yes," she said, stifling a feeling of disappointment. "Maybe that would be best."

"I'll tell you something, though," he went on. "I believe I have some old papers relating to Malthorp. One of my predecessors collected a lot of stuff when the house was closed up years ago and I think it's in a box in the vestry. If you're happy to wait a moment I'll go and see if I can find it. If it would interest you, that is."

"Yes, it would very much, thank you," said Beth. "I think maybe that the more I can find out about Malthorp, the better."

As he left, she heard Janet's voice in the hallway. There was a low conversation as he obviously explained why Beth was there and a few moments later, Janet bustled in.

"Well, my dear, I hear you and Peter have got the village gossips going! Are you feeling better?"

"Much, thank you. I'm so sorry to have caused all this trouble."

"Oh, stuff and nonsense! I love giving Maureen Tidy something to talk about – she really is the most objectionable woman! One of these days she'll be given enough rope to hang herself, with any luck. Not very Christian, I know, but that's how I feel. Now, how are those two lovely boys of yours?"

She chatted away until Peter came back bearing a large cardboard box.

"Goodness knows what's in it," he said. It's quite heavy so I think there are some books in there as well as papers. I'll carry it over to your car for you."

Janet took Beth's hands as she left.

"Now, don't forget, my dear, we are always here if you need us. If Peter's not around I usually am. If you need anything, don't hesitate to call."

"I will," promised Beth. "Thank you both for being so kind."

Peter put the box on the back seat of the Land Rover.

"Don't forget to let me know if you find anything interesting," he called as she put the car in gear.

Beth raised a hand in a farewell wave, very much aware that Maureen Tidy was standing at the door of her shop tight-lipped, staring at her as she drove away.

CHAPTER 26

It wasn't until a couple of days later, on the Wednesday, that Beth had the chance to explore the contents of the box. For reasons she couldn't quite fathom, she had hidden it up in one of the cupboards in a spare bedroom. Inwardly she justified it by promising herself that if she found anything of interest she would share it with Adam, but she didn't want to have to explain to him why she had been to the vicarage in the first place. Besides which, he was working long hours; a consultant in the department had left suddenly and he had been obliged to take on his workload until such time as another one could be appointed, so that was another reason for not bothering him, she reasoned.

Debbie had taken the boys to school that morning. Jamie had gradually come out of his shell and seemed much happier; she'd thought she'd even heard him and Danny giggling away at some private joke that morning up in Jamie's bedroom. No other unexplained things had happened and Beth began to think she had been overreacting after the stress of Audrey's death.

She went into the spare bedroom and retrieved the box from its hiding place. Peter was right, it was quite heavy but even so she decided to take it down into her studio where it was light and airy. The bedrooms at the front of the house were quite dark, even on a sunny day.

As she knelt on the floor and lifted the lid of the box her first reaction was one of disappointment. It seemed to be full of old musty parish magazines. She looked quickly through them as she lifted them out, but they were dated from the nineteen-sixties and were full of news about flower shows, Mother's Union meetings and village events. Only one that was dated 1968 had anything relating to Malthorp; a grainy picture of the house with a caption underneath which read:

Malthorp House; part of village history for over fifty years.

As she lifted out the last of the magazines, she came across a yellowing newspaper, the *Hampshire Gazette*, dated May 19th, 1911. Beth felt a frisson of excitement. May 19th – the day after Valentine had so tragically died. She scanned the front page but there was nothing there so she began to turn the fragile pages carefully. On the third page she found it; a quarter page column.

Local child dies in tragic accident

A terrible tragedy occurred in the village of Upper Melcombe yesterday afternoon. Valentine Edward Taylor, aged 9 years, fell down a deep well in the grounds of his home, Malthorp House and was drowned. There were no witnesses as to the tragedy but Mr Richard Cartwright, the boy's stepfather said:

"The cover had been left off the well against my explicit instructions as the gardener had been watering the early vegetables. We can only think that Valentine leant over to look down the well, and slipped and fell. He had no hope of keeping himself afloat because of his disabilities (the boy had severe weakness in his legs). As you can imagine, the whole household is mourning his loss."

An inquest will be held tomorrow, but there is no doubt, in view of the circumstances, that a verdict of accidental death will be returned.

Beth felt quite tearful as she read the faded words. Despite his formal words of regret, Richard Cartwright's seeming sorrow at his stepson's death did not ring true somehow, especially in the light of what Bill had told her. She laid the paper to one side. Underneath were some tattered books, mainly copies of the history of the village, written by someone called the Reverend Percival Symonds. She lifted them out, intending to look through them later to see if there was anything included in them about the history of Malthorp. She was about to put everything back when she noticed that there was something caught underneath the bottom flap of the box. She lifted the flap and pulled out a red leather-bound book. It looked very much like a diary and as she opened it to reveal the first page her heart missed a beat. The writing was a fine copperplate and on the first page was written the name Beatrice Taylor. On the opposite page the first date was April 5th 1906.

Beth got up and walked over to the chair by the window. The sun had gone in and she felt suddenly cold. She shut the French doors and, sitting down, began to read.

BEATRICE – 1906

1906 – April 5th

I have decided that I will start to write down my feelings and thoughts, just for my own satisfaction. I have, in the past, kept so many of my hopes and fears in my heart and have often not been able to discuss them, even with dear Mama. And now my dearest Edward is so unwell – his chest grows weaker with each passing day and I cannot trouble him with my innermost anxieties.

Yesterday, I took Valentine to see Doctor Temple in Winchester. He was highly recommended to me by Mrs Paston, whose son Laurence suffers from a similar condition to poor Valentine, though not so severely, I think. I was so hopeful that he would be able to suggest something to allay Valentine's disorder and to enable him to walk more easily but alas; he tells me that Valentine's condition (that is known by the common name of Rickets) is a very severe form. Although some treatments have been known to help sufferers, we have done all we can and he did not feel that there is any more that can be done to help him. He spoke very kindly to Valentine and called him a fine young man, and my poor boy smiled his lovely smile as usual and said thank you so sweetly as we left. I must admit I felt the tears so very near. Valentine knew, in that way he always does, how upset I was, and on the train on the way home he said: "Don't worry Mama; I am sure I will soon be able to walk much better with these new crutches the doctor has given me." I love him so much!

April 16th

Great excitement today for Valentine, as it is his Fourth birthday. Mama and Papa have come to stay for a few days, and this morning we took Valentine to the park to feed the swans. After luncheon he had his nap, and then Cook provided us with a perfectly splendid birthday tea. Edward was able to join us for a while and we had quite a merry little party. Mama and Papa have bought Valentine a wonderful clockwork clown, which climbs up and down a ladder and can perform all sorts of wonderful antics. He was so taken with it that he insisted on taking it up to bed with him, where it now reposes on the chest of drawers by his bed.

April 28th
A dreadful day. My darling Edward has suffered a terrible attack – he can scarcely catch his breath, and lies there too weak even to cough. The doctors have told me there is little hope of him recovering this time and that I must prepare myself for the worst. When I went in the room to sit with him awhile, he looked at me with such tenderness and whispered: "Do not grieve too much, my love."

How can I go on living without him? But I know I must, for Valentine's sake.

May 22nd
I have not felt able to write down my feelings for the past weeks. Even now, as I write these words, I feel I will break down and slip down into the depths of despair. The loss of my darling husband has dealt me a bitter blow but I know I must be strong for my boy's sake. Mama and Papa have been wonderful and have given me so much support. They are trying to persuade me to return with them to Gloucester; they say they would be so happy to have us to live with them for as long as we wish; it is a tempting proposal but I feel I cannot bear to leave this house where Edward and I have spent five happy years. For now, we will stay and I shall devote myself entirely to caring for Valentine. I feel closer to him with each passing day...

CHAPTER 27

Beth suddenly became aware of the insistent ringing of her mobile. For a moment she could not think where she was, so caught up had she been in Beatrice's world. Then reality kicked in and she grabbed her phone off the table.

"Hello?" she said breathlessly.

"Beth? It's Simon. You sound a bit startled. Have I caught you at an awkward moment?"

"Simon! No, I'm sorry. I was just in the middle of reading something that was all. How are you?"

"Fine, thanks. I was just wondering if I could pop down and see you tomorrow. I've got a bit of news that I think you might find rather interesting."

Beth thought quickly. She didn't know if she really wanted to see Simon at the moment, but she couldn't think of a good excuse to put him off.

"That should be fine. It would have to be the morning, though. I have to pick the boys up around three – it's parents' evening at Danny's school so he's finishing earlier than usual."

"That's fine. I'll be over at about, say, eleven?"

"Is this about my father, Simon? You said at the funeral you thought you'd found something out about him. Is he still alive? Do you know where he is?"

"I don't really want to tell you over the phone, Beth. I'll see you tomorrow, okay?"

He rang off, leaving Beth feeling both frustrated and faintly annoyed. She still didn't altogether trust her brother-in-law, even though he had helped her over the incident in London. She also felt guilty that she was still keeping secrets from Adam. She decided that she would definitely talk to him tonight; tell him about her feelings about the house – maybe she would even tell him about her encounter with Kevin and what Simon had discovered. She looked at her watch. Midday already and she hadn't done a thing. She must at least go and walk Finn who was looking at her appealingly from under the table. She sighed. She would pack away the contents of the box, apart from the diary, and put it back upstairs. The rest of Beatrice's story would have to wait until later.

◦◦◦

In his flat in London, Simon put his mobile down and gave a satisfied smile. It had been well worth the bribe of a slap-up meal and two bottles of expensive red wine at the Dorchester; his friend Inspector Tony Wilmot of the Met had done some very worthwhile investigation for him on the police computer. He was sure Beth would be more than grateful when he saw her tomorrow. With any luck that gratitude might lead on to some of his darkest fantasies becoming an amazing reality...

"You look like the proverbial cat that swallowed the cream. Whatever are you thinking about, lover?"

He jumped and turned round. He hadn't heard Fiona come in, so lost had he been in his dreams. An attractive, dark-haired woman she stood, hands on hips, in the doorway regarding him quizzically through piercing blue eyes. He looked away and pretended to be searching for his cigarettes.

"Oh, it's nothing really, Fi. I've just been speaking to Oliver Finch. He wants me to go up to Birmingham tomorrow to cover a story about teenage vandalism in the city. I'm sorry, I know we'd planned to meet for lunch but I should be back by early evening, so can we make it dinner instead?" The lie came easily to his lips, even though he couldn't meet her eyes.

Fiona looked at him quizzically. She always knew when he was lying to her but she loved him and, over the past three years, she had put up with his occasional bouts of infidelity with remarkable fortitude, but she was beginning to wonder where their relationship was going. She knew Simon was not the type to commit himself to one woman for life and she was under no illusions about his feelings for her; she was a convenience for him, that was all, and she didn't know how much longer she was prepared to accept that situation. She smiled sweetly at him.

"That's fine," she said. "As a matter of fact, I've had a better offer for lunch. Martin Nash called me today. He's over here for a few days and said he'd really like us to meet up again before he flies back to Boston, so I was going to cancel anyway. I'll tell you what; let's go to dinner at Franco's tonight to make up for it, just in case you don't get back tomorrow. I'll book a table for seven-thirty. I'm going shopping with Kate now so I'll see you later darling. *Ciao!*"

Simon smiled ruefully as she left. Franco's was the latest trendy restaurant in Kensington and would cost him an arm and a leg. Seducing Beth was turning out to be an expensive business. He only hoped it would be worth it in the end.

Beth's hopes of talking things over with Adam were dashed when he arrived home late, looking pale and tired.

"Sorry, my love. It's been a hell of a day. Mike Johnston was off sick so we were even more short-staffed. Are the boys asleep?"

"Ages ago. Have you eaten? There's a chicken casserole keeping warm in the Aga if you want it."

"No thanks," he said releasing a wide yawn. "I grabbed a meal in the canteen about two hours ago. I think I'm going to go straight up to bed. I've an early start again tomorrow. How are you doing Finn?" He fondled the dog's golden, silky ears. "Are you coming up, Beth?"

"It's a bit early for me. I'll be up in a while. Goodnight, my love."

"Goodnight darling." He kissed her and made his way wearily upstairs, Finn following closely behind. Beth went into the kitchen and took the casserole out of the Aga. She tidied round quickly then went to the bottom of the stairs. There was no sound; Adam must already be in bed. She made her way into her studio, drew the curtains and switched on the gas fire as the room felt a little chilly. Then she picked up Beatrice's journal once more.

She seemed to have written in it only briefly from the last entry Beth had read, and the next few pages covered her day-to-day struggle to cope with her lonely widowhood. Up until the end of 1907 she seemed to have spent most of her time caring for her young son with an occasional visit to her parents in Gloucester.

Then there came a change of tone. Beatrice's lonely existence was about to be transformed. Beth sat up and began to read with growing anticipation.

BEATRICE – 1907-1908

December 12th
Margaret Paston has kindly invited me to a Soiree at her house tonight. At first I declined the invitation, fearing that I might be the only lady there alone, but Margaret has assured me that there will be several single ladies (and gentlemen, though of course I could not contemplate starting a conversation with any of them) and has begged me to attend. She has been such a good friend to me that it would be churlish to refuse. Valentine is very excited for me and has begged to be allowed to stay up a little later, so he can see me, as he so sweetly puts it, "all dressed up". Nanny Bartlett has given this her seal of approval so all is well with the world. I am so pleased for Valentine's sake that I have found such a treasure to care for him. She has endless patience and encourages him greatly in everything. He insists on calling her 'Baba', a name she seems very happy with. I am beginning to look forward to tonight.

December 13th
I do not even know how to begin to write down what has happened, so I will start from the beginning.
I arrived at the Soiree at about half-past-six. There was quite a gathering there already; Margaret had invited about twenty-five people and had engaged a string quartet to play as everyone arrived. She and her husband, Henry, were there to greet me at the door and, after the maid had taken my coat, Margaret introduced me to a group of ladies who were very friendly and immediately included me in their conversation so I did not feel at all isolated. They were all beautifully attired and I was so glad I had decided to wear the cream organza dress trimmed with blue lace. The evening flew past; at about nine o'clock light refreshments were served and I found myself separated from my new acquaintances as I sat down near to the window with a small plate of food.

"May I join you?" a voice said and I looked up to see a tall, very handsome gentleman standing before me.

"Of course," I replied, feeling a little flustered. He sat down and we began to eat in a silence that at first felt a little uncomfortable.

"Do you know the Pastons well?" he suddenly asked. I began to explain about my son and how he had similar disabilities to theirs and that we had been good friends before Edward had passed away. Before I knew it, we were chatting away as if we had known each other all our lives. He told me his name was Richard Cartwright and that he was from Oxfordshire. Henry Paston and he had been at university together and they had run across each other quite by chance whilst Richard was in the area visiting an elderly aunt.

"I am sorry to hear about your husband," he said. "You must find it very hard being on your own with a child to bring up."

"It has not been easy," I replied. "But Margaret and Henry have been very good and my Mother and Father have also helped me greatly."

"Do they live near to you?"

"Not too near now. I was brought up in Lancashire – my father was a mill-owner, but he sold his business some years ago and moved to Gloucester. They have several times offered to buy me a house there so I can be nearer to them, but I do not feel I could leave Hampshire at the present time, where Edward and I have been so happy."

He nodded sympathetically, and then said rather hesitantly, "Mrs Taylor... I hope you will not think me presumptuous, but I have so much enjoyed our conversation and I would very much like to call on you tomorrow, if that is acceptable? Perhaps you would do me the honour of accompanying me on a drive in the park if the weather is not too inclement?"

I felt very flustered.

"Oh, Mr Cartwright, I really do not think..."

"Please," he said simply. "It would give me the greatest pleasure if you would allow it. Could I call, say, at about two o'clock?"

So, I have agreed and he will be here at any moment. I do hope I am doing the right thing. I did very much like him, though, and I feel sure that Edward would not want me to mourn forever...

January 31st
The last six weeks have passed in such a whirl of activity that I have not had a moment in which to write down everything that has happened. Suffice it to say that I have been out nearly every day, visiting museums, art galleries and lovely little village churches, all with dear Richard. He decided to stay with his Aunt, of whom he seems very fond, for a while and he has been such an attentive and amusing companion and such good company. We have taken tea out several times in a delightful tea-room near to the park; we seem to have so much in common and are agreed on so many things. It sometimes seems to me that we have known each other all our lives, not for just six short weeks.
I have felt a little guilty, because I have been so occupied that I have spent very little time with my dear Valentine. He seems quite content though; Nanny Bartlett more than compensates for the neglect on my part and has taken him out in his wheeled chair nearly every day; sometimes to the park or, on several occasions, to visit Margaret and play with dear Laurence.

The weather has been unseasonably mild which has meant that Richard and I have been able to go out and about with little disruption. He is such a wonderful companion and I must confess I am becoming more than a little fond of him...

February 5th
Now, for my Great News. Richard has proposed to me! It happened yesterday as we walked by the cathedral in Winchester. He tells me that he has loved me from the moment we first met, and that he wants to marry me without delay and devote the rest of his life to making me happy. I have told him I must think about it for a day or two. I have Valentine to consider after all; I do not know how he will feel about my marrying again. He and Richard have met only briefly,

but Richard has told me he will be willing treat Valentine as his own son, despite his disabilities.

I think I already know what my answer will be...

The next few entries described Beatrice's joy and her preparations for the coming wedding which was to take place in six weeks.

March 16th

Tomorrow is my wedding day! We are to be married very quietly in the registry office in Winchester. Our only guests are to be Margaret and Henry, Mama and Papa and my sister Lydia and her husband James. I very much wished Valentine to be there too, but Richard dissuaded me, saying that the building would be unsuitable for him as there are steep steps leading up to the door and it will be difficult to get his wheeled chair into the room where the ceremony will take place. Valentine was bitterly disappointed and shed a few tears, but I have promised him that he may come to the wedding luncheon at the George Hotel so he is a little happier now.

I had so hoped Mama and Papa would like Richard and be happy for me, but I fear it is not to be so. Papa had a long talk with me last night and expressed his doubts about the wisdom of my marrying a man I had only known for so short a time. He does not seem to have taken to him, despite Richard being so charming when they met, and I am sorry to say that we came as near to quarrelling as we have ever done; Mama had to intervene as we exchanged high words. She, too, voiced her reservations but said that I must do what I felt to be right, both for myself and Valentine. Lydia was the only one who seemed truly happy for me; she and James embraced me warmly and wished me happiness.

Valentine is to go with Nanny Bartlett to Gloucester while we are away on our honeymoon. I know I will miss him so much but Richard is taking me to Venice and then on to Rome! We will be away for a month. On our return we will be looking for a new house. Richard's house in Oxfordshire has already been sold he tells me, and Henry has kindly agreed to oversee the sale of our dear house while we are away. He will also ask the agent to look for a suitable property for us in the local area.

In twenty-four hours I shall be Beatrice Cartwright.

I pray that you will give me your blessing, Edward...

CHAPTER 28

Beth read the last entry in the diary with a profound sense of disappointment. She had been hoping that Beatrice would continue the story and describe some of the events that had happened later at Malthorp. She suddenly became aware that she had cramp in her legs where she had curled them up under her while she read. Her mouth felt dry as well; she would make herself a cup of tea, she decided, before going up to bed. She stood up, wincing slightly at the pain in her legs and stretched, yawning.

As she walked towards the studio door Beth suddenly became aware that she could hear a woman quietly weeping. She remembered vividly that she had heard the same sound the day of Danny's accident and gasped, frozen with shock, conscious that her heart had skipped a beat. The sound of the weeping seemed to be coming from some distance away as before and, as she cautiously opened the door, she realised that it was emanating from somewhere upstairs. Maybe it wasn't a woman at all, she told herself firmly. Perhaps it was one of the boys having a bad dream.

She went to turn the hall light on but inexplicably she couldn't seem to locate the switch. For a moment the hall seemed to shimmer in front of her eyes and everything felt dreamlike, almost surreal; she steeled herself to climb the stairs which were lit only by the pale moonlight which shone through the fanlight over the front door. As she did so the sobbing became louder and she took a shuddering breath as she forced herself to continue. As she reached the top of the stairs she blinked in confusion. The wall in front of her looked different somehow and for a moment she could not think why; then she realised that where before it had been painted in a pale smooth cream emulsion, now it seemed to be deeper and more textured somehow. She remembered the old flock wallpaper that had been there originally when they first viewed the house. She reached out to touch it and felt the raised surface under her fingertips. Surely it couldn't be…?

As she withdrew her hand and stepped back, a dark shadow passed before her. She recoiled and clutched the banister as the shadow shifted and changed, taking on the shape of a man. It became clearer and she saw it was a well-built, dark-haired man, dressed in what looked like an old-fashioned frock-coat. He did not seem to see her as he strode along the corridor and entered Jamie's bedroom.

Beth's frozen limbs at last came back to life and she gave a short cry as she flew along the corridor after him, her only instinct to protect her son. At the bedroom door she stopped and gasped in disbelief at what she saw.

It wasn't Jamie's bedroom, at least not as she knew it. The tall bookcase which housed his books and games was no longer there and neither was his wardrobe, nor his toy garage with its multitude of cars, or his bright blue carpet. Instead, the room consisted of a massive dark wood wardrobe, a high chest of drawers and an old-fashioned washstand which stood on the polished floorboards. Next to a narrow, iron-framed bed with its high mattress was a low table on which stood a small oil-lamp which burned with a subdued, flickering light. Half-leaning across the bed was a woman wearing a long white dress, who was sobbing bitterly into a small lace handkerchief. The tall man strode across the room towards her, anger apparent in his every gesture. The sobbing ceased abruptly as he addressed the woman in a low, vindictive tone.

"When are you going to stop behaving in this unseemly manner, Beatrice? I will not tolerate this excessive grieving for much longer!"

"Richard, please! You must see how much I miss him – I cannot forgive myself."

"Enough!" he grabbed her arm roughly and she gasped in pain as she tried to pull free. "You still have a living child to care for in the nursery. I'll not stand for this a moment longer!" He swore at her as he lifted his hand and struck her sharply in the face. Beth cried out in horror and started forward to help the woman who had fallen to the floor...

She found herself standing at the foot of Jamie's bed. Bewildered and disorientated she looked around the room. Although the room felt icy-cold everything was back in its place and her small son was on his side, snuggled under the duvet sleeping peacefully. She was shaking as she sank to her knees beside the bed and put her face close to his on the pillow. He stirred slightly in his sleep and she stroked the thick dark hair back from his forehead.

The landing light came on and Adam appeared in the doorway.

"Beth? Is everything okay? I thought I heard you call out. Is Jamie restless?"

Beth nodded weakly and put her finger to her lips. She got up and came out of the room, pulling the door behind her.

"You're as white as a sheet," he went on. "Are you not feeling well?"

"I'm okay, really, Adam. I just fell asleep downstairs that's all, and… and then I heard Jamie stirring so I went in to check on him. I'm coming to bed now."

"Good." He smiled at her sleepily. "See you in the morning, love."

Beth was still shaking as she used the bathroom. She stared into the mirror and saw a white, shocked face staring back at her. Had she really seen the ghosts of Beatrice and Richard Cartwright or had her imagination been working overtime after reading Beatrice's diary? No, it had been all too real; the images had been too definite and she could still feel the texture of that flock wallpaper on her fingertips. Somehow, time had slipped back and she had briefly been in the Malthorp of the past. A Malthorp that was haunted by the family who had lived there over a hundred years ago; the family that was not at rest because of the terrible events that had happened there. And the boy, Valentine, Beatrice's adored son who had died so tragically, seemed able to somehow communicate with their small son, and use him to try and tell them something. Tomorrow she would ask Peter Bowers to come and say prayers in the house as he had promised, to see if that would help to bring some peace to this troubled house. Maybe she would also try to get in touch with Gloria Nash, who had sensed the unhappiness and who might be able to help her if she could persuade her to come back. Then she remembered that Simon was coming the next day to tell her what he had found out about her father. Well, he wouldn't be staying all day so with any luck she could speak to Peter in the afternoon.

She slid into bed beside Adam who was deeply asleep. She knew now that she could not confide in him; he would say, as he had before, that it was all in her imagination, that she was overtired and overwrought, that the strain of everything that had happened had affected her. But she knew that she had not imagined what had happened to her tonight and she lay awake thinking about it for a long time before she slipped at last into an uneasy slumber.

CHAPTER 29

Beth awoke the next morning with a pounding headache. She opened her eyes and groaned as Adam came out of the bathroom, a large bath towel wrapped round his waist.

"I feel like hell!"

He frowned with concern. "You don't look too good. Do you want me to give Debbie a ring? I'm sure she wouldn't mind running the boys to school this morning. I only wish I could stay home today but it's so manic at work."

"No, I'll be okay after a cup of tea and a couple of aspirin." She looked at him thoughtfully. "Did you hear anything strange last night, Adam?"

"No, I went out like a light." He pulled on his trousers. "I vaguely remember coming into Jamie's room to see if you were alright but otherwise I slept like a baby. Why – did you?"

"No, not really." Beth drew her knees up. "Well… I thought I heard… I saw… oh, never mind." She put her hand to her aching head. "I'd better get the boys up."

"I'll do that. You have your shower and I'll get their breakfast and bring you up a cup of tea and some aspirin before I go to work." He finished buttoning his shirt and bent to give her a swift kiss. "I'll try and leave a bit earlier today; it's time I spent a bit more time with my family!"

He hurried out and a few minutes later she heard him chivvying the boys to get up. She went into the bathroom and got in the shower, standing blissfully in the stream of hot water, feeling it wash away the trauma of the night before. It all seemed rather unreal now but she knew she had not imagined it. Today, after Simon had been, she would definitely go and see Peter Bowers. If anyone could help her discover what was going on she was sure he would be the best person to talk to. When she came out of the bathroom a cup of tea and two aspirin sat on the bedside table. She smiled, thinking how lucky she was to have Adam's love and support. She only wished she could share her fears with him.

When she came downstairs, the boys were sitting at the big, scrubbed kitchen table eating cereal. Danny looked up, his face full of concern.

"Are you okay, Mum? Dad says you're not feeling very well. Only, me and Jamie don't have to go to school today, you know. We can easily stay home and look after you."

"Nice try, Dan," laughed Adam, ruffling his son's sandy hair. "Mum will be fine. Debbie's going to take you to school today; I've just rung and asked her. "No, Beth," he went on as she started to protest. "It will do you good to have a bit of a break. Sit and put your feet up; you don't have anything urgent on today, do you?"

Beth, stifling a slight feeling of guilt about Simon, shook her head.

"Okay, that's settled then. Look at the time! I'd better get going." He kissed her and gave the boys a swift hug. "Bye fellas – see you later!"

Debbie arrived about half-an-hour later to pick the boys up. Unusually, Jamie clung to Beth when she went to say goodbye.

"Want *you* to take me, Mummy. Don't want to go with Debbie!" His bottom lip quivered.

"Maybe I should take him," Beth said to Debbie. "He hasn't done this for a long time."

"Come on Jamie!" said Debbie. "If you're a good boy you can sit in the front today. Danny won't mind, will you, Danny?"

"Course not. And you can play on my DS, Spud. Come on, let's go and sort out a game for you."

To Beth's relief, Jamie let go of her and went to the car with Danny. Debbie grinned,

"Danny's a marvel with him, isn't he?" She peered at Beth closely.

"Are you okay, Beth? You're looking very pale and tired this morning, if you don't mind me saying so."

"I just had a bad night, that's all. Thanks so much for taking them this morning, Debs. I hate calling you in on your day off."

"No problem. If you're still feeling rough later, just call me and I'll pick them up for you as well. Bye!" She gave a cheerful wave as she drove off and Beth was relieved to see that Jamie was bent over Danny's DS and seemed to have got over his distress at leaving her.

The phone was ringing as she went back indoors and she hurried to answer it. It was Guy Turner, her agent.

"Beth! How are you? Sorry I haven't been in touch for a while." He hesitated. "Look, I was so very sorry to hear about Adam's mother. That must have been an awful shock."

"It was," said Beth. "But we're coping alright. How are you, Guy?"

"Fine. Look, Beth, I'll get straight to the point. I don't know how you'll feel about this but an amazing commission has come up and I think it's going to be right up your street. I've had a call from Sam Toovey, the film director with Excalibur, the US film company that launched earlier this year. He's been in negotiation with Desmond and they've finally reached an agreement. Filming starts on the first of the White Wizard books in August and they want you to be the concept artist working closely with Desmond on getting the artwork right for the film. Beth, it's a terrific opportunity. What do you say?"

"It sounds marvellous. But I've never done anything like that before. Would I be able to work from home?"

"That's the snag, Beth You see, Excalibur's based in New York. It would involve you working over there for a time."

"How long are we talking about? Weeks? Months?"

He paused. "It could be for up to a year. It might mean you moving over there for a while, Beth – I mean all of you, and it would be all expenses paid. What a terrific opportunity, eh? Now, I know there's a lot to consider but don't say no straight away; promise you'll think about it, please. Talk it over with Adam, I know he has commitments and it would mean him taking a sabbatical, but it would be marvellous for all of you. I'll be in touch soon."

She put the phone down, her head in a whirl. It certainly was an incredible opportunity, but one that she couldn't even contemplate; there was no way she could disrupt her whole family's life to satisfy her own selfish desires. They would have to leave everything – family, friends, poor Finn… She dropped to her knees and put her arms round the dog's furry neck.

"We couldn't do that to you, could we feller?" she said. He licked her nose and she laughed. "Besides, it would mean leaving this house."

This house… well, perhaps leaving here wouldn't be such a bad thing, she thought as she let Finn out in the garden. She was beginning to feel distinctly uncomfortable about Malthorp. But, New York? Maybe that was taking things a bit too far.

Simon arrived on the dot of eleven and Beth led him into the sunny kitchen. She had made a pot of fresh coffee and he sniffed appreciatively.

"Wonderful! Just what I need. The traffic was horrendous on the M25. How are you, Beth? You're looking a bit pale."

"I'm getting a bit tired of everyone telling me that. I'm fine, Simon. How's John doing?"

"He's coping really well. David went back last week and we've all been ringing to make sure he's okay, but you know Dad. He wouldn't admit it even if he wasn't."

"We're going to try and get down and see him soon. Laura and Geoff have offered to have the boys again for a weekend so we'll probably take them up on that." She put a steaming cup of coffee down in front of him. "Right, I'm dying to know. What have you found out about my father?"

He reached in his pocket and took out a couple of sheets of paper.

"Well, a friend of mine's been doing a bit of digging and he's discovered that your father left Wales shortly after you went to Liverpool. He then disappeared for quite a while but my friend's pretty sure he traced him a couple of years later, living in Southern Ireland."

"Ireland!" Beth stared. "Why would he have gone to Ireland?"

"No idea," Simon said. "Anyway, the next trace of him is nearly fifteen years ago, when an Owen Morgan is listed as living in Penzance, in Cornwall."

"Are you sure it's my father?" asked Beth. "How would he know it's the same Owen Morgan?"

"Because he traced a life insurance application that was made about nine years ago," said Simon, "and on it he had to state any beneficiaries. You were named, Beth. He must have been keeping tracks on you because he even knew your married name."

She swallowed.

"So, he didn't forget me." She felt the tears welling up. "But why didn't he get in touch, if he knew where I was? Why didn't he want to see me?"

"I don't know the answer to that, I'm afraid. But there's more, Beth," said Simon gently. "Your father married again some years ago. He's got two more daughters."

She stared at him in utter disbelief.

"No! No, I don't believe you!"

"It's true, I'm afraid. There's no doubt about it."

Beth bent her head and looked at her rapidly cooling coffee. She could hardly take it in. Not only had he deserted her, leaving her to suffer all she had gone through on her own, but he had started a new family without a second thought for his eldest child. So, he had never really cared, from the day he had sent her away. She felt the tears spill over and run down her face.

Simon stood up and came round to her, putting a comforting arm round her shoulders. She leant against him, sobbing in earnest now and he leaned over and grabbed a piece of kitchen towel.

"I'm so sorry, Beth. This must be awful for you. If it's any consolation, he obviously thought about you as he made you a beneficiary on his life insurance. I'm only sorry I had to be the one to tell you."

She blew her nose and gulped back the tears.

"It's no consolation – it was him I needed, not his money!" She made an effort to smile at him. "I'm really grateful you found out, Simon. For years I've hoped that one day I would know what had happened to him. Well, now I know. He's alive and well and living happily with a new family." She smiled bitterly. "I presume that he divorced my mother then, or else she's dead."

"I tried to trace her as well," said Simon gently. He hadn't, but he thought it sounded good. "But there are no records of her."

Beth gave a watery smile.

"It's been a shock, but thank you so much, Simon. I really am glad I know."

"Let me take you out to lunch," he said. "I think you need cheering up."

"No, I'll get us something here," she said. "If you don't mind, I don't really feel up to much. I've got plenty of salad and stuff in the fridge."

"Lovely." He sauntered over to the window. "The garden's looking great, Beth. That mutt of yours obviously loves it out there."

"Finn! I'd forgotten he was out there." She opened the door. "Come on, boy!"

He ran in, wagging his feathery tail. Simon watched as Beth fussed him, giving him a treat out of the tin. Staying here suited him very well. Lunch and a couple of glasses of wine might relax Beth enough to make her unwind and let down her guard. He fancied her more than ever and it had been difficult to restrain himself when she had leant against him just now…

An hour later when Beth had loaded the dishwasher and they were in the lounge relaxing over another glass of wine she told Simon about Guy's phone call and he had agreed that it was something she should think about very carefully. She had begun to feel that she could safely confide in him, so she told him about some of the strange things that had been happening in the house and of her fears for Jamie, though she didn't tell him everything. He listened without interruption until she had finished.

"What does Adam say about all this?" he asked.

"He doesn't believe it; of course, I know it sounds crazy. Oh, Simon, I wish he would listen!"

He stretched and reached out for the bottle of wine.

"Oh well, that's Adam for you, ever the cynic." He thought smugly that things were turning out far better than he had hoped. Top-up?" he added casually as he got up.

"No, I mustn't or I'll be over the limit and I have to pick Jamie up at three."

"Why don't you ring Debbie? I'm sure she won't mind. Then you won't have to worry." He topped his own glass up and moved to sit beside her on the sofa. "Are you feeling better now?"

"Yes, much better. I really am very grateful to you for listening, Simon."

"How grateful?" he asked; leaning forward he put his hand behind her head and pulled her to him kissing her deeply on the lips.

Beth froze with shock and tried to pull away.

"Simon – no. You've got the wrong idea... I..."

He laughed softly.

"No, this is the right idea, Beth. You and I – we're meant for each other, always have been. You'd be much better off with me rather than my milksop brother. I can show you what it's like to be with a real man."

He kissed her again, pinning her down and ignoring her struggles. She closed her eyes as he slid his hand up her thigh and again tried to wrench herself away, but he was too strong. She could taste the stale wine on his breath and opened her eyes, looking round desperately for something she could grab to hit him with. Then she realised...

It wasn't Simon holding her. It was Kevin; his thick lips parted and his narrow piggy eyes gleamed with desire. She screamed and began to struggle more forcefully against the weight of his body.

Suddenly there was a low growl and a furry golden shape threw himself at her attacker. He cried out in agony and let her go, rolling off the sofa and cradling his hand where a deep bite was bleeding profusely.

Beth jumped up as Simon stared in disbelief at his injured hand. "Beth," he said. "Beth, I…"

She was shaking with shock and anger. "I think you'd better leave, Simon."

"But, my hand…"

She went into the kitchen and fetched a clean tea towel which she handed to him in silence. He wrapped it round his hand, wincing in pain.

"Bloody hell, that hurts! I need to see a doctor or something."

"There's a walk-in clinic in the next town on your way back," she said coldly. "I suggest you go in there and get it properly dressed. You'd better make sure your tetanus shot is up to date as well. Now, please go, Simon and let's forget this ever happened."

She went into the hall and opened the front door. He pushed past her and down the steps to his car, his face flushed with anger.

"That fucking dog of yours should be put down!" he called as a parting shot. "He's bloody dangerous!"

Beth slammed the door and then sank down to the floor as she heard the car roar away. Finn came up and sat as close to her as he could get. She found herself shaking as she cuddled into him. "Oh, Finn," she murmured, "what the hell is happening to me?" It felt as if her whole world was falling apart.

CHAPTER 30

In the end Beth decided to say nothing to Adam about the offer from Guy to work in New York. She just wanted to put the whole awful day behind her; the traumatic news about her father and Simon's unforgivable behaviour afterwards were things she did not want to dwell on. She still felt very guilty about keeping everything from him, but she knew he would be furious if he found out about Simon and would also be very hurt to think that she had confided in his brother instead of him.

It wasn't until a couple of days later that she made her way with Finn to the vicarage to see Peter. Nothing untoward had happened in the house; Jamie had seemed more settled and content, Adam less stressed about work and Danny… well… was just Danny. Beth had begun to relax, although she still felt very emotional. They had invited Laura and Geoff over for dinner that evening. They had married very quietly a few weeks earlier and Adam and Beth had promised them a celebratory meal. Beth also thought it might be a good opportunity to get Laura on her own for a while and talk to her about at least some of the bizarre things which had happened. She felt that if she didn't confide in someone soon she might just go mad, and sensible, level-headed Laura seemed the ideal person. That decision made, she thought that now was the time to speak to Peter as she had planned and see what he thought of her strange experience; ask him if he thought it was worth coming up to the house as he had suggested.

She was destined to be disappointed. The cleaning lady, duster in hand, answered the door. She stared at Beth for a few moments.

"If you're after the vicar I'm afraid you're out of luck. He and Mrs Bowers have gone up to London to a convention. He'll be back Saturday afternoon."

"Oh, thank you. It wasn't important; I'll catch up with him then." Beth turned to go but the woman spoke again.

"Mrs Ellis, isn't it – from up Malthorp?" She folded her arms and regarded Beth quizzically. "I'm Irene Stokes from the village. How are you getting on up there? Strange old place, isn't it?"

"We're fine," Beth replied. "As a matter of fact, we've settled in very well."

"Oh, yes?" Irene Stokes shook her head disbelievingly, her grey, permed curls bobbing. "My family's been here years, you know; in fact, my great uncle worked up at Malthorp in the gardens many years ago. Nasty business about that dreadful accident up there though, wasn't it. Must have knocked you for six – Maureen Tidy tells me you had a bit of a bad turn the other day and vicar had to bring you in for a cup of tea. Quite recovered are you?"

"Quite," said Beth, trying to keep her temper. Honestly, Maureen Tidy must have rushed around the village telling everyone. Irene's small, shrewd eyes narrowed as she looked Beth up and down.

"Well, can't stand here chatting all day. Sorry the vicar isn't in. Want me to give him a message, do you?"

"No thanks," said Beth shortly. "I'll see him and Janet when they get back."

She walked down the path seething, but by the time she reached the gate she'd begun to see the funny side of it. She decided to walk through the churchyard and have another look at Valentine's grave. On the way she stopped to pick a few wild flowers.

It was very quiet and as she approached the spot where the grave stood, she felt none of the sense of menace that had been here on the day they had lost Jamie. Even the little stone angel seemed to have a calm and gentle expression on its face. She bent to lay the small nosegay of flowers on the grave and, as she did so, she thought she heard a long whispering sigh. She spun round but there was nobody in sight. Shivering slightly, she walked a little way down the path looking at the other old gravestones, most of which were leaning at precarious angles with lettering carved into them that was barely legible. Then she noticed a large, more elaborate grave, topped by an ornate stone urn. Something made her stop to read the inscription:

> **Here Lies**
> **BEATRICE CARTWRIGHT**
> **Beloved Wife of Richard**
> **Born: 2nd July 1880**
> **Died 25th June 1912**
> **Eternally Sleeping in Peace**

She bit her lip. So, this was Beatrice's final resting place; a few yards away from her beloved son. Beth felt tears prick her eyelids. Poor Beatrice! She had only survived him by a year. It made her more determined than ever to find out more about the woman she had last seen sobbing by her dead son's bedside. She wondered how she could go about it. There surely must be some way of researching Beatrice's life and death. She would look on the internet when she got home to see if there were any websites that could help her; in fact, she was almost sure she had read about people using them to look up their family history. From Beatrice's diary she already knew where her parents had lived; the name of her sister and she had the date of her second marriage to Richard Cartwright. She should also be able to roughly pinpoint the date of her first, to Edward Taylor, using Valentine's age as a guide. Laura might have some ideas as well.

Feeling quite excited at the prospect of doing something positive Beth made her way along the path leading from the church towards home.

On Valentine's lonely grave, the little nosegay of flowers fluttered slightly in the breeze. Then quite suddenly they were lifted into the air by an unseen hand and thrown violently against the wall.

CHAPTER 31

Beth and Adam had a lovely evening with Laura and Geoff. It was the first time they had seen the house completely redecorated and refurbished and they were suitably impressed. Beth had made a huge moussaka and the boys were allowed to stay up and have dinner with them; they were delighted to see Laura and Geoff again and more than happy to show them every nook and cranny of Malthorp.

After they had gone to bed, not without protest, at about nine o'clock, the adults drifted into the lounge for coffee. Adam and Geoff started looking through Adam's collection of DVDs with a view to choosing a film they could all watch, so Beth suggested to Laura that they took a walk round the garden.

"It's good to see Adam looking so relaxed," Laura said as they wandered along the path. "He's been massively overloaded with work. Hopefully, now we've got this new consultant starting on Monday, things will be a little easier." She stopped and looked at Beth. "You're looking a bit washed-out though, if you don't mind me saying, Beth. I know it's all been an awful strain on you, too, what with poor Audrey and everything. Are *you* okay?"

Beth bit her lip.

"Not really. Actually, Laura, I really need to talk to you about something. That's partly the reason I suggested we came out here."

They strolled on and came to the bench which stood near the front door. Laura sat down and patted the seat.

"Come on then. Sit down and tell Auntie Laura all about it."

Beth took a deep breath and told her everything, leaving out only the news about her father and the fact that Simon had been to the house and made a pass at her. She still found it hard to speak about her father's betrayal and she thought that Laura might think that she had been wrong to involve Simon in the first place because she worked so closely with Adam and was very fond of him. Beth also didn't want her to feel in an awkward position. Laura listened in silence until Beth had finished.

"Wow, that's quite some story," she said. She shivered. "There certainly do seem to have been some strange things happening. Are you saying that Jamie's in any danger from this Valentine? And what about Audrey's accident – do you think any of this could have had anything to do with that?"

"I honestly don't know," Beth said. "But I think I need to find out more about the story before I can fully understand what is going on here. I thought I might try and research some more about Beatrice. I want to know more details about her life here with Richard Cartwright. Was their marriage happy? If what I saw was real or if it was… I don't know, spirits, ghosts, or just some weird echo of the past… he seems to have been a bit of a brute to her. From what Bill Tidy told me I don't think he treated her son very well either, and the newspaper report certainly didn't give the impression that he was exactly devastated by Valentine's death. I think that finding out more about her could hold the key to the unhappiness that still seems to be here. That's one of the things I was going to ask you to help me with. I know you can research family trees through the internet but I don't have a clue where to start. I thought two heads might be better than one when it comes to that."

"Funnily enough," said Laura. "My older brother Paul is a bit of an amateur historian and he's been researching our family history. He's found out quite a lot about our ancestors, good and bad, in fact he's been driving us all up the wall on the subject. He'll know the best way to go about it, so give me what you know and I'll see what he can find out for you. I can't promise he'll come up with the goods but he'll do his best that's for sure."

"Would he really? That would be brilliant," said Beth. "I'll email you the details tomorrow if you don't mind passing them on."

"What does Adam think about all this?" asked Laura curiously. "He hasn't mentioned anything about it."

"He doesn't believe in any of it," said Beth. "He just puts it all down to coincidence. That's why I can't talk it over with him so please don't say anything to him about this, Laura. I will tell him when the time is right, but let me find out a bit more about what's happening first." She looked pleadingly at her friend. "As long as you don't believe I'm going nuts, because I feel as if I am at the moment."

"Of course I don't. You're one of the sanest people I know. What are you going to do about this offer you've had from Excalibur?"

"I'm going to put that on the back burner for now. We've only just settled into here; I don't want Adam to feel pressured into making such a big life change at the moment. They can wait for their answer."

"Come on, girls!" Geoff's booming voice echoed through the garden, making them jump. "We're about to put a scary film on and Adam's made more coffee."

"What's the film?" Laura asked him as they made their way back to the lounge.

"*Lady in White*; it's a real hair-raiser according to Adam. You might want to look under the bed tonight, babe!"

"Very appropriate!" muttered Laura. "Come on, Beth, let's sit down and be suitably terrified. After what you've told me tonight, I think we might find it quite tame!"

Upstairs, Jamie turned restlessly under the covers. An owl hooted outside his window and he woke suddenly. The moonlight was shining through a crack in the curtains casting a long shadow across his bed. After a moment he threw the covers off and padded softly to the window. Looking down into the garden he smiled as he saw the figure of the small boy who waited for him, the moonlight reflecting off his round wire spectacles.

"Valentine!" he whispered. "I'm coming."

He opened his door very quietly. From downstairs he could hear the muted sound of the television. Instead of using the main staircase he turned to the right, crept past Danny's room and made his way down the narrow wooden staircase that led to the kitchen. The back door was locked but he knew where the key was kept, hanging in the small pantry to the left of the door. He struggled a bit to turn it in the lock, but eventually he managed it and slipped through into the garden.

Jamie shivered a little in his thin cotton pyjamas. He hadn't stopped to put his trainers on, so it was with bare feet that he made his way across the lawn to where he had seen Valentine standing. There was no sign of him and he looked around, puzzled. Then he saw a small shadow slip past the summerhouse and into the woods and he laughed delightedly and ran to join him. His friend moved on swiftly ahead, despite his crutches, and Jamie tried desperately to keep up, ducking as low branches and bushes brushed his face. Then the tall gateposts loomed up ahead, topped by snarling stone lions and Jamie realised they were near the road. He stopped in confusion. Mum and Dad had always told him that he mustn't go outside the gates on his own. Valentine had stopped, too, and was standing on the other side of the road, leaning on his crutches. He didn't seem at all out of breath and his thin face was alight with anticipation.

"Come along, Jamie!" he called. "It's alright; you're safe with me. I'll look after you. Come and play!"

Jamie hesitated for only a moment. Then he ran across to join his friend.

The film had finished and they were laughingly discussing it.

"I don't think I'll be able to hear that song again without looking over my shoulder," said Laura. "Some of the acting was a bit wooden though."

"I don't know how anyone can believe in all that stuff," stated Geoff. "I've never believed in all this supernatural crap! Too practical and earthy, that's me."

"Absolutely," agreed Adam. "I can't believe anyone does."

Laura and Beth exchanged wry glances.

"There are more things in heaven and earth Horatio…" Laura began. Geoff gave a huge guffaw.

"Come off it, babe. You don't mean to tell me you believe in any of it, surely?"

"I might do."

Geoff snorted with laughter again, grabbed her and began waltzing her round the room, singing the film's haunting song in a high falsetto:

> "*Did you ever see a dream walking?*
> *Well I did…*"

Laura thumped her husband hard in the chest and he let her go and collapsed laughing into the nearest chair.

"Pack it in, Dunbar! A lot of people do believe in ghosts, you know, so don't mock!"

"Well, I certainly don't!" Adam stated again emphatically. "I grew up with it, remember. My poor mother was well into all that, for all the good it did her." He put his arm around Beth. "I think we're too concerned about the living in our job, eh Laura?"

She nodded slowly. "I suppose. Well, we'd better make a move – it has gone midnight and we've got to be up early tomorrow."

They made their way into the hall, Geoff still teasing Laura, while Adam fetched their coats. There was a sound on the stairs and they all looked up as Danny appeared, rubbing his eyes sleepily.

"There, you've woken the kids, Dunbar," Laura said crossly.

"Okay, Dan?" said Adam. "Sorry if we woke you."

"'S'alright," he muttered. "I just wanted to say goodbye."

"I'll just see him back to bed and check on Jamie," said Beth. "Come on, Danny."

Laura and Geoff gave him a quick hug and he stumbled sleepily up the stairs back to his room. They heard Beth's murmured goodnight and then the sound of her opening Jamie's door. A few moments later she came running back down the stairs, her face white.

"Jamie's gone! He's not in his room."

"Have you checked the bathroom?" said Adam, not seriously worried for the moment. "Or the attic? He might be up there playing."

Between them, they combed the whole house, but Jamie was nowhere to be found. Then Adam discovered the unlocked back door.

"I know I locked it earlier tonight," he said. "He must be outside somewhere. Perhaps he's sleepwalking."

Beth felt a cold dread wash over her.

"He's not sleepwalking," she said. "He's with Valentine."

"Who's Valentine?" asked Geoff, bewildered.

"It's Jamie's imaginary friend," Adam replied. "Look, let's split up and look for him. He can't have gone far, surely?"

He fetched some torches and they went off in different directions, calling for him. Beth went towards the old kitchen garden to see if Jamie had wandered off to sit beside the old well again, but there was no sign of him. She felt sick with fear. She was certain that he had been lured away by Valentine and that the boy meant him some harm.

Suddenly, she heard Finn barking and then Geoff's shout.

"Beth! Adam! I've found him!"

"Thank God! Oh, thank God!" she cried on a sob as she hurried in the direction of Geoff's voice. He was carrying Jamie in his arms and she could see that the little boy was motionless.

"Where was he?" asked Adam.

"Finn saw him first; he was way up the road, near the path that leads towards the church," said Geoff. "Let's get him indoors, he's frozen."

He laid Jamie gently on the big settee in the lounge. Laura knelt down beside him and felt his pulse.

"I think he's just passed out," she said. Beth brought a blanket and wrapped him in it. Make him a hot drink, Adam, he's very cold."

They rubbed his feet and hands and Jamie's eyes gradually flickered open as Adam came in with a mug of hot chocolate. He frowned, and then smiled sleepily at Beth.

"Valentine and me was playing a good game, Mummy. He wanted me to come with him to his special place."

She put her arms round him and hugged him tightly.

"Jamie, darling. You must promise us you won't go out with Valentine again. You might have got lost."

He sat up, looking at her solemnly and his next words sent a chill down her spine.

"No, I won't, 'cos Valentine says he'll look after me but I've *got* to do what he wants, Mummy. He says if I don't, he won't be my friend anymore." His lip quivered. "An' he says that I won't see any of my family again, *ever!*"

CHAPTER 32

Beth decided to keep Jamie home from school the next day. He was very pale and listless and, unusually, very clingy and besides she didn't want to let him out of her sight. She was beginning to feel increasingly that the threat from Valentine was becoming very real. It was a miserable day; the weather had turned very wet and windy so Adam said he would drop Danny at school; he was staying at a friend's for tea after school and was being dropped home later. After emailing all the information she had about Beatrice and Valentine to Laura, she felt that she needed to take her mind off things so she decided to do some baking and sat Jamie in the kitchen with her with his cars and colouring books. He soon lost interest in them and came over to the table to watch her, so she lifted him on to the high stool near her, gave him his own bowl with some cake mix in it and he sat happily stirring it with a small wooden spoon. Then he helped her decorate the fairy cakes they had made.

Later that morning she sat with him in the lounge watching *Shrek*; after about half an hour he fell asleep so she went back out into the kitchen to make herself a cup of tea. The house phone rang while she was boiling the kettle and she saw it was Laura. She picked it up quickly so it wouldn't disturb Jamie.

"Hi, Beth. How is Jamie doing? I haven't had much of a chance to speak to Adam but he said you'd kept him home today."

"He seems okay, just very tired and a bit quieter than usual. He's asleep at the moment."

"Good. Look, I just rang to let you know I passed those details on to Paul. He said he's going to research some of it on the Internet sites he uses, and he also has some other resources that might prove useful. Hope you don't mind – I gave him your email address and he's going to email you directly with any information he can find out. I thought it would be more sensible than him ringing in case Adam's about."

"Thanks, Laura, that's great. I still feel really guilty about not telling Adam, but I think it's for the best at the moment. I'll let you know what I find out."

"If it's any consolation I think you're wise not to say anything until you find out more about what's going on. You know, that was pretty scary last night with Jamie. There does seem to be something strange going on, and I think you are right to be concerned. But, Beth…" she hesitated for a moment "…don't take too much on your shoulders and get out of your depth. This might turn out to be something you shouldn't be handling on your own."

"I know. Don't worry, Laura, I will be careful. But if I'm going to protect Jamie, I have to know all the facts."

She put the phone down and picked up her tea. In the lounge Jamie was still peacefully sleeping while on the screen Shrek and Donkey argued. She smiled, turned the volume down and picked up her sketchbook. She would have an hour's sit down then see about sorting out what to have for lunch.

The shrill, insistent ring of the doorbell woke her. The rain was still lashing against the windows. On the settee, Jamie stirred and sat up.

"Mummy…" He held out his arms.

She picked him up and went to answer the door. To her amazement Gloria Nash was standing there, swathed in a voluminous black raincoat and clutching a large pink umbrella, regarding her with anxious eyes. Her red Corsa was parked some way down the drive.

"Beth, my dear, I am so sorry. I just felt I had to come. I should have come before this, but I just felt I couldn't. I've had such strong messages, you see, and I just couldn't ignore them any longer."

"Messages?" Beth stared at Gloria. "What sort of messages?"

"Can I come in, dear? I'm sorry, I am very wet."

"Of course." Beth stood back, putting Jamie down, allowing Gloria to enter. "Please, let me take your coat." She hung the damp raincoat on the coat stand in the hall and indicated the umbrella stand next to it into which Gloria thrust the dripping umbrella. "Come into the kitchen and I'll make you a cup of tea."

"Thank you, dear. As I said I'm so sorry to turn up like this out of the blue. I was going to phone you first but for some reason I felt strongly that I had to see you face to face." She hesitated. "I know I should have made the effort to come to poor Audrey's funeral but it was all such a shock, you see."

"I do understand, Gloria, really," said Beth. She led the way through the green baize door and into the kitchen and sat Jamie at the table before going to put the kettle on. "It was a terrible experience for you, and Adam and I weren't at all surprised that you couldn't face it."

"But I *should* have come… I knew, you see, that I could have perhaps prevented it if I had listened to the warnings and taken more notice of the signs."

"Nobody could have prevented it," said Beth sadly. "No one could have predicted that the branch would snap at that particular moment. You mustn't blame yourself, Gloria."

"That's just it, Beth." She went and sat down next to Jamie, who gazed up at her solemnly. She smiled at him gently and then leant forward earnestly. "That's what my voices have been telling me. I could have stopped it if I had only had the courage to speak to him before he caused it."

Beth stared at her.

"What do you mean? Speak to whom?"

"Why, *him*, the boy I saw," she bit her lip and glanced again at Jamie. "The boy in the tree of course. It was no accident – he made it happen, Beth. You know who I mean, don't you?" Beth opened her mouth to deny it, but then slowly nodded. She glanced at Jamie who had picked up his crayons and was occupied with his colouring book.

"That's why we have to try and communicate with him." Gloria laid her hand gently on Jamie's head. "And we have to do it soon, before something else happens in this house!"

Beth suddenly realised the significance of what Gloria had just said.

"You… you mean… you actually *saw* him? When… how?"

"Why, that day, of course, when it happened. He was right there, up in the tree looking down at us. Jamie saw him, too, didn't you dear?"

Jamie plugged his thumb in his mouth, his eyes still fixed on Gloria and slowly nodded.

Beth frowned and shook her head.

"No, Gloria, Jamie wasn't there. He was up in bed, fast asleep, weren't you, sweetheart? I checked on him to make sure he was okay." She caught her breath suddenly, remembering the oak leaf she had found in Jamie's bed.

"Nevertheless, he *was* there," said Gloria firmly. "Things are not always as they seem. And you know that things are not right in this house, Beth. There is a presence here that is not at rest and I believe you have felt that as strongly as me. Please, won't you tell me what has happened so that I can perhaps help you to communicate with this poor child and find out what he is trying to tell us, and why he is not able to leave? We need to do that soon as I think there is considerable danger here for you and your children, especially Jamie."

Beth took a deep breath and sat down.

"You're right," she said shakily. "I know that this is getting worse. I'll tell you everything I know."

CHAPTER 33

The bar was crowded and noisy with lunchtime drinkers. Simon Ellis was sitting on his own at a corner table, staring broodingly into a large glass of whisky. He couldn't remember if it was his fourth or fifth; he only knew it wasn't helping him to forget the fact that Fiona had left him.

He had arrived back from Hampshire in a foul mood, his bandaged hand still throbbing from the deep bite inflicted by Finn. He had taken Beth's advice and stopped at the walk-in centre where they had dressed it and given him a tetanus jab as a precaution, but it still hurt like hell. Fiona wasn't home so he had slumped in front of the television, opened a bottle of cognac and proceeded to get utterly and gloriously drunk. Fiona discovered him there a few hours later; she had been worried as she'd had to work late and had been unable to reach him as he had turned his mobile off. She had rung the news editor, Oliver Finch, to find out where he was and had been told that he didn't know but that he certainly hadn't sent him to Birmingham to cover a story. When she was eventually able to rouse Simon, a flaming row had ensued and she had stormed out. The next day he arrived home from work to find her packing her clothes.

"I've had enough, Simon," she told him. "I'm not putting up with it any longer. You don't want a two-way relationship and I don't believe you're even capable of it. I don't know where you were yesterday, or who you were with, or how you injured your hand but, quite frankly, I certainly don't want to hear whatever lie you were planning on telling me." She banged the suitcase shut. "I'll send for the rest of my stuff later." Then she was gone, leaving him speechless and devastated. He had tried to ring her several times and had sent her innumerable messages and voicemails but she'd ignored them all and he had finally decided to give up.

He took another large gulp of the whisky and reflected bitterly again about that disastrous afternoon at Beth's. He had been so sure of himself and that had been the problem. If he had only been prepared to wait for a while, things might have been so different. On the other hand, after all he had done for her, you would have thought the frigid bitch would have been more grateful. Now she had caused him not only deep humiliation but the loss of the one woman he had been truly fond of. But she wouldn't get away with it; he would find some way to get even with her and his holier-than-thou brother…

"Simon! What's this, a liquid lunch break? I didn't expect to see you in here at this time."

He looked up blearily, to see Tony Wilmot standing by the table looking at him quizzically.

"Hi, Tony. No, I'm not at work at the moment, taking a few days off. I haven't been feeling so good."

"I can see that. What on earth's happened to your hand?"

"I got bitten by a dog. Fucking vicious brute belonging to my bloody brother. If it wasn't him, I'd be taking it further but, well, you know me – wouldn't want to cause a rift in the family and all that."

"Still, bloody nasty thing to happen. Is this the brother whose wife wanted all the information about her father?"

"Yes." A thought struck Simon and he leaned forward. "As a matter of fact, I needed to talk to you about that, Tony. She was really happy to find all that out but she desperately wants to contact her dad, find out all about his new family and, if possible, meet up with him. Is there any way you can give me his address or his phone number?"

Tony shook his head.

"Afraid I can't do that, old man. I stuck my neck out as it was; it wasn't easy, you know and I'd be in deep trouble if anyone found out. Sorry."

"I understand," said Simon. "Pity, though. I had a case of Jameson's with your name on it if you'd been able to help me out, plus a few quid to go with it. Never mind, let me get you a drink anyway."

An hour later they parted company amicably. Simon called a taxi and settled back comfortably in the back seat as it drove him home. He smiled contentedly as he reflected on a satisfactory outcome to the afternoon. In his pocket was a phone number and as soon as he got back to the flat, he rang it from his mobile.

"Is that Mr Morgan?" he asked the male voice on the other end, trying not to slur his words too badly. "You don't know me, but my name is Simon Ellis. I'm ringing you because I want to talk to you about your daughter, Beth."

Afterwards he paused for a few minutes before lighting a much-needed cigarette and then glanced at his watch. Two-thirty. With any luck he might catch Adam. He took another long drag and picked up the phone again.

CHAPTER 34

Adam put his phone down and stared into space. The call from Simon had come like a bolt from the blue; he still couldn't take in what his brother had told him. He sat thinking for a few moments, then buzzed through to his secretary.

"I'm afraid I have to leave early, Mary. Sorry it's such short notice but can you cancel that meeting with Dr Nolan? Tell him I'll rearrange it as soon as possible."

"Of course, Mr Ellis. Oh, Laura Dunbar has just come in to speak to you. Is it alright if I send her in?"

"Very well." A moment later the door opened and Laura looked in.

"Sorry Adam, I won't keep you long. I just wanted a quick word about the operating schedule for tomorrow. I thought we ought to get the Potts boy in first thing, but…" her voice trailed off and she looked at him and frowned. "Are you okay, Adam? Is this a bad time?"

"I don't know," he looked at her bleakly. "Laura, please tell me the truth. Has Beth told you anything about what she believes is happening in the house?"

Laura bit her lip and looked away. "I… I don't think I should say anything, Adam. Beth spoke to me in confidence."

He stood up and began pacing up and down.

"I need to know, Laura. I've just had an extraordinary phone call from my brother Simon and I don't know what to make of it. He thinks Beth is suffering from delusions, that she's seeing things that can't possibly be there. He's worried about her mental state; he thinks the boys could be at risk."

"That's ridiculous, Adam!" Laura interjected indignantly. "Yes, Beth has been having some strange experiences, but she is *not* delusional. Some odd things have been happening, but she's been worried about telling you about them because she knows how you feel about… about…"

"Supernatural occurrences?" finished Adam. "Yes, I think that's all a load of rubbish, as you know; but if she's worried about it, then why not talk to me? Instead, she seems to have confided in Simon, you, and God knows who else. Anyone, in fact, except her husband! And what about this offer of work in New York? Did you know about that?" He flushed with anger and shook his head disbelievingly as he saw her face. "Oh, I see you did. I wonder when, or even if, she was planning on telling me about *that*?"

"Look, Adam, she thought she was doing the right thing. I don't know how Simon knows about all this or what exactly he's said, but you know what he's like; he's always been jealous of you and, let's face it, he loves making trouble. At least give Beth the benefit of the doubt, and don't jump to conclusions before speaking to her. I know she was going to talk to you; she probably just wanted to pick the right moment. You've had a lot on your plate lately and she knows it. At least give her a chance to explain."

He nodded slowly, his anger subsiding. "Of course, I will. You know I love her so much, Laura, and I know she's worried about Jamie at the moment. I am too. And what happened to my mother hit us both so hard. I just can't bear to think that there have been secrets between us. Our marriage has always been so open; I thought we could talk about anything."

"You can," said Laura gently. "Just give it a chance and don't judge her too hastily – and certainly not on your brother's say-so."

She sighed as she watched him walk down the corridor and wondered if she should ring Beth to warn her. But then she decided she should leave well enough alone. She would stay out of it and let them work through this and hope that Adam would see that things were not right at Malthorp; not right at all.

CHAPTER 35

Gloria put a comforting hand over Beth's. They were sitting in Beth's studio and she had just finished reading Beatrice's diary. She glanced at Jamie, who was sitting on the rug in front of the fire playing with his cars. Beth had made them sandwiches and they had eaten them in silence while she read.

"It's quite a story, my dear. I can see why you have been so distressed and confused and why you want to find out more about Beatrice. But you must be careful, Beth. This could be dangerous territory. I can fully understand why you are so worried about your children."

Beth nodded. "Particularly about Jamie. He's so little, so vulnerable. I couldn't bear it if anything happened to him." Tears came into her eyes. "I need to know how to protect him. Danny could be in danger, too. We still don't know exactly how his accident in the woods happened. That's why I need to find out more of what went on in this house; what happened to Beatrice and Valentine. I think that could hold the key to everything. If we could help them somehow."

"It won't be easy," said Gloria. "I believe our first step must be to see if I can communicate with Valentine." She lowered her voice and glanced at Jamie, but he seemed absorbed in his cars. "I think I must go up into the attic as that seems to be where some of these manifestations have occurred." She stood up and moved towards the door.

"Do you want me to come with you?" asked Beth, feeling she should offer, though she very much hoped Gloria would say no.

"This is something I have to do alone, my dear. Stay here with Jamie and promise me that you will not let him out of your sight. I do not know what reaction I will get, but I do sense that this child seems very angry and frustrated and that he is using Jamie as some sort of link so that he can express those feelings. This attempt to communicate with him could well be quite a disturbing experience. Jamie needs to be safe so please do not leave this room, whatever you may hear."

"Gloria…" began Beth, but she had already closed the door after her. She shivered and moved towards the fire. Jamie glanced up and she smiled at him.

"Jamie thirsty, Mummy."

She crouched down beside him.

"I'll get you a drink in a moment, sweetheart. When Gloria comes back."

He nodded and returned to his cars, lining them up in neat rows; reds together, blues together. She sat beside him and glanced upwards. No sound as yet. She sent up a silent prayer, even though her belief in God felt shakier than ever.

❦

Gloria climbed the stairs to the first floor, feeling her usual mix of trepidation and anticipation. Over the years she had experienced several encounters with souls that were not at rest; most had been relatively peaceful but one or two had been angry or distressed. This one had felt different from the start and she was not quite sure what to expect. The house seemed very silent; almost too silent as she made her way along the passageway towards the steps which led up to the attic. As she put her foot upon the first one, she thought she heard a whispering sigh which echoed faintly.

"Who is there?" she asked quietly. "Is that you, Valentine? Will you speak to me?"

The silence grew heavier; she felt it like a thick, dark cloak surrounding her in its folds, smothering her. She could hear voices in her head, unclear like a badly tuned radio – the man's tone angry, bullying, the woman's pleading, tremulous. She shuddered, but forced herself to mount the stairs. Halfway up, the voices stopped abruptly.

"Will you speak to me, Valentine?" she asked again, then a chill ran down her spine as she saw the small wet footprints on the wooden treads leading upwards.

From above, a child's voice started singing faintly: the tune, vaguely familiar from her childhood, drifted softly down the stairs…

> *In the sky so clear above me*
> *The moon doth brightly shine*
> *Give me your heart then I will be*
> *Forever your Valentine*

She reached the top of the stairs and stretched her hand out towards the door handle, aware that the singing was becoming louder, echoing in her head.

> *Please say you'll always love me*
> *With a promise oh so true,*
> *And if you say that this is so*
> *My heart will belong to you.*

The singing stopped abruptly and she felt the temperature drop as the door swung open of its own accord…

Gloria took a deep breath and stepped into the room.

CHAPTER 36

Adam pulled up outside the house and frowned as he saw the red Corsa. It looked familiar but he couldn't think for a moment who it belonged to. Then he remembered – Gloria Nash. Had Beth known she was coming? If so, it was yet another thing she hadn't mentioned to him. He climbed out of the car and made a dash for the door through the pouring rain.

The house seemed very quiet. He hung his coat up, noticing the unfamiliar black raincoat hanging there. He thought that maybe Beth was in the kitchen and started towards the door but just then the door to the studio opened and she appeared.

"Adam! I wasn't expecting you. Why are you home at this time – is something wrong?"

"We need to talk, Beth." He frowned. "Is that Gloria's car outside? What's she doing here?"

"She – she came to apologise about missing Audrey's funeral, and to see how we were. Is there something wrong, Adam?"

"I don't know, Beth. That's what I want to ask you. I had an extraordinary phone call from Simon today. He seems to think that you've been imagining a lot of things; he says you've told him about some strange incidents that have happened and that you've been holding back from me. What on earth's going on – and why the hell are you confiding in him and not telling me what's bothering you?"

Beth flushed, and pulled the studio door to. "It's not like that. I was going to talk to you, but you've been so busy lately, so preoccupied with work. I didn't want to…"

"So, it's my fault, is it?" He had meant to remain calm but he was growing angry again. "That's your excuse. You felt you couldn't approach me, so you confided in my brother, Laura, Gloria Nash too, I daresay – where is she, by the way?"

"She just went upstairs for a moment." Beth stared at him in despair. "Honestly, Adam, I didn't mean to shut you out, but I didn't know how to tell you what's been happening. Listen, I think there's something very wrong here and I believe it's all to do with the people who lived here in the past. I think Jamie, and maybe Danny, could be in terrible danger. I've had some very, very strange things happen to me and then there was Danny's accident, your mother, Jamie disappearing…"

"Beth, just stop and listen to yourself," he said wearily. "You're beginning to sound like my poor mother. For God's sake, *nothing's* happened that can't be explained rationally. Okay, Danny had a horrible accident; kids do; we see it all the time at the hospital. My mother's death was also a tragic accident. As for Jamie; he was sleepwalking – again, lots of kids do."

"But there have been other things…"

"I need a cup of tea," he moved towards the baize door. "Do you want one?"

"No." She moved towards him. "You're right Adam. I should have talked to you before. Gloria will be down in a moment and then I want to show you something."

Before she could finish there were a sudden series of loud crashes and then a piercing scream from above them. For a moment they stood motionless in shock. Then as one they ran towards the stairs.

CHAPTER 37

They burst through the attic room door and stopped, staring in disbelief. The room was in utter chaos. The windows were wide open and the curtains were soaking wet from the rain that was blowing in. Bookcases had been thrown on their sides, books were scattered all over the floor, the television had been moved to the other side of the room. The doors of the big cupboard stood open and games, puzzles and toys were spilling out in a jumbled heap. In the corner of the room Gloria Nash crouched, hunched up with her hands over her eyes.

"Gloria!" Beth rushed over to her. "Are you hurt?" She knelt down beside the older woman and put an arm round her. She could feel that the woman was trembling uncontrollably. "Gloria?"

Gloria made a strange sound, somewhere between a moan and a sob. Her glasses had slipped down her nose, and she fixed unfocused eyes on Beth for a moment then gave a violent shudder.

"Has he gone? Please tell me he has." She suddenly seemed to focus again and clutched Beth's arm. "You *must* leave this house, my dear, all of you. You are in great danger. He will not stop until he has exacted his revenge."

"What did you see?" asked Beth. "What happened?"

She shuddered again. "I tried to speak with him, with Valentine, to communicate my desire to help him, and at first he seemed to respond but something dark and vindictive stood between us. I tried hard to break through but it would not let me and the child is so *angry*. He cannot be at peace until this impasse can be overcome somehow. Beth, I have communicated with so many unhappy souls but I have never experienced such hatred, such malice before. The other malevolent presence is, I believe, that of his stepfather, whose soul is also in torment. *His* malice is so forceful and so strong that it is feeding the boy's hatred. The only positive force coming between them, and trying to help her son overcome this, is Valentine's mother, Beatrice. But he resents her, too."

She rose to her feet shakily, pushing her glasses back on her nose. "Beth, I cannot emphasise this enough, you and Adam cannot stay here with the children; Jamie must be removed from here especially. He needs to use him to achieve his desires."

"What utter rubbish!" Adam stepped forward his face white with anger. "Is this how you make your money Mrs Nash? By coming into people's homes, throwing a few things around and then feeding them some tripe about evil spirits? Well, it won't wash with us. You may have been my mother's friend but that doesn't give you the right to walk in here and upset my family. I suggest you leave – now!"

"Adam, please!" Beth put her arm around Gloria. "Gloria is here to try and help us to protect Jamie and Danny. These things are really happening, you have to believe me!"

"I've heard enough!" Adam snapped. "Now, if you wouldn't mind, Mrs Nash, I'd like you to leave our house. Think yourself lucky that I'll not be informing the police about the damage you've caused."

Gloria rose shakily to her feet.

"Mr Ellis, believe me, I understand your anger and disbelief. But I can assure you that I was not responsible for what has happened here today. As I have said, there is grave danger here for you all if you stay. The forces that reside within these walls are more powerful than you can possibly imagine."

Adam shook his head disbelievingly.

"What part of 'leave' do you not understand, Mrs Nash? Beth will show you out."

He stood back, stony-faced, and held the door open. Gloria walked unsteadily past and Beth followed her, flinching at the furious look on his face. They walked downstairs in silence. Jamie stood by the studio door clutching one of his precious cars, his eyes wide and scared. At the front door Beth said

, "Gloria, I am so very sorry. It's so unlike Adam to react like that.

He's very angry with me for not telling him what has been going on. I don't know what to do now." Her eyes filled with tears. Gloria put her coat on and leant forward to give her a swift hug.

"Don't worry about me, Beth. I'm used to people reacting in the way that your husband has done. It is hard enough for those of us who believe to accept some of these manifestations. But…" through her pink spectacles her gaze travelled to Jamie and she lowered her voice, "…but you must be vigilant. Don't let Jamie out of sight because he is particularly vulnerable and Valentine will take advantage of that. By all means find out what you can about the family but be very careful; you could be treading on very dangerous ground. Remember, I am only a phone call away if you should need me."

Beth nodded, not trusting herself to speak. As she closed the door behind Gloria she turned and saw Adam was halfway down the steps. She hoped he hadn't heard the last part of her conversation with the medium. His face was still taut with anger. She turned to Jamie, who was looking at her in bewilderment.

"Jamie thirsty," he said tentatively. "Jamie want a drink *now*, Mummy."

"Come into the kitchen darling and Mummy will get you some apple juice. I'll talk to you later, Adam. We can't discuss this now."

Adam shrugged.

"As it seems I'm the last person to be told about anything, that remark doesn't surprise me. Anyway, as far as I'm concerned there's nothing to discuss. You seem to have decided that there is a problem where there obviously isn't. That woman has pulled the wool over your eyes, so believe whatever you choose to believe, Beth, but don't involve the rest of our family, or our friends, in it. Discussion ended."

He stormed down the stairs and into the lounge, banging the door behind him. Jamie jumped and began to cry. He had rarely, if ever, heard his father raise his voice in anger. Beth led him into the kitchen and poured him his drink, picking him up and sitting him on her knee while he drank it, sniffling in between sips.

"Daddy *cross*," he said tearfully. "Daddy *shout*."

"I know, darling," Beth sighed. "Daddy didn't mean to frighten you. He's just tired."

He looked at her solemnly.

"Valentine's cross too. He didn't like that lady. She told him to go away. But he *can't*, Mummy. He can't go away."

Beth leaned forward and took his face in her hands. For once he didn't flinch or move away.

"Why can't Valentine go, Jamie? What does he want?"

Her son held her gaze and his lip trembled.

"He wants the bad man to feel his pain. He wants the bad man to *die*."

CHAPTER 38

Adam barely spoke to Beth that night. After she had cooked dinner, which neither of them could eat, and put the boys to bed he went to his study and shut the door. She heard him switch his music on and the strains of Vivaldi's *Four Seasons* echoed faintly from the room. She sighed and went into the lounge, sat down and opened her laptop. An email alert pinged up and she saw it was from Paul Simmonds, Laura's brother. She opened it and read with mounting excitement.

> From: Psimmonds78@hotmail.com
> Subject: **Family of Beatrice Taylor**
> Hi Beth
> Found out quite a few interesting facts about Beatrice and family. She was born in 1880 in Lincolnshire. Her father was George Joseph Lawson, a mill owner, pretty wealthy according to the 1881 census, as he had a large household with several servants. He died in 1911. Her mother was Amelia, who passed away the following year. There were two siblings; a brother who died young and a sister who, as I think you already know, was called Lydia. Lydia married James Halliwell in 1906; he died in 1946 and she in 1962. They had three children, Sidney (b.1908), Michael (b.1914) and Constance (b.1924). Beatrice herself, as again you know, married twice, first to Edward Taylor (in 1901) by whom she had Valentine Edward (b.1902) and then, in 1908, to Richard John Cartwright (b.1869), by whom she had Robert John (b.1909).
>
> After Valentine and Beatrice died, the trail is more difficult to follow but I did manage to find Richard Cartwright on the electoral register in 1925. He was still living at Malthorp but

there is nobody else of the name of Cartwright living there so one assumes that he didn't remarry after Beatrice. Whether his son Robert, who would have been about sixteen by then, was still living with him is a matter of conjecture, of course, as he is not mentioned. Cartwright died in 1927.

Now for the news you might find really interesting. Constance, Lydia's daughter is still alive! I managed to track her down, again through the electoral register, and she's living not far from you in Alton. She is nearly ninety and lives with her daughter, Mrs Sheila Finchcombe. The address is 4 Cresswell Close and the phone number is 07234 682566. I took the liberty of giving Mrs Finchcombe a preliminary ring and explained that I was researching the history of Malthorp on your behalf. She spoke to her mother and says she would be willing to see you if you wanted. So, I'll leave it with you. If I can help in any other way, please let me know. It seems to be a fascinating story!

All the best, Paul.

Beth shut the laptop after printing Paul's email and saving to her secure document file. Adam knew the password for her account and she didn't want to risk him finding it. She felt awful about deceiving him again, but she told herself it was for the boys' sake and she couldn't take the chance of him finding out just how far she was prepared to go to protect them. She picked up her mobile and went out through the French doors into the garden. It was still dusk; a few birds were singing in the trees and there was a gentle breeze blowing. Adam's study window was open so she walked round to the other side of the house and, flipping open the mobile, dialled the number she had saved in it a few moments ago. After a couple of rings, a woman's voice answered.

"Sheila Finchcombe."

Beth's voice stuck in her throat for a moment.

"Hello, who is that?" The woman's voice sounded impatient and Beth took a deep breath.

"Hello Mrs Finchcombe. My name is Beth Ellis. I believe you spoke to Paul Simmonds today about the possibility of my speaking with your mother, about her aunt, Beatrice, who used to live in Malthorp House?"

"Ah, yes. Well, I have to tell you, Mrs Ellis, that my mother is very frail. She was quite ill a few weeks ago and her memory is deteriorating quite considerably. I don't know how much she will be able to tell you."

"I quite understand," said Beth. "I promise I won't ask her too many questions. I just thought she might be able to fill in some gaps for me about her aunt's life here."

"She has told me a few things but she does get quite distressed. I don't think her aunt had a very happy life at Malthorp. She has mentioned that there were some letters, but she's never shown them to me. To be honest I'm not really that interested in the family's past; I suppose I'm too busy dealing with the here and now, so I have tended to cut her off when she's been talking about it; especially as it makes her a bit tearful."

"I see," Beth hesitated. "Are you sure she will be okay to see me?"

"Oh, yes. In fact, she was quite adamant she would when I told her you were living in that house. She said that some memories shouldn't be forgotten, whatever that might mean. When would you like to come and see her?"

"I could make it tomorrow morning. About eleven?"

"That would be fine. She's at her best in the mornings, gets very tired after lunch and sleeps quite a bit in the afternoon. We'll look forward to seeing you then. Goodbye, Mrs Ellis."

Beth hung up and slipped her mobile into her pocket. She walked back to the rear of the house to hear Finn scratching at the kitchen door so she opened it to let him out. She went over to the bench near the garden wall and sat down watching the big golden dog as he sniffed around. She suddenly felt very tired; the day had taken its toll on her and she was drained. She called Finn and he came over, wagging his tail and sat by her feet. She fondled his soft ears and he put a large paw on her knee.

"Oh Finn," she sighed. "Am I doing the right thing? Maybe I should let it go. Perhaps we should all go away to the States for a year; get the boys away from all this."

Finn stiffened suddenly and gave a faint growl. Beth frowned.

"Hey, boy, what's the matter? What is it?"

The dog's hackles rose and his growling grew louder. He took his paw off Beth's knee and stood up, staring at the house intently, his whole body shaking. Beth followed his gaze and her breath caught in her throat.

There was a face staring out at her from the French doors. The image was grainy, like an old black and white photograph, but it was clearly a woman's face, white as death, her eyes black with despair. As Beth rose from the seat and stepped towards the house, her heart racing, another face appeared beside the woman who shrank back; this time it was a dark-haired, swarthy man. She had seen them both before, that night in the house when everything had changed and she had somehow slipped back in time – Richard and Beatrice Cartwright.

Suddenly their images faded and the child appeared, small and thin, his eyes gleaming brightly through round wire spectacles. His image was clearer, sharper than the man and woman and as he smiled slowly Beth felt her blood run cold. Somehow, he was more frightening than either of the others. "Valentine?" she whispered.

Without warning there was a loud explosion as the glass of the doors shattered and blew outwards into the night. Shards of glass flew towards her and Finn, still by her side, yelped loudly as one pierced his leg. Adam appeared from the house, his face white with shock.

"Beth! God, what happened?"

"I... I don't know. Adam... *Finn!*"

They knelt down beside the distraught dog who was whimpering and trying to bite his injured leg.

"We must get him to the vet straight away. See if the boys are okay and I'll ring Henry Selway in the village. He might come out."

An hour later they were sitting round drinking hot chocolate and comforting Finn who had a large bandage round his front leg and looking very sorry for himself. Henry Selway, the vet, had cleaned the wound, given him a painkilling injection and left them with a large plastic hood which Finn would have to wear so he didn't try to get the bandage off. Fortunately, Henry had managed to get the shard of glass out without anaesthetic as it hadn't penetrated too deeply.

"I don't understand how the hell it could have happened," Adam said for the twentieth time. "The only thing I can think is that somehow a stone flew up and cracked it. It was old glass so I suppose it could have weakened over time."

Beth said nothing. She was still in deep shock from what she had seen but she knew it was no use trying to tell Adam, he just wouldn't believe her. Still, at least he was speaking to her again.

"I've got some sheets of plywood in the shed. I'll just fix them over the doors until we can get the glazier out tomorrow. You're not going out are you?"

"I've an appointment at eleven," said Beth, thinking quickly. It would take her half an hour to drive to Alton. "Do you think you could be here?"

"Well as it happens, I've not got anything urgent on. I'll take the morning off. I'm sure Laura and the new guy can cover it. Where are you going?"

"I'm having my eyes tested in Winchester," said Beth, the lie coming quickly. "I can cancel if you want."

"No, it's okay." He put his mug down and walked over to her.

Squatting down he took her hands in his. "Look, Beth. I'm sorry I got so angry earlier, but it's so hurtful that you felt you couldn't talk to me. Can you understand that?"

She gave him a sad smile. "Please, Adam, it's me who should be apologising. I should have told you, but…"

"It's okay, my love. He kissed her gently. "But, please, no more secrets, eh?"

Beth took a deep breath. She would have to tell him what she intended to do.

"Adam, I know that and that's why I have to tell you…"

"I know… New York; that *is* something we'll need to discuss, but not tonight." He stood up and stretched, yawning widely. "Come on, I'll just fix that plywood on and we'll go to bed. I don't know about you, but I'm shattered."

Beth closed her eyes. She had tried to tell him, but she knew it was hopeless. She would just have to go on living the lie until she could prove to him that there really was something malevolent in this house. She would do anything to protect her boys and if that included deceiving her husband then so be it. She stroked Finn's head gently.

"Don't worry, boy," she said softly. "I won't let him hurt you again."

CHAPTER 39

Number four Cresswell Close was a neat bungalow with a large front garden on the quiet outskirts of Alton. Sheila Finchcombe, a plump, motherly woman who looked to be in her mid-sixties, opened the door with a welcoming smile.

"Come in, come in. Glad you could make it, Mrs Ellis. Mother is in good form today and so looking forward to meeting you."

"Please, call me Beth. It's very good of you to allow this."

"Not at all, and you must call me Sheila. I'm afraid I know very little about Great Aunt Beatrice; as you know she died long before I was born, but I think my grandmother Lydia confided in my mother and I believe it was quite a sad story." She smiled warmly. "Now, before I take you in to meet Mother can I offer you a cup of tea or coffee?"

Before Beth could reply a querulous, but surprisingly strong, elderly voice called out from a room on the right of the hallway.

"Is that Mrs Ellis, Sheila? Please don't keep her standing out there, bring her straight in."

Sheila smiled ruefully. "Coming, Mother."

She ushered Beth through the door into a light and airy room which overlooked the front garden. The cream walls were hung with paintings, mainly of birds, and against one wall was a single bed with a small washbasin next to it. A small bookcase jammed with books stood against the opposite wall to the door and there was a fireplace with a coal-effect gas fire; above it the mantelpiece was lined with family photos. A small, upright chair stood to one side of it and to the other was a rise and recline chair opposite a large television set. Sitting in the riser chair was a frail, elderly lady with fine, snowy-white hair and surprisingly bright blue eyes behind her gold-rimmed spectacles.

"Do come in, Mrs Ellis, how perfectly lovely to meet you. I'm Constance Dawson. Now Sheila, how about some tea or coffee for our guest?" Sheila nodded and pulled the upright chair round so Beth could sit opposite her mother.

"It's all in hand, Mother. Which would you prefer, Beth?"

"Oh, coffee would be lovely. Milk, no sugar please."

"I'll leave you two to chat while I make it. Have you taken your tablets, Mother?"

"Yes, dear, please don't fuss. Now Mrs Ellis," she continued as Sheila left the room. "Please do sit down and tell me how I can help you. I understand you and your family are living at Malthorp House?"

"Yes, but please call me Beth."

"And you must call me Constance, my dear. My son-in-law, Derek, is a lovely man but he will insist on calling me Connie, which I hate. Now, how are you getting on at Malthorp?"

Beth frowned. "Well, I don't know how to put it really, I love the house but there have been some rather strange incidents…" She paused, not really knowing how to begin to explain.

Constance gazed at her intently for a moment, then leant forward and laid her hand on Beth's arm "You know, my dear, that doesn't surprise me at all. My mother, Lydia, told me many times that it was a very sad house. I was the youngest of her children, you know; there were over twelve years between me and my eldest brother and, being the only girl, my mother and I were very close. She confided in me that Aunt Beatrice was desperately unhappy there; you obviously know that she lost her eldest son, Valentine, under very tragic circumstances. And sadly, she herself died only a year later."

Beth nodded and reached into her bag. "I found a diary written by Beatrice in the months leading up to her wedding to Richard Cartwright, her second husband."

Constance's face darkened at the sound of his name.

"Richard Cartwright was an abominable, cruel man who treated

Beatrice appallingly both before and after Valentine's death. He had affairs with other women while he was married to Beatrice you know. My mother found it difficult to even speak his name. When Beatrice died the family would have nothing to do with him – even his own son, Robert, left home as soon as he could and apparently never made any contact with his father afterwards. Money was tied up in a trust fund for both the sons, which Beatrice's father had set up, but after Valentine died it would have all been Robert's when he became twenty-one. Apparently, Cartwright tried everything to get his hands on the money, but the trustees would have none of it. He died alone in poverty, still at Malthorp. It was rumoured he drank heavily and that he also had syphilis; Mother said that he went raving mad in the end, cursing Beatrice and her dead son. Well, he deserved such a horrible end in her opinion. When he had gone, Robert shut the house up for a time. He didn't wish to live in it and I don't blame him, though I believe eventually he went back there. May I see the diary please, my dear?"

Beth handed over the book just as Sheila bustled in with the coffee.

"Now, there are some nice biscuits there, Beth, please help yourself. Shall I put yours here, Mother?"

"Yes, yes, dear," Constance said impatiently, screwing up her eyes as she perused the diary. "We'll call if we need anything else."

Sheila threw Beth a look of amused resignation and went out, shutting the door firmly behind her. Constance handed the book back to Beth.

"Will you read it to me please, dear? My eyesight is not so good as it used to be and I find this handwriting quite hard to decipher."

Beth took the small book and began to read. When she had finished, she looked up to see Constance's eyes were full of tears.

"That poor, poor girl! She sounds so full of excitement and anticipation and she must have thought this was her chance to find happiness again, plus a new father for little Valentine. If only she had known what was in store for them." She took a tissue from the box on the little table by her side and wiped her eyes. "Thank you so much for bringing that to me, Beth, it is good to know that she was happy, if only for a short while."

"You should keep this," said Beth, as they drank their coffee. "After all, you are her closest living relative. It's yours by right."

"Oh, no, I don't think so. As I'm sure you know, my family aren't really interested in our past. I trust you to keep it safe, my dear." She pointed to the bookcase. "Now, on that bottom shelf there is a wooden box. Would you bring it over to me, please?"

She took it from Beth and rested it on her knee. As she opened it, she smiled. "Ah, I thought it was in here." She handed Beth a photograph in a gilt frame. "That's my mother on the left with Beatrice when they were quite young girls."

The black and white photograph was a little faded but nothing could dim the beauty of the two girls who stood with their arms around each other. They looked to be in their late teens and were very much alike, their thick, dark hair curling to their shoulders. Beatrice was the slightly taller of the two and they were both smiling at the camera, looking carefree and relaxed.

"That is a lovely photograph," she said, handing it back to Constance. "They were obviously very close."

"Indeed. And this is one of Beatrice and her first husband Edward with their son, little Valentine."

Beth looked at this one with even greater interest. It was a more formal, posed photograph and this time Beatrice was sitting on a chair in front of her husband, a handsome, fair-haired man with a small moustache. He rested a proprietorial hand on her shoulder while gazing at the camera and Beatrice was looking down lovingly at the little boy on her lap. He was a dark-haired, very frail-looking child, dressed in a long smock and looked to be about three years old. He was gazing adoringly back at his mother. It was a lovely family picture, but Beth felt a chill run through her as she looked at the child. So, this was Valentine, the boy who had died at Malthorp, the boy who was still not at peace. He looked so young and innocent in the photograph. So engrossed was she that she almost missed what Constance was saying.

"Now, my dear, *these* were what I was looking for." Beth looked up to see her holding out a large brown envelope. "These are a few letters that Beatrice wrote to my mother. I haven't read them for many years, but I seem to remember that they become increasingly sad and strange as time goes on. Please take them with you and read them. It might give you some insight into Beatrice's unhappiness and what really happened at Malthorp all those years ago."

"Are you sure? It feels wrong to read your mother's private letters."

"I'm quite sure. I feel that someone needs to know the truth. It's preyed on my mind for many years. Now, if you don't mind, I am feeling a little weary now. Come and visit me again soon, my dear, and let me know how things are going. Sheila will show you out." She laid back in her chair and closed her eyes. Beth put the diary and the letters carefully into her bag and crept out of the room. Sheila came hurrying out of the kitchen.

"All done?" she asked brightly. "Was Mother able to help you?"

"Very much so," said Beth. "She's rather tired now. I hope I haven't worn her out too much" She indicated the brown envelope. "Look, I must tell you that she's given me some family letters to read. I hope that you are happy with that?"

Sheila shrugged. "It's fine by me. As I told you, I'm really not that interested, so I'm glad Mother's found someone who is." She ushered Beth to the door. "Do come and visit again. I think it's done Mother good to see a different face."

She waved goodbye cheerfully as Beth drove off. It was nearly one o'clock and she decided to stop off at a nearby garden centre for a bite to eat before heading homewards. She rang Adam on his mobile.

"Hi," he said. "How did the eye test go?"

"Fine, no change," Beth answered feeling a pang of guilt. "Did the glazier sort the doors out?"

"Yes, all done. He couldn't explain how it happened either. It's rather strange because he said it couldn't have been anything hitting the doors from the garden, because the glass shattered *outwards*, but there was no sign of anything or anybody hitting it from inside. So, it's a bit of a mystery. I'm off back to work in a minute. You okay to pick the boys up?"

"Yes, fine. I'm just going to grab some lunch, then I'll do a bit of shopping and get them. Is cottage pie okay for dinner?"

"Great! See you later."

She hung up, relieved that things seemed back to normal between them. She drove into the garden centre and went into their tea room where she ordered herself a chicken sandwich and a pot of tea. Settling down in a comfy chair in the corner she reached into her bag and pulled out the old brown envelope containing the letters. She carefully slid them out as the paper was quite fragile. With mounting anticipation, she unfolded the first one and saw the date, written in rather faded ink, in Beatrice's by now familiar hand. The twenty-seventh of May, 1908.

Taking a bite of the sandwich she began to read.

BEATRICE 1908-1909

Malthorp House
27th of May 1908

Dearest Lydia,

Well, here we are at last in our new house! It has taken so much longer than expected because the weather, as you know, has not been kind and the workmen were quite unable to finish working on the roof during April. But it is finished at last, and I am gradually getting used to the size of Malthorp House after living in the dear little cottage in the village whilst we were waiting. Richard has been <u>so</u> particular about having every detail right for us and it is wonderful to have everything brand-new. It has been so kind of father to help us furnish it as well as his generosity in paying the builders (Richard has said he will, of course, pay every penny back); our rooms look wonderful and the kitchen has been fitted with every modern convenience; Mrs Stoller, our cook, is delighted with the new range and says that cooking on it is a delight. We also have a beautiful bathroom, with a <u>water closet</u> (so different from the cottage where we had only an earth privy at the bottom of the garden!).

The gardens will be wonderful too when they are landscaped as Richard desires. I offered to take charge of that task as I feel sure I would enjoy so doing, but Richard refused my offer saying that I would have enough to do running the household, and that in any case he had strict ideas on how he wants them laid out. I am a little worried about the expense, but he reassures me that it is all in hand. He has already supervised the setting out of the kitchen garden; it is a little way from the house, which is not ideal, but while work was being carried out an underground spring was discovered and Richard has caused a quite deep well to be dug so that there will be a constant supply of water available for the fruit and vegetables. He has hired a man from the village, an old soldier named Albert Stokes who, with his son Jim, is proving to be an excellent gardener.

We have six indoor servants in all; Mrs Stoller; Florrie Baker, the kitchen maid; Mrs Calder, the housekeeper; Daisy Phillips, the housemaid; Mr Yates, the butler and John, the footman. We also employ Mrs Fox from the village to help with the washing and rough work and Billy, Daisy's brother, to clean the shoes. So, you can see my dear that I am <u>quite</u> busy supervising them all if nothing else!

Now to my dear little Valentine.

It is taking him quite a little while to adjust to such a great change in his life and, of course, to having a new Papa. When we were living at the cottage he was quite content, as we were there on our own for most of the week as Richard had his work in the City to go to and stayed at his club, only joining us at weekends. He is finding it rather harder now as Richard is only going up to the City once or twice a week and we cannot do just what we want. Nanny Bartlett is wonderful with him, but Richard is somewhat strict and says I have spoiled and indulged him, which may be true of course. I so wanted to furnish one of the rooms downstairs for him, because it would have made it much easier if he had not to struggle upstairs, but Richard said that was quite out of the question and that he intends to make the attic into a nursery and eventual schoolroom. Valentine will take all his meals up there with Nanny and his bedroom will be on the floor below. I ventured to say that he would find it hard to climb the steep stairs, but Richard insists it will be good for him to exercise his legs and that I am only encouraging his laziness. I <u>will</u> try and persuade him, but he has little patience where Valentine is concerned. I do hope things will improve between them; I hate to see that hurt look on my boy's face when Richard calls him a 'cripple'.

Well, dearest Lydia, please write back soon and let me know how you and James are faring. I do so envy you your little house, though I am sure I will soon get used to Malthorp.

Your loving sister
Beatrice

Malthorp House
12th September 1908

Dearest Lydia

Thank you so very much for your letter. I am so sorry that I have not written sooner but time seems to fly past <u>so</u> quickly; here we are into the Autumn months, although the weather remains pleasantly warm and the trees are still very green. I do hope you received the jars of Apricot Preserve safely that I sent you recently; I sent a hamper containing some to Mama and Papa also – our fruit and vegetables have been <u>splendid</u>, considering this is the first year we have attempted to grow them. Admittedly the fruit trees were here already, so I suppose we cannot take the credit for those. Mrs Stoller has been working non-stop and the pantry is now full of jars of preserves and pickles so we shall be well prepared for the harsh winter months!

Richard has been away for a few days; he had important business in the City, so he has been staying at his club again. I do miss him when he is away, but between you and me it is easier as regards Valentine who, I am sad to say, still cannot seem to form any sort of relationship with his step-papa. Indeed, to my constant dismay, he seems almost to fear and dislike him; I know he is only young but I am very distressed that they cannot like each other's company more. I have to admit that I feel Richard is sometimes quite harsh with Valentine; he does not seem to understand or accept my dear boy's infirmities and indeed is positively unsympathetic at times. I am so saddened; I fear that Valentine is even withdrawing from me and you know how close and affectionate we have always been. I understand that there may be some natural jealousy on his part – he is but six years old – however it nearly broke my heart the other day when he said, "Mama why did you have to marry again? Were you not happy when it was just we two?" Unfortunately, Richard heard him and was very angry – he ordered Valentine to bed early with no supper and told him he would be confined to the nursery for the rest of the week for his ingratitude and the sin of resentment, and that he should feel thankful that he was cared for at home instead of being sent to an institution for the infirm. Valentine went to bed weeping, but Richard would not allow me to go in and comfort him, saying he must learn his lesson.

I must close now, dearest Lydia, for I hear Richard downstairs; he is home somewhat early and will expect me to be there to greet him.

Write to me soon.

Your loving sister

Beatrice

⸙

Malthorp House
3rd October 1908

My Dear Lydia

Thank you, dearest sister, for your letter and the lovely books you sent for my Valentine. He was <u>so</u> thrilled with them – Nanny Bartlett is reading Mr Kipling's excellent 'Just So' stories to him every night and he is enjoying them immensely. I am trying to spend a little time listening to him read every day if I can, and think he is progressing well though, when Richard came in the other day to listen, he remarked that he considers Valentine <u>very</u> backward for his age as he was stumbling over some of the longer words. I believe, though, it was because Richard made him a little nervous as he normally copes very well when we are on our own. Richard mentioned again that next year he will consider sending him away to Boarding School, but I protested <u>quite</u> vehemently, saying that Valentine is very young yet and not nearly strong enough to cope with such a change. Nanny Bartlett does a wonderful job with him; she too reads with him every day and is teaching him simple arithmetic; I feel this is all he needs at present. Perhaps next year, when he is seven, we can think about a tutor. He is so very fond of Nanny Bartlett and she of him.

It is Richard's birthday next week and he has arranged for us to go to a hotel in Bath for four days. Whilst there we are going to take the

Waters and go to a ball at the Assembly Rooms. I am looking forward to it very much; Richard has ordered me a new gown – I went into Winchester last week for my fitting. He chose a beautiful peacock-blue watered silk with a cream lace trim and I was quite taken aback when I saw the dressmaker's bill, but Richard laughed when I mentioned it and said only the best for his beautiful wife. He can be <u>so</u> generous sometimes!

Whilst we are away Nanny Bartlett, accompanied by John, is going to take Valentine to see the Pastons for the day so he can spend some time with Laurence, whom he has not seen since we left our old house. It will do him good, I am sure, to be in the company of a child of his own age since, apart from the village children, there are none nearby to Malthorp. Sometimes I think perhaps Richard is right and that he would be better off at school making friends, but I am afraid he would be terribly teased and bullied because of his condition. Perhaps when he is a little older and stronger I might consider it. I have even thought about suggesting he attends the village school, where he could at least come home every day, but I know Richard would never countenance such an idea.

I must confess that I, too, feel a <u>little</u> isolated here at Malthorp. We have no immediate neighbours and Richard does not encourage visitors. I have tried to persuade him to invite Mama and Papa and you and James for Christmas, but he is insistent that he would prefer our first Christmas here to be on our own. It is <u>such</u> a contrast to my life with Edward who, although he had no living family, loved nothing better than gay company and spending time with us all. I must say that I do find it rather strange because Richard has always told me that he has no family of his own apart from his elderly Aunt and yet he doesn't even wish to visit her any more, or to invite her to visit us. Indeed, I have never met her as she did not even attend our wedding. I would love to do so but have never made her acquaintance because Richard insists she is too frail for visitors.

Well, my dear, I think that is all my news; I will be sure to write soon

and tell you about our little trip to Bath – I confess I am <u>so</u> looking forward to it. Please give James my love.
Your ever-loving sister,
Beatrice

⁂

Malthorp House
3rd January 1909

My dearest Lydia
A very Happy New Year to you all! I confess that I am very surprised not to have received any letters from you lately; I wrote twice, once at the beginning of November and again in December, and can only think your letters must have gone astray. It is strange because I did not hear from Mama either for a while; however, I received a long letter in her Christmas Card telling me all the news.

We had a pleasant, but very quiet Christmas Day. A large Christmas Tree was ordered and Valentine was permitted to help decorate it, which he enjoyed very much. For once Richard was much more tolerant of him and he was allowed to join us downstairs for dinner on Christmas Eve and, of course, for Christmas Day luncheon. He was delighted with his Christmas Presents – thank you for Treasure Island, he is looking forward to Nanny Bartlett reading it to him when she has finished Through the Looking Glass. I gave him a Fort, complete with toy soldiers and he spends hours playing with it. Nanny Bartlett kindly bought him a beautiful Music Box which plays his favourite tune; My Heart Will Belong to You – do you remember that it was Edward's favourite song and we always used to sing it together when you came to visit? I think he loves it so much because it reminds him of Edward who used to say it was <u>his</u> favourite because it has Valentine's name in it!

Richard gave him a beautiful illustrated Bible and Valentine thanked him very prettily, but I think he is a little apprehensive, because Richard says he will expect Valentine to read set verses every day and perhaps memorise some to improve both his reading and his moral attitude. I did not say anything but I think that is a lot to expect of a child of his age.

Now, I have some very Exciting News to tell you. I am expecting a child! I went to see Doctor Williams yesterday and he has confirmed that the happy event will take place in July. Richard is <u>absolutely</u> delighted and is insisting that I rest every afternoon, even though I feel <u>extremely</u> well; not at all sickly as I did when I was carrying dear Valentine. I have not told him yet; I do hope he will be thrilled at the idea of a baby brother or sister.

Richard has gone to the City today; he has urgent business and may have to stay for a night or two, so I am going to walk to the village this afternoon accompanied by Nanny Bartlett and Valentine. The weather is good, quite cold but bright sunshine, so we are going to wrap up well and make sure Valentine has plenty of rugs in his wheeled chair. I'm sure Richard would not allow it if he was here but – while the cat's away as they say! I will post your letter myself whilst we are in the village so this one should <u>not</u> go astray!

I do hope all is well with you and James, <u>please</u> do write soon and let me know how you, James and little Sidney are faring.

Your loving sister

Beatrice.

CHAPTER 40

"Excuse me, have you finished? May I clear your table?"
Beth looked up in startled confusion at the plump woman hovering by the table clutching a tray. She had been so caught up in reading Beatrice's letters that for the moment she could not think where she was. She smiled apologetically as the woman regarded her quizzically.

"Of course – I'm so sorry, I was miles away."

She glanced at her watch. Quarter past two. She was due to pick Jamie up in just over an hour. Much as she would like to finish reading the four letters that remained, she had better pick up the few bits of shopping she needed before heading to Hopelands. Just then her mobile rang, and she saw it was Tom Mitchell.

"Beth?" He sounded anxious and her heart sank.

"Tom, hi. Is everything okay? Is there a problem with Jamie?"

"Well, yes, I'm afraid so. Beth, could you come over straight away please? I need to see you."

"What is it? Oh God, is he hurt? Has there been an accident?" Her voice rose.

"No, no, nothing like that – he's fine. But there has been an incident involving another child. I don't really want to discuss it over the phone but Jamie is a little upset. I think you need to get here as soon as possible."

"Of course. I'll come straight away."

She put the phone down, her head in a whirl. Tom had sounded very serious and concerned. What on earth could have happened? She grabbed her jacket and bag and hurried out to the car.

Jamie had been having a good day. First, they had been outside playing on the obstacle course, which he loved and then they had moved indoors to play 'School Shop' where they took it in turns to be the shopkeeper or the shopper. Jamie particularly liked being the shopper and pushing the small shopping trolley around the tables which were loaded with miniature packets, tins and bottles. Then it was time for lunch, which the children ate in the bright, colourful hall and he felt really happy that Mum had packed his one of his favourite cheese triangles. But as he went to unwrap it the boy sitting next to him, Zac, made a grab for it.

"I like them!" he declared, pouting. "They're my favourite. I want it, Jamie, give it to me!"

"No! It's Jamie's. You can't have it!" Jamie pushed him away.

Zac screamed loudly and grabbed it from him. He was considerably bigger than Jamie and easily held him off as they struggled. Before Jamie could stop him, he had torn off the rest of the wrapper and stuffed the cheese in his mouth. Doreen, the dinner lady, heard the commotion and rushed over to see what had happened but it was too late.

"Now then, what's the matter?" she asked, seeing Jamie in tears. "Why are you two fighting?"

"Zac... Zac take my cheese..." wailed Jamie.

"No, it was *my* cheese!" retorted Zac. "I like cheese!"

Doreen got a tissue and wiped Jamie's eyes. "Never mind, Jamie," she said. "You've got plenty of lunch left, though it was very wrong of you to take that, Zac You need to say you're sorry to Jamie."

Zac's bottom lip stuck out and he glared mutinously at Doreen. "Won't! I not sorry!"

Doreen frowned, but decided not to pursue it. She knew Zac of old, and if she insisted, he would be very likely to have a meltdown. "Very well, we'll talk about it later. Come on Jamie, we'll sit you over here to finish your lunch."

She led the still-sniffing Jamie over to another table, and smiled at her colleague Jane who was standing nearby.

"Keep an eye on Zac," she said. "He's very prone to pinching the other children's food." She set the rest of Jamie's food onto a plate and gave him a cup of water. "There we are, Jamie," she said kindly. "You eat that nice sandwich up now."

Jamie sat at the table on his own with his head down; he didn't feel like eating any more of his lunch and pushed the plate away. He took a sip of water; then he felt the bench sag slightly as if someone had sat down next to him. He looked up quickly, thinking it might be Zac. Then he gave a wide grin as he saw who it was.

"Hello Jamie!" said Valentine. "That was horrible of Zac, wasn't it? I think we need to teach him a lesson."

When Beth arrived at Hopelands Tom Mitchell was waiting by the front doors for her. She ran up the steps.

"Tom! What is it? I've been worried sick, imagining all sorts of things. What on earth's happened?"

"Come into the office, Beth. We need to talk somewhere private." He ushered her into his private office and shut the door. "Please sit down."

"You said there has been an incident with another child."

"Yes, a boy called Zac Harper."

"Zac? Yes, Jamie's talked about him a few times. But I thought they were quite friendly. In fact, I was speaking to Zac's mum only the other day and she was saying that he had been asking if Jamie could come over to play one day soon."

Tom nodded. "Yes, well, there was an unfortunate incident at lunchtime. Zac pinched some of Jamie's food and he and Jamie had a bit of a tussle. Jamie ended up in tears and Doreen, the dinner lady, had to separate them. I think Jamie may have taken it harder than we realised at the time."

Beth stared at him. "So, this is just about Jamie and another boy having a bit of a fight? I don't understand, it doesn't sound that serious – I mean, did Jamie hit Zac or something?"

Tom bit his lip. "No, not then – everything seemed fine. Then, this afternoon, the children had an art and craft class. The class are painting a big mural and Jamie and Zac were working on the sky. Sarah Miles, the art teacher, turned her back for a moment to sort out some paints and the next moment she heard a scream. When she turned round, Zac was on the floor; Jamie was sitting on him, pinning him down and pouring a pot of blue paint all over his face. It was in his hair, his eyes and his mouth. Apparently, he was choking and Sarah had to turn him on his side because he was fighting for breath."

"Oh my God!" Beth was horrified. "Is he going to be okay?"

"Well, he's been taken to hospital for a check-up. The paramedics don't think he'll have suffered any permanent damage because the paint was well diluted and, of course, all our craft materials are non-toxic, but they will possibly keep him in overnight to be safe."

"Where's Jamie?"

"Marie's taken him into the sensory room to calm him down. Although it was strange; he didn't seem to be at all aware of what he had done, indeed he seemed to shut down after it had happened. You know, he's made such good progress lately and it's very unlike him to react in such an aggressive way to another child. I know you said he's been having some problems at home lately and that certainly seems to be borne out by what he said just after it happened."

"What was that?" asked Beth faintly, though she had an idea what was coming.

"Well, this imaginary friend of his, that you've been so concerned about – Valentine? He told Sarah, quite adamantly, that it was Valentine's idea. Jamie's blaming the whole thing on him."

Jamie was very pale and silent on the way home in the car. Beth rang Adam from Hopelands to tell him what had happened and he was as horrified as her. He said he would go and look in on Zac, see what the situation was, and maybe talk to Zac's parents, then leave work early to go and pick up Danny so that Beth could take Jamie straight home. As they headed up the road towards the village Beth glanced in the mirror at her small son, who was curled up in his car seat, thumb firmly plugged in his mouth.

"Jamie," she said, "it's okay, darling. Mummy knows you didn't mean to hurt Zac. Tell me the truth. Did Valentine tell you to pour that paint all over Zac, like you told your teacher?"

In the mirror she saw his eyes swivel in her direction. Slowly, he nodded.

"And how about that day in the woods when Danny was hurt? Was that Valentine too? "

He nodded again and unplugged his thumb. His bottom lip trembled, "An' Valentine told Jamie to tear Danny's books up."

Beth didn't dare ask him about Audrey. She slowed down as they approached the turn-off for the village.

"Why do you think Valentine makes you do bad things, Jamie? What does he want?"

Jamie wriggled in his car seat and tears sprang into his eyes. "He wants us to tell what the bad man did a long time ago. He's angry 'cos his Mummy didn't help him and she let the bad man hurt him so he can't leave the house."

"What did the bad man do? Who was he?"

Jamie put his thumb back in his mouth and closed his eyes.

Beth frowned. She hated questioning him like this, but she had to know. "Jamie! Please darling, you have to try and help me understand. Does Valentine want you to find out what happened and help him?"

Jamie shook his head and muttered through his thumb. "No, Mummy. He wants *you* to help him."

Beth sighed. I only wish I could, she thought, then maybe this nightmare would be over.

"I'm doing my best, Valentine," she whispered. "What else can I do?"

The skies began to suddenly darken as she approached the lane leading up to Malthorp and the first fat raindrops began to fall. As she turned into the lane the heavens opened and she turned her wipers on full blast as the windscreen was obscured by the torrential downpour. They were nearly at the entrance to Malthorp when to her horror, through the blurred glass, she saw a small figure standing motionless in the middle of the road. She stood on the brakes and swerved hard. She felt a sharp pain in her left wrist as the steering wheel spun uncontrollably; despite her efforts it twisted out of her hand, then she lost control completely as the Land Rover skidded and slewed violently across the road. As the car tipped, she caught a glimpse of one of the sinister stone lions glaring down at her, and heard the sound of Jamie's terrified screams as they hit the stone gatepost of Malthorp head on, then she remembered no more.

CHAPTER 41

Beth opened her eyes slowly to see Adam's concerned face looking down at her. She screwed up her eyes against the light; her head hurt and she ached all over. She suddenly realised she was lying in a hospital bed and the memory of the crash came surging back, together with the echo of the last thing she remembered hearing – Jamie's screams. She tried to sit up.

"Jamie?" she asked.

"It's okay, my love. He's fine." Adam put his arm round her and gently stroked the hair back from her face. "He wasn't hurt, just very shaken up. The air-bag went off, thank God, otherwise you might have been more seriously injured."

Beth looked down to see her left wrist in plaster.

"Did I?

"Yes, broken wrist I'm afraid and a slight concussion. You'll be in here for a couple of days." He sat down next to her and took her uninjured hand in his. "Can you remember exactly what happened, Beth? The police say it looks as though you just lost control. It was a clear road, a bright afternoon and there was no other car involved as far as they know. It was lucky you were found so soon; one of the people from the village was walking her dog and heard the crash so she rang for the emergency services right away."

Beth stared at him disbelievingly.

"A bright afternoon? Adam, what are you talking about – it was bucketing with rain; I had to have the wipers on at full speed!" She hesitated. "And there *was* someone else involved; I swerved to avoid him and that's what made me lose control." She met his eyes. "I'm pretty sure that it was a child, in fact I... I think it was Valentine, Adam. I definitely saw him standing in the middle of the road."

"No, it can't have been, Beth, the police said…"

"I don't care what they said! I tell you Adam it was Valentine – he caused the crash." She struggled to sit up as he looked away, biting his lip. "Please, you have to listen to me, I know it sounds crazy, but this is real. Just think about it; Danny's accident; the strange things that have been happening, Audrey's death; what happened with Zac – he's at the root of it all. We have to get away from Malthorp before something else happens. Gloria was right and we're all in terrible danger. Valentine is still there and he's using Jamie to get what he wants." She bit her lip. "Adam, that's not all, it's not just Valentine; twice I've heard a woman sobbing, and one night I had such a weird experience – I seemed to slip back in time and I saw her, his mother, and someone else, a man I think was his stepfather… it was terrifying! And… and I saw them again last night; I swear I saw their faces at the window before the glass exploded…"

"For God's sake, Beth, enough!" Adam stood up and walked over to the window. He stared unseeingly at the red brick hospital buildings for a moment and then turned and walked back, taking a deep breath as he did so. "Look, I don't know what it was that you believe you saw, but I *know* there are no ghosts or evil spirits or whatever you want to call them. Look, things have been getting out of hand lately; bad things have happened, admittedly, and I've been having to work long hours so you've had to cope with the kids and we've all been under a lot of pressure. Listen, I've been thinking a lot about it and, when you're out of here, why don't I take some time off and we'll all go away for a couple of weeks? Somewhere abroad, say Spain or Portugal? We could get a villa with a pool and everything. We've never taken the boys out of the country and I know they'd love it, especially the flight. It won't hurt them to miss school for a while. What do you say?"

Beth closed her eyes. It was hopeless; she so badly wanted to tell him about her visit to Constance and to show him Beatrice's letters, but she knew that he wouldn't want to listen. She felt weak and shaky, her wrist hurt like hell and she felt tears seep from under her eyelids.

"Whatever you think," she murmured, her voice catching in her throat and she turned her head away. Adam bent over and kissed her cheek.

"That's it, you rest and think it over when you feel up to it my love. I'll let you get some sleep now – I'll bring the boys in to see you later. Debs is going to stay for a few days, she's been absolutely marvellous so you don't have to worry about a thing. See you later."

When he'd gone, Beth dozed for a little while before the staff brought round her lunch. She managed to eat a little, though she had no appetite and then sat and half-heartedly flicked through a couple of magazines Adam had left for her. Then she got out of bed, still feeling sick and a bit dizzy, and looked around for her handbag. She finally found it in the bottom of her bedside cabinet; to her relief Beatrice's letters were still safely inside in the brown envelope. There were four left and, despite the headache she now felt coming on, she decided to carry on reading them. Climbing back into bed, she opened the envelope. She needed to know how Beatrice had coped with the increasing hostility between her son and her husband.

BEATRICE

Malthorp House
July 24th 1909

My Dearest Lydia

Well, as Mama has no doubt told you, Richard and I have been blessed with a beautiful son, Robert John, born a week ago at two o'clock in the afternoon. He weighed a very healthy seven pounds, and is perfect in every respect. Richard is naturally delighted and spends every moment he can in the nursery. He has, as is his way with <u>every</u> aspect of our lives, taken charge of the nursery arrangements and has engaged a young girl from the village, Jenny Somers, as Nursery Maid to assist Nanny Johns who is a very capable and efficient woman that he employed from a London agency. I was having some difficulty feeding Robert and she suggested that I supplement his milk with a powdered solution of cow's milk in a bottle and he seems very content with this and is thriving.

Valentine is fascinated with his little brother and wished straight away to hold him, but Richard would not countenance such a thing, saying that Valentine is neither responsible nor robust enough to hold such a small baby and, indeed, has forbidden him from even visiting the Nursery. I did protest, saying I felt Richard was being unnecessarily harsh and that naturally Valentine wanted to get to know his brother, but Richard grew quite angry with me and I must confess to feeling a little weak and tearful after the birth so I did not venture to argue the point. I am hoping he will relent in the future. I could see Valentine was upset; he misses his beloved 'Baba' so much still, although he is progressing well under Mr Hopkins, his new tutor and seems to like him well enough.

My dearest, you and James must come soon and visit us to see your new little nephew. I know how much Valentine would love to see you too; only the other day he mentioned his Aunt 'Lydie' and asked when we would visit you. He had such fun flying the kite with James – I do wish that Richard would make time to do that sort of thing with him, but he still has very little time for my dear boy and is so impatient and intolerant towards him. Indeed, he has even ventured to suggest lately that Valentine should perhaps be sent to live in an Institute for the Disabled – a suggestion against which I most vehemently protested as you may imagine! I am telling you this in the <u>strictest</u> confidence, of course; <u>please</u> don't mention it to Mama or Papa as I know they would be very angry indeed that Richard should propose such a thing.

Robert will probably be christened at the local Church; that is my wish anyway. Reverend Beech, is a delightful man and the Church, St Andrew's, is very lovely with such a tranquil and peaceful feeling within its walls.

We have not been there to worship as much as I would have liked, as Richard is not a great devotee of church-going – even though he insists on Morning Prayers every day for the family and servants, but I am determined to go when I am up and about again.

Well, my dearest Lydia, it is nearly time for Nanny Johns to bring Robert to me for his afternoon feed, so I will close now. Please, please do write to me soon and let me know all your news and tell Mama I will write and hope and pray to see her and Papa very soon.

My very fondest love to you, James and little Sidney

Your ever-loving sister, Beatrice

There was a break in the letters then of nearly a year and when they resumed the tone had changed.

Malthorp House
September 5th 1910

My dearest Lydia,

I cannot tell you how wonderful it was to see you and James during our visit to Gloucester. I cannot believe how quickly the week passed; to spend so much time with dear Mama and Papa was splendid, though I do feel a little concerned for Papa, he seems to have lost much weight and is so short of breath that it seems an effort for him to do anything. He was wonderful with the boys though, especially Valentine, who loves him so dearly in return. Mama is also looking very tired and unwell; I think she is very concerned for Papa though she tries very hard not to show it.

I felt so distressed that Richard has made little effort to form any relationship with the family, indeed he and Papa had high words over his treatment of Valentine. I attempted to speak to him about it when we returned home but he grew very angry with me, saying I thought more of you all than I do of him. I denied this, of course, saying that there are different types of love and my love for the Family took nothing away from him but he became quite enraged and we exchanged a few heated words.

Lydia, I tell you this in <u>strictest confidence</u> and I beg you not to repeat it to anyone, not even James, but during our quarrel Richard violently struck me, causing me to double up in pain. He then overpowered me and (I do not know how to relate this to you, but you are a married woman and will know to what I refer), proceeded to force himself upon me quite brutally and against my will. He was very contrite afterwards, of course, but it has left me shaken and unwell, even a week after it happened. This is not the first time he has threatened me or Valentine with violence but it has never come to this before. Since it happened, he has been very considerate and very attentive, explaining that I am sometimes very unreasonable and provoke him (though I do not feel I do), so perhaps I need to put it behind me and try harder to please him.

I think Valentine senses something has happened; he has been very nervous and unhappy since our return three days ago and Richard has done nothing but criticise him – he examines his School Work every day and says that his handwriting and arithmetic are appalling for a boy of his age. Valentine drew me such a lovely picture the other day of the house but Richard poured scorn on it before tearing it in half, saying that it was no better than a two-year-old child would produce. He then sent Valentine to bed early without supper because he naturally shed tears at Richard's unkindness. Valentine has not spoken since except to say he hates Richard.

My dear, I'm sorry to sound so despondent but life is not easy for me and I do feel quite wretched at the present time.

Your loving sister, Beatrice

Malthorp House
December 15th 1910

Dearest Lydia

I do hope you and James are well. Christmas is nearly upon us once more and the weather here has been unseasonably mild after the dreadful gales we suffered in the Autumn, but today the temperature has dropped and we are threatened with snow.

How is Papa? I wrote to Mama last week but have not had a reply yet. I do hope he is a little better and that he has been able to get about a bit more. I so wanted to come up to see him, but Richard would not countenance it, saying my place is here with him and Robert. Please give them my <u>dearest love</u> when you next visit.

I must admit to feeling rather low, my dear; I have not seen my darling Valentine for a few days. Richard will only allow him to be brought down once a week and he may only spend half an hour with me in the parlour. He is so unhappy, hardly like my boy anymore; he speaks seldom and then only to answer any questions I ask him. He has lost all his lovely cheerful nature and has grown very thin and pale, dragging himself round painfully on his crutches. I know he pines for me and I have begged and begged Richard to allow him to become part of our household again, as I know he is very sorry for what happened with Robert. There was a distressing incident which I will tell you about another time, but Richard refuses to relent. So, my poor boy must suffer his banishment to the attic and it breaks my heart to hear him singing 'our' song so sadly up there sometimes.

Richard has been away for two days, he says it is on business, but I do not know whether to believe him; indeed, I am beginning to suspect him of having another woman, as I found a lace handkerchief on the floor in his study the other day which is certainly not mine, and I have smelt perfume upon him several times when he has returned home from the City. I dare not venture to say anything because I fear his anger so. His outbursts of temper have become very much worse; indeed, I feel I hardly know him anymore. He was furious with me yesterday because I dared to ask him if I could take Valentine to Winchester to see Doctor Temple again.

He struck me so violently across the face that I have had to stay in my bedroom today as my eye is quite swollen and bruised. I know he says I deserve such punishment but I do try not to say anything to provoke him, though he insists I bring it upon myself.

He is away tomorrow and so I shall have a chance to go to the Village if my eye is better, and I will post this myself. I have written before this but I suspect he is taking my letters from the posting tray downstairs as I know you do not always receive them.

Love as always, dearest sister

Beatrice

Beth put the letter down feeling a deep sense of sadness and outrage. Poor woman – Richard Cartwright sounded a sadistic bastard. She remembered back to the night she had seen everything change in the house, how he had spoken so brutally to Beatrice and raised his arm to strike her. So, he had raped her, probably more than once, and she had not been able to do anything because in those days such treatment of a wife was considered acceptable within marriage; by law a husband had the right to treat his wife however he wanted. Constance had spoken of him being unfaithful to Beatrice and that seemed to be true also. So, his treatment of Valentine had also worsened; she wondered what the boy could have possibly done to his little brother to warrant being treated so harshly, banned from seeing his mother and banished to the attic room. No wonder the poor child still haunted the house and was so angry – he must have spent many unhappy hours in this place. And Beatrice; no wonder she could not find peace and seemingly was also trapped at Malthorp with her son and the man who had detested him and brutalised her.

"Poor little Valentine," she murmured out loud. "What on earth did you do to make him hate you so much?"

VALENTINE
September 1910

The great storm has raged for two days. Gale-force winds have relentlessly lashed both land and sea; torrential rain has flooded huge tracts of the countryside; lightning has struck periodically, splitting ancient oak and elm in the nearby woods. Two fishing-boats have been lost in the heaving seas near the Needles, with the loss of fifteen lives. People in Hampshire have said they cannot remember worse weather.

But now the worst of it has abated and the inhabitants of the county are beginning to resume their daily activities and count the cost of the devastation the storm has wrought. Farmers gloomily survey their sodden fields and ruined crops; roofs are repaired and roads and tracks cleared of fallen trees. The villagers of Upper Melcombe have suffered their share of the misfortune and are counting themselves lucky to have escaped the storm relatively unscathed compared to many. A few tiles are missing from roofs, there are some fallen elms in the woods, an overturned cart in Tupps Lane and, of course, there is the sad loss of Mrs Bellman's old dog, which was hit and killed by a falling branch. It is counted a miracle that the church spire, well over four hundred years old, has weathered the storm.

Malthorp House, too, has escaped the worst of it, although here too the roof is missing some tiles, and a bucket has had to be placed in the nursery maid's room to catch the water from the resultant leak. The Cartwrights, but recently returned from Gloucester, where they have been visiting Beatrice's parents, have instructed Albert Hudson, the roofer, to call as soon as possible to repair the damage.

Jenny Somers can hear the sound of the gentle *plink-plonk* the water is making in the galvanised bucket as she sits on the nursery chair mending one of baby Robert's fine wool vests. The rain has all but stopped though there is still a fine drizzle coming down from the leaden skies. It is nearly half past seven and she has not long lit the gas lamp. The early September evening is chill and the nursery fire has been burning most of the afternoon, so the room feels warm for once. It is one of the things Jenny does not like about working here at Malthorp; the Master will not allow the fires to be lit too early and the nursery, here at the top of the house, becomes chilly. Today, though, little Robert has been suffering from a slight cold, so the Mistress has ordered the lighting of the fire. Jenny does not care for the Master at all; he gives her the shivers with those piercing cold eyes of his, and the way he uses them to look at her as if she was beneath contempt. She likes the Mistress, though; she feels sorry for her, being wedded to *him*. There is one other thing she doesn't like, and that is the way Richard Cartwright treats young Master Valentine. It is wrong for him to be so spiteful and she has told Nanny Johns so.

"It's not our place to say anything about that, Jenny," Nanny Johns will never allow a word to be said against the family. "I'm sure the Master doesn't mean to be unkind to Master Valentine. It's just his way."

Jenny doesn't agree. She has seen first-hand how horrible he is to Master Valentine, and the poor little lad being the way he is and all. It is cruel and heartless in her opinion. She always tries to be as kind as she can to the boy, dear little thing he is, though so quiet and withdrawn at times. It tears at her heart to watch him dragging his poor wasted legs as he hobbles around on those crutches. However hard he works at his lessons with his tutor, Mr Hopkins, it seemed that it was never good enough for his step-papa. She smiles slightly at the thought of Mr George Hopkins, who always says "Good Morning" to her so politely on his way through the nursery to the schoolroom beyond. He is nice-looking in his way and she likes him very much. But he will never really notice a lowly nursery-maid like her, she is sure of it. She sighs a little wistfully and bends more closely over her mending, squinting a little in the dim light. It is Nanny's afternoon off and she has been left in charge of baby Robert. She puts the vest down on the mending-basket and creeps over to the cradle. He is sound asleep, one fist clenched and thrown above his head, his fine blond hair tangled and curled around his flushed face. She pulls the covers over him a little more. Bless him, Jenny thinks fondly; just over a year old and a little angel. Now *he* is his father's pride and joy; unlike Valentine, Robert can do no wrong. He has recently started taking his first uncertain steps and you'd think that he was the only child in the world to achieve such a thing to listen to the Master talk. The Mistress has tried to get Valentine to show an interest in his little brother but it is hard because, if the Master is around, he will not countenance it.

That is another thing Jenny has noticed; on the rare occasions young Master Valentine is around little Robert, she is sure she has caught a strange cold look of resentment on his thin face when he looks at the baby, indeed the look is almost akin to hatred... She shakes herself mentally. Really, she must be getting fanciful; it must be because she is tired and, yes, *hungry*. She sighs as her stomach grumbles. It is an hour before she can get her supper, and she knows for a fact that Cook has made a nice lamb stew. The thought of it, bubbling, savoury and hot, makes her stomach growl again... She looks thoughtfully at the sleeping baby. He won't stir, she's certain of it. Dare she risk popping down to the kitchen for a bowlful of stew and a gossip with young Florrie Baker the kitchen maid? She'll be back in less than twenty minutes. The Master and Mistress are at dinner, and Master Valentine is safely tucked up in his bed in his room, so no-one will know. She's done it before, even though she isn't supposed to. Yes, she *will* take the risk. She draws the heavy wooden shutters over the barred windows, slips out of the nursery and shuts the door.

Valentine, lying awake in his cold bedroom, hears the nursery door shut and Jenny's soft footsteps as she creeps down the stairs. He shivers and pulls the thin bed-covers more tightly around him. Earlier, he had asked his mother if he might have a fire in his room, but she had frowned and said,

"You know your stepfather does not allow it at this time of year, my dear. I will ask Daisy to put an extra blanket on your bed."

Richard Cartwright had come in just then and caught the end of the conversation. He had said immediately,

"Nonsense, Beatrice, don't mollycoddle the boy. It will do him no harm to shiver a little. I won't have him complaining and whining at every opportunity."

Valentine clenches his fists tightly as he thinks of his stepfather. His passionate hatred of him does not lessen with time. He thinks that the animosity between them has grown even worse since their visit to his grandparents' house in Gloucester. Grandpapa Lawson had shown Valentine a great deal of affection; he did not seem to think less of his grandson despite the fact that his legs are twisted and weak. Indeed, he tried to suggest that Valentine be taken to London where there were several famous consultants who might be able to help him live a better life despite his deformity. Valentine overheard him telling Mama of a special brace he had heard of that could be fitted to the legs to help the sufferer walk without the need for crutches. He had offered to pay for the treatment, but his stepfather had treated the suggestion with the cold contempt he showed for everything related to Valentine, and Valentine's well-being.

"That will not be necessary," he had said coldly. "The boy shows no regard or consideration for others. His mind seems as twisted as his body; he shows no aptitude for learning and at times appears almost an imbecile. You would be wasting your money on him. It would be better by far to lavish care on your *normal* grandson, little Robert."

There had been high words between them, and Grandpapa had ordered Richard Cartwright to leave the room. Valentine had heard his mother pleading with her father not to be hasty, but he had replied,

"I'm sorry, Beatrice, but you were a fool to marry the man. I'll tell you, my dear, not a penny more of my money will you see while he remains your husband. I'll put it all in trust for the boys until they come of age; that way at least *he* will have no benefit from it."

Valentine turns restlessly again. He is so very cold; his feet are like ice and he feels that he cannot bear it a minute longer. Then he remembers his mother ordering a fire to be lit in the nursery. It will be warm in there and Jenny has gone downstairs. He will go in and sit by the fire for a while. Even if he falls asleep, he knows Jenny will not tell if she comes back and finds him. He likes Jenny; at seventeen, she is young enough to remember what it is like to be a child and he loves it when she tells him of her life in the village with her five brothers and sisters. He pulls himself awkwardly out of the bed, wraps the thin blanket round his shoulders and reaches for his crutches. His door creaks slightly as he opens it, but there is nobody to hear and he makes his way as quietly as he can along the passage and slowly and painfully climbs the steep wooden stairs to the nursery.

A soft light is burning and the firelight flickers welcomingly as he opens the door. He hobbles over to the low chair by the fire, moving the work-basket full of wool and sinking down comfortably into the chair. He sits for a while watching the flames, and feels his eyelids grow heavy as he grows warm and comfortable…

All at once there is a low wail from the crib in the corner of the room. Then another, as little Robert wakes up. Valentine tries hard to ignore it, but the wailing grows louder and more persistent. With an impatient sigh, he gets up and shuffles painfully over to the crib. The baby is kicking and crying fretfully, fat tears on his chubby cheeks; his little face is red and his nose is running with snot. Valentine leans over the crib and looks at him dispassionately.

"Why do they like you?" he says. "Look at you. You're ugly and you smell and you make a lot of noise. Maybe if you weren't here they might like me better. What do you think?"

But Robert screws up his eyes and screams even louder. Valentine puts his hands over his ears.

"Stop!" he yells. "Stop it at once you *horrible* child!" But the child screams even louder, and Valentine looks around the room in desperation.

Surely there is something that will make him be quiet? Should he try and fetch Jenny? Then he sees, by the crib, the answer – the lacy pillow that Jenny uses to prop Robert up in his feeding-chair. Without conscious thought, he picks it up and holds it firmly over the baby's face. Time seems to stand still as he looks down. Robert's cries became muffled, then weaker, and gradually they stop.

"There!" says Valentine smiling down at his brother. "Better now."

Suddenly, he hears the door open, and the room seems full of noise. He moves away from the cot, dropping the pillow. People are shouting and screaming; he hears his mother's voice saying "No! No!" and the sound of Jenny Somers sobbing. Then Nanny Johns, saying, "It's alright Madam, he's breathing, poor lamb." This is followed by an indignant yell from the baby. Then above his head he hears, most terrifyingly of all, his stepfather's voice, thick with anger.

"You'll leave this house today, girl. How dare you neglect your duties and leave my son alone; you worthless slut!"

Then his hard hands descend on Valentine's shoulders and he is lifted bodily, carried back down to his room and flung roughly on his bed. Valentine cries out in pain as his crippled legs hit the iron bed frame, but Richard Cartwright pays no heed. His voice is still shaking as he leans over the bed and his dark, swarthy face is distorted with fury.

"*You* are an evil and wicked boy! You will be locked in here and punished severely for what you have done to my son!"

Valentine, terrified, raises his eyes at last to the furious countenance and stammers,

"S-Sir, I... I didn't mean to hurt him... he wouldn't stop crying!"

"Be silent, boy! I have always known you to be a twisted and unnatural child, but now you have proved it to everyone beyond any reasonable doubt. After I have thoroughly chastised you for the sin you have committed, you will no longer be considered part of this household. I will not send you away for your mother's sake, though I am sorely tempted, but from this moment you will have no contact with any member of the household without my express permission. Perhaps one day, when you have shown sufficient remorse for your actions, I may relent a little, but do not depend upon it. Now stay here and reflect upon your evil actions and tomorrow you will receive the severest punishment!"

When he has gone, slamming and locking the door behind him, Valentine lies shivering and staring up into the darkness. Is he really evil? Had he really meant to harm his little brother? He tries hard to recall his feelings as he bent over the crib, but all he can remember is the feeling of power that had come over him as he had pressed the pillow to Robert's face.

That emotion still lingers, together with the overwhelming need within him to hurt his stepfather and one day deprive him of the person he loves best in the whole world, as he has robbed Valentine of his Mama.

Then he realises fearfully that almost certainly his mother will despise him too for what he has done, and Valentine feels a deep despair within as tears well up in his eyes. She will not be there to protect him anymore. Will she, too, hate him from this day?

Richard Cartwright was as good as his word. Valentine received a rigorous beating at his hands the next day and was banished to the nursery, which was stripped of all comfort and made into an austere schoolroom. Apart from his daily lessons with his tutor, Valentine was rarely allowed any contact with other members of the household. He scarcely saw his mother, and knew nothing of her pleas to Richard for leniency. Little Robert was moved into a nursery room of his own downstairs.

As for Jenny Somers, she was summarily dismissed and her place taken by a nursery maid of more mature years, who could be relied upon never to leave her young charge alone.

CHAPTER 42

"Simon? Are you okay?"

Adam's voice, on the other end of the phone sounded puzzled and a little impatient. Simon sat up in bed and tried to clear his aching head. He remembered little of what had happened last night; he had gone to some bar, in Soho he recollected vaguely, and had drunk innumerable beers and whisky chasers until he had nearly passed out. Hadn't there been some girl with him? Jane… Janet… no, *Joanne*, that was it. He'd got into a taxi with her and… He glanced to the right and saw a huddled shape next to him. Bloody hell, she was still here, must have spent the night! He honestly couldn't remember a thing. He tried to clear his mind and concentrate.

"Adam, yes, hi. Sorry, bit of a bad night last night; I've only just surfaced. What can I do for you?"

"I just thought I'd better let you know that Beth's in hospital. She had an accident yesterday afternoon when she was bringing Jamie home from school."

"Oh my God, is she badly injured? What happened – was Jamie hurt?"

"Jamie's fine, but Beth's suffering from concussion and a broken left wrist. She lost control just near the house and crashed the car into the gatepost. Car's a write-off but that doesn't matter of course. I just thank God it wasn't worse."

"Quite so. Look… er… give her my love, won't you. Hope she makes a good recovery."

"You'd be welcome to come down and visit. I'm sure she'd be glad to see you."

Simon hesitated, thinking quickly. "I… I don't think I'll be able to, I'm afraid. Got a lot going on at the moment. I'll get over to see you soon."

He hung up and got out of bed, holding his aching head as he made his way to the bathroom. He splashed some cold water on his face and grimaced as he looked in the mirror at his bloodshot eyes and three days of stubble.

"You're losing it, Ellis," he told himself. "Better get yourself together."

After a long hot shower and a shave, he dressed with care in his designer jeans and Armani shirt. In his tiny kitchenette he took a couple of aspirin, drank some tea and then carried a mug into the bedroom. Setting it down, he poked the huddled shape under the bedclothes.

"Hey, Joanne! Rise and shine – time to get up."

There was a muffled groan and a tousled-haired brunette emerged from beneath the covers.

"Wha…What? What time is it, for God's sake?"

"Time you were going home," he grinned. "Come on, I've got things to do and people to see. I made you tea."

"Thanks." She sat up yawning and stretched sensuously. "That was some night, wasn't it? Are you sure you want me to go? I reckon I can think of a few entertaining things for us to do that we didn't think of last night."

"Sorry, love, no can do. As I said, I've a busy day today. Why don't you leave me your phone number and I'll give you a ring sometime."

"Is that it?" She narrowed her eyes. "I'm just another one-night stand, I suppose?"

"Come on, Joanne." He reached out and stroked her naked breast. "We had fun, didn't we?"

"It's Janine!" she snapped, knocking his hand away. "And I'm surprised that you can even remember anything, you were pretty well off your face you know. And I've got news for you, *lover boy;* you weren't even that good in bed. Don't bother ringing me, I've got far better things to do with my life!"

She threw back the covers, almost knocking the mug of tea to the floor and flounced into the bathroom stark naked, glaring at him before slamming the door violently. Simon grinned; he could see why he'd been attracted to her. He took the tea back to the kitchen, pouring it down the sink. Somehow, he didn't think she'd be in the mood to drink it before she left. He picked up his phone and checked the message he'd received the evening before. He would have to get a move on if he was to get to Winchester to meet the man who was arriving that afternoon. Beth's accident had changed his plans slightly, but on the other hand it might work out even more satisfactorily with her being in hospital. She wouldn't have any choice but to see her visitor.

His plans for revenge were coming together nicely.

BEATRICE

Malthorp House
May 22nd 1911

My Dearest Lydia,
I do not know if I can bear to tell you what has happened, and so soon after dear Mama's passing.

My boy, my Angel, my darling Valentine has left me – he has gone to a better place than this Earth to be with his dear father, whom I trust will love and protect him in Heaven.

I will never, never forgive myself for being away from the house when it happened. If only I had not gone to Town on that day, but Richard was so insistent that I go and call on Margaret and Henry Paston. It seems strange as he has always discouraged me from visiting my former friends, even though he knows them well, but he was adamant that I visit them, saying the servants were all going to the village fair and he wished to take advantage of the house being quiet to do the accounts.

I suppose we will never know why Valentine was out in the gardens – he seldom went out on his own; indeed, he knew he was not allowed to do so without Richard's express permission, but it seems that he did on this occasion and – I can hardly bear to write these words – must have ventured too near the edge of the well and somehow slipped and fallen in. As you know, the well is not raised up, but sunk straight into the ground with only a low wall around it and there is a cover that should be kept on it at all times when it is not in use. Stokes is beside himself with guilt – he swears he did not leave the cover off after watering the vegetables, but there is no doubt that it was not put back.

Oh, Lydia I hate to think what my darling boy suffered, and how terrified he must have been in those last few moments of his life! <u>How</u> can I go on living without him? I cannot stop weeping for him, even though it makes Richard so angry.

His Funeral is to take place on the seventh day of June. I cannot believe dearest Mama passed away from us only two weeks after poor Papa and I cannot even come to <u>her</u> funeral but Richard will not countenance me travelling to Gloucester and indeed I do not feel I can, so stricken as I am with Grief. I know it will be so difficult for you so soon after Mama, but I beg you and James to come to Valentine's funeral. You are my only family now and I feel quite, quite alone. I know that you will feel unable to leave your darling baby, Sidney, but you can bring him and he can stay with Nanny Johns and my little Robert. I cannot even take comfort from him as Richard will not let me see him in my present state and refuses to allow him to attend the funeral, so he will be left in the nursery.

I cannot write more. <u>Please</u> come.
Your Heart-Broken sister
Beatrice

JUNE 7th 1911

A steady, soft rain falls over the small, sad procession as they follow the tiny white coffin to the far corner of the churchyard. There are only two pall-bearers, for the little body within weighs practically nothing. As they prepare to lower the coffin gently to the ground the simple wreath of lilies and roses slips off and falls into the open grave.

Beatrice Cartwright gasps and emits a low cry of distress. She instinctively moves forward, as if to reach down into the grave and retrieve it, but her husband tightens his grip on her arm and shakes his head.

"Leave it, my dear. Stokes will get it." He nods sharply at the old man who, his face screwed up with grief, unsteadily steps forward from the few servants who stand on the opposite side to the family and retrieves the wreath from the muddy hole. The Reverend Thomas Beech, vicar of Upper Melcombe, begins the burial service.

"We have entrusted our brother to God's merciful keeping, and we now commit his body to the ground. Earth to earth, ashes to ashes, dust to dust..."

Beatrice stifles another sob, aware of her husband's stiff disapproval as he stands silent and unmoved beside her. Her sister Lydia and her husband James stand behind them and Lydia, tears also falling, leans forward and takes Beatrice's hand. They are the only other family mourners present, as her parents are now both deceased. The words of the burial service, spoken but a short time before in the church, echo through Beatrice's mind.

"Man born of woman has but a short time to live – like a flower we blossom and then wither, like a shadow we flee and never stay..."

The pall bearers slowly lower the tiny coffin into the ground. At last Richard Cartwright releases his iron grip to allow his wife and her sister to step forward and throw a handful of earth onto the coffin. He glares disapprovingly at the servants, many of whom are in tears. He had already called them together that morning and warned them that he wants no unseemly show of emotion at the graveside. He frowns suddenly. Surely that is the Somers girl standing there behind old Stokes. How dare that slut show her face at a family gathering? He will see to it as soon as possible that her family are informed of his disapproval. Their cottage is on land owned by him and if they are not very careful, he will see them turned out.

The rain has ceased and a watery sun is now breaking through the clouds. Everyone bows their heads as the Reverend Beech says a short prayer, but Richard Cartwright curls his lip scornfully and does not join in. *He* will say no prayers for the boy he detested. He raises his eyes and looks instead at the great yew which stands a few yards away. He frowns and narrows his eyes in disbelief at what he thinks he sees, before a shaft of sunlight momentarily dazzles him.

There is a child standing in the dark shadow of the tree. A small, very thin boy. Wearing round wire spectacles and leaning upon two wooden crutches...

Richard's breath catches in his throat and he takes an involuntary step forward. Surely not... Beatrice raises tear-drenched eyes to look at him as he gazes in disbelief.

"Richard? What is it?"

He turns to her then looks again, but the apparition is gone. He takes a deep shuddering breath and composes himself, though he is shaking as if with a fever.

"It is nothing, my dear. I am chilled with the damp. Come, now, the service is over. We must return to the house."

"Let me stay a little longer, *please* Richard. I need to say goodbye to Valentine properly."

"Certainly not! You must accept with fortitude that Valentine is gone and remember that you have Robert to think of now." She gives a despairing cry and he frowns. "Come, Beatrice, this behaviour is unseemly; pray do not make an exhibition of yourself. I hope the servants have not neglected their duties and that there will be a hot meal awaiting us."

He once again takes his wife's arm in a vice-like grip and she winces, but obeys him. As they make their way down the narrow path that leads to the lych-gate, Beatrice glances back. Young Jenny Somers is standing sobbing by Valentine's grave, holding a small posy in her hand. She stoops and drops it gently on to the coffin. As she turns away the gravedigger steps forward and Beatrice hears the first clods of earth being shovelled onto her beloved son's coffin. She looks down and feels her throat contract again with grief as she raises her sodden handkerchief once more to her eyes.

CHAPTER 43

Beth put the last letter down with tears in her eyes. How terrible it must have been for Beatrice, alone in that house with her devastating grief and a husband who treated her with increasing brutality and contempt. It seemed that he even stopped her from taking comfort from her baby. She wiped her eyes and opened the envelope to slide the letters carefully back inside. As she did so she noticed there was another piece of paper at the bottom of the envelope but because this one was folded in four, she hadn't seen it when she pulled the others out. She cautiously slid it out; it seemed even more fragile than the rest. It was not headed like the others and was only a few lines long. It read:

18th May 1911

Lydia

I am writing this in haste and am giving it to Daisy to post when she goes to the village – she has sworn not to let Richard know that she is doing so.

    I know you may think me insane, but I have to tell you what has been occurring here at Malthorp. Dearest sister, a year ago we buried my poor boy but – <u>he has not gone from this place</u>. I must tell you that I see and hear him nearly every day and, sister, he is not at peace! He looks at me with such reproach and sometimes, though it causes me such pain to say it, with an expression I can only describe as loathing. I cannot tell you how <u>distraught</u> this makes me feel; I do not understand what it is that he wants of me or why he should haunt me like this. His Spirit (if indeed that's what this apparition is) is not at rest and he seems to infer that I am somehow responsible for this. I have tried to talk to Richard about what is occurring but he becomes so enraged with me that I am afraid of what he will do; he may strike me as he has done so many times, or worse. But I know he sees Valentine too; I see it in his face often and know that he, too, is frightened.

I am so weak and tired, Lydia. I cannot go on like this; I <u>beg</u> of you to come with James and take me away from here without telling Richard. I cannot stay in this house a moment longer – I am so fearful for my very life. I have to close now – <u>He</u> is coming…

Here, the letter abruptly broke off and Beth felt a deep chill running through her, despite the warmth of her hospital room. <u>He is coming</u>… did she mean Valentine or Richard Cartwright? Beatrice was obviously terrified of them both. So, Valentine had haunted her, too, obviously believing that she was in some way responsible for his death. Perhaps because he felt she hadn't protected him enough from his stepfather's brutality, or was it that she had not been there to save him on the day he died? But his death was a tragic accident, wasn't it? Nobody was to blame, except perhaps Albert Stokes the gardener, but Valentine hadn't haunted *him* as far as anyone knew, though according to Bill Tidy the servants had heard strange noises in the house.

And, Valentine was still there; only now he was haunting her youngest son. What did he want from Jamie and why couldn't he rest? He was trying to tell them something and Beth knew she had to find out what it was before someone else got hurt. One thing she knew for sure, her boys, especially Jamie, mustn't go back to Malthorp; even though Valentine was obviously able to get to him outside the house, Malthorp was at the heart of whatever was happening. She was suddenly struck by a thought – could Valentine have been responsible for her terrible experience in London when she had seen Kevin? It seemed to her now that anything was possible. She found her mobile and dialled Laura's number, praying that she wasn't in the middle of a meeting. To her relief, she answered on the second ring.

"Beth! Geoff and I were going to come and see you this evening. How are you feeling? We were so sorry to hear about the accident…"

"Laura, listen. Sorry to cut in but this is important. I need you to do me a huge favour."

"Of course, my love, anything."

"Is there any way that you can have Danny and Jamie to stay for a couple of days? I know you've got work but they'd be at school during the day. It's just until I'm out of here and can try and sort things out."

"Of course, you know we love having them. But what's the problem?" she lowered her voice. "Is this to do with the ghost?"

"Yes. I've found out quite a lot more, and there are some things I have to do to try and sort this out. Until I do, I don't think it's safe for them to be at the house."

"Oh, Beth, I don't like the sound of this. You're getting in really deep. Don't you think you should tell Adam everything? You shouldn't be doing this on your own."

"I've tried to tell him, Laura, but he doesn't want to listen. Look, please don't tell him I asked you to have the boys, just make the offer. Debs is holding the fort at the moment but I know she has other commitments, so he'll think you having them will be a good idea. Maybe you can persuade Adam to stay too."

"Well… I don't like keeping the truth from him."

"Please, Laura, I need you to do this for me. I *have* to know they're safe!"

"Okay… okay. Don't get yourself stressed. I'll do it."

"Thank you. Thank you so much! I promise I am going to sort it and it will all be alright."

Beth hung up and lay back on her pillows. Her head was pounding again but she felt a tremendous sense of relief. At least she knew that Jamie and Danny would be safer for a while. She closed her eyes, trying to ignore the pain in her head. Barbara, the duty nurse came bustling in.

"Ah," she said brightly, seeing Beth's expression. "Time for your painkillers."

Beth sat up and swallowed the tablets with some water. "Thanks. My head is aching a bit."

"Well, I don't know if you feel up to a visitor, but you have one. He's been hanging around for a while but I thought you were asleep. He says he's a relative."

"Okay, well if he's been waiting." Beth wondered who it was. She hoped it wasn't Simon. He was the last person she wanted to see. Maybe it was John. She knew he'd been very upset to hear about the accident and had told Adam that he would try and get down and see her.

It wasn't John. Instead, a small, thin man with a head of wiry grey hair walked into the room. Beth stared. She was certain she didn't know this man, but yet… there *was* something familiar about him and she felt a frisson of fear for a reason she couldn't quite understand. Then he spoke and she knew.

"Beth. Beth, *cariad*, do you know me?"

"Dada? *Dada* – no, it can't be." She was white with shock. "What… what are you doing here… how did you know…? I don't understand."

CHAPTER 44

She felt a sense of utter disbelief as her father walked slowly towards her and spoke in his familiar Welsh lilting voice.

"Oh, Beth, I'm so sorry. I know this must be an awful shock for you but I felt I had to come. I've wanted to for years but I didn't know how you'd feel, see? Then, when your brother-in-law said you'd been trying to find me and that you wanted to see me, I thought…"

"*Simon?* Simon contacted you?" She stared at him open-mouthed. "But I told him quite categorically that I *didn't* want to see you! When I found out you'd been around all those years and you hadn't bothered; found that you'd even remarried and had another family, I couldn't believe it. How could you do that, Dada – how could you just forget me and Mam like that?" Her voice rose. "Years I waited when I was a child – years – just hoping, praying for a letter. You promised me – the last thing you said when you put me on that coach was that you'd write! But you didn't bother did you? Not ever. I was out of sight, out of mind. You just left me there with Auntie Glenys and Kevin. Do you even know what happened to me when I was there?" Tears filled her eyes.

Owen's face was contorted with grief and guilt. "*Cariad*, believe me I didn't know what you went through, not for a long time. Please, give me a chance to explain. I know this has been a great shock and I'm so sorry because I certainly wouldn't have come if I had realised this is how you still felt. I took Simon's word for it, that you wanted to see me I mean."

Beth wiped the tears from her eyes. "Yes, well, Simon has his own motives for doing this. You'd better sit down," she added shakily. "I'm willing to listen, at least."

Barbara popped her head round the door. "Is everything alright?" She looked at Beth with concern. "I thought I heard raised voices. Your visitor will have to leave if it's too much for you, Beth."

"No, it's okay," Beth said shakily. "I'm just feeling a bit emotional, that's all,"

"If you're sure. Would the two of you like a cup of tea by the way? The trolley's just coming round."

They nodded and waited until she'd put the tea on Beth's table and left the room. There was an awkward pause and then Owen smiled and said, "You've grown into a beautiful woman, Beth. You look so much like your Mam."

Beth blinked back the rising tears and managed a shaky smile. The disbelief that she was actually face to face with her father was gradually subsiding and she felt a great sadness well up within her as she looked at Owen more closely. It was a shock to see that his hair was completely grey and his face was so lined. Whenever she thought of him, she had visualised the virile and fit man she had known as a child and she was suddenly struck with the realisation that he must be close to seventy.

"What happened, Dada?" she asked. "Why did you never write to me?"

"I meant to, *cariad*, I always meant to. But after you were gone, I couldn't seem to think or feel anything. I left Wales and found a job on another farm in Herefordshire and tried to carry on working, but I knew it was no good. I saw you and your Mam in every tree, in every blade of grass and I knew that I had to get away, far away and find a whole new life free from all the memories. So, I went to Ireland."

"Why Ireland?" Beth asked.

"I met an Irishman from Dublin in the pub, who was over here visiting family and he told me they were looking for cheap labourers over there. The country wasn't doing so well and a lot of people had lost their jobs, so they were replacing them with unskilled workers they could pay less to. He was going back over the following week and wanted someone to share cheap lodgings with. I decided to go, but I honestly intended it to be for just a few months and then I'd come back and get you and we'd start over, just the two of us."

"So, what happened? Why didn't you come back for me?"

Owen took a sip of his tea and closed his eyes for a moment.

"Well, I worked on this building site for a few weeks, in a daze, like, and then I had a sort of breakdown. I hated the job and one day I just left and didn't go back. I left Dublin and decided to start walking and see what happened. I lived rough, doing a bit of work here and there to earn enough money to eat, then one day I fell ill. Someone found me by the side of the road and I didn't know who I was or what was happening. I was taken to hospital and I don't remember anything much about the next couple of years; I had viral encephalitis which affected my brain and made me lose a lot of memories from the past. They put me in a hostel for homeless men, run by the Catholic Church, and I was given some work and a small wage. When I finally remembered who I was and that I had a daughter in England I came back over as soon as I could. I eventually found Glenys. She told me you'd caused nothing but trouble and that you'd run away and been taken into care. I knew she was lying; I felt it in my bones that there was more to the story, but she wouldn't tell me the truth."

Beth winced. She thought Glenys had at least liked, if not loved her, but it seemed that she had not forgiven Beth for being the cause of her husband's imprisonment.

"So did you find out that Kevin had …" she swallowed, "… raped me."

"I spoke to young Trevor and he told me what his Dad had done." He clenched his fists. "That evil bastard! I never liked or trusted him, but if I'd known that he'd hurt you…" His lip trembled. "I wanted to kill him, Beth, for what he did, but he was in prison, see, and I couldn't get to him."

Her eyes filled once again. "He died in there – he was killed by another prisoner. So why didn't you come for me then, Dada? Did you not know I was in the children's home?"

"Glenys lied again. We had a terrible quarrel after I found out about Kevin. I said she should have protected you knowing what he was like, but she still put all the blame on you. Then she said you hated me for leaving you and that the social services had put you out to foster parents; that you were settled in a new home and they would never let me see you because I'd deserted you in the past. Fool that I was, I believed her! Consequently, I gave up and went down to Cornwall. I found work down there on a farm and met Jane. We married a couple of years later."

Beth leant forward.

"What about my Mam?" she said, her voice breaking. "What happened to her?"

"Oh Beth, *cariad*, I'm so sorry. Your Mam... she died not long after we parted. She was with another man but he deserted when she was... well, she was having a baby. There were complications and she died during the birth, the baby along with her. It took me a long time to find out because she'd changed back to her maiden name. I had to know because we never divorced and Jane and I wanted to marry."

Beth felt numb. Her father was looking at her with such love and compassion, and she could feel nothing except grief, loss and sorrow for what might have been.

"Beth, I have two more daughters, your stepsisters." Owen hesitated then slipped his hand in his pocket. "Would you like to see their pictures? They're called Nerys and Olwen."

"No, Dada," Beth swallowed back more tears and reached out a hand to stop him. "I understand now the reasons why you deserted me, and I know it's not been entirely your fault so I don't blame or hate you, but I don't think we can just pick up the pieces as if it had all never happened. You have a new life and so do I. Go and be happy in it and forget me. It's the best way for us both, I think."

Owen looked devastated. "But I don't want to lose you again and I know you have your two boys. They are my grandsons, Beth, and I'd love to get to know them. We could be a family again."

For a moment, Beth was tempted, but tears filled her eyes again as she realised that it couldn't be. "No, Dada, I'm sorry. They don't need that complication in their lives at the moment and neither do I. You have a family that love you and I'm glad for you, and glad that you came today and helped me understand what happened all those years ago. Now I feel that I can accept and finally close that part of my life. But I think it has to be this way."

She saw that Owen, too, was close to tears as he bent forward and embraced her.

"I'll always love you, Beth," he said shakily. "And I wish you and your family joy in your lives even though I can't be part of it."

He turned and was gone before she could answer. She lay back on her pillows, sobbing in earnest now. For years she had dreamt of her Dada finding her and now that he had, she had rejected him. She had hoped for a joyful reunion with her Mam but she was gone forever and Beth had never even had a chance to say goodbye. Her whole world seemed to be collapsing around her.

CHAPTER 45

Adam had been tied up in an important meeting since he had left Beth. It was nearly three o'clock and he was very hungry. They'd had coffee and biscuits earlier, but he was desperate for something a bit more substantial so he made his way to the hospital canteen and sat down by the window with a sigh of relief, a cup of tea and a sandwich in front of him.

"Adam." He looked up to see Laura standing over him. "How did it go?"

"Not too well, I'm afraid. More cutbacks – honestly if we pare down the service much more there won't *be* a service." He regarded his sandwich gloomily, his appetite suddenly gone. "They're talking about amalgamating some departments and it may well affect us. I sometimes feel we're banging our heads against a brick wall because they don't seem to want to listen to the people who really know what's best."

Laura smiled sympathetically.

"I know, I feel much the same but they always seem to get their way in the end no matter how much we kick and scream." She hesitated. "How's Beth? Geoff and I are going to pop up and see her later."

"A bit groggy, as you can well imagine, but she's going to be fine. She's very confused, swears it was pouring with rain when the accident happened but the police say it was a perfectly clear afternoon, a bit cloudy but good visibility." He paused for a moment. "She's also insisting she saw someone standing in the road, a young boy, but there was definitely nobody else involved. I think she just got distracted, maybe by Jamie, and the rest of what she thinks she remembers is probably caused by the concussion."

"How is Jamie?" asked Laura.

"He was pretty shaken up as you can imagine. He's not been

sleeping very well and keeps asking for Mummy. Debbie will be picking them both up soon and she'll bring them in to see her."

"Look, Adam," Laura took a deep breath, "I've been thinking; why don't you and the boys come and stay with us for a few days – Beth too when she comes out? It would give you all a break and it might be better for Jamie to be away from the house, help him get over the trauma of the accident. We'd be more than happy for you to come and you know how much we love the kids."

Adam frowned. "It's a really lovely offer, Laura, but are you sure? There's Finn to think about as well…"

"Finn would be more than welcome too; but if you're worried why not ask Debbie to look after him at hers for a few days? That way you'll know he'll be getting his walks and so on."

"That's a good idea," said Adam, biting into his sandwich. "Look, I'll run it by Beth but I'm sure she'll agree."

"I'm sure she will," replied Laura, inwardly cheering. "Come over today. I'll get Geoff to make his special lasagne; I know how much the boys love it." She frowned and leaned forward to look out of the window. "Hey, isn't that your brother Simon down there near the car park?"

It was pouring with rain and Adam had to squint through the blurry window to see that it was indeed his brother. "What's he doing here?" he wondered out loud. "When I spoke to him earlier he said he wouldn't be able to make it to visit Beth. Perhaps he changed his mind. I wonder who that old guy is he's talking to."

"I don't know, but it looks to me like they're having one hell of an argument."

Adam saw what she meant. The older man talking to Simon was gesticulating angrily and his body language seemed very hostile. He watched with interest as Simon held his hands up and started to back away.

"It's probably some guy who's lost his girlfriend to my brother. He looks pretty pissed off."

Simon was by now walking rapidly away from the confrontation towards the multi-storey car park as the older man pulled up the collar of his coat against the rain, hunched his shoulders and walked away in the direction of the pedestrian exit. Adam shrugged. "I'll find out at some point I suppose. I'd better go up and see Beth quickly now before Debbie turns up with the boys. I'll speak to her about us staying but I'm sure she'll like the idea. She still seems to have some crazy idea that the house is haunted and that the boys are in danger. I've tried to reason with her, but I think everything that's happened has just really spooked her. I'll let you know as soon as possible."

"That's fine; just turn up whenever this evening. We'll be home by five-thirty."

They stood up and he gave her a hug. "Thanks so much, Laura, don't know what we'd do without you two sometimes."

"Don't mention it. Just make sure you bring a nice bottle of red wine when you come!"

Adam poked his head cautiously round the door of Beth's room. The room was quite dim because of the overcast sky and she was lying on her back. He thought for a moment that she was asleep and walked over quietly to sit by her bed. Then he saw that actually she was wide awake and her eyes were red and swollen.

"Beth! Oh, my love, whatever is it? Are you in pain?"

She shook her head slowly and gave a muffled sob. He wrapped his arms round her as she sat up, being careful of her injured wrist. "Oh, Adam…"

"What is it? Tell me."

He listened with growing disbelief as she told him about her father's visit and what he had told her.

"Beth, I'm so sorry. That must have been a hell of a shock – I only wish I'd been here with you."

"The worst of it is, I don't know if I've done the right thing by sending him away," she said miserably. "I've spent all these years not knowing and pushing it all to the back of my mind and now I just don't think I could cope with getting to know him again, let alone meeting his new family. Do you think I've done the right thing, Adam?"

"I can't tell you that, my love. Maybe you need to give it a few weeks, get over the shock and then think about it again. I'm sure he understands how you must be feeling." He frowned. "What *I* don't understand is how he found you – and how he knew you were here in hospital. Even if he'd gone to the house, Debbie would never have given a stranger any personal information about you."

Beth took a deep breath.

"It was Simon, Adam. Simon brought him."

"*Simon*? So that explains why I saw him in the car park having an argument with a guy... that must have been your father!" He unwrapped his arms from round her and looked perplexed. "But why would Simon have done that? I mean – out of the blue. Why would he contact him at all?"

She met his eyes. "He was getting his own back, Adam. He wanted to hurt me."

"Why on earth?"

"I didn't tell you because I knew how angry you'd be but I asked Simon to see if he could find out what had happened to Kevin Webster. Something really weird happened to me when I was up in London a few weeks ago and Simon just happened to be there." She told him the whole story.

Adam listened with growing incredulity as she spoke. "So, you actually imagined you saw Kevin and you never said anything to me?"

"I couldn't, Adam. I just thought I was going mad and when Simon offered to help."

"You thought you'd enter into a cosy little conspiracy with my brother. Well, thanks for that!"

"This is exactly the sort of reaction I knew I'd get," said Beth, desperately trying to get him to understand. "That's why I didn't say anything at the time. I was going to tell you – you have to believe that."

"I don't know what to believe any more," he said. "Just a moment; you said he had contacted your father to *hurt* you. Why on earth would he do that if he was trying to help you?" He shook his head as he saw the look on her face. "What else haven't you told me, Beth?"

She took another shuddering breath and told him everything; how Simon had discovered her father's whereabouts and how he had come to Malthorp to see her that day. When Adam heard how he had made a pass at her he jumped up, his face dark with anger.

"So *that's* why he's been avoiding us lately! He always was a devious bastard. I heard that Fiona had walked out on him and I was all prepared to be sympathetic but now I see why. He's always made it plain that he fancied you and that he's jealous of us. Well, he's overstepped the mark this time – I'm going to have it out with him!"

"No, please Adam, leave it. I just want to forget it ever happened and, in a way, he's done me a favour by letting me meet my father and come to terms with the truth. I think he'll get the message that he can't hurt me anymore. Let him get on with his sad life as long as he stays out of ours." She was very near to tears again and Adam relented, sitting down and putting his arms round her again.

"Well, perhaps you're right. Look, the boys will be here any minute. Laura's made us a really kind offer." Adam told her and Beth smiled, feeling a great sense of relief and gratitude to her friend. He continued to hold her, letting her think he agreed with her about forgetting what his brother had done. In reality he was determined to have it out with him.

After a while the boys came running in and threw themselves at her. She cuddled them closely as best she could with her injured wrist.

"I've missed you so much!"

"Not as much as we've missed you, Mum!" exclaimed Danny. He looked closely at her plaster cast. "Does it hurt a lot? Can we write on it in a minute?"

"No and yes," laughed Beth. "You'll need a marker though."

"Cool! I've got a red and a green one in my bag. C'mon Jamie; you can draw a picture on Mum's wrist!"

But Jamie stayed cuddled up to Beth, looking at her with his big blue eyes.

"Mummy, Jamie didn't want the car to crash. I was scared."

"I know, my darling. But mummy's okay, see? Just a silly broken wrist and a few bruises. As long as you're not hurt, Jamie, that's all that matters."

"Hey, guys, guess what?" Adam had been chatting to Debbie while Danny signed his name on Beth's cast with a flourish. "Debbie's going to look after Finn for us and we're going to stay with Auntie Laura and Uncle Geoff for a couple of days until Mum comes out of hospital. In fact, Mum might come and stay too for a while."

The boys cheered; Jamie got off the bed and, with Danny's help, wrote his name in large blue letters under his brother's. They stayed for a few more minutes chatting to Beth then the nurse appeared to say it was nearly time for the evening meal and she thought Beth should have some rest. Danny and Adam went into the corridor and started chatting to the nurse, but Jamie came over to the bed and climbed up to put his arms round her once more.

"Mummy," he whispered in her ear. "Mummy; Valentine won't be at Auntie Laura's house, will he?"

She hugged him tightly to her with her free arm. "No, darling," she whispered back. "He won't be there, I promise." He looked away, his eyes filling with tears; his bottom lip trembled.

"'Cos Jamie doesn't like Valentine now, Mummy. Jamie doesn't want to be Valentine's friend no more. He tried to hurt us in the car."

"You saw him, darling?" Beth asked softly. He nodded and a tear trickled down his cheek.

Her heart went out to him. He was so little, so vulnerable and it broke her heart to see him looking so scared. She turned his face towards her.

"Mummy's going to sort it all out, Jamie. I'm going to tell Valentine he has to go away from the house and leave us alone and I promise he won't make you do anything else that you don't want to."

"Not ever again?"

"Not ever again." She kissed him. "Now go with Daddy to Auntie Laura's and I'll see you tomorrow."

He gave her a final squeeze and slid off the bed. She felt close to tears again as she saw him take Danny's hand and, as they left, she lay back feeling intensely tired and helpless.

Would she be able to keep her promise to Jamie?

CHAPTER 46

Debbie took the boys back to Malthorp in her car and Adam followed. They packed a few clothes and the boys chose some books and toys they wanted to take. Adam also threw some things in a bag for himself; he would fetch Beth's stuff when she came out of hospital which should be in a couple of days. Debbie had agreed to take Finn back to her house; his leg was healing well, and he jumped joyfully into the boot of her estate car with his own bag of necessities along with his dog bed.

"Could I ask you another big favour, Debs?" said Adam. "It would be great if you could just drop the boys off at Laura's for me. I won't be long. But I just have something to do before I go there."

"Sure, no worries. Come on you two."

Adam waited until they had driven away then went back into the house to check all the doors and windows were securely locked. It felt very empty suddenly and he hurried round eager to get back into Winchester. He was determined to speak to Simon and had a pretty good idea where he might be. As he came out of Beth's studio into the hall he thought he heard a whispering sigh.

"Who's there?" he asked sharply. He listened intently, aware that he was holding his breath but he could hear nothing. "Old house, it's probably the pipes," he murmured to himself. "Beth's getting me spooked now with all her talk of weird goings on!"

He went out through the front door locking it behind him. Faintly, in the distance, he thought he heard singing. The song sounded vaguely familiar though he couldn't quite make out the words. It seemed to fade in and out like a badly tuned radio. Must be coming from the church, he told himself – probably choir practice. Either that or somebody had their radio on very loudly in the village. He shrugged and got into the car. Now he was going to find Simon.

Adam drew into the forecourt of the Hampshire Hog public house on the outskirts of the city. He knew it was one of Simon's favourite watering holes and smiled grimly to himself when he saw his brother's black BMW in the car park. It was just after six and he knew Simon would have been there since they opened at five so, hopefully, hadn't had too much to drink yet. They did bed and breakfast accommodation so he assumed Simon would have booked a room for the night.

It was fairly quiet inside and spotted Simon straight away sitting in a corner nursing a large whisky. He seemed deep in thought and didn't look up until Adam pulled up the chair opposite and sat down. He gave a slow smile.

"Well, brother dear, what the hell are you doing here?" he said, his voice slightly slurred. "Thought you'd be at the hospital holding your lovely wife's hand or something."

"Shut up, Simon, and listen." Adam leant forward and stared coldly at his brother. "I've come to tell you that from now on you stay away from us. We want nothing to do with you. As far as I'm concerned, you're a malicious, unscrupulous bastard who thinks nothing of using whoever he can for his own petty schemes. I'm ashamed to call you my brother."

Simon went white, then his eyes narrowed and he gave a short laugh. "I see Beth's told you all. Wasn't she thrilled to see dear Dada again then? Wasn't it the happy reunion she'd hoped for? Mind you I can understand why not – he's a bit of a pathetic old git isn't he; how he ever managed to father a stunner like Beth is a mystery. Wonder if his other two daughters are as tasty."

"You really are the lowest of the low."

"Did Beth tell you everything?" Simon continued as if Adam hadn't spoken. "Did she tell you how she practically offered it to me on a plate?" He took a huge gulp of whisky. "I tell you, dear brother, she's wasted on you with those lovely tits and that sexy arse."

He got no further. Adam reached across the table and grabbed the front of his shirt. He pulled him forward and hit him full on the nose; Simon fell back with a crash onto his back, breaking the chair and smashing his glass as he did so. A couple of women screamed and the landlord came hurrying out from behind the bar.

"Oi! What's going on? We'll have none of that in here – I'll call the police!"

"Sorry." Adam put down five twenty-pound notes. "That's for any damage caused. He looked down at Simon who was holding his bleeding nose and groaning. "You might want to get my brother a cold flannel."

He walked out, leaving them all staring in disbelief, got into his car and drove to Laura's. His hand hurt like hell but he felt strangely satisfied and realised that he had wanted to do that to Simon for a long time. Geoff opened the door to him and grinned.

"Come in old mate, you've timed it just right for the lasagne. Sorted out what you needed?"

"Oh, yes," Adam said. "I think you can safely say I have. Tell you all about it later. Now, lead me to the lasagne; I'm starving!"

The skies have cleared and a bright full moon shines over Malthorp. It casts dark shadows outside and within the house; the air is still and all is silent until a single discordant note sounds from the piano in the sitting room. The woman weeping quietly in her child's room raises her eyes and whispers his name – "Valentine?" His voice echoes through the house, pure and clear in the moonlit room.

> *In the sky so clear above me*
> *The moon doth brightly shine,*
> *Give me your heart then I will be*
> *Forever your Valentine.*
> *Please say you'll always love me*
> *With a promise oh so true,*
> *And if you say that this is so*
> *My heart will belong to you.*

"Ah Valentine, my love, I am so sorry!" she cries. *"Come back to me…"*

"You let me die, Mama." His voice is low and full of malice. *"You let me die."*

"No, Valentine, no! I could not help you… I was not here; I would do anything to go back and prevent it now. You must believe me!"

"You let me die…" the relentless voice continues, *"and now you must suffer as I do."*

Her hand flies to her mouth as she sees him at last, her boy… but not her boy, this small wizened creature leaning upon his crutches, his face twisted with hatred. He moves towards her and she cries out in terror…

Then the dark shadow, their nemesis, comes swiftly between them, she recoils and the boy screams with frustration. Suddenly a fierce gust of wind howls through the house, and the moon briefly disappears behind a cloud.

When it lights the room again, the shadows have gone and, for now, all is still at Malthorp.

CHAPTER 47

The Hampshire Hog was holding a quiz evening and by nine o'clock the pub was bursting at the seams. Simon had gone up to his room after his encounter with Adam; the landlord had not been best pleased but had allowed Simon to keep his room on condition that he left the bar, refusing to serve him any more drinks. Simon had been tempted to drive back up to London once his nose had stopped pouring blood, but decided that it wasn't worth taking the risk as he knew he was well over the limit. He had a feeling the landlord would have reported him anyway had he attempted it. Instead, he took a sandwich up to his room; he had a full bottle of Glenlivet in his bag anyway. After a couple of hours, the sound of the quizmaster belting out the questions through a microphone and the resulting shouts of response from the punters began to get on his nerves. He went to the bathroom and looked at his swollen nose in the mirror. It looked and felt very sore.

"You sanctimonious bastard, Adam," he muttered thickly. "You and that frigid bitch deserve each other." He poured another slug of whisky into the water glass by his bed. "You think you're so great, with your wonderful career, your big house, your sexy wife and your spoiled kids. Well, I've got news for you, brother dear, you're not going to get away with this. Let's see how you like it when you get a taste of your own medicine!"

He took out his mobile and called a taxi. He'd go over there now and confront his brother – tell him what he really thought of him and his oh-so-perfect life, maybe give *him* a swollen nose, see how he liked it. His resentment grew as he contemplated bitterly that it was because of Adam that he, Simon, had never had a real chance in his life. His parents had been so busy giving everything to their golden boy that he had always come last in their eyes. He resented Neil and David, too, but at least they weren't always around to rub his nose in it, not like Adam. He lurched unsteadily downstairs and out to the front of the pub where he lit a cigarette as he waited for the taxi to turn up.

※

Danny woke with a start. For a moment he didn't know where he was; the bed and window seemed to be in the wrong position, then he remembered he was lying in the top bunk in the room he was sharing with Jamie at Laura and Geoff's. He turned over to go back to sleep, then realised he could hear Jamie quietly crying below him. He leaned over and saw his brother sitting bolt upright in his bunk, tears trickling down his cheeks.

"Hey, Spud, what's wrong? Did you have a bad dream?" He swung his legs over and jumped down, "Come on, tell me what's up. Are you missing Mum?"

He nodded. "Jamie sad… but that's not why me crying."

Danny fished out a crumpled tissue from under his pillow and dried his brother's tears. He put a comforting arm round Jamie's shoulders. Usually Jamie shied away from physical contact but this time he snuggled into his brother. "Mummy promised," he said miserably. "Mummy promised that Valentine wouldn't be here."

Danny looked round the room.

"There's nobody here, Jamie. It's okay… you just had a bad dream."

"But he *was* here and so was the bad man; Jamie saw them."

Danny switched on the bedside light. "Look, honestly, there's no one here. You just imagined it, Spud."

"NO!" Jamie shouted suddenly, pulling himself violently away from Danny. "Valentine *was* here, just now! He wanted Jamie to go and play again, but I didn't want to. Then he got angry with me. He said if I didn't then someone would *die*. Danny – I'm scared, I'm really scared!"

CHAPTER 48

Simon paid the taxi driver and clambered unsteadily out of the cab.

"Do you want me to wait, mate?" asked the cabby. "Doesn't look like there's anyone at home to me."

It was true, the house was in complete darkness. Maybe they'd gone to bed early, Simon thought blearily. The whisky had really kicked in now and he almost changed his mind – go back to the pub and crash out; then he felt the pain of his sore nose and remembered why he was there. He was going to teach his holier-than-thou brother a lesson.

"No, it's alright," he mumbled. "I'll call for a cab back later."

The taxi driver shrugged and, as the taxi drew away, Simon staggered up the steps to the front door and raised the knocker, crashing it down hard a few times. Then he held down the bell for good measure but there was no answer.

He stood back and looked up at the darkened windows. No sign of life. He lurched along the front of the house, cursing as he almost tripped over the wooden bench under the sitting room window. He tried to peer through but could see nothing, so decided to try his luck at the back; maybe Adam was in the kitchen, though Simon wasn't sure why he wouldn't have heard the front door.

Again, round the back of the house, everything was in darkness. Simon felt his anger and frustration mounting as he tipped back his head and yelled at the top of his voice:

"Adam! Hey, Adam you prick – answer the fucking door! Are you in there?"

There was still no response, but he could have sworn he saw a flicker of light in one of the upstairs rooms. His lips tightened. So that was the way Adam wanted to play it; to ignore him and hope he would go away. Well, it wasn't going to work – Simon was determined to have it out with him once and for all. He tried the back door, but it was firmly locked. Then he noticed the small window next to it that led into the scullery. It had never fitted properly and he remembered Beth telling him that they were intending to get a replacement. He looked around for something to use as a lever, but there was nothing around.

"What the hell?" he muttered. Then he saw there was a pile of bricks at the corner of the house so he picked one up and used it to smash the window. He quite expected lights to go on and to hear indignant voices but still there was nothing. He took off his jacket and wrapped it round his hand as he carefully reached in through the jagged pane and released the catch. He hauled himself up and squeezed through the window. It was a tight fit, but he managed it and jumped to the floor, cursing again as he caught himself on the deep butler sink that stood next to the window. He strode across the scullery into the kitchen and pushed his way through the baize door which shut with a gentle whisper behind him.

"Adam!" he yelled. "I know you're here. Come out and talk to me, you fucking miserable bastard!"

The moon shone eerily in the hall – all was silent. He took a few steps forward and then paused; he was sure he had heard a childish giggle somewhere in the darkness.

"Danny? Jamie?" He looked around for the light switch, swept his hand along the wall but he couldn't seem to see one, only the gas brackets above his head. "Is that you? Stop playing stupid tricks and go and tell your Dad I want a word with him."

The soft laughter came again, but this time it seemed to be more distant. Then, from upstairs, he heard a soft scampering sound and the sound of an echoing voice.

"Uncle Simon! I'm up here!"

His mind felt fuddled as he headed unsteadily towards the stairs. He looked for the light switch, but once again it eluded him.

"Stop this, Danny!" he shouted angrily. "Go and get your Dad. Surely you two aren't here on your own?"

"Come and find me, Uncle Simon. I'm up here!"

Swearing softly under his breath he climbed the stairs, the soft moonlight showing the way. It cast deep shadows on the red flocked wallpaper and he frowned as he saw a swift, swirling movement to his right as he reached the top. He caught his foot on the last step and lurched unsteadily down the corridor, reaching the bottom of the steep stairs which led to the boys' attic playroom.

"Are you up there, Danny? Jamie?" Again he heard the soft laughter. "You little devils… wait till I find you – you'll be sorry for playing silly buggers!"

He began to climb the stairs but they seemed to shift and waver in front of him. He passed his hand across his eyes. He'd meant what he'd said, when he got hold of those little sods, he thought belligerently, he'd teach them a lesson for leading him on.

The door at the top was closed but as he reached out it slowly opened. He stepped inside, fully expecting to see one or both of his nephews standing there laughing but the moonlight shone brightly through the bars across the window, tiger-striping bare floorboards where before there had been brightly-patterned carpet. He looked round in bewilderment, seeing no sign of the children's possessions – their big TV, crammed bookcases and beanbags had gone – instead, over to one side there appeared to be a blackboard on a wooden easel and on the wall some sort of faded map of the world. Deep shadows were cast into the corners of the room which was somehow devoid of human occupation. Then suddenly one of the shadows seemed to shift and Simon frowned, trying to focus his eyes.

"Danny?"

It was then he realised, with a jolt of horror, that it was not Danny he was seeing but an indistinct, hazy outline of another child; a child far too small and hunched to be either of his nephews. Gradually it seemed to sharpen and come into focus and he saw that it was a slight, stooped young boy leaning on a pair of wooden crutches. A cold chill of fear shuddered down his spine as he realised that the boy was soaking wet; water dripped from his old-fashioned clothes and hair. As Simon recoiled, the boy's piercing eyes stared malevolently at him through round wire spectacles.

"Who... who the hell are you?" he said hesitantly, but as he felt the waves of implacable hatred and malice emanating from the boy, a feeling of the utmost horror and dread swept over him. He knew the boy meant him harm and that he had to escape but he could not seem to move or tear his eyes from that malignant gaze. He suddenly found the strength he needed and began to back out of the room. The child moved towards him leaving small wet footprints on the bare boards. Simon felt for the door and tried frantically to grasp the stair banister behind him. It eluded his grip... he tried to turn his head to find it but could not... then, with a cry of despair, he felt his foot slip as he lost his balance. He plunged helplessly, inevitably, backwards down the steep staircase. As he hit the bottom there was an ominous crack; he felt pain shoot down his entire body then he gasped once and was still.

Above him, though he could no longer hear it, a child softly giggled.

CHAPTER 49

The young doctor smiled warmly at Beth as she finished her morning examination.

"Everything seems fine, Mrs Ellis. I think you'll be okay to go home today; there are no further signs of concussion though your head may feel a bit sore for a couple more days. You'll be in plaster for a few weeks, I'm afraid, but do try and keep the arm elevated as much as possible. The nurse will give you a sheet with some exercises to do which will help the circulation in your arm and help the healing process." She picked up her stethoscope. "Shall I ask the nurse to call your husband?"

"Yes please. I think he's here today, but if you can't get hold of him then perhaps you can ask Laura Dunbar to come up. We're staying with her and her husband for a few days."

"Of course. I'll also prescribe some painkillers for you to take home." She hurried out and Beth sat back in the upright chair next to her bed feeling exhausted. She'd hardly slept a wink the night before; everything had been going round and round in her mind and she had been trying desperately to think what to do next. She looked up as the nurse came in carrying a cup of tea.

"Good news that you can go home today!" she exclaimed breezily. "We couldn't contact your husband but I believe Mrs Dunbar is coming up as soon as possible. Now, shall we get that plaster covered and get you showered and dressed?"

"Yes please," murmured Beth, hating the feeling of helplessness that her broken wrist engendered. But she did feel better when a while later, newly showered and dressed, she saw Laura arrive in the corridor by the nurses' station. She was out there for a few moments and Beth assumed that she was sorting out her medication. It wasn't until she saw Laura's face when she walked in the room that she realised that something was very wrong.

"Laura – whatever is it? Oh my God, is it the boys... or Adam? What's happened?"

"No... no, Beth it's not them." She paused and shook her head. I've just had a phone call from Adam. He went to Malthorp to pick up some things for you and he found..." She swallowed and bit her lip.

"What? Please, Laura, tell me!"

"Oh, Beth, he found his brother – Simon? He was at the bottom of the attic stairs. He must have fallen – his neck was broken. Beth, I'm so sorry to have to tell you, but Simon is dead!"

Adam was still in deep shock. He had arrived at Malthorp at eight-thirty that morning and let himself in through the front door. Before going upstairs to fetch the things that Beth would need when she came out of hospital, he had decided to go through to the kitchen and fetch a couple of bottles of wine from the rack to take back with him. As soon as the baize door shut behind him he saw the smashed window in the scullery.

"Oh no!" he said out loud. "We've had a break-in." He hurried back into the hall and quickly checked the downstairs rooms. As far as he could see, nothing had been disturbed. "Perhaps they got cold feet," he murmured. "Better check upstairs as well." He ran up the stairs and turned to the left, checking the bedrooms on that side of the house. As he walked back along the corridor towards the boys' rooms, he saw a huddled figure lying at the bottom of the attic stairs. He couldn't believe it when he realised that it was Simon. He knew immediately when he saw the twisted angle of his head that he had broken his neck. With shaking fingers, he had dialled the emergency services and they had arrived within half an hour.

Now he was at the police station waiting to be told if he could go home. The police had questioned him closely, especially when he had told them how he and Simon had parted on such bad terms. Adam felt he would never forgive himself for his bitter words to his brother and the fact that he had punched him. He looked up to see Geoff standing in front of him.

"Adam? Come on, old son; let's get you back to ours."

"I think the police wanted to speak to me again."

"No, it's fine. They know you were at ours when… when it happened. You're not under any sort of suspicion."

"God!" Adam buried his face in his hands and then looked up at his friend. "You know, Geoff, I'm beginning to think that Beth is right; that bloody house is cursed or something. First my mother, now Simon – and all the things that have gone wrong since we've been there. It's got to be more than coincidence, hasn't it?"

Geoff shook his head. "I don't know, but I think Beth needs you right now; in fact, you need each other. Come on, Laura's expecting us and you know you can stay as long as you need to."

"Thanks, I appreciate that. How is she – Beth, I mean."

"She's okay; just really shocked at the news and worried about you. And Jamie's not too good; he had one of his screaming fits just before Beth got back this afternoon."

"What brought that on?"

"No idea. He's okay now though; Debbie came over and managed to calm him down. She's taken him and Danny to MacDonald's for a treat, then they're going to go back and walk Finn in the park."

"Thank God for Debbie; don't know what we'd do without her at times. I've spoken to Neil and he's breaking the news about Simon to Dad; it's awful for him to hear about this so soon after losing my mother."

When they arrived back at the house Beth and Laura were in the kitchen, a pot of tea in front of them. Beth jumped up and ran to Adam putting her arms round him as best she could with her injured wrist.

"Oh, my love, I'm so, so sorry about Simon. I know he hadn't been the best lately but he certainly didn't deserve this. Do you know how it happened?"

"The police seem to think he'd had a lot to drink and he just lost his footing – though why he went up to the boys' playroom we'll never know. Did you know I went to see him last night?"

"Geoff told me you'd had an argument."

"It was a bit more than that," said Adam and a look of anguish crossed his face. "He said some pretty crude and unpleasant things about you and I'm afraid I punched him on the nose. I can't believe that was the last thing I did before…" He closed his eyes and Beth hugged him tightly.

"So why did he go to Malthorp?" Laura asked.

"Presumably to have it out with me. Though quite why he broke in when it was obvious that there was no one at home, I don't understand."

"If he was drunk and angry, he probably wasn't reasoning things out very well," said Geoff. "Whatever happened you mustn't blame yourself, Adam. Nobody could have foreseen what Simon would do or what the outcome would be."

"I suppose you're right," said Adam. He sat down and took the cup of tea Laura was holding out to him. "Doesn't make it any easier though." He looked at Beth and took a deep breath. "I'm beginning to think you're right about that house, Beth. So many strange things have happened and I believe it is affecting Jamie quite badly because he certainly has had some issues to contend with. Maybe we should cut our losses and sell – look for somewhere else. I'm not saying I believe in all this haunting nonsense, though," he added intractably, "and I love that place and I think we'll miss it, but after everything that's happened I'm not sure we'll be able to settle back in there again."

Beth nodded, the relief palpable on her face. "I agree. Listen, I didn't talk to you properly about it before, my love, because I didn't think at the time that it was feasible, but you remember I've had that fantastic offer from Guy Turner."

She filled him in with all the details about the opportunity to go to New York. Adam was sceptical at first, feeling that it would be a huge step to take for the family but gradually he began to come round to the idea and they all started to discuss it in depth. He thought he should be able to take a year's sabbatical from the hospital; with the money that Beth would be earning, and the fact that the trip would be all-expenses paid, they should be able to afford it. They could sell Malthorp, put all their possessions in storage, and leave the money from the sale of the house in the bank to buy somewhere when they came back to England. "That's if anyone wants to buy it!" Adam commented gloomily, still feeling pessimistic.

They would obviously have to find schools for the boys over there, but hopefully Guy would help them sort that out and they felt sure that Tom Mitchell would also be able to recommend somewhere suitable for Jamie. Gradually, Adam became more positive and he and Beth began to feel quite excited about the prospect. They decided to discuss it with the boys when they came back from Debbie's.

As they'd expected, Danny was thrilled with the idea. "Oh, that's so cool!" he kept saying. "Wait till I tell them at school. New York! Will there be loads of gangsters and shoot-outs and things?"

"You've been watching too many films, mate!" laughed Geoff, ruffling his hair. Danny grinned, and then his face fell.

"But, Mum," he said suddenly. "What about Finn? Can we take him with us?"

Beth put her arm round him.

"I'm afraid not, Danny. It wouldn't be fair to take him on a plane, and he might have to be quarantined when we got there. It just wouldn't be feasible."

"But what's going to happen to him? We can't leave him behind!"

Debbie stepped forward. "Listen Dan, Jamie, I'm going to miss you all so much, so do you think I could look after Finn for you for a year? He'd be really great company for me and you know how I love him." Beth and Adam looked at her gratefully as she smiled warmly at the boys.

"What do you think, Jamie?" Danny asked his brother, who had been very quiet while the discussion was going on. "Do you think Finn would be okay with Debbie?"

Jamie gave a small nod of assent.

"That's okay then." Danny's face was wreathed in smiles once more. "New York here we come!"

Beth knelt down beside Jamie, "Is that okay, sweetheart? Would you like to go to America?"

Jamie looked at her wide-eyed. "Jamie like to go to 'merica if Valentine won't be there, 'cos Valentine can't go on planes either can he, Mummy?"

"No," Beth said. "Valentine won't be there." She whispered quietly to him. "Mummy's going to make sure of that, my darling."

CHAPTER 50

Adam went back to work a couple of days later. He had travelled to Berkshire to see John the day after Simon's death. His father was, naturally, devastated at the news about his son but very concerned about Adam and Beth after yet another terrible incident at Malthorp. He agreed entirely that they should seriously consider moving and thought that the idea of going away to America for a year was a good one.

"I shall miss you all, of course," he said as he dished up lunch. "But it's not a million miles away and you never know I might even come over for a visit. Have you told the boys about Simon?"

"We told Danny last night," Adam said. "He was pretty upset, but they didn't see a lot of him so I think he'll get over it pretty soon. We haven't said anything to Jamie yet; I don't think he'll really understand. Dad, you know the funeral won't be for a while, don't you? There will have to be a post-mortem and an inquest, I'm afraid. Suspicious circumstances and all that. I'm so sorry."

"Not your fault, my dear boy." His father's eyes were filled with sadness. "Poor Simon," he said, "he never really found his niche in life, and he was always very bitter about what he considered his unfair deal. I just wish he could have been happier. Fiona rang me, you know; she is so upset and blames herself, feeling that their split-up hit him very hard. But, as I told her, Simon was always his own worst enemy. After all it was just a terrible accident wasn't it?"

"Yes, of course," said Adam, putting a comforting arm round his dad's shoulders. "Just a terrible accident."

◦∽∘∽∘

Beth found it hard to adapt to being back at Laura and Geoff's and she knew that the boys were finding it difficult too; they had always liked being there but she knew they missed the space and freedom of

Malthorp. On the other hand, Jamie seemed more settled in himself; he had not woken up at night and had not mentioned Valentine at all. However, Beth was determined that she must do something to resolve the unfinished business at the house and help the unhappy souls who still dwelt there to find some sort of peace. Otherwise, she felt she could never be sure that Valentine would go away and leave her family alone.

When everyone had left for work and school on the third day and she was on her own, she decided to ring Gloria Nash and ask her advice. The medium answered her phone almost immediately.

"Beth, my dear girl, I felt instinctively that I would be hearing from you soon. I was so shocked to read in the paper about what happened to your brother-in-law; I am so very sorry."

"Yes, it has been a pretty bad time, and it wasn't the only thing." Beth told her about her accident and what had led up to Simon being in the house.

"Are you still at Malthorp? Because if you are…"

Beth filled her in and Gloria listened in silence until she had finished talking.

"My dear, I think you are very wise to stay away. Things are escalating rather alarmingly aren't they, as I was afraid they would. This child, Valentine, is becoming increasingly frustrated and vicious; I fear these incidents, awful as they are, could be just the beginning."

"That's what I'm afraid of too," admitted Beth. She told Gloria about Beatrice's letters and said, "I'd like to show them to you. Can we meet?"

"Of course. How about tomorrow? I can meet you in Winchester at, say, ten o'clock?"

"Yes, that would be great. I can get a lift in with Adam after he's dropped the boys off. Obviously, I'm not driving at the moment because of my wrist. Shall we say by the Butter Cross?"

"Lovely, dear, see you then."

Beth rang off with a feeling of relief tempered by guilt. She knew that she should really tell Adam of her plan to meet Gloria but she was afraid of his reaction. No, it was better to keep quiet and see what Gloria had to say. No sense in tempting fate.

※

Beth arrived in Winchester early the next morning as Adam was dropping her and he had to be in by nine-fifteen. He hadn't been too happy about her going in at all and she had used all her persuasive powers to get him to agree.

"I'm going stir-crazy sitting around," she told him. "I promise I'll be careful; I just want to have a mooch around and I can easily get a taxi back."

Eventually he reluctantly agreed. "But promise you'll ring me, or Laura, if you have any problems."

She wandered round the shops for a while and then made her way to the old Butter Cross, remembering nostalgically how she and Adam had first met there. Gloria was on time and they decided to walk round to the Cathedral and have coffee in their café. Only a few people were in there and they settled near the window with their cappuccinos and a toasted teacake each. They chatted for a while, then Beth pulled the brown envelope out of her bag and handed it to the medium. She stared broodingly out of the window at the ancient flint wall outside and watched the noisy starlings quarrelling over a crust that someone had dropped while Gloria read, totally absorbed by Beatrice's letters.

"Fascinating! Absolutely fascinating!" she said softly when she had finished. "Poor woman; she had so much to contend with, torn between her love for her son and her duty to her husband, for it was 'duty' in those days. It's no wonder she and her child are not at rest."

"But what can we do?" asked Beth, "Can we help them, Gloria? I can't go away to New York and leave this unresolved. Even if we have gone, whoever buys Malthorp could be in danger too. It could be another child like Jamie for all we know."

Gloria nodded, "I agree." She took a sip of her cappuccino and leaned forward. "Beth," she said earnestly. "I will endeavour to help you, though it will be very challenging. But I am willing to try." She hesitated. Neither of them had touched their teacakes. "It will mean us, and by *us* I mean you and I, going back to Malthorp and trying to fully communicate with Valentine and possibly Beatrice who I believe is also there. And…" she paused again "…I definitely sensed that the other malevolent presence in the house will add to the problems we will encounter."

"Richard Cartwright," said Beth. "I think he is the main reason why Valentine cannot leave."

"Yes, the hatred between them is a palpable force that cannot be easily broken. But if we can find out *why* it is so potent then we may be able to resolve it. But it won't be easy; in fact it will very likely be unpleasant and downright dangerous. Are you sure you want to take that risk?"

Beth drew a deep breath.

"When can we start?" she said.

MAY 12TH 1911

Richard Cartwright stares blankly at the wall opposite his study desk. He has just received the news he has been waiting for and he now has to decide what his next course of action should be. This news has changed everything; there remains only one obstacle in his way. Now his mother-in-law has joined her husband in death he must endeavour to break the terms of the trust; only then will he be able to get his hands on the money he desperately needs. He has invested, heavily and unwisely, in several dubious ventures and his gambling debts have spiralled out of control; not to mention the money he owes to the lady who is willing to accommodate his particular sexual tastes. Beatrice's money that her father gave her upon their marriage has all but gone and his only hope now is the fortune split between her useless, crippled son and his own child, Robert. Cartwright rises and walks to the sideboard on which stands the decanter. Pouring himself a large brandy he stares broodingly out of his study window. From here he can see quite clearly the kitchen garden and old Stokes drawing a bucket of water from the deep well to water the spring cabbages. He nods thoughtfully. It will take careful planning but he is sure he can do it; it is just a question of when and how.

It will be no onerous task for him, he reflects; in fact, it is one which will give him the utmost satisfaction.

CHAPTER 51

Jamie waited impatiently as Geoff paid at the entrance to the swimming pool. It was a Saturday afternoon two days later and Adam had taken Danny to his friend's to stay the night, so as a special treat Geoff had said he would take Jamie swimming. It was the first time Jamie had ever been to the swimming pool without Danny and he was very excited. It was the first time Geoff had been for a long time as well and he was looking forward to it; especially to taking Jamie on the pirate ship and the water flumes which were a new feature.

They spent a very happy hour and a half, and when they came out of the changing rooms Geoff bought Jamie a burger to tuck into at the café. "I'll get you an ice-cream as well," he said. "What would you like?"

"Jamie likes a rocket lolly," he said. "They my favourite!"

They looked in the ice-cream cabinet but couldn't see one so they went up to ask the lady behind the counter, but she smiled apologetically at Jamie, "Sorry, sweetheart, we don't have those. We've got a fruit ice lolly with ice-cream in the middle, they're nice."

Jamie looked very disappointed. "But Jamie likes rocket lollies." He looked at Geoff appealingly, his eyes huge. "They sell them in the shop at home."

Geoff gave a mock sigh and rolled his eyes then exchanged a smile with the serving lady. "Okay, I suppose we can do a detour and go back that way. We can't have you telling Auntie Laura that I wouldn't buy you a locket rolly!"

Jamie giggled. "You silly, Uncle Geoff – it's a rocket lolly!"

They went out to the car and Geoff strapped Jamie carefully into his car seat. It didn't take them long to reach Upper Melcombe and as Geoff drew up in front of the shop he saw that Jamie, worn out by the swimming was nodding off in the back. Geoff turned and gave him a grin.

"You coming in with me young man, or are you too tired? You can stay there if you like."

"Jamie stay here, Uncle Geoff," he said sleepily. "I'm a bit tired."

"Won't be a tick. I'd better pick up some more milk and bread for Auntie Laura while I'm in there."

He got out of the car and strolled into the shop. Jamie stretched and yawned. Geoff had left the radio on and one of Danny's favourite songs, *There Must be an Angel* by the Eurythmics was playing. Jamie started humming along, but frowned as the radio suddenly crackled and then stopped. He had recently learned how to undo the buckle on his seatbelt but Beth had given him strict instructions that he mustn't do so unless she was there. But he wanted to listen to the rest of the song. He sighed and looked out of the window. There was no sign of Geoff so he decided to get into the front and see if he could get the radio to work again. He managed to undo the buckle without any trouble, slid out of his seat and squeezed between the two front seats. Sitting in the passenger seat he pushed the button on the radio several times but nothing happened. Suddenly he heard a gentle scratching sound on the window. Thinking it was Geoff playing a trick he looked to his left and his eyes widened with fear. Valentine was standing outside looking in at him and smiling. Then the window slid down, even though Jamie hadn't touched it.

"Hello Jamie," Valentine said softly, " I want you to come and play…"

"Don't want to," Jamie began fearfully, but he knew it was no use. The car door swung open and Valentine held his gaze as Jamie slid slowly out of the seat and climbed out of the car.

Valentine led him away, past the houses and shops and through the gate which led into the churchyard.

"Come on, Jamie," he said. "We're going to play hide and seek again."

An hour later the village was besieged by police cars as the hunt began for James Adam Ellis, aged six.

But he had completely and inexplicably vanished.

CHAPTER 52

"Is there any news?" said Laura rising quickly as Geoff appeared at the car.

Geoff shook his head and looked at her despairingly. "Christ! I'll never forgive myself. What the hell was I thinking, leaving him on his own in the car? But I thought he'd be fine; I was only gone five minutes."

"Beth and Adam are on their way. They should be here any minute."

Geoff groaned and buried his head in his hands. "I don't know how I'm going to face them."

"Look, the police don't believe anyone else is involved. They think he just wandered off – someone in one of the cottages saw a little boy on his own go past their window. I'm sure they'll find him soon."

Beth and Adam arrived a few minutes later. White-faced they got out of the car and ran over.

"What happened?" asked Beth, her voice breaking. "My God… *Jamie!*"

Adam went over to talk to the police while Laura did her best to comfort Beth. A few minutes later he came back, looking pale and distraught. "There's still no sign of him. They are going to organise a search party and I'm going over to the house with them now to make sure he isn't there."

"I'll come with you," Beth said, but he put his hand out to stop her.

"No, you stay here, just in case he turns up."

"Don't you worry, Mrs Ellis, we'll find him." She turned to see Bill Tidy standing behind her. "He'll have just wandered off, you'll see. He'll be back with you before you know it."

Peter and Janet Bowers hurried over as Adam and a white-faced Geoff left to join the search party.

"Beth, we're so sorry," said Janet her eyes full of compassion. "Do you want to come and wait in the vicarage?"

Beth shook her head. She felt sick and dizzy. "No thank you," she said faintly. I want to stay by the car in case he comes back."

"Of course," she squeezed Beth's hand. "I'm sure he's alright."

Beth felt she'd go mad if anyone else said that to her. She went and sat on the wall by the shop, feeling that her legs wouldn't support her any longer. Maureen Tidy bustled out with a cup of tea for her which she didn't really want, and Laura came and sat next to her.

"Beth…" she began.

"Please, Laura, I don't want to hear you telling me he'll be okay. If you don't mind, I'd just like to be left alone for a few moments."

"Of course, I understand." There were tears in her eyes as she walked away and Beth felt a pang of guilt as she stared sightlessly at the ground. Suddenly her mobile rang. She snatched it up eagerly, but then her shoulders sagged as she realised it was Gloria.

"Beth, my dear, I'm in Winchester. Now listen, I think we should…"

"Gloria, I can't talk now… something awful has happened."

"Whatever is it?"

Beth explained, her voice breaking. Gloria cut in.

"Beth, my dear, I think this is Valentine's doing. I think he has taken Jamie!"

"But what… Why… Oh God he's going to hurt him, isn't he?"

"I don't know, but we must act, we have no choice. Where are you now? I am coming straight over."

"I'm in the village. Adam and the police are checking the house to see if he's there."

"I don't believe they will find anything. Listen, when they come back and the house is clear then you and I must go there. This is probably our only chance to resolve this and save Jamie. Will you meet me there?"

"Of course, I'll go as soon as I can."

Adam came back about half an hour later, his face haggard. "We've looked everywhere but there's no sign of him. I'm going out again to look around the area with the police. Are you going to stay here?"

"Yes. I'll stay with Laura."

He hugged her. "We're going to find him, Beth, I promise."

As soon as he'd gone Beth turned to Laura. "There's something I have to do. Will you please stay here in case there's any news?"

"Where are you going? Let me come with you."

"No, please, I have to do this alone. I think I might be able to find him."

"Beth?"

She hurried off before Laura could argue any further, and ran down the path to the lane which led to Malthorp. A few moments later Gloria's car pulled up beside her. Beth got in and burst into tears. Gloria patted her arm and fished in her handbag for a tissue which she handed to Beth.

"Now, my dear girl, I know how you must be feeling but I am sure that Valentine has Jamie," she said her voice shaking.

"But Adam and the police have checked the house and the surrounding area," said Beth despairingly, blowing her nose loudly. "There's no sign of him."

"No, there won't be," Gloria said grimly. "He will make sure of that. But we *will* find him, Beth. I don't think Valentine will harm him."

"But what does he want?" Beth's voice broke on a sob.

"I don't know, but we will soon find out." She let out the clutch and they drove off.

CHAPTER 53

Malthorp looked very tranquil and serene in the evening sunlight. It seemed as if nothing bad could ever have happened within its solid walls or in those peaceful gardens which surrounded it. Beth and Gloria stood looking at it for a few moments, both unwilling to break the spell, to shatter the illusion of complete and utter well-being that the scene before them engendered.

Then, as one, they shivered as they remembered the tragedy, sorrow and anguish that had taken place there and the terrible death of the young boy whom they believed had Jamie in his grasp. Gloria took a deep breath.

"Are you ready, my dear?"

Beth nodded and they walked towards the front of the house. The stone eagle above the porch watched them with its menacing glare and all was still; it seemed that even the birds had fallen silent. As Beth inserted her key into the front door and they entered the ice-cold hallway, Gloria gave a shudder.

"He is waiting for us. I feel his presence very strongly."

"Valentine?" whispered Beth tremulously. She felt as if every nerve in her body was on edge.

"Yes, I think so. Now, you have to be very brave, Beth. We need to go up to the playroom. That is where the manifestation seems the strongest and that, I believe, is where I should be able to communicate with him. He was very hostile to me before, but I have a strong feeling that it is your presence that he and his mother need to help him to tell us his story."

"But we need to find Jamie; I have to look for him Gloria. He must be so frightened!"

"I don't think we will find him easily. But, as I said, I don't believe that Valentine intends to harm Jamie; he seems to need him and we have to find out why."

"And what about Richard Cartwright? You said that he is a threat too?"

"I believe that Richard's spirit may be an evil force we have to overcome; that is my instinct. However, we will see. Now, my dear, whatever happens, stay with me. We are stronger together and we are facing a formidable power. You will have to stay focused and follow my lead."

Beth wanted nothing more than tear Malthorp apart brick by brick, screaming Jamie's name until she found him, but she felt she must trust Gloria. Her heart thumped in her chest as they mounted the stairs. As they reached the top and turned to walk down the passageway towards the attic stairs, she heard a child singing softly. She recognised the song immediately. It was the one Jamie had sung so plaintively that day when they had found him in the garden sitting by the old well.

She felt sick with fear for her son as she listened and heard the poignant words:

> *In the sky so clear above me*
> *The moon doth brightly shine,*
> *Give me your heart then I will be*
> *Forever your Valentine.*

The words faded into an eerie silence; then they heard the desperate sobs of a woman echoing through the house.

"Beatrice?" whispered Beth.

Gloria nodded, grasping Beth's hand as they walked resolutely along the passage to the foot of the stairs. Beth shuddered as she realised that this was where Simon's body had lain for several hours before Adam had found him. She tried not to think about it; tried desperately to focus as they mounted the stairs to the door. Looking up, her heart almost missed a beat as in the half-light she saw the unmistakably thickset figure of Kevin leering down at her. She stopped dead, her legs refusing to function. Gloria grabbed her arm.

"Don't surrender to it Beth, it's just an illusion! Think of Jamie."

Beth forced herself to visualise her son's face in her mind and Kevin vanished at the same time as the woman's bitter weeping fell silent. The silence seemed to thicken around them, becoming increasingly menacing, and Beth felt it wrap itself around her like a thick cloak. As they reached the top of the stairs and faced the closed door, it slowly swung open.

"Ready?" asked Gloria, and Beth nodded. They stepped in and gasped as they faced the scene before them.

All the furniture and the carpet that had been in the room had vanished. Instead, there were bare floorboards, covered only partly by a faded red-patterned rug. In the middle of the room, pitted and stained with ink, stood an old-fashioned school desk with a bench. The cupboard was still at the end of the room, its door wide open and they could see that it was filled with books. To one side was a blackboard and easel. It was like looking at an old black and white film, grainy and indistinct, yet at the same time it appeared very real.

Although they took all this in, both were transfixed by the sight of the young boy who stood beside the school desk. He looked no more than nine or ten years old; his back was hunched and Beth now saw with pity how withered and wasted his legs were. He leaned upon the two wooden crutches looking at them coldly through his round wire spectacles. His face was lined and drawn with pain. Water dripped from his dark hair on to the bare floorboards. Gloria stepped forward, focusing all her mind upon him.

"Valentine!" she said softly. "Valentine – we see you. Will you speak with us? Will you let us help you?"

The boy laughed softly, maliciously and Beth shuddered as he pointed at her with one of the crutches. His voice was thin and tinny and echoed around them,

"You cannot help me. Only *she* can."

"How can I help you, Valentine?" Beth asked softly though she was very frightened; the sense of malevolence emanating from him was terrifying.

"Your child must become one with me. The strength of your love for him will atone for my mother's betrayal, and that strength combined with mine will allow me to revenge myself upon the one who caused my death."

Beth felt her heart lurch. "Where is he? Where is Jamie? Please don't hurt him."

Gloria put her hand out towards the boy. "Valentine, if you harm another innocent child then you will never find peace. You cannot use Jamie – that is not the way."

"I have waited too long!" His face contorted in anguish. "She took Jamie away from this house and it is only through him that I can find enough power to destroy that evil which holds me here!"

"I tell you, Valentine, you cannot find the peace you seek down this path!" Gloria cried, her voice shaking but resolute. "You must let us help you in another way."

There was a crash as the blackboard was hurled to the floor and, as books began to fly out of the cupboard, a howling wind blew up. Valentine screamed with rage, his face horribly distorted and Beth cried out in terror as a book struck her in the face. Blood began to trickle down her cheek There was a sharp pain in her injured wrist as if some unseen force was gripping it tightly. "Valentine," she cried, "please, stop!"

Gloria took her good hand again and held it tightly, though she, too, was shaking. "Beth!" she shouted above the cacophony of noise. "Remember we must stay strong for Jamie. We have to call upon the one person he may respond to."

She closed her eyes, once again summoning all her strength, and spoke in a firm and decisive voice, "Beatrice! Beatrice, I ask that you show yourself; for his sake come now to your son Valentine and help us to resolve this."

For a moment nothing happened, then they saw an ethereal,

indistinct figure materialise on the other side of the room by the window. As her form became gradually clearer, Beth recognised the woman she had seen sobbing by Valentine's bedside. Her face was filled with anguish as she looked at the ghost of her son, his face still a mask of fury.

"Valentine?" Her voice was weak and fearful.

"Go! I do not wish to see or speak with you. You betrayed me, whom you professed to love! Go with *him* for that is what you wished. He will face his judgement and you should face it with him!"

"Please, Valentine, please," she implored. "I feel your hurt and anger but you must show me *why*. Show me what happened to you that day and why it is that you hold me responsible."

"I cannot." The boy's face changed suddenly; the anger and hatred drained from it and he seemed to shrink into himself. Beth saw him for what he was; for what he had been; a little boy, as vulnerable and dependent as Jamie. "Mama! Oh Mama! I want to so very much but I cannot. I do not know how."

Then, without warning, a dark menacing shape came between them. Valentine shrank fearfully back into the shadows and Beatrice cried out in terror.

"No, Richard! Leave him, I beg you; let him speak!"

The shadow materialised into the man Beth had seen before in the house, Richard Cartwright, his once-handsome face bloated and grotesque. He gave a chilling laugh as he loomed over them.

"Why should I, you feeble, useless bitch? Know this – I will never release you or that wretched useless cripple! I will see you both wallow forever in your misery, as I do in mine. You will never be free!"

Gloria released Beth and took a step towards the terrifying figure and she seemed to grow in strength and stature as she faced him fearlessly. "It is *you* who deserves that fate, Richard Cartwright!" Her voice was loud and fierce and her face stern and unforgiving. "Step back from here and we will hear the truth at last!"

Cartwright roared in fury, but he flinched from her as she held his gaze and shrank back, becoming an indistinct and dark shadow again. Gloria turned once more to the boy and said firmly but gently, "Listen to me, Valentine, I *can* help you. You can use both of us to show us what happened to you and to find that peace you desire. Be strong and let me help you do what you need to."

He faltered, and then nodded slowly, "Very well, I will try."

"Beth, take my hand again and close your eyes," said Gloria urgently. "I don't know if this will work but we have to both try if we're to save Jamie. The strength of your love for your child is powerful."

Beth did as Gloria commanded and, as she did so, she was sure she felt Beatrice's gentle presence close beside her. Cartwright's dark shadow still hovered in the corner.

"Close your eyes," Gloria said, "and empty your mind. Now Valentine, please, through us all, show us the truth of what happened to you…"

MAY 18th 1911
VALENTINE

Valentine hobbles unsteadily down the path. His wooden crutches make a hollow tapping on the flagstones and, as one of them catches in a crack, he stumbles and nearly falls. He rights himself with some difficulty and carries on, eager to reach his destination. At the end of the pathway, he turns past the kitchen garden, where old Stokes is usually to be found digging and humming patriotic songs under his breath. But today there is nobody about and the boy limps painfully on towards the outhouse where Jim has told him that he will find the puppies.

His legs are aching badly now, especially the right one, the one that is wasted so badly, for this is a lot further than he usually goes without his wheeled chair. There is a rare smile on his thin, eager face and his bright blue eyes behind the round wire spectacles are alight with anticipation. He is never usually allowed out alone like this but most of the servants have gone to the village fair, his tutor has given him a day's holiday, and his mother has gone to town for the day to visit her old friend, so he is determined to take a chance and see the puppies for himself. Valentine has told Mama that he would dearly love to have one of the litter for his very own, but he knows he will never be allowed. If his stepfather sees him out in the garden there is bound to be a severe telling-off and probably another punishment because, although he has relented a little of late and has reluctantly given in to Mama's pleading, allowing Valentine to sleep downstairs in his old room, he is still remorseless when it comes to the smallest transgression. However, he is usually in his study in the afternoons and Valentine has sneaked out through the back entrance so he feels sure he hasn't been seen.

Down by the kitchen garden Valentine stops suddenly and frowns as he notices that the cover is off the old well, the one Stokes uses to water the vegetables. It is lying on the ground beside the low wall which surrounds the well. If his stepfather sees this he will be very angry; only last week after family prayers, which all the household is required to attend, Valentine remembers him telling the servants that the well should never be left uncovered in case little Robert, nearly two years old and becoming very adept at escaping Nanny's clutches, should go near it.

He decides that he will put it back if he can. His stepfather is hopefully still in his study doing the wages for the servants, but if by chance he comes out and sees that the cover has been left off then he will be furious, and old Stokes, who is always so kind to Valentine, will get into trouble. He leaves the path and stumbles over the uneven ground towards it; laying his crutches down he bends awkwardly and grasps the sides of the round wooden lid. It is far heavier than he has anticipated and he only manages to lift it a few inches off the ground then is forced to drop it. Gasping, he straightens up and prepares to have another try.

There is the faintest sound of footsteps behind him. He half turns in relief, thinking it is Stokes, or perhaps Jim. But he has no chance to see, for, without warning, two arms like steel bands close round him lifting him effortlessly into the air. He kicks feebly and tries to struggle, but he is powerless against the strength of the arms as they propel him forward and over the low wall into the well. He opens his mouth to scream but, before he can do so, he drops like a stone and the ice-cold, murky water closes over his head as he sinks to the bottom.

He kicks violently, fear lending strength to his wasted limbs, and surfaces briefly, choking and spluttering. He scrabbles frantically at the rough brick sides of the well, searching in vain for a handhold but, finding none, looks up to see the face of the monster who kneels at the edge of the well looking down at him dispassionately.

"Help me!" Valentine screams, arms flailing, "Mama!" But his final cry of desperation is cut short; the merciless, freezing water fills his mouth and nose as he sinks again. When he surfaces for the last time, his lungs bursting as he tries in vain to gasp for air, he sees that his stepfather has gone. In those final, brief seconds of his life he experiences two emotions – one the sharp pain of despair as he realises he is going to die; the other is that all-too-familiar, powerful, deep-seated hatred of the man who has done this last dreadful thing to him. As his lungs flood with the ice-cold water and his tiny hand sinks below the water for the final time, the burning desire for revenge fills the whole of his being, and his last conscious thought is the forming of a deep and lasting vow.

Someone will pay dearly for the taking of his young and innocent life.

The ripples that disturbed the hitherto peaceful water at the bottom of the well gradually subside so when they come to look for him later that day, the only sign of Valentine Taylor is a pair of crutches lying near the well and a pair of round wire spectacles, floating forlornly on the black surface of the water.

CHAPTER 54

Beth opened her eyes slowly, shocked and dazed by what she had witnessed. The experience of seeing Valentine's murder had been terrible but somehow fascinating; it had almost seemed as if she was watching some old black and white horror movie, surreal yet at the same time tangible. It had felt so real she felt she should cry out a warning to Valentine as Richard Cartwright had crept up behind his young stepson and cold-bloodedly murdered him.

She became aware that Beatrice was still beside her and that she was weeping softly again. Then she felt a soft breath as the woman moved away and towards her son who was now hunched over his crutches, his head drooping. Gloria sank to the floor, exhausted by her ordeal and Beth knelt down and put a comforting arm round her. She heard Beatrice speak as she bent towards her son.

"Valentine, oh, my dearest boy! I swear I did not know what he had done, or how very wicked he was. I understand now why you could not rest. I am so sorry that you suffered this." Her son pointed his crutch at Cartwright as he cowered before them.

"*He* prevented it, Mama, his presence stopped me from telling you in life and… and afterwards."

Beatrice straightened and looked towards the hovering shadow in the corner of the room. Cartwright seemed to be gathering strength again and began to move towards them. Beth could see him quite clearly now, his dreadful bloated face leering at them all. His malevolent gaze fell on Valentine and his expression became even more filled with hatred and loathing. He loomed over the boy, fists clenched and Valentine shrank back fearfully but, as they watched, Beatrice glided towards him and drew back her lips, her face changing from sadness to pure fury, her eyes blazing. As the shape of Richard Cartwright shrank back and seemed to diminish, so she grew in stature until she towered over him like an avenging angel.

"*Why?* Why did you murder my poor child?"

He shrank further back, his face full of malicious hatred.

"I drowned him as you would any useless runt! That fortune should have been mine... mine, I tell you!" His hands reached out trying in vain to reach Valentine.

"NO!" she shrieked. "Your filthy greed killed him before, but this time you shall not prevail. I shall not let you touch him again!"

Without hesitation she threw herself at the dark shadow that was Cartwright, her hands clawed, wrapping herself tightly around him, tearing savagely at his face. He gave a roar of agony as they twisted and fought, but her fury and ferocity were more than equal to his. As Gloria and Beth watched, with a last shriek she finally overcame him and he howled in pain as they spiralled up and away, becoming fainter and more diaphanous until they vanished altogether, Cartwright's final agonised scream echoing in the room around them.

The women found they were clinging tightly to one another, and turned as one to look with apprehension at Beatrice's son who had not moved.

"Valentine!" Beth stepped towards him. "Are you free? Has he gone forever?"

He looked towards them and his expression had changed to one of hope. "I do not know," he replied, his voice faint. "My Mama protected me from him this time. But I do not know whether he is gone forever. You must pray for me that I am finally released and can now leave this place where I have lingered so long."

He looked away; they realised he had begun to fade slowly before their eyes and Beth cried out despairingly,

"Valentine – wait! You must tell me; where is Jamie?"

"He is safe... Look for him where I sleep; where I hope now to sleep forever..."

His voice faded as he slowly disappeared. Beth clasped Gloria's arm.

"I know where Jamie is! He's in the graveyard. Quick, Gloria we must go there now!"

It was dusk as Beth ran down the path which led to the church gate, closely followed by Gloria who was gasping for breath. In the distance they could hear voices and Beth stopped for a moment.

"Gloria, please go to the village, find Adam and the others and bring them here. Tell them to bring blankets and the paramedics!"

"Of course, my dear, but are you sure he'll be there?"

"I know it; I feel it. Please just hurry!"

Gloria rushed off and Beth ran down the path past the front of the church and round the side. She sped across the grass to where the huge yew stood by the churchyard wall. She stopped, squinting in the half-light and her heart sank. There was no sign of Jamie. Half-sobbing, she approached the grave where the words that had started her on her quest were etched so deeply into the stone beneath the weeping angel:

> **Here lies**
> **VALENTINE EDWARD TAYLOR**
> **Beloved Son of Beatrice and Edward Taylor**
> **Born: 16th April 1902**
> **Cruelly taken: 18th May 1911**
> **Sleep today, Oh Early Fallen,**
> **in thy Green and Narrow bed.**
> **Dirges, from the Yew and Cypress,**
> **mingle with the Tears we shed.**

Then her heart missed a beat as she saw a small trainer-clad shoe poking out from behind the grave. She rushed round to see her young son lying curled up with one arm outstretched in the deep shadow of the yew.

"Jamie!" she cried and knelt down beside him. For a moment he didn't move and her heart sank. Then she gasped with relief as he stirred and opened his eyes:

"Mummy!" He held out his arms. "Jamie cold."

※

"I can't understand it," said PC West, scratching his head. "I checked the church and the graveyard twice. How could I have missed seeing the lad? All I can think is that he must have been well hidden by that old yew tree. I tell you, Bill, the Sarge isn't very happy with me. But, honestly, that's the last place I thought the kid would hide anyway."

"Bit of a mystery that," said Bill Tidy. "Mind, some funny things happen in this village. Why, my old Gran could tell you some tales."

"Shut up, Bill!" Maureen snapped. "He don't want to hear your stupid stories. Mind you," she said under her breath, "always did think there was something funny going on up at Malthorp with that Ellis family. Still, the little lad's found now so that's alright."

Adam and Beth drove back to the Dunbar's house in silence. Jamie, who was well wrapped up in a blanket, was now sound asleep in his car seat. He had been checked over by the paramedics at the scene and pronounced none the worse for his experience. Adam had questioned him gently about what had happened but he had just said he couldn't remember anything. He didn't mention Valentine at all, much to Beth's relief. She had no intention of telling Adam what had happened at Malthorp; she only knew that they were never going back. Before they had left the village, she had given Gloria a hug and thanked her for everything she had done. Gloria had hugged her back and whispered:

"I very much hope that this will be an end to it, my dear, and that those poor souls have found peace. But one can never tell. Be happy, Beth, I wish you and all your family the very best of everything for the future."

She had walked swiftly away and Beth knew that they would probably never meet again.

They drew up at Laura and Geoff's and Adam took a deep breath. "We'll get the house on the market tomorrow," he said. "I don't know about you but I think we need to leave as soon as possible and put all this behind us."

Beth nodded her agreement. "We will." She smiled at him. "We'll be okay, Adam, things will be fine from now on." She looked back at her peacefully sleeping small son, "As long as we have our family, nothing can hurt us."

CHAPTER 56
FOUR MONTHS LATER

Beth walked slowly along the path and saw that Peter Bowers was waiting for her where they had arranged to meet. He smiled warmly as she approached him and held out his hands, "Beth! Good to see you."

She grasped his hands and squeezed them tightly. "And you, Peter. Thank you so much for agreeing to do this."

"Well, it is a little unorthodox but it sounded as if it was important to you. When do you leave for New York?"

"Tomorrow morning."

"Have you sold?"

"No, not yet, but there are several interested parties. There is talk of it being bought as a conference centre again, but nothing is settled yet."

He noticed that she shivered slightly even though it was very warm in the bright sunlight. The huge yew cast a dark shadow over the path as they approached Valentine's grave. They looked at it in silence for a few moments then Peter asked, "Ready?"

Beth nodded and stood to one side, her head bowed while Peter clasped his hands together, shut his eyes and began to speak.

"Oh, Heavenly Father, we beseech you to look down upon this thy servant, Valentine, taken so cruelly before his time and bring him close to Thy loving care. We ask you humbly to allow him to take his place where he belongs, safe in your arms, free from the troubles and afflictions that burdened him in life. Bestow your blessings upon his innocent soul, Lord, as we remember the words that your Son spoke. 'Suffer the little children to come to me…' Amen."

"Amen," echoed Beth. She bent and laid the small posy of flowers she had brought on Valentine's grave.

"Now rest in peace, Valentine," she whispered.

EPILOGUE
PRESENT DAY

"What an amazing place!" Matthew Drayton said enthusiastically as he jumped out of the BMW and gazed up at the house in awe. "Bloody hell, I never expected anything like this!"

"It looks as if it needs a lot of TLC to me," said his wife, Ruby. "Can we really afford to do it, Matt?"

"Course we can. Look, it's been empty for a few years but there's nothing that a lick of paint and a bit of updating won't do. Come on, Rubes, this is our dream, isn't it? An upmarket B and B is just what this area is crying out for." He frowned as he glanced into the back of the car. "C'mon kids, go and check out the garden while Mum and I look inside."

Tiffany, their thirteen-year-old daughter, yawned dismissively. "No thanks, Dad. I'm waiting for Sophie to Snapchat me. The signal's not brilliant; I don't want to move and lose it."

Matthew rolled his eyes. "What about you, Ryan? Come on, son, don't tell me you want to stay in the car as well?"

Eight-year-old Ryan scowled. "S'ppose not," he grumbled. He got out reluctantly and ambled off in the direction of the wooded area to the side of the house. Matthew sighed. Kids and their smartphones! In his day a place like this would have been like paradise… oh, well…

Matthew and Ruby spent the next half an hour exploring their potential new house. When they finally emerged, Matthew was grinning triumphantly. He had known that Ruby would love it. Malthorp House was something special and they would really be able to make something of their lives here, he felt it in his bones. He glanced into the car and then sighed impatiently. Tiffany was still sitting in exactly the same position glued to her phone, but there was no sign of Ryan.

"Where's your brother?" he asked, but Tiffany shrugged.

"Ryan!" he shouted. There was no response. He cupped his hands around his mouth and shouted as loudly as he could in the direction of the woods where he had last seen his son. "RYAN!"

Ryan crawled reluctantly out of the old den he had discovered in the woods. This place was great; the garden was awesome and he'd had a lot of fun but his dad sounded impatient; he had better get back or he would be in trouble. As he stood up to brush the dead leaves and twigs off his grey hoody, he thought he heard someone giggle and there was a faint rustling in the undergrowth. He felt suddenly uneasy as if he was being watched. "Is that you, Tiff?" It would be just like his sister to try and scare him. There was no response and a cold wind sprang up, chilling him through his thin top. He turned and hurried back towards the house where his parents were waiting impatiently. He saw that his sister was still sitting in the car. It couldn't have been her, then, in the woods…

"What do you think then, Ryan? Like the garden?" asked his mum.

"It's cool. I found an old den. Only…. the woods are a bit spooky." He glanced back at them, still feeling uncomfortable. "So, what about the house – are we going to buy it?" His voice trailed off as he gazed at the house, frowning. "Dad? Who's that strange guy there?"

Matthew followed the direction of his pointing finger.

"Where, son? I can't see anyone."

"*There*, at that downstairs window to the right of the door. He's staring at me; he's got horrible eyes and he looks really angry."

Matthew and Ruby frowned as they looked at the window. "There's nobody there, Ryan," said Ruby. "It was probably just a reflection, love."

"It *wasn't*, Mum – he was right there and he looked straight at me!"

Tiffany yawned and stretched, finally looking away from her phone.

"Stop making things up, Ry."

"I'm not! He was there, I tell you, I saw him. His face was all white and he was looking straight at me!"

"Okay, okay, you two, don't start." Ruby ushered her small son into the car. "Come on, you've had to wait around for a long time so we'll stop for a McDonald's on the way home to make up for it." She smiled at her husband. "Then we'll ring the agents and put in our offer."

As they pulled away, Ryan looked back at the house. He knew he *had* seen the angry man, and that there had also been something scary in the woods, but he also understood that the grown-ups wouldn't believe him. He bit his lip. He had to try and persuade them...

"I don't *want* to live there," he said softly.

But nobody heard him.

THE END

Printed in Dunstable, United Kingdom

68539415R00198